Dear Reader,

When I ask people to  hundred or so heroes of names occur consistently. Waite, appeared in an older book, *The Notorious Rake,* first published in 1992. Edmond has earned his reputation, but he is also one of my most complex, troubled heroes. It did not take me long to fall in love with him while I was creating him, and it did not take readers long to love him when they read his story. Now, more than twenty years later, you can fall in love with him all over again—or for the first time. His heroine, Mary Gregg, Lady Mornington, is an intelligent, refined widow, apparently his polar opposite. She spurns his attempts to woo her at the same time as her heart inexplicably yearns toward him. It is still one of my favorite books.

Mary was first mentioned in *A Counterfeit Betrothal* as the supposed mistress of the hero of that book, though in reality they were just friends. This story, also one of my favorites, is that rarity—a romance with two love stories of equal value. I really enjoyed writing it as one of the romances, involving the daughter of the other main couple, is light and humorous, whereas that of her long-estranged parents, whom she has schemed to bring together again by faking an engagement to a young rake she has known since childhood, is far more seriously passionate.

I am delighted that these two books are in print again, and I know many of you will be, too. I hope you will enjoy this two-in-one offering. Do let me know at my web site, www.marybalogh.com, or on my Facebook page, www.facebook.com/AuthorMaryBalogh.

Mary Balogh

"One of [Balogh's] best books to date."
—A Romance Review

AT LAST COMES LOVE

"Sparkling with sharp wit, lively repartee, and delicious sensuality, the emotionally rewarding *At Last Comes Love* metes out both justice and compassion; totally satisfying." —*Library Journal*

"*At Last Comes Love* is the epitome of what any great romance should be. . . . This novel will leave you crying, laughing, cheering, and ready to fight for two characters that any reader will most definitely fall in love with!" —Coffee Time Romance

THEN COMES SEDUCTION

"Exquisite sexual chemistry permeates this charmingly complex story." —*Library Journal*

"Balogh delivers another smartly fashioned love story that will dazzle readers with its captivating combination of nuanced characters, exquisitely sensual romance, and elegant wit." —*Booklist*

"Mary Balogh succeeds shockingly well."
—Rock Hill *Herald*

FIRST COMES MARRIAGE

"Intriguing and romantic . . . Readers are rewarded with passages they'll be tempted to dog-ear so they can read them over and over." —McAllen *Monitor*

"Balogh has once again crafted a sensuous tale of two very real people finding love and making each other's lives whole and beautiful. Readers will be delighted."
—*Booklist*

SIMPLY LOVE

"One of the things that make Ms. Balogh's books so memorable is the emotion she pours into her stories. The writing is superb, with realistic dialogue, sexual tension, and a wonderful heart-wrenching story. *Simply Love* is a book to savor, and to read again. It is a Perfect Ten. Romance doesn't get any better than this."
—Romance Reviews Today

"With more than her usual panache, Balogh returns to Regency England for a satisfying adult love story."
—*Publishers Weekly*

SIMPLY UNFORGETTABLE

"When an author has created a series as beloved to readers as Balogh's Bedwyn saga, it is hard to believe that she can surpass the delights with the first installment in a new quartet. But Balogh has done just that."
—*Booklist*

"A memorable cast . . . refresh[es] a classic Regency plot with humor, wit, and the sizzling romantic chemistry that one expects from Balogh. Well-written and emotionally complex." —*Library Journal*

SLIGHTLY DANGEROUS

"*Slightly Dangerous* is the culmination of Balogh's wonderfully entertaining Bedwyn series. . . . Balogh, famous for her believable characters and finely crafted Regency-era settings, forges a relationship that leaps off the page and into the hearts of her readers."
—*Booklist*

"With this series, Balogh has created a wonderfully romantic world of Regency culture and society. Readers will miss the honorable Bedwyns and their mates; ending the series with Wulfric's story is icing on the cake. Highly recommended." —*Library Journal*

SLIGHTLY SINFUL

"Smart, playful, and deliciously satisfying . . . Balogh once again delivers a clean, sprightly tale rich in both plot and character. . . . With its irrepressible characters and deft plotting, this polished romance is an ideal summer read." —*Publishers Weekly* (starred review)

SLIGHTLY TEMPTED

"Once again, Balogh has penned an entrancing, unconventional yarn that should expand her following." —*Publishers Weekly*

"Balogh is a gifted writer. . . . *Slightly Tempted* invites reflection, a fine quality in romance, and Morgan and Gervase are memorable characters."
—*Contra Costa Times*

SLIGHTLY SCANDALOUS

"With its impeccable plotting and memorable characters, Balogh's book raises the bar for Regency romances." —*Publishers Weekly* (starred review)

"The sexual tension fairly crackles between this pair of beautifully matched protagonists. . . . This delightful and exceptionally well-done title nicely demonstrates [Balogh's] matchless style." —*Library Journal*

"This third book in the Bedwyn series is . . . highly enjoyable as part of the series or on its own merits."
—*Old Book Barn Gazette*

SLIGHTLY WICKED

"Sympathetic characters and scalding sexual tension make the second installment [in the Slightly series] a truly engrossing read. . . . Balogh's sure-footed story possesses an abundance of character and class."
—*Publishers Weekly*

SLIGHTLY MARRIED

"*Slightly Married* is a masterpiece! Mary Balogh has an unparalleled gift for creating complex, compelling characters who come alive on the pages. . . . A Perfect Ten." —*Romance Reviews Today*

A SUMMER TO REMEMBER

"Balogh outdoes herself with this romantic romp, crafting a truly seamless plot and peopling it with well-rounded, winning characters."
—*Publishers Weekly*

"The most sensuous romance of the year."—*Booklist*

"This one will rise to the top." —*Library Journal*

"Filled with vivid descriptions, sharp dialogue, and fantastic characters, this passionate, adventurous tale will remain memorable for readers who love an entertaining read." —*Rendezvous*

WEB OF LOVE

"A beautiful tale of how grief and guilt can lead to love." —*Library Journal*

A Counterfeit Betrothal

The Notorious Rake

MARY BALOGH

DELL

NEW YORK

2013 Dell Mass Market Edition

A Counterfeit Betrothal copyright © 1992 by Mary Balogh
The Notorious Rake copyright © 1992 by Mary Balogh
Excerpt from *The Proposal* by Mary Balogh copyright © 2012 by Mary Balogh
Excerpt from *The Arrangement* by Mary Balogh copyright © 2013 by Mary Balogh

Published in the United States by Dell, an imprint of The Random House Publishing Group, a division of Random House, Inc., New York.

DELL is a registered trademark of Random House, Inc., and the colophon is a trademark of Random House, Inc.

A Counterfeit Betrothal was originally published in paperback in the United States by Signet, an imprint of Dutton Signet, a division of Penguin Books USA Inc., in 1992.

The Notorious Rake was originally published in paperback in the United States by Signet, an imprint of Dutton Signet, a division of Penguin Books USA Inc., in 1992.

This book contains an excerpt of the forthcoming title *The Arrangement* by Mary Balogh. The excerpt has been set for this edition only and may not reflect final content of the forthcoming book.

ISBN: 978-0-440-24547-6
eBook ISBN: 978-0-345-53869-7

Cover design: Lynn Andreozzi
Cover illustration: Gregg Gulbronson

Printed in the United States of America

www.bantamdell.com

9 8 7 6 5 4 3 2 1

Dell mass market edition: June 2013

A Counterfeit
Betrothal

1

"*A*nyway," Lady Sophia Bryant said, "I have no intention of marrying anyone. Ever." She gave her yellow parasol a twirl above her head and looked into the flowing waters of the River Thames, which sparkled in the May sunshine.

It was a rash statement to make considering the fact that there were three perfectly eligible gentlemen in the group that adorned the grass on the riverbank at Lady Pinkerton's garden party in Richmond. There were two other young ladies there, too, one Lady Sophia's close friend and the other one of the greatest gossips of the younger generation. By nightfall the whole of London would know what she had just said, including her papa, who had brought her to London for the Season, doubtless with the intention of finding her a husband despite the fact that she had not quite reached her eighteenth birthday.

But she had meant the words.

"Then there will be no further point in being in town," Mr. Peter Hathaway said. "We gentlemen might as well pack our trunks and retire to the country, Lady Sophia." He caught the eye of Lord Francis Sutton, who was sprawled on his side, propped on one elbow, his chin on his hand. He was sucking on a blade of grass. He raised one expressive eyebrow and Mr. Hathaway grimaced.

"Were it not for the presence of Miss Maxwell and Miss Brooks-Hyde, of course," he added hastily.

"But why, Lady Sophia?" Miss Dorothy Brooks-Hyde asked. "Would you prefer to be a spinster dependent upon your male relatives for the rest of your life? You do not even have any brothers."

"I shall not be dependent," Lady Sophia said. "When I am one-and-twenty I shall come into my fortune and set up my own establishment. I shall cultivate the best of company about me, and all the married ladies will envy me."

"And you will cultivate the label of bluestocking into the bargain, Soph," Lord Francis said, first removing the blade of grass from his mouth. "It won't suit you."

"Nonsense," she said. "You are going to be horribly covered with grass, Francis."

"Then you can brush me down," he said, winking at her and returning the blade of grass to his mouth.

"I do not wonder that the name of rake has sometimes been attached to you in the past few years, Francis," Lady Sophia said severely.

"Sophia!" Miss Cynthia Maxwell said reproachfully, dipping her parasol in front of her face to hide her blushes from the gentlemen.

Sir Marmaduke Lane entered the conversation. "Seriously, Lady Sophia," he said, "it is neither easy nor advisable to avoid matrimony. Our society and the whole future of the human race depends upon our making eligible connections. Indeed, one might even say it is our duty to enter the married state."

"Fiddle!" was Lady Sophia's reaction to this rather pompous speech. "Why would one give up one's freedom and the whole of one's future happiness just out of a sense of duty?"

"I would rather have said that happiness comes from marriage and the bearing of children," Dorothy said.

"What else is there for a woman, after all?" She glanced at Lord Francis for approval but he was occupied with the absorbing task of selecting another blade of grass to suck upon.

"Marriage brings nothing but unhappiness," Lady Sophia said hotly. "Once the first flush of romance has worn off, there is nothing left. Nothing at all. The husband can return to his old way of life while the wife is left with nothing and no means of making anything meaningful out of what remains of her life. And there is no getting out of marriage once one is in, beyond praying every night for the demise of one's partner. I have no intention of allowing any such thing to happen to me, thank you very much."

"But not all marriages are so unfortunate, Sophia," Cynthia said soothingly. "Most couples get along tolerably well together."

"Well, my parents' marriage is a disaster," Sophia said, twirling her parasol angrily and glaring out across the water. "My mother has not left Rushton in almost fourteen years and my father has not set foot there in all that time. Don't talk to me of getting along together."

"Sheer stubbornness is the cause, I would guess," Mr. Hathaway said. "I am not acquainted with your mama, Lady Sophia, but I can imagine that your papa is stubborn to a fault. They ought not to have carried on a quarrel for that long, though. Were they always unhappy together?"

"How would I know?" Sophia said. "I was only four years old when they separated. I scarcely remember their being together."

"They should make up their differences," Sir Marmaduke said. "They should find comfort in each other in their old age."

Mr. Hathaway snorted while Lord Francis grinned. "I don't know the countess, Lane," the former said, "but I would wager that Clifton would not enjoy being informed that he is in his dotage. You cannot find some way of bringing them together, Lady Sophia?"

"Why?" she said. "So that they may quarrel and part again?"

"Perhaps they would not, either," he said. "Perhaps they would be delighted to see each other again."

"Of course," Dorothy said, "ladies do lose their looks faster than men. Perhaps he would be shocked to see her aged."

"Mama is beautiful!" Sophia said. "Far lovelier than . . ." But she would not complete the comparison. Lady Mornington was undoubtedly Papa's mistress, discreet as they both were about their relationship. But Mama was lovelier for all that. Ten times—a hundred times—lovelier.

"Then you should bring them together," Mr. Hathaway said. "It was probably a foolish quarrel, anyway."

"Oh, how could I possibly accomplish such a thing?" Sophia said irritably.

"Say you want your mama here for the Season, Sophia," Cynthia said. "It is perfectly understandable that you would wish her to be here for your come-out."

"Papa asked me if I wanted her or him to bring me out," Sophia said. "If I had said Mama, then he would have stayed away. I would not choose. I refused. Anyway, I do not believe Mama would have come. She has been in the country for too long."

"You will have to get yourself involved in some scandal, Soph," Lord Francis said after working the blade of grass to the side of his mouth. "That will bring her at a trot. Find someone quite ineligible to elope with."

"Oh, do be serious, Francis," she said crossly. "Why would I want to elope with anyone? I would be forced to marry him and probably would not bring Mama and

Papa together after all. That is the silliest idea I ever heard."

"Conceive a grand passion for someone ineligible, then," he said. "Refuse to listen to reason. Threaten to elope if your father will not consent. Be as difficult as you girls know how to be. He will send for your mother out of exasperation before you know it."

"He would be more likely to pack me off to Rushton," Sophia said. "I do wish someone would change the subject. How did we get started on this, anyway?"

"By trying to guess who would be betrothed or married to whom by the end of the Season," Mr. Hathaway said. "Could you not betroth yourself to someone your papa will disapprove of, yet would not like to reject out of hand, Lady Sophia? Can you not present him with a problem that he would need your mama to help solve?"

She tutted. "One of the royal dukes, perhaps?" she said.

"One of your papa's friends, perhaps," he said, his brow furrowed in thought. "Or the son of one of his friends. Someone he would not quite want for his daughter, and yet someone he would not like to send packing because of his friend. A younger son, perhaps—with something of a shady reputation."

"Did someone mention my name?" Lord Francis asked. "You should conceive a grand passion for me, Soph. My father would be delighted and my mother would not stop hugging me from now until doomsday. Clifton would have an apoplexy."

"What a ridiculous idea," Sophia said.

"Not necessarily," Mr. Hathaway said thoughtfully. "Clifton and the Duke of Weymouth have about as close a friendship as they come, do they not? And Sutton is certainly the type of man I was just describing."

"Thank you," Lord Francis said dryly. "Don't forget,

Hathaway, that there are only three older brothers and four nephews between me and the dukedom."

"But you are something of a rake, Francis, you must admit," Sophia said. "And what Papa calls a hellion into the bargain."

He grinned at her and winked again. "Fancy me, do you, Soph?" he said while Cynthia dipped her parasol again, and Dorothy was almost visibly storing up details to share with her mama as soon as she decently might. "It would work, too, by Jove. I'll wager Clifton would send his most bruising rider tearing off on his fastest mount for your mama if you just whispered your intention of making yourself into Mrs. Lord Francis."

"How stupid," she said. "As if I would ever in my wildest moment consider marrying you, Francis."

He shuddered theatrically. "It is as well, then," he said, "that I would never in the deepest of my cups consider asking you, Soph. Don't glare. You started the insults."

"Besides," Sir Marmaduke said, "it would not be fitting to use the institution of holy matrimony as a charade to accomplish another goal entirely."

"But Sophia," Cynthia said, "do you not think it worth a try? Wouldn't your papa really be in a dreadful dilemma?"

"I believe," Sophia said unwillingly, "that he and His Grace once expressed a wish that their families be united by marriage. But unfortunately for them, Papa had only me and I was too young. Francis is the only son still unmarried."

"And the black sheep into the bargain," that young man said. "Clifton has been ominously silent on the old topic since Claude, my last respectable brother, married Henrietta two years ago."

"The question is," Mr. Hathaway said, "are you willing to try it, you two?"

"Enter into a passion with Soph?" Lord Francis said. "The idea has its appeal, I must admit." His eyes laughed at Sophia as they traveled over her seated figure in its flimsy sprigged muslin dress.

"How stupid," she said. "Stop looking at me like that."

"But do you think your papa might send for your mama if you announced your intention of marrying Lord Francis, Sophia?" Cynthia asked.

"If I got into what Papa calls one of my stubborn moods and insisted that she be consulted, perhaps," Sophia admitted. "But perhaps not, too. They have managed to solve all problems for the past fourteen years without once meeting face-to-face."

"But are you willing to try?" Mr. Hathaway asked. "That is the question now. Sutton?"

Lord Francis was grinning at Sophia. "Soph?" he asked.

"I certainly am not marrying you," she said. "If you have any secret hope that that is how it will end up, Francis, forget it."

"There is nothing to forget," he said. "It will be all charade, Soph. All panting and pretended passion. A counterfeit passion. I rather fancy it. Life has been tedious lately."

"What do you say, Lady Sophia?" Dorothy asked, a note of suppressed excitement in her voice.

Sophia twirled her parasol and prepared to say one more time that the whole idea was ridiculous and that she would not, even in pretense, show a romantic interest in her old childhood tormentor. There was no bringing Mama and Papa together anyway. If they had remained irrevocably apart for fourteen years, there was doubtless no way of changing things now.

"I would strongly advise against it, Lady Sophia," Sir

Marmaduke said. "The holy institution of matrimony is not to be taken in jest."

That did it. "I say yes," Sophia said, lifting her chin and looking indignantly at Lord Francis's lazy and very white grin. "I say let's try it. But I am not marrying you, mind, Francis."

"Good," he said. "You had better be careful not to fall in love with me in earnest, Soph, or you will be doomed to a terrible disappointment, you know. And if you puff up like that, my girl, you might explode. You gave the first set down. I merely took my cue from you."

"This will not work," she said. "It is a remarkably foolish idea."

"It might, too," Mr. Hathaway said hastily. "But one thing we must all do is swear secrecy. Not a word or a hint. Miss Brooks-Hyde?"

Dorothy looked to be in an agony. She would fairly burst with the story. "Oh, very well," she said. "But I hope for your sake that this charade will not go for too long, Lady Sophia. It will do your reputation no good at all."

"Thank you," Lord Francis said.

"I mean when she breaks off the betrothal," Dorothy said, coloring. "Or the connection, if it does not quite come to a betrothal."

"I do hope the scheme works for you, Sophia," Cynthia said. "I know how you adore both your mama and your papa. And it is not as if you do not know Lord Francis at all. You have known each other forever, have you not?"

"For at least that long," Lord Francis said. "Or is it longer, Soph? I can remember outrunning you when you could scarcely walk."

"Lane?" Mr. Hathaway asked.

"You may depend upon me," Sir Marmaduke said. "I can only applaud your efforts to effect a reconciliation between your parents, Lady Sophia, even if I must frown upon your methods. But I shall say nothing."

"And I shan't, of course," Mr. Hathaway said. "So all is settled. And since the Earl of Clifton is at this garden party, I would suggest that the two of you link arms and stroll off and start falling desperately in love."

"Done," Lord Francis said, getting unhastily to his feet and stretching out a hand to help Sophia to hers. "You will be able to brush me off after all, Soph."

"I absolutely will not," she said indignantly. "You may brush yourself off."

"You see?" he said, appealing to the rest of the group. "She is afraid that if she once lays hands on me, she will not be able to remove them again."

Miss Cynthia Maxwell tipped her parasol once more to hide her blushes.

SHE LEANED FORWARD in her seat the better to see out of the carriage window. It looked amazingly the same, the village of Clifton, though she had not seen it for well over fourteen years. She looked half eagerly, half unwillingly at the parish church with its tall, elegant spire and its cobbled path that wound through a sleepy churchyard.

They had run along it after their wedding, hand in hand, laughing, eager to escape from the boisterous greetings of family and friends and villagers, eager to reach the carriage outside the gate, eager to be behind the curtains where they had found the privacy in which to kiss lingeringly and gaze into each other's eyes and smile with the novel and incredible knowledge that they were man and wife, that she was his viscountess.

Almost nineteen years ago. She had been seventeen, he twenty-one. Their parents on both sides had been reluctant to consent to the match on account of their youth, but they had persisted. They had been caught up in all the wonder of young love.

Olivia Bryant, Countess of Clifton, leaned back in her seat and closed her eyes. She did not want to view the ghosts of those young lovers rushing from their wedding to a happily ever after world—a world that had lasted not quite five years. She did not want to think of it. She had stopped thinking of it a long time ago.

The carriage proceeded on its way through the village and to the gates leading to Clifton Court half a mile beyond. Her father-in-law's home when they were married, now her husband's.

Despite herself she felt her stomach churning with apprehension. What would he look like now? Would she recognize him? He had been tall and slim when she last saw him, his dark hair thick and always overlong, his face handsome and boyish and ever alight with eagerness and a zest for life—except the last time she saw him, of course. He had been twenty-six years old at that time. He was forty now. He had turned forty in May, two months before.

Forty! He was middle-aged. She was middle-aged. She would be thirty-seven in September. They had an eighteen-year-old daughter. Sophia had celebrated her eighteenth birthday in London one day after her father's birthday. Although in labor all through his birthday eighteen years before, the countess had been unable to give birth until two hours into a new day. They had laughed about it, gazing fondly and triumphantly into each other's eyes after he had been allowed into her bedchamber to view his new daughter.

She would give him a son the next time, she had promised him. But there had been no next time. She had not conceived in four years, and after four years he had left, never to return.

Would she recognize him? She felt rather sick.

Sophia's letter had been abject and pleading, Marc's cool and formal and to the point. But both had made her see that it was necessary for her to come. She had shown both letters to her friend Clarence—Sir Clarence Wickham—and he had agreed with her. She should go, he had advised. Clearly a family decision must be made, and it was the kind of decision that could not be discussed by letter.

Sophia was deeply in love with Lord Francis Sutton, youngest son of Marc's friend the Duke of Weymouth. Deeply, head over ears, forever in love, according to her letter. He was handsome and charming and intelligent and kind and everything that was wonderful. And if ever he had given in to a youthful wildness, it was all behind him now. He worshiped her and was going to love her and care for her for the rest of their lives. And though he was a younger son and had lived somewhat extravagantly for some years, he was not without prospects. Apart from the settlement his father would make on him when he married, he was the favorite and heir of an elderly great-aunt, who was very wealthy indeed. Please, would Mama come and see for herself just what an eligible husband he would be for her, and persuade Papa that his wild days were at an end? Please would she come? *Please?*

Their daughter had conceived a quite ineligible passion, the earl had written, and had declared her intention of marrying the young man or running away with him. Lord Francis Sutton was a hellion, no less, an irresponsible puppy who would lead Sophia a merry dance if they were wed. Besides, she was far too young to be thinking of marriage. And yet the situation was awkward. The young people had been unfortunately vocal in their intentions, and Weymouth and his wife were delighted at the proposed connection. He had been forced to invite them and the young man to Clifton with a few other guests, hoping that somehow the betrothal could be avoided. Weymouth, on the other hand, seemed to believe that it was a betrothal party that was in the making. Would Olivia please come to Clifton to help talk sense into their daughter?

"You always seem to have had more influence over her than I," he had written graciously.

And so she was coming. She felt the carriage rumble over the humpbacked stone bridge and knew that the house would be visible out of the left window. She turned her hands palm up and examined them closely.

Surely there must have been some other way. But there had not, she knew. Sophia must be dissuaded from making a disastrous marriage. The countess could remember Lord Francis only as a young and mischievous little boy, three or four years older than Sophia. But Marc had said in his letter that the young man was wild. That would mean that he was a daredevil, a gambler and drinker, a rake. A womanizer.

Not that for Sophia. Anything but that. If they were in love now, it would not last. He would return to his old ways once the gloss had worn off their marriage. Sophia would end up with a lifetime of misery, an unfaithful rake for a husband.

Not that for Sophia. *Please not that,* she begged an unseen power silently. *Please not that.* Sophia was all she had. If she had to live to see Sophia rejected and desperately unhappy, she would not be able to bear it.

When finally she could ignore the approach of the house no longer, she saw that the front doors to the house were open. And Sophia herself was eagerly rushing down the marble steps, looking pretty and fashionable with her dark hair cut short and curled—very like her father as the countess remembered him. She had a young man by the hand and was dragging him after her—a tall and slender young man with fair hair and a laughing handsome face.

"Mama!" Sophia stood beside the carriage almost bouncing on the spot in her impatience, waiting for a footman to open the door and lower the steps. She continued speaking as soon as the door was opened. "I thought you would never get here. I said you would be here yesterday, but Papa said no, that you could not possibly come all the way from Lincolnshire to Gloucestershire before today at the very earliest. Perhaps even tomorrow, he said. But I knew it would be today once it became obvious that it would not be yesterday."

She hurled herself into her mother's arms as the latter descended the steps.

"It seems forever," she said. "I wish you had come to London, Mama. It is so splendid there. This is Francis." She turned to smile dazzlingly at the fair young man and to link her arm through his. "Do you remember him?"

"Only as a very young boy who had a gift for getting into mischief," the countess said, smiling and extending a hand to him. She noted with a sinking of her heart his very attractive grin. "I am pleased to meet you again, Lord Francis."

"I do not wonder that you have kept yourself in the country, ma'am, rather than come to London," he said, taking her hand in a firm clasp. "I see that you have been keeping yourself close to the fountain of eternal youth."

The Countess of Clifton was far from pleased by the young man's flattery. If he used it on Sophia, it was no wonder that he had turned the girl's head. And he was far too handsome. But such thoughts fled from her mind as she became aware without looking—without daring to look—of someone else coming out onto the steps of the house and beginning to descend them.

Was it? she thought in some panic when it was no

longer possible to keep her eyes from straying beyond Lord Francis's shoulder. Could it be? Her heart was beating so painfully that she thought she might completely disgrace herself and faint.

He was broader. Not fat—there was not one spare ounce of fat on his body as far as the eye could tell. But broad and powerful of shoulders and chest. He looked fit, well-muscled, strong. He was taller than she remembered. His hair was still thick—he had not lost any of it, as she had expected he might. It was still dark, but liberally flecked with silver. Oddly enough, the silver hairs added to rather than detracted from the overall impression of virility that he gave.

His face was different. Just as handsome—more so, in fact. It was a man's face now, not an eager boy's. But there was a hardness there, about the jaw and in the dark eyes, a cynicism that had been totally absent before.

It was him. Of course it was him. So very different. So very much the same.

"Olivia," he said, stretching out a hand. She remembered his hands, the long strong fingers, the short, well-manicured nails. "Welcome home."

"Marcus," she said, placing her hand in his, watching it close about hers, feeling with some shock its warmth and its firmness, almost as if she had expected to watch but not feel.

And she watched and felt more shock as he raised her hand to his lips. She looked up into his eyes and realized that his thoughts must be occupied in the same manner as her own. He was noticing the changes, the sameness.

Mostly changes, she thought, dropping her gaze again. She had been twenty-two years old when he had left her—no, when she had driven him away. A mere girl.

"Papa," Sophia said, clapping her hands, "does Mama not look beautiful?"

"Yes," he said. "Very. Come inside, Olivia. My butler and housekeeper are eager to be presented to you. Then Sophia will take you to your room and you may rest and refresh yourself."

"Thank you," she said and laid her hand on the arm he extended to her.

She heard Sophia laugh in delight behind them.

2

*H*E HAD NOT KNOWN HOW HE WAS TO TREAT HER when she arrived. He had agonized over the possibilities for days. And he was not at all sure that he had made the right decision.

Perhaps he should have treated her as a guest rather than as the mistress of Clifton Court. Perhaps he should have had her put in a guest chamber rather than in the countess's room next to his own. Perhaps he should have had the connecting door between their dressing rooms locked. Perhaps he should have stayed inside the hall to greet her instead of going outside. Or, perhaps he should have insisted on going out ahead of Sophia. Perhaps he should not have given her the function of hostess at dinner, seating her at the foot of the table, facing him across its length, Weymouth beside her. Perhaps he should have been all business and taken her aside soon after her arrival to discuss the matter of Sophia's imminent betrothal.

Perhaps he should not have summoned her at all. Perhaps he should merely have invited her opinion and advice by letter. He had done so several times over the years. Her letters were invariably lucid and sensible.

He felt like a gauche schoolboy again, the Earl of Clifton thought later in the evening as he completed the third hand of cards opposite the duchess. He should be more like his wife. She had been a calm and unruffled hostess all evening and was at present conversing quietly at the other end of the long drawing room with Weymouth and Sutton and Sophia and a few of the other guests.

His wife! It seemed impossible, he thought, glancing across the room at her. His wife of almost nineteen years. Livy. A stranger.

"They make a charming couple, do they not, Marcus?" the duchess said as he took her elbow and steered her in the direction of the tea tray. She was smiling fondly across the room. "Such a lovely and prettily behaved girl. Better than Francis deserves, I must confess, though he is a dear boy and will appear so to all the world once he has sown his wild oats, as William puts it. And I do believe that perhaps they are already sown. Sophia is having a steadying effect on him."

"It seems a long time since they used to play and quarrel interminably," the earl said, avoiding the basic issue. Sutton had offered for Sophia already, but had been given no final answer. He had been told that the matter must be discussed with Lady Sophia's mother. He had been told that there was the serious matter of Sophia's very young age to be considered. And yet the earl's friends, the Weymouths, were behaving as if the delay in consent was a mere formality.

"And he is closer in age to her than Claude would have been," the duchess said, "or Richard or Bertie."

"The christening of Claude's son went well?" the earl asked, trying to turn the subject.

It was a fortunate question. The duchess, accepting a cup of tea from his hands, seated herself, summoned about her a court of younger ladies with a gracious smile, and proceeded to entertain them with an account of the christening of her son's heir. Lord Clifton stood watching her politely.

Sophia, he saw, had moved with several of the young people and seated herself at the pianoforte. Sutton was behind her, leaning past her to set a piece of music on the stand before her. His arms were on either side of her so that when she turned her head to smile warmly at him they almost kissed. The earl felt his jaw tightening. If that young puppy ever laid so much as a single finger on Sophia without his personal say-so, he would . . .

He looked toward his wife. Olivia must help. She would doubtless know what to do to put an end to such an undesirable connection. Just as she had known how to persuade a much younger Sophia to spend Christmas with him that one year when the girl had wished to return home to her mother, with whom she had always lived for most of the year. And when the time came, she had known how to talk their daughter into going to school, although Sophia had been angry and rebellious. She loudly exclaimed that Mama would take her part and not insist that she be packed off to an institution just as if she were not wanted.

It was not easy having a daughter, he had found, with no wife close by to advise him on how best to bring her up. He had never asked Mary's advice, though she was a woman of sense and doubtless would have been willing to give it. Mary and Sophia belonged to quite different aspects of his life.

His wife was talking with Weymouth and smiling. She looked quite at her ease until she glanced his way, catching his eye. She turned sharply away, and seemed discomposed for a moment.

He had wondered if he would recognize her. And perhaps he would not have, if she had not been alone and in Sophia's arms. Perhaps he would have passed her on a crowded street. Though he would undoubtedly have turned his head for a second look. She had been very pretty as a young woman—unusually lovely, in fact. She had had a slender, pleasing figure and a bright, expressive, smiling face surrounded by masses of almost blonde curls.

She was beautiful now, quite extraordinarily beautiful. Her figure was fuller, more alluring, her long hair combed smoothly back from her face and coiled at the back of her head—there was no sign of gray in it. But her face was the part of her that had changed most. Although she smiled now, and had smiled through dinner and most of the evening, it appeared to be an expression she had deliberately assumed. The animation, the brightness had gone, leaving behind only beauty and serenity.

Livy! She had been only seventeen when he had first seen her. Her parents had had no intention of marrying her off so young. She was making her come-out only because an older cousin of hers was also to be presented and the two families had decided to make it a joint occasion.

They had spent most of the evening on opposite sides of the ballroom. He had been very young himself, just down from Oxford, just about to embark upon the life of a man about town. He had been eager to acquire some town bronze, some town swagger—until he had seen her and known all through the evening that she had also seen him, though their eyes never quite met.

But their eyes had met and held, after he had arranged an introduction to her and danced with her after supper. And her cheeks had flushed and her lips had parted, and he had been smitten by a whole arsenal of Cupid's darts. Poor foolish young man, believing that young love could last for a lifetime.

The earl returned his attention to the Duchess of Weymouth in time to make an appropriate comment on something she had said. Sophia must be prevented from making the same mistake, he thought. She must be protected from coming to the same fate as her mother. And yet he himself had not even been a rake—not as Sutton was with his large array of ladybirds and just as large a following of respectable young ladies sighing for his favors. He himself had been an innocent. A dangerous innocent, who had made one mistake and had not had the sense to keep quiet about it.

Livy!

He bowed and turned away from the ladies as the conversation turned to other topics. He strolled across the room in the direction of his wife and Weymouth. And he remembered how she had been as a young bride and how he had been. A pair of young innocents deeply in love and eager to consummate that love, the one as virginal and unknowledgeable as the other.

He had been fumbling and awkward. He had hurt her dreadfully and had been forced to finish the consummation to the sound of her smothered sobs. And yet she had turned in his arms afterward and looked at him with that eager young face and consoled him, one hand smoothing his hair. *She* had consoled *him*! It did not matter, she had assured him. She was his wife now and that was all that mattered.

"And it will be better next time," she had told him. "It will be, I promise you. Marc?" Even in the near darkness he had seen the radiance of her smile. "I am your wife. Not just because of the church and the vicar and the ceremony and the guests. But because of this. You are my husband."

"Forever and ever, Livy," he had promised her, kissing her warmly and lingeringly. "Forever and ever my wife, and forever and ever my love."

Poor fool. Forever had lasted not quite five years.

She looked up as he approached. The smile that she had imposed upon her face stayed in place.

"I have just been telling Olivia how good it is to see her again," the duke said. "She is in good looks. We had some good times together, all of us, did we not, when the boys were small and Sophia a mere toddler?"

"Yes," the earl said. "Bertie and Richard and Claude were always her champions against the various atrocities Francis devised to be rid of her."

The duke laughed. "I think I had a permanently stinging hand that one time you all stayed with us for a month," he said. "I doubtless gave myself far more pain than I meted out to Francis's backside. Do you remember the orchestra pavilion, Olivia?"

The earl chuckled and looked at his wife to find that her smile had changed to one of genuine amusement.

"If it is possible for one's heart to perform a complete somersault," she said, "I think mine did when I saw Sophia sitting on the very peak of the dome, as cool as a cucumber, refusing to admit either that she was frightened or that she did not know how to get down."

"And she was barely four years old," His Grace said.

"I did not know," the earl said, "that I was capable of shinning up smooth pillars and up an even smoother dome in less time than it would have taken me to run around the pavilion once."

"And Olivia standing below admonishing you to be careful," the duke said with a chuckle. "And holding out her arms as if she thought she could catch you if you fell."

Lord Clifton met his wife's amused eyes and felt his smile fade with hers.

"And Francis nowhere in sight," His Grace continued, "after luring her up there. He had gone fishing, if I remember correctly. And it was Olivia weeping in your arms, Marcus, after it was all over, not Sophia. She was on her way to join the fishing party, I believe."

"Yes," the earl said. "I believe I was so shaken that I even forgot to spank her."

"They were good days," the duke said with a sigh, "when the children were all young and about us. But who would have thought that Francis and Sophia would ever develop an attachment? He would never let her play with him even when they got older. Is that not right, Marcus?"

"Fortunately," Lord Clifton said, "they did not see much of each other once they were both off at school and Sophia was spending most of her holidays at Rushton. They have not met for four years before this spring."

"And now it seems, Olivia," the duke said, "that they want to make us related by marriage. How will you like it, eh? Do you fancy having my scamp of a youngest son for a son-in-law? I would not blame you at all if you were to say no." He laughed heartily.

The earl looked at his wife.

"Marcus and I have had no chance to discuss Lord Francis's offer," she said quietly. "It would be unfair to give my opinion until we have done so, William."

A good answer, the earl thought, looking at her admiringly. Marcus? She had called him that earlier outside. Prior to that, she had not called him by his full name since before their marriage. It had always been Marc. But then he had been calling her Olivia since her arrival.

Which was as it should be. They were, after all, strangers. Strangers who happened to share some memories and a daughter.

"This is neither the time nor the place to discuss terms anyway," the duke said. "Ah, the young people are leaving the pianoforte."

Sutton was taking Sophia by the hand, the earl saw, and threading his fingers with hers. They were smiling at each other as if they saw the whole world mirrored in each other's eyes. And they were approaching.

"Your permission, sir," Lord Francis said, bowing, "to take your daughter walking on the terrace outside. Miss Maxwell and Lady Jennifer, Mr. Hathaway, and Sir Ridley will be coming, too, if the ladies' parents permit."

"It is a heavenly night," Sophia said. "We looked out through the windows a short time ago—did we not, Francis—and all the stars are shining and the moon is bright. Do say yes, Papa. It is too warm in here."

She was looking very pretty, her father thought, her dark eyes bright, her cheeks flushed, the radiance of young love giving her a certain glow. She reminded him of her mother, although he had never before thought them alike. There was something in the expression. Olivia had used to glow like that.

"Mama," Sophia was saying, "the fountain looks quite breathtaking in the moonlight. Do you remember that from when Grandpapa used to live here? You should come outside with us. You should come with Papa." She laughed and turned toward him. "What better chaperons could there be, after all, than my parents?"

"I think your mother is probably tired from her journey, Sophia," he said.

"And yet," Lord Francis said with a bow, "there is nothing better calculated to lull one to sleep than a short walk outdoors before retiring. Is there, Lady Clifton? Won't you come?"

There was a brief silence.

"Olivia?" the earl said and found himself almost holding his breath. "Would you care for some fresh air?"

"Thank you," she said after another brief pause. "I think that would be pleasant."

"I shall send up for your cloak, then," he said.

* * *

"LOOK BACK WHEN you have the opportunity," Sophia said. "Not now. Casually, just as if you are looking at the stars. I cannot look without seeming very obvious. Are they walking together, Francis? Are they talking? Don't do it now or they will think I have asked you to do so. *Not now!*"

Lord Francis had turned his head over his shoulder without any attempt at casualness or subterfuge.

"She has her arm through his," he reported. "They are not talking. At least they were not when I looked. But perhaps one of them had just stopped speaking and was pausing to draw breath while the other had nothing to say."

"I said not now," she hissed at him. "They will think we are spying on them."

"If I had only thought," he said, "I would have brought my telescope out with me. Except that I did not bring it with me to Clifton, of course. And now that I come to think of it, I do not possess one at all. I shall slink across into some bushes if you wish, Soph, to observe the proceedings. Do you think they will miss me? I don't know how they could when Lady Jennifer is shrieking with such mirth. Whatever can Hathaway be saying to her, do you suppose?"

"This is all a joke to you, is it not?" she asked. "My mama and papa are together for the first time in fourteen years and all you can do is talk about stupid things like slinking off into bushes. Do you ever take anything seriously?"

"I do, Soph," he said. "I would worry about getting my knee breeches snagged by thorns."

"Oh!" she said, tossing her head.

"I think it is time for a melting glance," he said. "We cannot have them thinking that our ardor has cooled. I think we have done remarkably well so far, don't you? I don't know about you, Soph, but I am giving serious consideration to going on the stage."

"You might as well," she said tartly. "You would be close to all your actresses."

"Smile, darling," he said seductively, turning his face sideways in order to give an image of his profile to those walking behind them and smiling dazzlingly down at her. "Come on, Soph. It is worth a mint to see you do it."

She turned her head to look up into his eyes and smile slowly and meltingly. He bowed his head a fraction closer and looked down at her lips.

"Don't you dare," she said, her expression not changing at all. "If you want your cheek smacked and your nose flattened and your eye blackened, just come half an inch closer, Francis."

His face moved perhaps a quarter of an inch closer. "That is quite far enough," he said. "Not that your threats would deter me if I really were tempted in even the smallest way to steal a kiss, Soph. But I have a distinct feeling that your father's fist might cause my nostrils to part company with each other if I did."

They both turned their heads to face the front again, the radiant smiles fading as they did so.

"What next?" he asked. "My parents are already planning wedding journeys and drawing up guest lists and wondering which church the wedding is to be in. And my mother is already dreaming of new grandchildren and wondering if there will be time to wash and iron the family christening robes after Claude's baby and before ours. All while I stand by looking complacent and rather as if a falling star had hit me in the eye."

"I don't like to disappoint them," Sophia said, "but I would not marry you, Francis, if you were the last man on earth."

"In some ways we are remarkably well suited, Soph," he said pleasantly. "We think alike. I do not believe I would marry you even under similar but reversed conditions to the ones you mentioned."

"You are no gentleman," she said. "You never have been."

"There is no point in being cross just because I refuse to marry you, Soph," he said. "I was gentleman enough to allow you to refuse to marry me first. But enough of this quarreling. What happens next? We suddenly find that our love has cooled so that my parents and I can take ourselves off tomorrow and I can get back to the congenial life of raking?"

"You would like that, too, would you not?" she said. "You would like to abandon me just as if I were a hot potato to be dropped at all cost?"

"In short, yes," he said. "But I gather from your tone that you have further use for me."

"Of course I have further use for you," she said indignantly. "If you leave tomorrow or the next day, Francis, Mama will have no further need to stay here and she will go home and never see Papa again. And that will be that. And if that happens, I shall never marry anyone for I will not allow myself to be lured into such a life of misery. What are they doing? And *don't look now*!"

Lord Francis looked. "Strolling and talking," he said.

"Talking?" She looked up at him eagerly. "That is promising. Don't you think so, Francis?"

"We have been talking, too," he said. "Quarreling."

She sighed. "Do you think they are quarreling, too?" she asked.

"No idea," he said. "But you can depend upon it that they are too well-bred to come to fisticuffs, Soph. So I am to stay in order to keep them together, am I? Do you think they are going to allow us to become betrothed?"

"Not if Papa can help it," she said. "He says that I am far too young even though I have had my eighteenth birthday already and am older than Mama was when she married. But that would be his meaning, would it not? We are going to have to be distraught, Francis. We are going to have to threaten elopement or suicide."

"By Jove," he said. "Quite a choice, is it not? The devil and the deep blue sea, would you say?"

"No," she said. "But I would fully expect you to do so. I would choose suicide without the slightest hesitation. It will be best if they do consent, though." She frowned in thought. "We will want to marry without delay, of course. A summer wedding. Mama will have to stay to plan it. There will be a great deal for her and Papa to discuss. And perhaps our wedding will remind them of their own."

"Ah," he said, "I hate to interrupt this pleasant train of thought, Soph, but did you say our *wedding*? What do we do afterward? Neglect to consummate it and go begging for an annulment?"

"Oh," she said. "You are right. There cannot actually be a wedding, can there? But just the planning of it will remind them. Don't you think? And how could you say what you just said? It would be just like you to humiliate me by annulling our marriage and having the whole world say that I could not even attract you sufficiently to tempt you on our wedding night."

"Soph," he said, "I am glad the moon is not quite full. I might hear some words of real madness from you."

"But really," she said, "you could not have said anything more insulting, Francis. I should die of mortification."

"Good Lord," he said. "And to think that I gave up a week or two or five of a life of genial civilization in Brighton for this."

"A life of gambling and carousing and womanizing, you mean," she said tartly.

"That is what I said, is it not?" he said. "Time to bill and coo again, Soph. A kiss on the hand, I believe?" He raised her hand to his lips and held it there while she smiled radiantly up at him.

3

THERE WAS A CERTAIN FAMILIARITY EVEN AFTER fourteen years. A familiar height, her cheek just above the level of his shoulder. A familiar and distinctive way of holding his arm, with her own linked through it. He held it tight to his body so that the back of her hand was against his side.

She had never minded before, of course. She had always walked close beside him. When they had walked unobserved, he had often set an arm about her shoulders while she had set hers about his waist.

"Your curls make a comfortable pillow for my cheek, Liv," he had often said. And sometimes he would rest it there and snore loudly while she had giggled and told him how foolish he was.

She minded now. She had hoped to avoid memories and comparisons. She had hoped to avoid all but purely business encounters with him. A foolish hope, of course, when the duration of her stay was indefinite and there were guests at the house looking for amusement. And when it was summertime at Clifton. Summertime at Clifton. She felt a welling of memories and nostalgia.

Marc. Oh, Marc.

"So what do you think?" he asked now, breaking the silence between them.

"About Sophia and Lord Francis?" she asked. "She is

too young, Marcus. Only just eighteen. She is still a child."

"Yes," he said, and they both remembered an even younger child who nineteen years before had insisted on marrying. Two young children.

"She knows nothing of life," she said, "and nothing of people. She finished school only a year ago and was with me in the country until after Christmas. How can she possibly be ready for marriage?"

"She cannot," he said.

"I know how it must have been," she said. "She got caught up in the whirl and glamour of the Season and met Lord Francis again for the first time since they have both grown up, and fell in love with him. It was inevitable. He is a very handsome and charming boy. But she does not know what a sheltered world she has been living in. She does not know that their love cannot possibly last."

"No," he said.

"I know what it is like," she said. "I know just how she is feeling."

"Yes," he said.

Because it happened just like that with me. She did not speak the words aloud, but she did not need to. They hung heavy on the air before them.

"You are agreed with me, then," he said, "that we must prevent the betrothal from happening?"

"Yes," she said. "Oh, yes."

"It will not be easy," he said. "They are quite besotted with each other and you know how stubborn Sophia can be. I have always avoided confrontations with her whenever possible. I am afraid I have sometimes found her unmanageable. You have always done better than I on that score, Olivia."

"Yes," she said. "You have always indulged her, Marcus. Perhaps you were afraid of losing her love. I have always shut my mind to the possibility and refused to allow her her way on every matter."

"I have seen so little of her," he said. "I never kept her long because I felt she needed her mother more than her father. And I always thought you would miss her."

"Yes," she said. "I always did. Oh, Marcus, look at them. They are totally wrapped up in each other."

Sophia and Lord Francis were still walking, but their faces were turned to each other, the moonlight catching his expression of tenderness and utter absorption in her. For one shocked moment Olivia thought that he was going to kiss her daughter, but he drew his head back and they strolled on.

"By God," the earl muttered quite viciously, "he would have been sorry if he had moved just one inch closer."

"Oh, Marcus," the countess said, "is he quite as wild as you suggested? He seems such a pleasant young man."

"There is nothing vicious about him, as far as I know," Lord Clifton said. "He has been known to gamble a little too much and he involves himself in too many of the more outrageous and daring exploits in the betting books—things like racing curricles to Brighton and drinking a pint of ale at as many inns in London as possible during one night before becoming insensible. And he spends too much time in the greenrooms of the theaters. Nothing he will not outgrow in time in all probability. He is only twenty-two."

But you did not outgrow them. She wondered with unwilling curiosity if Lady Mornington was still his mistress or if it was someone else now. She so rarely heard news of his doings. Lady Mornington might be four or five years in his past by now, for all she knew. And probably was. After all, he had remained faithful to his wife for less than five years.

"But why would he suddenly wish to marry Sophia?" she asked. "He is very young and his behavior has suggested that he is not yet ready to settle down. Why the sudden change? She is just an infant."

"But a very pretty and vivacious infant," he said. "We are looking at her through parents' eyes, Olivia. To us she is just a child and probably always will be. You were increasing when you were her age."

She closed her eyes briefly and remembered. The wonder of it. The sheer joy of it. Life growing in her. Her child and Marc's, the product of their love. The only cloud—the *only* one on what had remained of their married life together after Sophia had been born was the fact that it had never happened again, that she had never again been able to conceive despite the fact that they had made love very frequently.

"Yes," she said. "Marcus, she must be persuaded to give up this foolishness. I shall have to talk with her tomorrow. I have had no chance today. I shall explain to her all the dangers and disadvantages of marrying so young. She will listen to me. She almost always has. And if she will not, then you must exert your authority. You must reject Lord Francis's suit."

"Yes." He sighed. "It will not be easy, Olivia. William and Rose seem to think the betrothal is an accomplished fact already. They are more than delighted. And they have always been such good and such close friends."

"Then you must speak with them," she said. "We can do so together if you wish. We must explain that Sophia is too young, that her happiness is very precious to us because she is our only child."

The only link between us in all these years.

"And everyone else expects it, too," he said. "That is why they think they have been invited here. And everyone in the neighborhood, doubtless. It is why they think you have come. Sophia has persuaded me to organize a ball for the end of the week, you know. Everyone will be expecting the announcement to be made there."

"Then they will have to find that they are wrong," she said. "Marcus, don't make a scene. There are two other couples out here. And it is just her hand."

She had felt the tightening of his arm muscles and had looked up to see the hardening of his jaw as he glared ahead at a besotted Lord Francis holding Sophia's hand to his lips and keeping it there for altogether too long a time.

"Impudent puppy," the earl muttered. "I shall take a horse whip to his hide and do what Weymouth should have done years ago."

"His behavior is not so very improper," she said soothingly. "Now that I am here we can handle this together, Marcus. It will be all over within a few weeks, I daresay, and then we can return to normal living."

"I hope you are right," he said.

THE COUNTESS OF Clifton sat in the window seat of her private sitting room the following day waiting for her daughter to come. It was more than an hour past luncheon already and they had still not had their talk. It was very difficult, it seemed, to accomplish anything of a serious or personal nature while a house party was in full swing. There was always too much else to do.

That morning a riding party had been arranged for the young people, to be chaperoned by Lord and Lady Wheatley, Lady Jennifer's parents. The earl had joined them. And at luncheon Miss Biddeford had talked of nothing else except the bonnet in the village that she should have bought the day before. Finally Mrs. Biddeford had agreed to take her daughter back into the village.

"Though it will be straight in and out again," she had said. "I want to play bowls with the others."

Several of the guests were with the earl on the bowling

green at the back of the house. Sophia had been invited to accompany her friend Rachel and Mrs. Biddeford and had looked inquiringly at her mother. The countess had nodded.

But there was no sign yet of the returning carriage. It was really too beautiful a day to be indoors, Olivia thought, looking out beyond the fountain and the formal gardens before the house over the rolling miles of the park in the distance. She had fallen in love with Clifton Court during her very first visit there, though on that occasion her room had been the small Chinese one at the back of the house, overlooking the kitchen gardens, greenhouses, and orchards, and the lawns, bowling green, and woods to the west.

The woods. And the hidden garden. She wondered if it was still there: a small and exquisite flower garden in the middle of the woods, entirely enclosed by an ivy-covered wall and accessible only through an oak door that could be locked from the outside or bolted from within.

It had been designed for and by the crippled sister of Marcus's grandfather, long deceased by the time Olivia first came to the house. Marcus had taken her there the day after their betrothal became official and one month before their wedding—a time when it was deemed proper for them to be alone for short spells without a chaperon.

It was there that he had kissed her for the first time. . . .

THE COUNTESS GOT abruptly to her feet and walked restlessly about the room, straightening a picture, shaking a cushion before moving through the open door into her bedchamber and beyond it to her dressing room. She checked her appearance in the mirror, applied more perfume to her wrists. And looked at the closed door opposite the open one leading back into her bedchamber.

She had been curious about it since her arrival the previous afternoon. She was really not sure. Her apartments had been the former countess's. But perhaps his rooms were elsewhere. She set a light hand on the doorknob and listened. Silence. It was probably locked, anyway.

She turned the handle slowly and felt the slight give of the door. It was not. She pushed it inward, her heart pounding uncomfortably, feeling like a thief. It was probably an unoccupied room.

A shaving cup and brush were on the washstand, brushes and combs and bottles of cologne on the dressing table. A blue brocade dressing gown had been thrown over the back of a chair, a pair of leather slippers pushed carelessly beneath. There was a book on the seat of the chair.

She looked unwillingly beyond the room, through the open door leading to a bedchamber equal in size to her own, though its high bed, richly canopied and curtained, was more elaborate than hers. There was another book on the bed, visible through the side curtains, which were looped back.

The only other part of the room she could see was a side table that held a single, framed picture. It was turned away from her. It was doubtful that she could have seen it clearly, anyway, from the connecting doorway between their dressing rooms.

Would it be *her*? she wondered. She had been told that Lady Mornington was a lovely woman. But perhaps it was someone different by now. Someone younger. Someone no older than Sophia, perhaps. Either way, she did not want to see. It was one thing to know of his debaucheries, to think of them occasionally when she could not force her thoughts to remain free of him, to imagine the woman with whom he was currently involved. It was another to see. To see the face of the woman—of one of the women—with whom he committed adultery.

She did not want to see. And yet she was already in the doorway to the bedchamber, looking nervously at the hall door, half expecting it to crash open at any moment. She listened again. Again silence.

The picture was turned so that he would be able to see it from his bed. Was he so little able to live without her, then? Was he longing to have this business with Sophia settled so that he could go back to her? Olivia hoped she would not be very young or very pretty, as she reached out an unwilling hand and turned the picture.

She was indeed very young. And smiling and happy. And pregnant, though the painter had omitted that detail. But she was not in her best looks, she had protested to Marc. She had begged him to wait until after she had given birth. But Marc could be as stubborn as his daughter was now. He wanted her likeness, he had told her, so that he could always have her with him, even when she was busy visiting and gossiping with her friends. She could remember realizing with some shock that he was afraid to wait in case she died in childbed. And so she had consented.

And the painting was now on the table beside his bed, turned so that he could see it from his pillow. Was it always there—from force of habit, perhaps—noticed no more than the rest of the furniture in the room? Or had he placed it there for the occasion, in case she should have reason to look into his room, as she did now?

That smile had been for him. He had never once left her during the tedious hours of the sitting. He had talked and talked and told endless funny stories until the painter had looked reproachfully at him because she had laughed so much.

The smile had been for him.

Marc!

She closed her eyes and drew in a slow breath.

Her eyes flew open at the distant sound of a door opening. She turned the picture back to its original position with hasty fingers and dashed back through both rooms, pausing only for a moment to set his slippers side by side beneath the chair. His valet must have missed them. Marc had never been renowned for tidiness. She closed the door between the two dressing rooms and leaned back against it, breathing with relief.

What in heaven's name would she have said if he had caught her?

"Mama?" Sophia's voice came from the bedchamber.

"In here," the countess called, hurrying through from the dressing room. Her daughter was peering around the door from the sitting room. "I thought you had decided to stay in the village until nightfall."

"Mrs. Biddeford remembered all sorts of things she wanted once we were there," Sophia said. "And Rachel decided that she did not like the bonnet after all. But once we had left the shop and made all the other purchases and were back in the carriage, she changed her mind once more and nothing would do but we must descend again and go back for it. All the way home she entertained us with assurances that she should have waited until she returned to town." She laughed.

"Sophia," her mother said, "we have to talk."

"Oh, dear," the girl said. "I always know you are serious when you smile at me in just that way, Mama."

"Sit down," the countess said, ushering her daughter back into the sitting room.

"It is about Francis, is it not?" Sophia said, looking at her mother anxiously and standing in the middle of the room. "You do not like him, Mama? You are remembering him as he was as a young boy, are you, when he was forever playing nasty tricks on me because I was always following him about? But that was just boyhood, Mama. All boys are like that, horrid creatures. Or you have heard bad things of him recently. He has been sowing his wild oats, Mama. It is what young men do. But that is all behind him now. And it is said, you know, that reformed rakes make the best of husbands."

"Oh, Sophia." The countess laughed despite herself. "Do you have any more platitudes to mouth? Come and sit down, do, and tell me how this all began. You have not seen Lord Francis for several years, have you? I cannot remember your having a single good word to say about him before now."

Sophia sighed and sank down onto a sofa. "But all our aversion to each other has been converted into love," she said. "He is so very wonderful, Mama. I did not imagine it possible to feel this way. Is this how you felt about Papa?"

"I daresay," the countess said. "Sophia, I find this very difficult. Until the last year or so, it has been easy to deal with you. If we disagreed on any issue of importance, I would merely decide for you whether you liked it or not. Now it is not so easy to force you to do what I wish, even if my greater experience of life helps me to see reality more clearly than you."

Sophia got to her feet again and crossed the room to one of the long windows. "You are not going to forbid me to marry Francis, then?" she asked. "But Papa is preparing to do so, is he not? And you wish to do so, do you not? But why, when he is the son of a duke, Papa's close friend, and when he and I are so deeply in love?"

"Sophia," her mother said earnestly, "you are so very young. So very sure that nothing will ever change, that there is such a thing as happily ever after. How am I to explain to you that life is just not so, that your future should be planned with your head and not your heart? I know that such an idea will be quite beyond your comprehension and utterly abhorrent to you. It would have been so to me at your age."

Sophia turned to look at her. "Must I fall out of love with Francis merely because you fell out of love with Papa?" she asked. "Must history always repeat itself?"

"Sophia." The countess looked distressed. "I did not . . . that is not what happened between Papa and me. It is not because of that that I am advising you to think more carefully."

"Yes, it is," Sophia said. "Every girl I know has made or is planning to make her come-out at the age of seventeen or eighteen. And all their mamas and papas are eager for them to make suitable marriages. It is the thing to do. Else, why is London during the spring known as the Marriage Mart? And who could be more eligible than Francis? It is true that he is a younger son, but he is the younger son of a duke and has a large portion, even without the inheritance he expects from his great-aunt. It is true that he has something of a reputation for wildness, but what gentleman does not? Most girls I know, and their mamas, too, would kill for an offer from Francis. Cynthia still blushes when she so much as looks at him. Why is it you and Papa alone who say I am too young? Is it because you were too young, Mama?"

"Yes," Olivia said, sadly. "I do not want you to make the same mistake as I made, Sophia."

"But other marriages work," the girl said. "The duke and duchess are still together and Mr. and Mrs. Maxwell and Lord and Lady Wheatley and—oh, everyone but you and Papa. You are the only married couple I know who live apart. Why did you stop loving Papa?"

The countess felt horribly as if she had lost control of the encounter. It was not proceeding at all according to plan.

"That is not what happened," she said, looking down at her hands.

"What, then?"

She looked up. "Oh, Sophia, he is my husband and your father. I did not stop loving him."

"And yet you have not seen him since I was four years old until yesterday," Sophia said. "Was it his fault, then? Did he stop loving you?"

"No," the countess said, "I don't know. I don't know, Sophia. Something happened. It was nothing to do with you. I did not stop loving him."

"You love him still, then?" There was a gleam of triumph in Sophia's eyes. "You have not spent any time with him today, have you? But you are bound to feel strange together at first. You will be more at ease as time goes on."

"Sophia," the countess said.

"You are ten times lovelier than she is, anyway," the girl said.

"She?" Olivia raised her eyebrows.

"Lady Mornington," Sophia blurted. "You know about her, don't you? She is Papa's mistress. But not nearly so lovely as you and he must see it, too, now that you have come home."

Olivia swallowed. Still Lady Mornington, then? After six years? His liaison had lasted longer than his marriage? He must love the woman, then. A more lasting love than his first had been.

"Sophia," she said gently, "I am not here to stay. I am here only so that Papa and I can discuss your future with you and each other without the awkwardness of exchanging letters. As soon as everything is settled one way or the other, I shall be going home again. Rushton is my home. This is Papa's home. But we have strayed a long way from the subject I wished to discuss with you."

Sophia smiled radiantly at her. "No, we have not,"

she said. "When Francis and I are betrothed, you and Papa and I can discuss the wedding. It will be much easier than trying to do it by letter. And since we wish to have the banns read as soon as the betrothal is announced, you might as well stay for the wedding. It is too far to travel back here from Lincolnshire less than a month after you leave."

"Sophia," the countess said, "have you been hurt dreadfully by the fact that Papa and I have lived apart for most of your life? It has not been in any way your fault, you know. Papa and I both love you more than we love anyone else in the world. And I cannot call my marriage a mistake, you see, for without it there would not have been you. And I am as sure as I can be that Papa feels the same way. But what are we to do about you and Lord Francis? Do come and sit down again and let us talk about it sensibly."

"We want to get married in the village church," Sophia said eagerly, coming to sit beside her mother, "even though it will mean having only family and close friends as guests. I want to get married where you and Papa were married, and Francis says that he wants to get married wherever I happen to be the bride walking down the aisle." She laughed. "He says the most absurd things. Tell me about getting married there, Mama. Did Papa kiss you at the altar? Did you cry? I was born less than a year later, was I not? I think you must have been very much in love."

Olivia sighed. "Oh, Sophia," she said. "Yes, we were. You were a child born of love. You must never doubt that."

4

$\mathcal{L}$ORD FRANCIS SUTTON, STANDING BESIDE THE bowling green, having completed his own game, drew Sophia's arm through his. He smiled warmly at her, and strolled a little farther along with her, quite out of hearing of either the bowlers or the small cluster of spectators.

"It must be age that is coming upon me unexpectedly early," he said, "or some strange malady that has struck me within the past couple of months and is proceeding apace. It must be the country air, perhaps, or the country foods. A strange deafness. *What* did you say?"

"She can be won over," Sophia said eagerly, her cheeks flushed becomingly. Her look could easily be mistaken for one of complete adoration. "She is uneasy about the match, Francis, but it is merely anxiety for my happiness. She said—or she implied very strongly—that she will not forbid our marrying even if she does advise strongly against it."

"That part I understood very well," he said. "You must have been speaking more loudly and distinctly when you said that. It was the next part I misunderstood—or I think I surely must have, anyway."

"The part about the wedding?" she said. "I told her we were eager to marry in the village church, or that I was eager, anyway, and that you wished only to do what pleased me. I told her that as soon as our betrothal was announced, she could stay and help plan the wedding."

"You are getting close," he said. "I believe it was the next sentence."

"We want the banns read immediately after the betrothal announcement," she said.

"That was the one," he said. "And I might have saved you the trouble of repeating yourself, Soph. I heard correctly the first time. May I ask you something? Are you trying to trap me into marriage? Are you playing a more clever game than all the other females who fancy me? It is a good thing you don't wear stays, Soph—you don't, do you? You would be popping them all over the place at this moment."

"Well!" The word finally found its way past Sophia's lips. "The conceit. The unmitigated conceit. All the other females. *All*? How many dozen, Francis? How many hundred? Or should I go higher? I would marry a toad sooner than marry you. I would marry a snake sooner than marry . . ."

"I follow your meaning," he said, smiling even more warmly and lifting her hand briefly to his lips. "It is just that you are chuckleheaded then, Soph? Smile, darling."

She smiled. "Don't you 'darling' me," she said from between her teeth.

"When on the stage," he said, "you have to throw yourself heart and soul into the part. Once the banns are read, my darling, we are going to be dead ducks, you and I. It will be bad enough to have to face down a broken engagement, Soph. But that? It is out of the question."

Tears sprang to her eyes. "But she will go back home," she said. "As soon as this is settled one way or the other, she said she will return to Rushton. Whether we become betrothed or not, she will go. And what is the point of being engaged, Francis, if she does not stay?"

"What indeed?" he said.

"She will stay if there is a wedding to prepare for," she said.

Lord Francis scratched his head and apparently watched the bowlers for a few moments. "Maybe so, Soph," he said. "But will she go home anyway after we are married? That is the question. And what am I talking about, saying *after* we are married? Insanity is infectious. It must be."

"She still loves Papa," Sophia said. "She as much as admitted so to me. And he must love her, Francis. She is so much lovelier than his mistress."

"Good Lord, Soph," he said. "You are not supposed to know anything about mistresses, and even if you do, the word should never be allowed to pass your lips."

"His ladybird then," she said, exasperated. "His bit of muslin. His . . ."

"Yes," he said, tossing a look up to a fluffy white cloud that was floating by. "Lady Clifton is certainly a better looker than Lady Mornington. But it does not follow that he therefore wants her more, Soph. If you want my opinion, trying to bring them back together again after fourteen years is rather like trying to flog the proverbial dead horse. Oh, Lord, waterworks?"

"No," she said crossly, turning with hurried steps back toward the house. "Just a little insect in my eye, that is all. And the sun is too bright. I forgot to bring my parasol with me."

He caught up to her, drew her hand through his arm, and patted it. "Perhaps I am wrong," he said. "Perhaps I am, Soph."

"No, you are not," she said, fumbling about her person for a handkerchief, then taking the one he offered her. "She has been here for a whole day and they have scarce said a word to each other except last night out on the terrace when we forced them together. It is quite hopeless. She will go back home, whether it be tomorrow or next week or next month."

He curled his fingers beneath hers on his arm. "Perhaps all they need is time," he said. "It must be awkward meeting again after so long and with so many other people around to provide an interested audience. Perhaps in time they will sort out their differences."

"Oh, do you think so?" she asked, looking up at him hopefully.

"Yes, I do," he said. "No, you keep the handkerchief, Soph. It looks rather soggy. You certainly are not one of those females who can keep their eyes from turning red after a few tears, are you?"

"Oh," she said. "The word 'compliment' is not in your vocabulary, is it, Francis? I am sorry in my heart that you have to escort me about in all my ugliness. Perhaps you should resurrect one of your old tricks. You always used to be able to get rid of me, usually by stranding me somewhere."

"The island I always thought was the best one," he said. "How many hours were you there, Soph? And you would have been there longer if I had not eventually whispered your whereabouts to Claude."

"It was most cruel of you to row back to shore before I could get down from the tree," she said, "knowing that I could not swim and that the water was just too deep to be waded."

"I never confided another secret to Claude after that," he said. "He almost broke a leg in his haste to take the glad tidings to our father. I believe I was too sore to sit down for the rest of that day."

"There was not a great deal of it left," she said tartly.

He grinned.

"Do you really think there is still hope?" she asked.

He shrugged. "Your father has taken himself off from the bowling green already," he said. "Perhaps they are talking even now."

"Do you think so?" she asked. She looked back to the bowling green to verify the fact that her father had indeed disappeared. "You will do it then, Francis?"

"Do what?" he asked suspiciously.

"Allow the banns to be read if they will consent to our betrothal," she said. "Will you?"

"And allow the ceremony to take place, too?" he asked. "And the wedding trip in the hope that she will remain here to greet our homecoming? And our first child to begin his nine-month wait for birth in the belief that she will stay for the happy event and for the christening to follow? Perhaps we can have ten children in a row, Soph. Or an even dozen. Perhaps at the end of that time your mother will think it not worth returning to Rushton. Our eldest will be coming up to marriageable age."

"You are making a joke of my feelings," she said, "as usual. It will not get as far as that, Francis. Of course it will not. I shall break off the betrothal before the wedding, whatever happens. You have my word on it."

"Good Lord, Soph," he said. "Do you have any idea of the scandal there will be?"

"I do not care about scandal," she said.

"You will," he said. "No one will want to touch you with a thirty-foot pole after you have jilted a duke's son almost at the altar."

"That will suit me," she said. "I have already told you that I have no intention of marrying anyone. I don't want to be touched with a pole or anything else."

"I am not talking only of suitors," he said. "No one will want to invite you anywhere, Soph. You will be an outcast, a pariah."

"Nonsense," she said.

"Well," he said, "never say that I did not warn you. But go ahead and do it if you must. As long as I have your word on it that you will do the jilting, that is. I will certainly not be able to do it."

"Oh, Francis," she said, looking up at him with bright eyes, "how kind you are: I did not think I would be able to persuade you to agree. You are wonderful."

"Soph," he said, frowning, "a little less enthusiastic with the *kinds* and the *wonderfuls,* if you please. They make me distinctly nervous coming from you. I think we had better hope that your papa says no and sends me on my way. We had better hope quite fervently, in fact."

"A wedding in the village church," she said, her eyes dreamy. "With the bells ringing and the choir singing and the rector decked out in his grandest vestments. And the organ playing. Oh, Francis, it cannot fail to remind them and affect them, can it? *Can* it?"

"Ah, Bedlam, Bedlam," he said. "Your doors are wide open to me and beckoning, it seems."

THE EARL OF Clifton was almost finished with a game of bowls when he saw his daughter walking up from the house. Olivia must have had her talk with her, then. Mrs. Biddeford had come out almost an hour before.

He relaxed somewhat. Olivia would have talked sense into Sophia. She seemed to have a gift for doing so. It had been a great relief to read her letter announcing that she was coming. A great relief—but something else, too. He had not been at all sure that he really wanted to see her again, even though her portrait followed him about wherever he went. It always stood beside his bed, where it was the last thing he saw at night before blowing out the candles and the first thing he saw in the morning before getting out of bed.

But there was something quite different between a portrait and reality.

He excused himself at the end of the game and laughed when Lord Wheatley remarked that it would be a pleasure to let such an expert at the game go.

"I'll wager you spend every waking moment of your summers out here practicing, Clifton," he said, "just so that you may make the rest of us ordinary mortals look like clumsy oafs."

"I have an especially large umbrella that I use to keep myself dry during the rainy weather," the earl said, "so that I don't have to waste a single one of those moments."

Sophia and Sutton had strolled a little apart from everyone else, he noticed, and were deep in conversation. Was she telling him? But she did not look particularly tragic. He had no misgivings about letting them out of his sight. They were surrounded by his houseguests, including Sutton's own parents. He made his way back to the house.

His wife was not in her private apartments. Neither was she in the drawing room or the morning room or any of the salons. Her ladyship had stepped outside, a footman told him when he finally thought to ask. To the bowling green? But he would have passed her on the way. He went out onto the terrace and looked along all the walks through the formal gardens. They were deserted. The seat surrounding the fountain was empty, he discovered when he walked all about it to see the stretch that was not visible from the terrace.

Where could she be? The village? But she would have gone with the Biddefords and Sophia earlier if there had been anything she needed, surely. The hidden garden? Would she have gone there? Would she remember it?

It had been allowed to deteriorate during his father's

last years. The lock had been rusty and the garden hope-lessly overgrown when he had gone there after his fa-ther's funeral. He had stood on the spot where he had kissed Livy for the first time and felt even more bereft than he had felt in the churchyard looking down at the box that had held all that remained of a much-loved father. He had felt that the state of the garden somehow mirrored the state of his life. Tidying it up, putting it to rights seemed a monumental task and somehow futile.

Why tidy up a garden that almost no one knew about, that almost no one now living cared anything about? After all, there were the large gardens surrounding the house and the well-kept miles of the park beyond. Who needed a small garden hidden in the middle of a wood?

He needed it, that was who, he had decided. Like the portrait, it was one small memory he had left of her. She had loved the garden. He had always known during that month before their marriage where he might find her and he had frequently gone to her there. She had never bolted the door against him, though together they had bolted it more than once against the world so that they might enjoy a private embrace.

Would she remember it? Would she go there? Would it not be the very last place she would go?

And yet he had hoped from the start. He had left the door unlocked since he knew she was coming, hoping that perhaps she would find it again, hoping that no one else would do so. He did not want his guests, or even Sophia, in the hidden garden.

He strode through the woods, veering off the main path until he came to the ivy-covered wall. The arched door was almost hidden by ivy. It was shut. He set his hand on the latch. She would not be in there. It was the most foolish place of all to look. And even if she were, it would be wrong to go in. If she had come there, it would be because she wanted quiet and privacy. If she were there, she would have bolted the door from the inside.

But it was not bolted. It swung inward on well-oiled hinges when he lifted the latch.

The contrast between the scene inside the garden and that outside would have caught at the breath of a stranger not expecting it. Outside all was tall old trees and muted colors and semidarkness. Inside all was exquisite blooms and riotous cultivated beauty and color. A stone sundial in the center was surrounded by delicate fruit trees between the seasons of blooming and bearing fruit. Smooth green lawns were on either side of the cobbled path inside the door and sloping rock gardens, carpeted with a profusion of flowers, at the opposite corners. Roses climbed the walls.

The earl's gardeners spent a disproportionate amount of their time keeping the hidden garden immaculate.

She was sitting on a flat stone in one of the rock gardens, her arms clasping her knees. The green of her muslin dress was as fresh as the grass. He closed the door quietly behind him. He did not bolt it. She was looking steadily at him, her eyebrows raised.

"You have kept it, then, Marcus?" she said.

"Yes." He strolled toward her.

"Why?"

He did not reply for a while. How could he tell her the real reason? "Family sentiment, I suppose," he said at last. "And because when something is so exquisitely beautiful one feels the need to cling to it."

She nodded. She seemed satisfied with his answer.

She was exquisitely beautiful, he thought. The portrait beside his bed no longer did her justice. And yet the bloom of youth was no longer there. She was a woman, more lovely than a mere girl.

"Well?" he said.

"I do not know if it can be prevented, Marcus," she said. "She has her heart set on the match and I did not notice that anything I said made her feel even the slightest doubt about the wisdom of her course."

"You failed?" he said.

"I told her at the start," she said, "that I would no longer treat her as a child and make her decisions for her. I told her I would not forbid the betrothal, though you well might. But I also told her that I would do all in my power to persuade her that she would be making a big mistake in persisting."

"You did not forbid the match?" he said, frowning.

"She is eighteen years old, Marcus," she said. "I was a married lady at her age."

"But can she not see how foolish it is to lose her head over almost the first man she has seen?" he asked. "She is eighteen, for God's sake, Olivia. A child."

"But she reminded me," she said, "that all about her in London were the young girls of the *ton,* come to be presented and to find husbands. It is the way of the world. And she is right, Marcus."

"You approve of the match, then?" He set one foot on a stone a little below the level of that on which she sat and rested one arm across his knee. "You think we should approve the betrothal?"

She looked troubled. "I don't know," she said. "All my instincts are against it. I cannot believe that she will be happy with Lord Francis. And I cannot believe that she can possibly know her own mind or realize that being in love is not always a sound basis for a marriage. But she turned the tables on me when I gave her those arguments."

He looked at her while she plucked a carnation and held it to her nose.

"She says it is because of you and me," she said, raising her head to look at him. "She says we are opposed because our own marriage failed and we find it impossible to believe that hers will not. She listed other marriages that have not failed. In fact, ours is the only one that has, as far as she knows."

He swallowed.

"Marcus," she said, "could she be right? Are we being unduly pessimistic and overprotective? Would we feel the same way if nothing had happened and we had stayed together? Or would we feel rather pleased at the prospect of her marrying Rose and William's youngest son? Despite his reputation, would we be pleased? He seems excessively fond of her. I don't know the answer. I cannot put myself into the position of a normal, contentedly married woman to know how I would feel. I came here to try to think of the answer."

He could not think of the answer, either. He looked down at her bowed head, at the smooth, almost blonde hair parted neatly down the middle and combed back from her face. And he watched her twirl the carnation and bury her nose in it.

If nothing had happened. If Lowry had not decided to get married in London and invited him and Livy to the wedding. If he had not appeared quite so eager to go because Lowry had been a particularly close friend of his at Oxford. If Sophia had not come down with the measles just the day before they were due to leave and Livy had not persuaded him, much against his will, to go alone because his heart had been so set upon it. If there had not been that stupid party for Lowry two nights before the wedding and all the interminable drinking.

If the rest of their university cronies had not laughed at him for being such a staid married man when he was still so young and had not dared him to come with them to a certain tavern of low repute. If he had not been so drunk and so foolish, foolish, foolish. He had never afterward been able to remember either the girl's name or what she had looked like. Only the fact that he had bedded her and hated it while he was doing it and hated himself after he had paid her and staggered out into the street and vomited into the gutter to the hearty amusement of those cronies who were still with him.

Foolish idiot of a young puppy. Having behaved so, he should have found some salve for his conscience and pushed the experience out of his mind. The girl had meant nothing to him and he knew that none of his friends would ever tell what he had done. He had known that he would never be tempted to do such a thing ever again.

But he had gone home and shut himself away from Livy for four days, puzzling her with his insistence that he needed to be with his books and catch up with what had happened on his property since he went away. And at night he had been unwell and too tired to make love to her. On the fourth night he had been too unwell to sleep in her bed. He had gone into his own little-used bedchamber.

"What is wrong, Marc?" she had asked him, coming quietly into his darkened room half an hour later as he stood staring out of the window.

"Nothing is wrong," he had said. "Just this stomach-ache, Livy."

"What happened in London?" she had asked.

"Nothing," he had said. "A wedding. Parties. Too much eating and drinking, Livy. I'll feel better soon."

"Is there someone else?" She had whispered the question.

"No!"

He had almost yelled the word, turning to face her. It had been the time to cross the room and take her into his arms, kiss her, take her through to her own room again, and make love to her. He could have forgotten once he had been inside her familiar and beloved body. And even if he could not have forgotten, he should never have told her. Never.

"There was a girl," he had blurted. "A whore. Nobody, Livy. I cannot even remember her name or her looks. I was foxed and dared to it. It meant nothing. Nothing, Livy. It is you I love. Only you. You know that. She was no one. It will never happen again. I promise."

Even in the darkness he had seen the horror and revulsion on her face. She had said nothing as they stood and stared at each other, his hand stretched out to her.

And then she had turned and fled. Both her bedchamber and dressing room doors were locked by the time he had gone staggering after her.

She had refused to forgive him. And she had kept on refusing until he had been forced to believe that she never would.

She set the carnation down on the stone beside her.

"You think I should have a talk with Sutton, then," he said, "and find out what his intentions and prospects and plans are? You think I should give our consent if his answers are satisfactory, if it appears that he is in earnest and intends to be good to Sophia? Is that what you think I should do, Olivia?"

"I don't know," she said, looking up again. "We have to make the most important decision concerning her that we have made in her life, Marcus, and reason and good sense no longer seem good enough guidelines. What is the reasonable or sensible thing to do? Mama and Papa and your parents did not stop us from marrying when they saw that our hearts were set upon doing so."

"No," he said.

She spread her hands palm up on her lap and looked down at them. "Perhaps they should have," she said.

"Yes."

"But does that mean that we should stop Sophia?" she said. "Perhaps it will turn out to be a happy marriage."

"Yes."

"Oh, Marcus," she said, lifting her face to him, "what do you think? I would so like you to make this decision because you are her father. But I know that is not fair."

"It strikes me," he said, "that in six months' time or a year or two years we will be going through this all over again, Olivia, if we say no this time. And I believe Sophia will always be too young and there will always be something wrong with the young man."

"Yes." She smiled ruefully.

"I think I had better hear what Sutton has to say for himself," he said.

"Yes."

"I will not make it easy for him," he said.

She smiled. "I remember your saying that Papa was a veritable ogre," she said. "Though he was normally the mildest of men."

"You were seventeen," he said, "and his only daughter."

"Yes."

"You will be prepared to live with this betrothal, then?" he asked.

"I suppose so," she said. "Sophia said that they will want the banns read immediately, Marcus. They wish for a summer wedding at the village church."

"Do they?" he asked. And he had the sudden memory of Olivia, her face raised to his, its expression tender and wondering and utterly vulnerable as the rector pronounced them man and wife. It was a memory all mixed up with organ music and the smell of flowers and the pealing of bells. "You would stay until after the wedding, then?"

The color deepened in her cheeks. "If there is a wedding," she said. "Yes, if I may."

"This is your home," he said.

She shook her head. "No," she said. "Rushton is my home."

"Are you happy, Olivia?" he asked and wished he had not turned the conversation to such a personal matter.

She did not answer for a moment. "Contented," she said. "I have my home and my garden and my books and music. And the church and my charitable works and my friends."

"Clarence?" he said. "Is he still your friend? I rarely see him in town."

"He does not often go," she said. "He prefers to remain in the country. Yes, he is still my friend, Marcus. So are a dozen other people and more."

"I am glad," he said. "You have never been willing to use the house in London, even when I have assured you that I would not be there."

"No," she said. "I am happier at home."

"I always loved the place," he said. "I am glad you are contented there."

"Yes," she said.

He straightened up and lowered his foot to the grass. "Are you coming back to the house with me?" he asked. "Or would you rather stay here a little longer?"

"I shall stay here," she said.

He nodded and turned away. But her voice stopped him when he had his hand on the latch of the door.

"Marcus," she said. He looked back over his shoulder. "I am glad that you have kept the garden."

He smiled and let himself back out into the wood.

I kept it for you, he wanted to tell her. But it would not have been strictly true. It was for himself that he had kept it. Because it reminded him of Livy and the perfection of the life they had had for almost five years before he had destroyed it in one stroke by trying to prove to a crowd of drunken men who meant nothing whatsoever to him that he was a real man.

He closed the door quietly behind him.

5

SHE HAD NOT PLAYED CHARADES FOR YEARS, THE Countess of Clifton thought, laughing after a particularly energetic round and seating herself to catch her breath. She always attended every assembly and social gathering in the neighborhood of Rushton, but for years she had been considered a member of the older generation and had sat with them, merely observing the more energetic sports of the young.

But Sophia had insisted that she join in the game this evening and Mr. Hathaway had echoed her urgings. Marcus had left the drawing room soon after the gentlemen joined the ladies following dinner, taking Lord Francis with him. Sophia had been flushed and frenzied ever since.

A footman had come into the room and was speaking with the duke and duchess and then turned in Olivia's direction. "His lordship requests the pleasure of your company in the library, ma'am," he said quietly for her ears only and then looked about him for Sophia.

The countess smiled at the duke and duchess as all three of them made their way to the door.

"So we are to be put out of our misery, Olivia," His Grace said. "Is it to be yes or no, eh?" He chuckled.

"The interview has certainly lasted long enough," the

duchess said. "All of an hour. Have they been talking business all of that time, do you suppose?"

"And so, Olivia," the duke said, as they all paused outside the library for another footman to open the doors for them, "we are to be rid of our last boy and you of your only girl all at the same time. We will have nothing to trouble our old age except the arrival of grandchildren."

The earl was the only occupant of the library. He was standing with his back to the fireplace, his hands behind his back. He smiled at them.

"Well, Marcus," the duke said, "did that scamp of a son of mine impress you sufficiently, or did you send him packing?"

"I have consented to his making his offer to Sophia," the earl said. "I believe he is doing so at this very moment."

"Splendid, splendid," the duke said, rubbing his hands together while the duchess fumbled in a pocket for a handkerchief and the countess watched her husband. "And when are the nuptials to be? Before Christmas, I hope. There is no point in waiting around once the intention has been expressed, I always say."

"In one month's time," the earl said. "Your son wishes to have the betrothal announced tonight, William, if Sophia will give her consent—and I don't believe there can be much doubt that she will do so. He wants the first banns read on Sunday."

The duchess shrieked and buried her face in her handkerchief.

"Here?" His Grace said. "Not in St. George's like our other boys? Well, a quiet country wedding has its charm, I must admit. You and Olivia were married here, were you not, Marcus? A charming wedding, as I remember. So Francis is proving to be as impulsive as ever, is he, and insisting on no delay? Now don't take on so, Rose.

No one has died. And, indeed, little Sophia may yet refuse him."

"But how can we be ready in one month?" Her Grace wailed. "Olivia?"

"I am sure it can be done," the countess said soothingly. "The invitations can be sent off tomorrow. They are the most urgent. Then we can sit down and plan everything else."

"I think for this evening we might as well relax," the earl said, "and await developments. Do have a seat, Rose. Olivia? And you, too, William. What can I offer you to drink?"

"This is quite like old times," the duke said, beaming about him a few minutes later when they were all seated cozily, drinks in hand.

It was and it was not, Olivia thought. They were together, the four of them, talking and apparently relaxed, as they had often been in the past. But she was no longer seated beside her husband, their hands almost touching—they had never embarrassed their family or friends by showing open affection in public. He was sitting in a chair by the fireplace, she on the sofa beside the duchess. And she no longer felt quite part of the group. The three of them had continued the friendship over the fourteen years when she had been at Rushton.

She had agreed with Marcus that afternoon that the betrothal should be consented to if his interview with Lord Francis was satisfactory. She still did not know if they had made the right decision. Probably they would not know until several years had passed and they could see how the marriage developed. But she wished, after all, that they could have done something to prevent it.

If there were to be no marriage, she would be able to go back home without further delay. Home to the safety and familiarity of Rushton and to her friends—Clarence and Emma Burnett in particular.

But now she was to be at Clifton for at least another month, amid all the fevered excitement of an approaching wedding. And it was to be at the church in the village. It was going to be very difficult.

And difficult to be in company with him daily, both of them mingling with his guests. And there would be innumerable occasions when they would have to be alone together, working on the arrangements. It was going to be difficult to bear. Every bit as difficult as she had expected. More so.

He was so very attractive. She had never particularly thought of that word in connection with him before. He had been excessively handsome and vital and very, very dear to her. But she could not recall ever feeling this aching pull toward his masculinity. It was not a pleasant feeling. She had no wish to feel it. She was not a schoolgirl to be sighing over a handsome man. She was a mature woman.

Besides, he was Marc—Marcus—and she did not want to be reminded of a marriage that had failed a long time ago and from the misery of whose ending she had fought her way back to life through a year and more of hell. She wanted only to be away from him, to be at peace again. And she knew very well what had made him so very much more attractive than he had been when they were together. It was experience—experience gained with countless other women.

She wanted nothing to do with his experience. She had preferred her innocent Marc.

They were interrupted less than half an hour after sitting down by the sudden and unheralded opening of the doors and the arrival of Sophia and Lord Francis, hand in hand, their faces brightly smiling.

"Ah," Lord Francis said, "you are all together here. Very opportune. Sophia has just agreed to marry me."

"I have," she said, flushing and laughing.

They were all on their feet suddenly, talking and laughing. And the duchess raised her handkerchief to her eyes again.

"Oh, my boy," she said. "My baby. And it seems no longer than a year ago that you were in leading strings." She hugged him and wept over him.

"Sophia, my girl," His Grace said, opening his arms to her, "we have wanted you for a daughter-in-law from the time when you could climb stairs after our boys but not descend them again. And now our wish is to be granted. Come and have a father-in-law's hug."

Everyone had to hug everyone else, it seemed. Olivia submitted to a bear hug from the duke, who assured her that he could not be better pleased at the closer link there was to be between their families, and to a teary one from Her Grace. Sophia threw her arms about her and danced her in a circle, declaring that now they would have a whole month together, all of them. Lord Francis smiled sheepishly at her until she cupped his face in her hands and kissed his cheek and told him that she would be proud to have him for a son-in-law.

And then her husband was there as she turned, smiling, from Lord Francis and he was releasing their daughter. The duchess was sobbing loudly in her husband's arms and lamenting the fact that their baby was leaving them and there would be no more weddings to look forward to until Bertie's girls grew up.

"Well, Olivia," the earl said, smiling at her. "We are to be the parents of a bride, it seems."

"Yes." She bit her lip and felt the unexpected emotion of the moment work at her facial muscles.

And then his arms came beneath her own and about her and he hugged her hard against him. Her own arms, for lack of anywhere else to go, went about his neck.

All she could feel was shock. Shock that he was quite unmistakably Marc, this older, broader man with the silvering dark hair. Quite unmistakably. It was something about the way he held her, perhaps. Something about the way he caused her body to arch itself against his. Something about the familiar cologne he wore. And something else, quite undefinable.

Marc!

His cheek rested briefly against hers. "We must be happy for them, Olivia," he murmured into her ear. "We must believe that they will be happy."

"Yes." She closed her eyes and then was standing alone again, aware of the duke's booming laugh and the duchess's sniffles and Sophia's chatter.

And she watched as Lord Francis set an arm about Sophia's shoulders, drew her close against his side, and bent his head to kiss her briefly but thoroughly on the lips. The girl looked stunned, almost angry, for a moment, her mother thought, before flushing scarlet while everyone laughed.

"We want to be married just as soon as the banns have been read," Lord Francis said. "Don't we, Soph? It will not be worth anyone's going home. There is going to be a wedding to celebrate."

"Go home!" the duchess exclaimed. "Did you hear that, Olivia? We will be fortunate indeed, Francis, if there is even time to go to bed within the next month. Do you have any idea whatsoever of all that is involved in planning a wedding? No, of course you do not. You are a mere man. Olivia, my dear, I have the headache merely thinking about the coming month."

The duke chuckled. "What Rose actually means, Olivia," he said, "is that she is now in her element and woe betide anyone who tries to distract her from the sheer delight of wearing herself into a decline over the coming nuptials."

"Shall we adjourn to the drawing room?" the earl suggested. "Our guests will be wondering why they have been abandoned for so long, though I daresay they will have guessed. I believe my wife and I have a betrothal to announce. Olivia?" He held out an arm for hers.

"AND WHAT DID you think you were about in the library?" Sophia demanded as soon as they were clear of the others.

She and Lord Francis had been permitted to step outside alone for a breath of air in light of the fact that they were now officially betrothed. Everyone else had appeared too tired from a day of outdoor activities and an evening of charades to accompany them. Or too tactful, perhaps. They were strolling along one of the diagonal paths of the parterre gardens.

"What was I about?" he asked, frowning. "I was about announcing our betrothal and trying to look suitably besotted."

"Looking suitably besotted does not include kissing my lips," she said. "You will stay far away from them in future, Francis, if you know what is good for you. You were fortunate indeed not to find yourself with a fat lip."

"If you cannot control your passion sufficiently, Soph," he said, "it would be better to bite me on the neck rather than on the lips. I can cover up the evidence with my cravat."

"Oh," she said, "you are disgusting. Who in her right mind would wish to bite your neck? Ugh!"

"You turned an interesting shade of scarlet when I did kiss you," he said. "I thought perhaps you were about to swoon in my arms, Soph."

"Yes, well," she said, "you said yourself that when you are acting you have to throw yourself wholeheartedly into the part. I had to convince Mama and Papa that it was my first kiss."

"It probably was, too," he said. "Was it?"

"Wouldn't you like to know!" she said, tossing her head.

He chuckled. "The worldly wise look does not suit you, Soph," he said. "We are going to have to steal several kisses, you know, over the next days. People will expect it."

"Oh, nonsense," she said.

"There are probably a dozen people lined up behind the darkened windows of the house right now," he said, "just hoping to see our silhouettes merge."

"What a ridiculous idea," she said, glancing across to the house. "I do not see a single watcher."

"Naturally," he said. "You would not exactly expect them to be lined up there, a candle in each hand, would you, Soph? They are standing back out of sight or hiding behind the curtains."

"Sometimes, Francis," she said, "I think you must have windmills in your head."

"It sounds painful," he said. "Shall we thrill them?"

"What?"

"Your mama and papa might be among them."

"Mama and Papa would not spy on me," she said indignantly.

"They would not think of it as spying," he said. "They will want to see for themselves that they made the right decision concerning us, Soph. They will want to see that we are not out here quarreling or walking ten feet apart."

"Well, we are not," she said. "Walking ten feet apart, I mean. We are always quarreling."

"I think we had better do this right," he said. "Stand still, Soph, while I kiss you."

"Lay one hand on me," she said indignantly, "and I will . . ."

"It will have to be two hands," he said, "and my mouth. You aren't afraid, are you?"

"Afraid?" she said scornfully. "Of you, Francis?"

"It is as I thought," he said, stopping and setting one hand on her arm. "You are afraid."

"Well," she said. "Of all the . . ."

"Half a minute should be a decent enough time for a newly betrothed pair, I believe," he said. "Count to thirty slowly, Soph. It will take your mind off your jitters."

And while she still looked up at him in mingled indignation and embarrassment and fright, he set his mouth to hers, took her free arm in his other hand and merged their silhouettes.

"What are you doing?" She drew her head back when she had counted no higher than twenty-one and glared at him. "What do you think you are doing?"

"Trying to open your lips with my tongue, actually, Soph," he said. "It becomes a little tedious merely to rest still lips against still lips, don't you think?"

"No, I do not think," she said. "That was a quite unnecessary part of the act. It could not be seen from the house. And if it had, Papa would doubtless be out here by now brandishing a whip about his head. Don't you ever do that again. *Ever*, do you hear me? It made me feel all funny."

"Did it, Soph?" He grinned. "You had better not go falling in love with me, you know. I don't want to be responsible for broken hearts or anything like that."

"Do you know, Francis," she said, "I do not believe I have known anyone—*anyone*, male or female—who comes even close to you in conceit. Fall in love with you, indeed! I would be as likely to fall in love with a toad. I would be as likely to . . ."

". . . fall in love with a snake," he said. "Sometimes you are not very original, Soph. Let us change the subject, shall we? Are you happy, at least? Are you satisfied?"

"Oh, Francis." She looked up at him with a radiant smile as they resumed their walk. "Was it not wonderful? Even more wonderful than could possibly have been imagined? They hugged each other. Did you see? Actually hugged. And I do believe he kissed her cheek, too. And in the drawing room afterward he kept her on his arm while everyone came about to congratulate us and kept his hand over hers, too, and talked about 'my wife and I,' just as if they had the most normal of marriages. Did you notice, Francis? Everything is going to be all right, is it not? After a month everything cannot fail to be all right."

"It was definitely promising," he agreed. "But I cannot help feeling that we have got in a little deeper than we expected, Soph. Good Lord, my mother must have soaked three handkerchiefs. And they were all so very pleased."

"Your mother and mine are going to love planning the wedding," she said, smiling up at him. "We must not forget that the guest list is to be drawn up directly after breakfast tomorrow. You must think of any special friends you want to invite, Francis, apart from Mr. Hathaway and Sir Ridley, who are here already, and I will think, too. I don't believe I will be able to sleep tonight."

"Soph," he said.

"What?"

Lord Francis sighed. "Nothing," he said. "Just a little thought from that alien world of sanity that I used to belong to."

"Oh, that," she said, sobering. "Yes, of course."

THE EARL OF Clifton could have gone through the connecting door between his dressing room and hers. She was, after all, his wife, and there had been a time when the door between their rooms was permanently open. But times had changed, of course. Or he could have knocked on the door and waited for her maid to answer. He could hear the two of them talking behind it. But there was something demeaning about knocking on the door of his wife's dressing room.

He strode around to the door of her sitting room and knocked.

She was dressed when she came through from the bedchamber a few minutes after her maid had let him in. But he must have taken her by surprise. He should have left his call until a little later in the morning, perhaps. Her hair had not been done. It hung smooth and shining halfway down her back. She had pushed it behind her ears. He tried to keep his eyes from it. It used to be short.

"I came to see if you had had second thoughts," he said, smiling. God, but she was beautiful.

"Second and third and thirty-third." She returned his smile. "I suppose we have to realize that we cannot live her life for her, Marcus, any more than our parents could live ours."

"They seem happy enough," he said.

"He is a pleasant young man," she said. "I think his charm is more than just of the surface. I like him."

"It seemed strange," he said, "to see him kiss my little girl in the library and no longer have the right to plant him a facer."

"Oh, Marcus," she said, "she was such a sunny-natured little girl, was she not?"

"Do you remember how she used to try to run across the grass almost before she could walk?" he said. "She used to be angry rather than upset when she continually fell down." He laughed.

"And then you would take her riding on your shoulders," she said. "And she would clutch on to fistfuls of your hair so that you used to swear that you would be bald by the time you were thirty."

He turned away suddenly and crossed the room to look out of a window. "Did you notice what she kept saying last night, Olivia?" he asked.

"About our all being together for the next month?" she said. "Yes. She said it more than once."

"She has never said much," he said. "I always thought she accepted the situation for what it was. Perhaps she did. Perhaps it is only being here with us like this that has made her realize that she grew up without a family."

"Yes," she said. "I did not realize, either, Marcus."

"This month is going to be very important to her," he said. "*We* are going to be important to her. We together. Her mother and father."

"Yes."

He turned from the window to look at her broodingly.

"Can there be some peace between us for one month?" he asked. "I know you have not liked me for many years, Olivia, and have made a new life for yourself in which there is no room for an old marriage. And I know there has been a dreadful awkwardness between us since you arrived—married but not married, separate parents to the same child. Can we at least outwardly be more together—for Sophia's sake? Is it possible?"

She stared back at him, her face pale. She looked rather as she had looked the morning he left home never to return, he thought unwillingly, although at the time he had not dreamed that he would not see her again for fourteen years. He had gone away to give her a few weeks to come to terms with his infidelity. To give her a few weeks to forgive him.

She never had.

She licked her lips. "I would do anything in the world for Sophia," she said. "You know that."

"Yes," he said. "And so would I. It will mean a little more than being under the same roof for a month."

"It will be like last evening?" she said. "My hand on your arm? 'My wife and I'? 'Our daughter'?"

"Smiling at each other," he said. "Doing things together."

"Planning the wedding together," she said.

"Can you do it, Olivia?" he asked. "For one month can you hide your aversion to me—at least in public?"

She raised her eyes to his. "Yes," she said. "For one month, Marcus. For Sophia's sake."

"A family for one month," he said. "I think it will be important to her, Olivia."

"Yes," she said.

"Let's go down to breakfast then," he said, extending his arm to her.

"My hair," she said.

He smiled in some amusement. "It is lovely," he said. "I like it long, though I always liked the curls, too. Go and have it dressed. I shall wait for you here, shall I?"

"Yes," she said.

He watched her leave the room and turned back to the window. A family for a month. It was a sweet seductive thought. One he must not allow to take a hold on his feelings. After Sophia's wedding she would be going home again. Back to Rushton. He must not let down the guard on his emotions during that month. It had taken him too many years to build it up.

6

$\mathcal{I}$T WOULD BE IMPOSSIBLE TO INVITE ALL THE *TON*, AS the duchess seemed to wish to do. Large as Clifton Court was, there was a limit to the number of guests who could be housed in its rooms. And the village church was not large. Members of the *beau monde* would not enjoy sitting outside in their carriages or standing in the churchyard while the marriage ceremony was in progress, the earl pointed out, because there was no room for them inside.

The guest list would have to be drawn up with care. All of the guests then staying at the house were willing and eager to stay or at least to come back again. Family had to come next and then close friends—those of Sophia, Lord Francis, the duke and duchess, the countess, and the earl.

The meeting of the interested parties lasted for all of two hours until, at last, the list was just the length it needed to be. Then Her Grace, Olivia, and Sophia spent the rest of the morning writing the invitations while the men went into the village to visit the rector.

After luncheon, the earl insisted that everyone take a rest from the wedding preparations in order to ride for a few hours and take a picnic tea on the hill north of the house.

"After all," he assured the alarmed duchess, who insisted that there were not enough hours left in which to arrange everything satisfactorily, "we cannot have you and Olivia looking quite hagged on the wedding day, now can we? Rose? And I do assure you that I have a perfectly competent housekeeper and cook, who are even now making arrangements to ensure that we will not all starve. I have also sent for most of my staff from the London house to come."

"And it is a beautiful day, my love," the duke told her. "Far too lovely to be wasted on the hysterics indoors."

"We are not having the hysterics, are we, Olivia?" Her Grace said. "We are merely busy."

"Besides," Lord Clifton said, "the other guests have been neglected quite shamelessly for half of the day. Olivia, can the time be spared?"

"We do need half an hour to finish the invitations," she said. "And they really should be sent today, Marcus."

"Half an hour it is, then," he said. "Not one moment longer."

And so while the afternoon was still early, they all rode out, hats shading their eyes from the brightness of the sun. They rode along the smooth miles of the park to the south of the house and back along the wooded banks of the river that formed the border of the park to the east. Cultivated acres stretched beyond it to the horizon. The river circled back around the house until, finally, the riders branched away from it toward the heather-covered hill a few miles north of the house. There carriages of food and footmen awaited them.

The ride had been a long one, even though the trees along the course of the river had shaded them from the worst of the sun's heat. They all dismounted at the foot of the hill and set the horses free to graze on the grass there. Most of the guests were grateful for the blankets set down on a piece of level ground halfway up the hill and sank down onto them before accepting glasses of wine from the footmen.

"That is my riding done for this year," Lady Wheatley said. "And it is more than I did last year at that."

Several people laughed.

"I never feel quite right if I do not begin each morning with a three-mile ride," Mrs. Biddeford said. "Though I do not have quite the energy of these children, I must confess." She grimaced as she watched several of the young people and the earl and countess climb the remainder of the slope to stand on top of the hill.

"Dear Olivia," the duchess said. "She is looking well, is she not? She seems not to have aged like some of us."

"I am glad you said *some,* my love," His Grace said with a chuckle, "or you would have mortally offended several ladies here, I do not doubt. Though you, too, look quite as youthful as you did on the day I married you."

"William!" the duchess said scornfully and fanned her face with a napkin. "But how delightful it is to see them together again, is it not?"

"I never could quite understand what the problem was," Lord Wheatley said. "I was always under the impression that it was a love match."

"That is precisely what the problem was," His Grace said.

SOPHIA, WHO HAD ridden with her friend Cynthia for much of the way, the two of them with their heads together wondering over the success of the original plan and discussing how best the mock betrothal was to be put an end to when the time came, found her hand being taken by Lord Francis when they dismounted.

"What are you doing?" she asked.

"Lacing my fingers with yours," he said. "It looks far

more intimate, Soph, than linking arms or merely holding hands. And while good manners would demand that we be with and converse with our friends during the ride, sentiment now dictates that we steal a few minutes together." He smiled into her eyes and she smiled back.

"Mama and Papa have not been together all afternoon," she said. "This is not going to work, Francis."

"Nonsense," he said. "After being away from their guests all morning, of course they would have felt obliged to mingle this afternoon as we did. They did well enough this morning."

She brightened. "Cynthia said they came down to breakfast arm in arm," she said. "Do you suppose that means . . . ?" But she stopped and blushed scarlet.

"Probably not," he said. "But they sat side by side in the library when they need not have done so, and they were both very insistent that the other's friends be invited to the wedding."

"Yes, they were, were they not?" she said. "Where are we going?"

"To the top of the hill," he said. "Young lovers have boundless energy, you know."

"No, I did not know," she said. "But there is a rather splendid view from the top."

"I know," he said, grinning. "I remember."

She looked at him blankly for a moment and then her look became indignant. "You were quite horrid," she said. "I do not know why I even talked to you in town this spring."

"Don't you?" he said. "It is because I am a duke's son and have fairly or unfairly acquired a reputation as something of a rake, Soph. An irresistible combination to the ladies, I have found. And yes, that does make me conceited, I must admit. I have saved you from having to say it yourself, you see."

"You went fishing," she said accusingly.

"I did," he said. "With my brothers. Blissfully free of female companionship."

"While I kept watch at the top of the hill for hours and hours," she said.

"Oh, come now, Soph," he said, "it could not have been for longer than two at the most. And we needed someone to keep watch, you know, while the rest of us went hunting poachers and highwaymen and brigands. You did a splendid job. You kept them all at bay so that we were able to enjoy a peaceful hour or two of fishing."

"You were fortunate," she said, "that I did not tell your father on that occasion. Or your brothers, either. They did not know what story you had told me to keep me away. Claude would have punched you in the nose."

"A manly punishment at least," he said. "Bertie would have spanked me, and my father would have walloped me. A subtle difference, you know—something to do with the weight of the hand. My father's was invariably heavy."

"You would have deserved it," she said.

"Doubtless." He grinned. "But you should be hoping fervently that I have not changed, Soph. I always managed to get rid of you, did I not? I must say, I felt uncomfortably hot under the collar when we called on the rector this morning and started to discuss banns and weddings and such."

"Did you?" Her eyes widened. "Papa has already sent for half the staff from the London house. Have you heard?"

He grimaced.

"Here we are at the top," she said. "Oh, how lovely. There is a breeze. Look, Francis, half the others are coming up, too. I thought everyone was tired from the heat and the ride."

"Ah, an audience," he said, catching her about the

waist with one arm, drawing her against him, and kissing her soundly before releasing her and taking her hand again.

"I told you not to do that again," she said indignantly.

"Kiss you?" he said. "But we have probably restored the spirits of a dozen or so weary riders and climbers, Soph. And there is a play to be acted out, you know."

"I meant that business with your tongue," she said. "The breeze was just cooling me nicely. Now I feel hot again."

"Soph!" he said. "Only a total innocent would say such a thing aloud and expect it to discourage me from trying again. If we are going to have to steal kisses, we might as well make them enjoyable, after all."

"Enjoyable!" she exclaimed. "You may speak for yourself, Francis. For my part, I would as soon kiss . . ."

"I know," he said. "Look who is coming up there to your left, Soph. And with arms linked. And talking with each other and seemingly oblivious to everyone else."

She looked, saw her father and mother approaching, grabbed Francis's arm, and squeezed it tightly.

"Oh," she said, "it is working, I knew it would. I never doubted it for a moment. It will work, Francis, will it not?" She looked up anxiously into his face.

"I don't see how it can fail, Soph," he said, "with the weather cooperating so gloriously and you and me so deeply in love, and all the joy of a wedding beginning to catch everyone up in its excitement."

"Oh, you are wonderful to say so," she said, squeezing his arm again. "I could kiss you, Francis."

"Once is enough for the time being," he said. "And not too free with the *wonderful*s if you please, Soph. I might start to think that you mean them and really start to feel choked by my cravat."

Sophia turned with a bright smile to greet the group of

friends who were reaching the summit of the hill and beginning to exclaim on the splendor of the view.

HE HAD GIVEN her the details of the visit to the rector. She had told him of some of the plans she had discussed with the duchess as they wrote the invitations.

"Was it a good idea to agree to let the wedding take place here?" she asked. "Rose seems a little disappointed that it is not to be at St. George's."

"It is what they both want," he said. "And these large *ton* affairs can be cold, you know."

"Yes," she said. "I never regretted that we married here, Marcus. It was a wonderful wedding, was it not?"

"Yes," he said. "But then I think a clay hut would have seemed wonderful to us on that particular day, Olivia."

She could think of nothing more to say and indeed was embarrassed that she had spoken so freely and thoughtlessly. They did not need to speak of their own wedding. Doing so would only cast a blight on their daughter's and make them anxious for her happiness again.

"You are content to invite only two friends from Rushton, Olivia?" he asked. "It seems not quite fair when I chose five of my close friends."

"Emma and Clarence will be enough," she said. "But I would be sorry if they could not come for Sophia's wedding. Clarence said, after I had received your letter, that it was quite what was to be expected at her age. I suppose a mere friend can see more clearly than a parent that a child is growing up."

"Yes," he said. "I have not seen Clarence for many years. Or Miss Burnett, either."

"Emma has never been far from home," she said. "And Clarence has not for quite some time."

She was breathless from climbing the hill and talking

at the same time. He paused and drew her arm more closely against his side. It would be so easy, she thought, to relax into this new state of amity, to believe that their natural and mutual concern for their daughter was a totally binding force, to imagine that the truce they had agreed to was a permanent peace. It was a feeling she must hold firm against. She did not want to have to go home in a month's time to fight all the old battles again.

But it was easy to remember just why she had been so happy with him, why she had loved him so much.

"I think perhaps we have done the right thing, don't you?" he said. "None of our guests threw up their hands in amazement that we would allow the betrothal of so young a daughter. And the rector seemed to feel that it was the most natural thing in the world for Sophia to be getting married. They look good together. They look as if they belong together."

"Yes." Olivia looked to the top of the hill, where their daughter and Lord Francis stood close together in animated conversation, their fingers laced. "They have known each other all their lives. That must help. It is not as if they have just recently met and have had romance blind them to each other's faults. They talk to each other a great deal. They seem to be friends, Marcus."

"Do you remember this hill?" he asked.

They had walked there the day before their wedding, when they had been able to escape from the frenzied activities going on at the house. They had climbed right to the top, as they were doing now, and let the wind blow in their faces and wished that the following day were over already so that they could be married and alone together.

"I don't care about the houseful of guests and the feasting and all the rest of it," he had said. "I just want you, Livy."

"And I you," she had said, turning into his arms. "To-morrow, Marc. It seems an eternity away."

"Tomorrow," he had whispered against her lips. "And then no more separations. Night or day. Never or ever, Livy, until death do us part."

"I love you," she had told him, and he had kissed her long and deeply while they were buffeted by the wind.

"I wonder if they feel as we did then," he said, and she knew that he was thinking of the same memory. "I wonder if they feel their wedding to be a mere nuisance standing between them and eternal bliss."

"But it was a wonderful day after all, was it not?" she said.

"Yes," he said. "They will discover that, too."

Before they could remember that they should not reminisce together, they were at the top of the hill, and the breeze greeted them—and their daughter. She had released Lord Francis's hand and pushed her way between them, taking the arm of each.

"Is this not wonderful?" she said, her cheeks glowing from the wind and happiness. "Miles and miles of countryside to see, the lovely sunshine, the cool breeze, and the three of us together again. Is it not wonderful beyond belief?"

"Yes, wonderful, Sophia," Olivia said, and found herself fighting tears for some reason.

"You are truly happy, Sophia?" her father asked. "You have not rushed into anything merely because you are eighteen and it seems the thing to do to marry?"

"I am truly happy, Papa," she said, squeezing his arm. "I am betrothed to the most wonderful man in the world and the most wonderful parents in the world are here to help me celebrate. This is going to be the happiest month of my life so far. And then all the years ahead with Francis. We want you to spend Christmas with us—you and

Francis's parents, too, of course. And the New Year. Don't we, Francis?"

Lord Francis had been laughing and joking with some of the other young people. He turned at the sound of his name. "Don't we what?" he asked with a smile.

"Want Mama and Papa and your mother and father to spend Christmas with us," she said. "And New Year. It is what we were talking about a few minutes ago when we were coming up the hill, is it not?"

"The very topic," he said, smiling deep into her eyes. "And we were both agreed that by Christmas we will probably be able to take our eyes off each other for long enough to entertain relatives. We will be disappointed if all four of our parents cannot be there."

"Mama?" Sophia asked eagerly.

"We will have to see," she said. "That is a long time in the future."

"Papa?"

"I shall be there, Sophia," he said quietly.

"Doubtless there will be numerous other occasions, too," Lord Francis said. "Won't there, Soph?" Somehow he had possessed himself of the hand that had been linked through her mother's. "Perhaps for the christening of our first child in a year's time or less."

Olivia heard her daughter suck in her breath as Lord Francis smiled at her again and raised her hand to his lips. Good heavens, had they talked about such a thing already?

"It looks as if the food has been taken from the baskets," Mr. Hathaway said loudly enough for all to hear. "And I feel as if I could devour it all myself."

"You would not be so unsporting," Rachel Biddeford said.

"Oh, yes, he would," Sir Ridley said. "I think those of us who hope to eat a bite had better race for it."

"Well, Soph," Lord Francis said, "you must lift your

skirt above the ankles and grasp my hand. I don't intend to be the last to the chicken slices."

And they were gone, all of the young people, laughing and shrieking and rushing down the hill.

The earl looked at his wife and smiled. "What was that we have been saying about their having grown up?" he said. "Were we like that at their age, Olivia?"

"Christmas," she said soberly. "It is not really that far in the future, Marcus. Will Sophia be very disappointed, do you think, to have to entertain us separately? Surely she cannot expect everything to change just because she is marrying Lord Francis."

"We will have to wait and see," he said. "All we have agreed to is this month, Olivia. And we have done the right thing. She is very happy to have the three of us together again. Let us just live this month through, shall we, and worry about the rest when it is over?"

"Yes." She sighed. "I have not looked forward to Sophia's growing up. If I had known that it would lead to this sort of complication, I think I would have looked forward to it even less."

"Shall we go down?" he said. "Are you hungry?"

"I suppose so," she said, shrugging.

"I have had some of the trees cut back from the river bank down there," he said, pointing down the north side of the hill. "Those very old ones. Unfortunately, they kept shedding ancient branches and sometimes whole trunks into the water and caused flooding. It seemed sad at the time, but actually the cutting back has made for a pleasant walk or ride. Would you like to see?"

"Yes," she said. "Have you made many changes, Marcus? I remember that you used to accuse your father of being quite unprogressive."

"The ravings of a younger man who had not yet learned to appreciate tradition," he said. "It is a good thing, perhaps, that most men are older when they eventually inherit. I have far more sympathy with my father than I used to have. Take my arm, Olivia. This section is steeper than it looks. Yes, I have made changes, of course, but nothing to destroy the character of the place."

"What others have you made?" she asked.

A WHOLE HOUR passed and several of the guests, having finished their picnic tea, had already ridden back to the house before the earl and his wife came strolling around the bottom of the hill and began the climb to the remains of the feast.

"Oh, dear," the countess said as if suddenly recalled to the present, "we have been neglecting our guests dreadfully, Marcus."

"They do not look neglected," he said. "In fact, I would say they look remarkably well fed. Is that Hathaway stretched out fast asleep? And several people are actually beaming down upon us—most notably Sophia. And Rose. Are you hungry yet, Olivia? I could eat a bear."

"And I forgot to have bear patties packed in the hamper," she said without stopping to think. His comment and her reply had been common ones during the years when they were living together.

"Cucumber and cheese and chicken will have to do instead, then," he said. The old reply again.

Olivia felt a heavy ball of panic lodged deep in her stomach. Their plan must not be allowed to work too well. The plan was for public appearances for Sophia's sake, not for private exchanges.

SOPHIA AND LORD Francis rode off together, Cynthia and Sir Ridley Bowden a little behind them.

"What did you mean," Sophia said accusingly when they were on horseback and on their way, "talking about our first child like that in front of Mama and Papa. I could have died of mortification."

"Or of burst blood vessels in your head," he said. "To say you turned scarlet, Soph, would be to understate the case. I was merely following your lead, that's all. You are the one who started talking about Christmas and New Year and all that sort of sentimentality."

"Inviting them for Christmas and a christening are two entirely different matters," she said. "I scarce knew where to look. In one year's time or less indeed. What a disgusting idea. I would rather . . ."

He held up a staying hand. "We are not going to have to go through all this toad and frog and snake business, are we?" he said. "Have done, Soph. The thought of infants and nurseries actually is enough to make me run all the way to Brazil without stopping or even noticing the ocean, so you need have no fear. Especially if you were to be the mother."

"And that is just like you, too," she said indignantly, "to give me such a very ungentlemanly setdown. I would rather be childless to my dying day than have you father my children. So there."

"They were an hour alone," he said, "out of sight of the whole company. And looking quite pleased with themselves and the world at the end of it, too. Very promising I would have to say, Soph. Another few days like this and we will be able to put an end to this charade before the wedding guests start to arrive."

"Do you think so?" she said. "They did look almost like an ordinary married couple, did they not, Francis? But how are we to know that they will stay together after we have put an end to all this?"

He shrugged. "I don't know," he said. "You will have

to ask them, I suppose, Soph. You are their daughter, after all."

"Oh," she said, "how can I go up to them and ask if they are going to remain together?"

"Ask them one at a time," he said.

"I suppose so." She frowned. And then she smiled radiantly at him. "The Christmas idea might work, though, Francis, even if this does not," she said. "There is no time quite like Christmas for love and families and peace and warmth and everything else that is wonderful. If we can get them to come to us for Christmas, they surely will remain together afterward. Don't you think?"

"Christenings sometimes have the same effect, too," he said dryly. "Soph, I am coming more and more to the belief that you are either the wickedest schemer it has ever been my privilege to know or that you are a case for Bedlam. I rather lean toward the latter."

"Oh, yes, of course," she said, mortified. "It will just have to happen this month, then, won't it?"

"And sooner rather than later would be good for my peace of mind, too," he said. "Promise me one thing."

"What?" she asked, looking at him.

"That after this you will consider yourself fully revenged for all those nasty things I did to you as a boy," he said. "That we will shake hands and go happily on our separate ways."

"But you agreed quite freely to this," she said. "I never agreed to all those horrid tricks. Don't tell me that you are having second thoughts, Francis, and wish we had never started all this. You are, aren't you?"

"Who? Me?" he said. "Having second thoughts? Why ever would I do that, Soph, when I am having so much fun? And when I am in imminent danger of being dragged off to the altar just so that we can have your parents for Christmas? It has never once occurred to me to have second thoughts or to give in to an attack of acute anxiety."

Sophia looked doubtful. "Well, then," she said, "why are you talking about shaking hands and going our separate ways? If we do that, Mama will go home before she and Papa have realized that they cannot live without each other and I shall never marry because I will be finally convinced that no good can come of marriage. Do you want to be responsible for those two disasters?"

Lord Francis sighed. "When you get back to Bedlam, Soph," he said, "ask them to reserve a room for me, will you? There's a good girl. I am going to be needing it soon."

Sophia clucked her tongue and spurred her horse to a canter. Lord Francis shook his head and went after her.

7

$\mathscr{T}$HEY REALLY DID NOT NEED THE DISTRACTION OF the ball less than a week after the announcement of the betrothal, the duchess said. There was so much to do without all the preparations for that. She seemed oblivious to the fact that the earl had organized the ball several weeks before and that his servants were quietly and efficiently carrying out all the work that was to be done. She seemed equally oblivious to the fact that various competent persons had taken over the preparations for the wedding and that everything was progressing smoothly.

As His Grace commented to the earl and countess one afternoon when Her Grace had finally been persuaded to rest in her room for an hour on the understanding that the world would not collapse about her if she did so, her mind must not be disabused. She was entirely happy being in a panic about nothing.

Besides, the duchess had assured everyone, herself included, the ball was entirely necessary as an official celebration of the betrothal.

The countess and Sophia, accompanied by Lord Francis, were to go to London for a few days the following week in order to be fitted for wedding clothes and bride clothes. Olivia had mixed feelings about the approaching journey. So many years had passed since she had been to town. And yet, she had always loved it there. Her come-out Season had been magical.

The duchess kept her busy most days about real and imagined preparations for the wedding. And there were guests to entertain. She grew accustomed to being the hostess at Clifton, to spending hours in company with her husband, behaving for Sophia's sake as if theirs was a real marriage. And it was a worthwhile effort. Sophia glowed and was utterly happy.

And yet, there was the need to spend time alone. For fourteen years she had been a very private person, bringing up a daughter, having a circle of good friends, participating in the social life of her neighborhood, and yet being essentially alone. She had grown accustomed to the life.

She needed time to think. Time to regain her equilibrium, her sanity. Sometimes she found herself almost forgetting that things were not as they seemed. Sometimes she found herself seating herself next to her husband or speaking to him or even seeking him out when there was no real need to do so. She had strolled beside him throughout one afternoon walk, for example, and had realized, only after they had returned home, that she need not have done so since Sophia and Francis had gone with a few other young people to the village.

And there were the mornings, two of them, when he had mentioned at the breakfast table that he must ride out about estate business for a few hours and she had asked him privately afterward if she might accompany him. She had always done so when they had been together. She did not want to be merely the lady of the house, she had always said. She wanted to be part of his world. She wanted to understand the workings of his land. She wanted to be able to talk meaningfully with her husband about the things that really mattered.

It was training that had stood her in good stead during the intervening years. Although Marcus remained in close communication with his steward, he never came home and had learned to trust her with the day-to-day decisions concerning Rushton.

And so she rode with him about Clifton and enjoyed those mornings more than she had enjoyed anything else for a long time. She watched and listened and asked him questions and made comments. They scarcely stopped talking during all the hours they were gone. During those hours, she had not once felt any awkwardness with him, or any strain from their long separation and the knowledge that it would resume once Sophia was safely married. It had seemed quite like old times. They had felt like friends. Friends and comrades.

Dangerously like.

She needed some time to herself. And she found it not in her rooms, where she could in all probability have gone undisturbed, but in the hidden garden. It became almost a regular part of her day to steal away there for an hour in the afternoons. Only one rainy day had kept her away.

She would sit in the rock garden, merely thinking or dreaming, her eyes feasting on the beauty and color of the flowers, her nose drawing in the heady scent of the roses. Or sometimes she would take her book and read. Sometimes she stretched out on the grass beneath the shade of one of the trees and watched the clouds float across a blue sky and let the peace of nature seep into her very bones. Once, she fell asleep.

It was like a place apart, a dream world, a little heaven on earth. Not Clifton, not Rushton, not the past, not the present. Not of this world at all.

She never bolted the door behind her, but she always hoped that no one else would discover the hidden garden. It would not be the same once someone else had been there to exclaim on its beauty. Except one person, of course. She went there each day to escape from him—not so much from his physical person as from the influence he was beginning to have over her emotions. And yet, of course, she took him there with her, for it was there he had first kissed her. It had been their garden—Marc's and Livy's. Two different persons.

She fought against the knowledge that in reality they were still the same people.

She was sitting there on the afternoon of the ball, rather than resting in her room before getting ready, as the other ladies were doing. The sun was hot again and the sky cloudless, as it had been so often recently. She was beneath the shade of a weeping willow tree, beside a bed of hyacinths. She was wishing that the remaining three weeks until the wedding would pass by quickly. And she was wishing that time would stand still.

She did not know what she wished, she thought, smiling ruefully at the contradiction in her mind and reaching out to touch a purple bloom.

And then the arched door opened and she looked up to see him come inside. She was not surprised. She had been expecting him.

Had she? Certainly she had not consciously done so. If she had, then surely she would have sought out privacy elsewhere. Had she wanted him to come? Onto magical ground like this, no part of the real world. Did she want him there?

He leaned against the door as he shut it behind him and she knew, although she could neither see nor hear it happening, that he had bolted it. She had expected it. Wanted it?

"You are not resting?" he asked her, strolling toward her along the path and around the sundial.

"Yes," she said. "Here."

He smiled and stopped below her. She was sitting on a

rock on a level with his shoulders. "You come here every day, don't you?" he asked.

"Yes."

It was a dream world indeed. He stood there looking up at her, his eyes roaming over her face, her hair, her body. And she looked at him, at the man he had become while she had not been there to observe the gradual changes. Neither seemed to feel the embarrassment of silence or the need to say anything.

Surely he was more handsome now than he had been. Or perhaps it was just that she was looking at him through older eyes that demanded more than a slender, good-looking boy. There were lines in his face—not wrinkles exactly—but lines of maturity and character. Lines that revealed that he had some experience of life. And his silvering hair was unexpectedly attractive. It was as thick as it had ever been.

His shoulders were broader, and his chest, too. And yet his stomach was flat and his waist and hips still slim. He was not showing his age in increased flabbiness as Clarence was doing. Clearly he looked after himself, as he had always done. The muscles of his calves showed that he walked and rode a great deal. She wondered if he still liked to spar at Jackson's boxing saloon when he was in town.

When he reached out his arms to her, she did not hesitate to set her hands on his shoulders and lean forward so that his hands could grasp her by the waist and lift her to the ground in front of him. He held her above him for a few moments and she looked down into his upturned face.

It was inevitable. It was what she had known for days was going to happen. Had she? The conscious thought had not crossed her mind. But she had known it. She had been coming to the hidden garden and she had known that he would eventually come there, too. It was their garden, after all, and it was still as lovely and re-mote as it had been when they shared their first kiss. It was the one thing in their world that had not changed.

He lowered her slowly, sliding her along his body until her feet touched the ground. And then he lowered his head and kissed her.

She could only feel shock at the sameness and the dif-ference. He was Marc as he had always been, bending her body to his, his height arching her head back. And so familiar that the years instantly rolled back. There were no years. Only Marc and her and the rightness of their being together. He was the only man who had ever kissed her or touched her in any way intimately.

And yet so different. He had used to kiss her with parted lips. They had always enjoyed the warmth and intimacy of kisses. She had liked to curl against him on a sofa or on his lap, indulging only in kisses, without any particular thought to going to bed. It had been a warm and wonderful form of communication.

But he had never kissed her openmouthed as he was kissing her now, his mouth wide over hers, his tongue pushing up behind her lip and creating strange vibra-tions against the soft flesh there.

And then his face was above hers and they were look-ing at each other again, exploring each other's eyes this time. And he was lowering his head and pecking light kisses on her temples and cheeks. She ran the back of her fingers softly over his jaw, her elbows up over his shoulders. His jaw was smooth. He must have shaved very recently.

They had always been able to look into each other's eyes without embarrassment and had laughed together once after two friends had told them that they hated to sit opposite each other at table when alone because doing so forced them to look into each other's eyes as they talked. She had laughed about it with Marc, and the two of them had tried it, sitting opposite each other at a small card table, their elbows touching on its top, their chins cupped in their hands, trying to stare each other down. They had laughed and occasionally leaned forward to exchange brief kisses, but succeeded in staying where they were for half an hour before they had been called away to some unremembered task.

They looked at each other now until he wrapped one arm about her shoulders and the other about her waist, drew her close against him, and kissed her again.

And this time the unfamiliarity was total. He slid his tongue all the way into her mouth until she felt filled with its firmness and heat, and withdrew it as slowly before pushing inward again. And she realized, as her knees almost buckled under her, what act he was simulating and then had no more time for thought. Only for reaction.

She had never felt desire before, a strange truth in light of the fact that their five years together had been ones of almost daily intimacy, and that she had always—with the possible exception of their wedding night—enjoyed their couplings. She had enjoyed them because they always gave him such pleasure and because there was joy in being so intimately possessed by the man she loved more than anyone else in the whole world. If asked, she would have said that she felt both desire for and fulfillment with her husband.

But she knew now, beyond the realm of rational thought, that she had never felt desire before. Never this raw throbbing from her mouth to her throat to her breasts to her womb and lower. A throbbing and an insistent longing to be possessed. Never this uncontrolled need to have his body fill her and give her peace.

She arched herself into him as one hand twined tightly in his hair and the other went up under his coat and waistcoat to the warm silk of his shirt at the back. And she held her mouth wide to the rhythm of the simulated loving of his tongue.

He was looking down at her again, his dark eyes gazing knowingly and heavy-lidded into her own. And he was turning her until their feet discovered soft grass, and lowering her down onto it, raising her muslin dress to her waist as he did so. His hands stripped her of her lower garments, removed his coat to set beneath her head, and undid the buttons of his breeches.

Was this going to happen? Was she going to allow it? It was one thing to share kisses with him in the hidden garden, however intimate, and quite another to couple with him there. Should she not put an end to the madness? She looked about her at the trees and the grass and the banked flowers spilling over the rocks. She could see the sundial behind her and the clear blue sky above. And she knew clearly what was happening and what was about to happen. She would never be able to accuse him of ravishment, she thought quite deliberately.

And yet she was like two persons. The one was detached and rational. The other ached for him and wanted him and needed him and knew that it had all been inevitable from the moment when she had read his letter asking her to come. For how could she see him again and not love him? How could she see him again and keep dormant within herself the knowledge that she had always loved him, had continued to love him even when she had hated him the most?

There was no stopping what was about to happen. And she would not stop it now, even if she could. She would think later of the shame of it, of the complications she was adding to her life, of the hell she would be facing after she had returned home, alone again.

He was beside her on the grass, pulling free the sash beneath her breasts with one hand as the other slid up her naked body beneath her clothes and covered one of her breasts. She closed her eyes and opened her mouth in a silent cry.

What he did to her breasts, to first one and then the other, was achingly familiar to her. She bit down on her lower lip and smiled with the wonder of it after all these years. Marc. She wanted to open her eyes and speak his name, but that was one thing she could not do.

And his hand moved down between her legs as he kissed her again, and began to do unfamiliar things, things that brought her desire to a boil and had her arching up against his hand, crying out into his mouth, begging for a release she had never suspected a need of before.

And then his weight was on her and his hands beneath her and his knees pushing between her own and widening them and he came up into her with one sharp thrust and something shattered inside her and inside her world so that she clung to him with her arms and legs, her body shaking out of control as he moved quickly and deeply in her to his own climax.

She was hardly aware that he moved off her almost immediately because of the hardness of the ground, taking her with him so that she lay on her side against him, her head on his arm while he lifted his coat and spread it over her. She slept almost immediately.

HE HAD GUESSED that she came to the hidden garden daily, though he had not spied upon her. And he had tried to stay away from there himself, sensing her need to have somewhere to go where she could be alone. It must be difficult for her, coming into his world at a moment's notice and forced to remain in it for a whole month. He realized that. And difficult, too, to be forced by her love for Sophia into spending more time with him than inclination would lead her to do otherwise.

He had tried to leave her alone and had failed on this particular afternoon. The ladies were all in their rooms resting in preparation for the evening's ball. The gentlemen were all variously employed and did not need his company. There was no work that particularly demanded his attention. And the weather was glorious—perfectly sunny and hot. It was an afternoon made for love.

And he loved her. He had never doubted it, had never even tried in all the years of their separation to stop loving her. Olivia was his wife, the woman he had chosen to spend his life with. Nothing had happened to change those facts.

He had known that he still loved her even before she arrived. What he had not expected was the force of his need for her. Not just physical need, though there was that, too, but also emotional need. He needed her companionship again, her support and respect. Her affection. He had never found a substitute for those qualities, even with Mary.

He needed her, but knew what a strain he had put on her emotions by pressuring her into playing out a charade for Sophia's benefit. He tried very hard to keep conversation easy and light between them, to do or say nothing that would embarrass or distress her, and in some ways it had been easier than he had expected. She still had her interest in estate business and the well-being of his tenants. They were able to talk impersonally, but with genuine interest on those matters.

He tried very hard to keep anything personal out of their relationship. She had made herself very clear on that score years before and had always been quite adamant in her refusal to forgive him. He had written almost daily when he first left home. Six months had passed before he finally wrote to her to inform her that it would be the last time he would beg her forgiveness. If she refused it that time, then he would be forced to consider their marriage at an end in all but name. He would leave her alone to live her life in peace, writing to her only about business matters and matters concerning Sophia. He had informed her that he would never take Sophia from her, but would need to see their daughter with fair frequency.

He had informed her yet again that he had been unfaithful to her only that once, that there had been no repetition of the infidelity during the six months, and never would be if she would but forgive him and take him back. She had written to tell him that after deep and careful reflection she had concluded that she could never again be his friend or his wife or lover after what had happened. It would always be there to come between them. She would be grateful if he kept the promises made in his last letter. She would never deny him Sophia for visits.

He had done as she asked. And a month after her letter arrived he had set up Patty, a young dancer, as his mistress. He had found a measure of forgetfulness with her for the year after that—a very small measure. The girl had been a very experienced young courtesan. But it had not been experience he had been in search of. It had been a substitute for Livy. After a year he had paid her off and never repeated the experiment, though he had occasionally—rarely—hired a woman for a single night.

He rested his cheek against the smooth hair on top of his wife's head and looked at the roses climbing the wall opposite. He would not sleep, explosive as their coupling had been. He wanted to smell the sweet fragrance of her hair and to feel the warmth and softness of her lower body, still unclothed, against his own. He wanted to feel the weight of her head on his arm and to listen to her even breathing.

Except that he felt rather sick. He had come to her at

last, half hoping as he walked through the woods that she would not be there, but would be safely resting in her own apartments. He had come to talk with her, he had convinced himself as he entered the garden and slid home the bolt on the door behind his back. He had come to smell the flowers with her and enjoy the sunshine. He had come . . . because he had had to come.

He would just hold her, he had decided a few minutes after that. He would just kiss her as he had kissed her during those days of their betrothal. He would indulge in a little nostalgia. And in a little self-indulgence, too, he had decided very soon after that, using his tongue on her in the sensual, suggestive manner taught him by Patty many years before.

And then it had been too late. He closed his eyes and turned his face into her hair.

He was feeling sick and despairing. What further proof would she need that he was uncontrolled and selfish in his passions? Locking the door of the garden and taking her on the grass as if she had been any whore. As if he had come there for no other purpose.

And he was feeling sick for another reason, too. She had changed. Her body was more mature and voluptuous. That was understandable. She had been twenty-two years old the last time he had slept with her. She was thirty-six now. But that was not the difference. It was a difference in experience.

She had been an innocent when he had left her, just as he had been. She had never initiated anything in their lovemaking and had never given any signs of great physical passion. She had always enjoyed their beddings. He had known her well enough to realize that. And they had always made love in the literal meaning of the term. But he had never known her aroused beyond a hardening of her nipples and an increased warmth. Even after five years of a very intimate marriage, she had been an innocent.

The woman with whom he had just coupled was no innocent. He had been startled by her early and total arousal, by the way she had arched herself to him, explored his body with pressing palms, sucked on his tongue, moaned out her desire, and half dragged him down to the grass. She had touched him with knowing hands after he had unclothed himself and while he had touched her. And she had twined herself about him and abandoned herself to physical release at his first inward thrust into her body.

It was not the Livy he had known with whom he had coupled. It was Olivia as she had become in fourteen years. He lay on the grass, her body nestled warmly against him, and stared at the roses. He wondered who had taken her from innocence to the glorious flowering of passion and sensuality he had just been witness to.

Clarence, he supposed. Clarence almost certainly. He had been a handsome enough man and had always been her friend as much as his own. Not that he suspected even for one moment that there had been anything between the two of them before the separation. But there clearly was a great deal between them now.

There was a dull ache of despair in the pit of his stomach and a growing anger, too. An unfocused anger. Not entirely against her. He knew from experience that it was nearly impossible to remain celibate for fourteen years. And not entirely against Clarence, though at least partly so—oh, yes, at least partly. And not even entirely against himself for causing it all.

Just an anger against fate, perhaps, for bringing about this present pass. For allowing Sophia to break out with the measles just when she had, and not a day or two later. For making Livy the type of woman who would want him to go to that wedding alone because he had had his heart set on it. For making him go even though he would twenty times have preferred to remain at home with his wife and daughter. For that stupid party and his criminal weakness. For all the rest of the chain of events leading to the end of their marriage and to this bitter-sweet moment.

Perhaps they had loved too dearly. Had he loved her less, perhaps he could have kept quiet about his infidel-ity and punished only himself with it. Had she loved him less, perhaps she could eventually have forgiven him. Had he loved her less, perhaps he would have forced her to take him back and they might have eventually worked out some sort of peace. Had she loved him less . . .

It was all pointless thinking. Matters were as they were. And he found himself physically satisfied and mortally depressed. And disturbed by the beginnings of anger.

She was awake. He could tell by the change in her breathing and by the slight tensing of her body. He closed his eyes. If she smiled at him, he thought, then he would talk to her from the heart. He would ask her once more, after all these years, to forgive him even though there was now much more to forgive. He drew a slow breath, opened his eyes, and eased his head back to look down into her face.

She looked back at him, her eyes blank. Not the blank-ness of a consciousness not fully returned, but a deliber-ate blankness. A mask. A brick wall. There was not even the suggestion of a smile on her face.

He felt his jaw hardening as he clamped his teeth to-gether. He eased his arm from beneath her head, sat up, and adjusted his clothing. He lowered her dress beneath the cover of his coat and then lifted the coat away and pulled it on. He got to his feet and brushed the grass from his clothing. And he turned to look down at her.

She had not moved or changed her expression or uttered a word.

"After all, Olivia," he said, and he hardly recognized the coldness of his own voice, "you are my wife."

Then he strode across the grass to the door, unbolted it, and let himself out, closing it firmly behind him.

8

ALL OF HER FATHER'S NEIGHBORS WERE DELIGHTED at the news of her betrothal, Sophia discovered at the ball that evening. They were equally delighted by the fact that she and her prospective husband had decided that the nuptials were to be held at their own village church.

"It must be nigh on twenty years since there was such a grand wedding in these parts," Mr. Ormsby said. "Your mama and papa's, my dear Lady Sophia. And a lovely one it was, too."

"The sun was shining," Mrs. Ormsby added, smiling and nodding toward the earl and countess, who stood next to their daughter and future son-in-law in the receiving line. "And such a beautiful bride."

"But no lovelier than you will be, my dear," Mr. Ormsby said before extending his hand to Lord Francis. "So you are the fortunate young man, are you?"

"The very one, sir," Lord Francis said, bowing.

The neighbors were also pleased to see her parents together again, Sophia saw, and she glowed with hope and happiness. They looked so splendidly good together this evening, her papa in black with sparkling white linen, her mama in turquoise silk. They looked not old enough to be her parents, she thought fondly, despite

Papa's silvering hair. It only made him look more distinguished.

Sophia smiled and curtsied and turned her cheek for yet another series of kisses from beaming well-wishers.

Color glowed in her mother's cheeks, Sophia had noticed earlier when she had called at her room so that they might come downstairs together for dinner. It was such a deep color and so perfect that at first Sophia had thought that her mama had taken to wearing cosmetics. But no, the color was natural, and had not faded at all in the course of the evening.

Her father was rather stiff and formal this evening. He had scarcely smiled, though he was treating his guests with courtesy and friendliness. But it was understandable, Sophia thought fondly, that his manner would be a little unnatural this evening. It was not every day that a gentleman held a ball in celebration of his only daughter's betrothal.

Sophia felt a stab of guilt and darted a look up at Francis. He smiled warmly back at her and one of the Misses Girten sighed and simpered as she approached along the receiving line.

"Such a very fine-looking couple," she commented to the earl and countess. "And clearly a love match."

Sophia felt even more guilty. But she quelled the feeling instantly. It was all worthwhile if it would finally bring Mama and Papa together again. They so obviously belonged together.

It was a pity that Bertie and Richard and Claude were not present, the duchess said with a sigh when it appeared that all the guests had arrived and the dancing could begin. She still could not quite believe that her baby was to be married within the month. But then, she said, cheering up visibly, the boys and their wives and families would be coming to Clifton more than a week before the wedding. Soon she would have all her family about her again.

"And soon you will have another daughter-in-law to add to the flock, Rose," the duke said, patting her hand and looking about the ballroom, which they had all just entered. "And doubtless another occupant for the nursery, too, within the year. Our boys are nothing if not prompt about such matters. They take after their father."

"William, love!" the duchess said, embarrassed.

Lord Francis, in view of all the guests in the ballroom, smiled meltingly into Sophia's eyes and raised her hand to his lips.

"The moment can be likened only to standing on a trapdoor, a noose about one's neck, waiting for the door to be sprung," he murmured fondly into her ear. "And knowing that one did not commit the crime but has cheerfully admitted to it all along on the foolish assumption that the real culprit would come to take one's place at the last moment."

"How can you liken a ball to a hanging, Francis?" she said, looking about at the floral decorations that she had helped with earlier in the day. "And it is all in our honor. Was there ever a more wonderful feeling? Look." Her hold on his arm tightened. "Papa is going across to the orchestra to instruct them to begin playing. And I believe he is going to make an announcement."

"The trapdoor hinges are creaking," Lord Francis said.

The Earl of Clifton raised a hand for silence. He got it easily since almost all eyes were on him and the gathered guests were eager for the ball to begin.

"Welcome to Clifton Court," he said, looking about him at all his friends and neighbors and houseguests. "The reason for this evening's celebration is well-known, so I do not intend to give a long speech."

"Bravo!" a voice said from a far corner, and there was a flurry of laughter.

"This is just an official announcement of the betrothal and coming nuptials of my daughter, Sophia, and Lord Francis Sutton, youngest son of the Duke and Duchess of Weymouth," the earl said. "They will lead the first dance, a waltz. Please feel free to lead your partners onto the floor after a few minutes, gentlemen. And enjoy the evening, ladies."

Sophia flushed at the applause and looked anxiously up at Lord Francis as he led her to the middle of the dancing area. "Everyone is going to be watching," she said. "I shall have two left feet, Francis."

"You are fortunate," he said. "I will be dancing with a noose about my neck."

"How foolish," she said.

"Smile," he commanded, and she tipped her head back to show that she was already doing so, and they began to waltz.

"Oh, Francis," she said. "This is very wonderful, is it not? I had no idea quite how it would be. I think that, after all, provided Mama and Papa remain together, and perhaps even if they do not, I will marry." Her eyes grew dreamy. "At the village church. And make very, very sure that nothing stupid ever happens to keep me away from my husband for the better part of my life. I think I will live happily ever after."

"Er, those plans don't include me by any chance, do they, Soph?" he asked. "I mean, you aren't expecting me to play the part of radiant bridegroom and happy husband as well as besotted fiancé, are you?"

"Of course not," she said. "You do not have to worry that I will break my word, Francis."

"What?" he said. "Nothing to add about snakes and toads and such? You aren't coming to like me by any chance, are you, Soph? I don't particularly want any softening of feelings here for a while yet, you know."

"Oh," she said indignantly, "how could I possibly like you, Francis? You always go out of your way to be obnoxious."

"Now that I know the secret of my success with you," he said, "I shall be sure to continue with it, Soph. A little twirl about the corner here, I think. We have guests to entertain. Ah, our respective mamas and papas have joined us on the floor, I see."

"Papa does not look at all relaxed," Sophia said with a frown. "He looks almost as if he is not enjoying himself. But they waltz beautifully together, do they not? And how could he fail to fall in love with Mama all over again, Francis? I think it is happening, don't you? They have been together far more than they needed to be in the past week. She has even been out with him about estate business."

"Lord," her partner said, looking harassed before putting his smile firmly in place again, "my mother is going to weep floods of tears when you jilt me, you know, Soph. She probably will not talk to you for the next ten years or so."

"I am not going to jilt you," she said indignantly. "What a horrid word."

"Oh, yes you are," he said firmly, "even if the word were ten times more horrid."

"I am going to end the betrothal," she said. "That is all."

"And that is not jilting?" he asked.

"No," she said. "Is that what people are going to say, Francis? That you have been jilted? It is going to be dreadful for you, is it not? People will wonder what is wrong with you. I am most awfully sorry."

"I will live with the ignominy, Soph," he said hastily. "Believe me, I will live with it."

PERHAPS THE HARDEST thing she had ever had to do, Olivia thought, was come downstairs to dinner. Harder even than alighting from her carriage outside the doors on her arrival at Clifton. Yes, harder even than that. She was more grateful than she could say when Sophia came to accompany her down.

Her mind had refused to stop teeming with a whole host of conflicting thoughts and emotions since earlier that afternoon. She had lain on the grass in the hidden garden for a long time after he had left, reluctant to move, afraid to set her thoughts in motion, to face what she had done, to wonder at his final look and his final words.

She had lain there trying to cling to mere feeling and reaction. She was sore and her breasts felt tender. And it had been wonderful, quite wonderful. It had been such a very long time. She had dreamed of it, ached for it so often over the years, and yet when it had happened it had been so much more wonderful and so much more— physical than she remembered. She knew that she would want it again.

With him. Only with him. Emma had once suggested to her, during one of her dreadfully restless periods, which had mercifully become less frequent over the years, that she go to one of the spas or even to London and take a lover for a month or two. Emma had always prided herself on being enlightened and had quite deliberately chosen the spinster life for herself. Olivia had been horrified. She was a married lady, she had protested. She could not dream of doing that with anyone but her husband.

She would not want to do it with anyone but Marc

even if he were not her husband. She had always known that.

Taking a lover had never been an option in her life. And yet her aloneness, her loneliness, her celibacy were her own fault. She had recognized that almost from the start. Refusing to forgive him after one infidelity, which he very clearly had regretted bitterly, was harsh and foolish. She should have forgiven him. She had wanted to forgive him. She *had* forgiven him in the privacy of her own heart. But she could not live out that forgiveness, she had realized during those first months alone, when his letters were coming almost daily. She could not live with him as before, be intimate with him, be his friend. There would always be that between them.

Olivia had finally left the garden, returned to the house, and sent down for hot water for a bath, recognizing the fact that her thoughts could not, after all, be kept at bay. The real world intruded, even into the hidden garden.

She had been too deeply in love. She knew that. Their marriage had been too perfect. She had not known it at the time, but had only realized it since, looking about her at the marriages of her friends and acquaintances. Her marriage had been unreal. Quite perfect for an unbelievable five years. There had never been a cloud on their horizon.

The storm, when it came, had killed everything. She had not afterward believed she could live with an imperfect marriage. She had believed that she could not be fair to him any longer. She would surely always look on him with suspicion and disappointment. He could never again be her Marc as she had known him. And she was afraid even to try to get to know a new Marc. Perhaps she could not love the new Marc.

The thought of not loving him had filled her with

panic. Better never to see him again. Better to live on alone as if he were dead.

And so she had written to him at the end of six months to tell him—untruthfully—that she could not forgive him. She had tried to explain her reasons, but she had been unable to explain.

She had been very young. Very immature. Very ignorant of life.

Making love with him that afternoon had surely been the most wonderful experience of her life. But of course she had given in to the unreality of the hidden garden. She had believed that that one experience could erase all the bitterness of fourteen years. She had believed as she woke up and remembered where she was, and with whom, that it would all be at an end, that he would smile at her, kiss her, and say something that would erase the past just as if it had never been.

Foolish woman. Even in fourteen years she had not fully matured. She had looked up at him with anxious eyes to find his own unsmiling and hooded. And then he had got up and dressed himself without a word or a look just as if it had all meant nothing to him. And finally his voice. His cold voice telling her that after all she was his wife.

She had just been one of his women. One of his countless women. But on this occasion, he had been able to excuse his promiscuity with the irrefutable truth that she was his wife.

She had been no more to him than any of his women! And she had been forgetting during the past week—deliberately forgetting, perhaps—that things had changed, that there was now a great deal more wrong with their marriage than just that first regretted infidelity. There had been other women in his life, probably untold numbers of them. There was Lady Mornington.

She had felt sick as she dressed reluctantly for dinner

and the ball. Physically sick. And dreaded meeting him again more than she had dreaded anything in her life. Going downstairs, seeing him again, behaving as if nothing had happened between them, was the hardest thing she had ever had to do.

He was dressed in the newest fashion, one she had heard of but never seen before. His evening coat and knee breeches were black, his waistcoat silver, his shirt and stockings white. White lace frothed over his hands. He looked far more handsome than any other man present. And she had to allow Sophia to take her across the drawing room to where he stood, talking with Mrs. Biddeford and Lord Wheatley. She had to smile at them all and accept a glass from his hand.

"Thank you," she said as he complimented her on her appearance, her eyes on the contents of her glass.

Sophia took a hand of each of them in hers and joined them, her two hands holding them together.

"This is going to be the most wonderful night of my life," she said. "And you are both here to celebrate it with me. Mama and Papa, how wonderful this all is."

He was looking broodingly at their hands, Olivia saw when she glanced up at him and then smiled at their daughter. His face was quite unsmiling.

They sat facing each other at dinner, but such a length of table lay between them that there was no necessity of even looking at each other and no possibility of talking. It was relatively easy. And then there was the receiving line, where they stood shoulder to shoulder for almost an hour, greeting guests, making small talk, and smiling and smiling. And not once glancing at each other or exchanging a single word.

"We must dance, Olivia," he said to her finally, after Sophia and Lord Francis had been waltzing alone for a few minutes. "It is what is expected."

It was the hardest moment of all, the necessity of

standing face-to-face with him and setting one hand in his and the other on his shoulder, the whole roomful of guests watching. And she had no doubt that they had drawn eyes from Sophia and Lord Francis. All these people, after all, knew that she and her husband had been estranged for many years.

"We must smile," she said, smiling.

He did not respond. "I suppose I must say I am sorry," he said after a few moments of silence.

"Why?" she asked. "You are not sorry, are you?" And she looked up into his cold eyes.

"And you are never in the business of forgiving, are you?" he said. "I would be wasting my breath."

"Do you apologize to all your women?" she said. "It must become tedious."

His jaw tightened. "All my women," he said. "No, Olivia, there is never any need. They always enjoy what they get. As you did this afternoon."

"Yes," she said. "It would be hard to resist such expertise."

"Well," he said, "no great harm has been done, then, has it? We are, when all is said and done, man and wife. And you have looked after yourself over the years, Olivia. You are still beautiful."

"A crumb thrown to the dogs?" she said. "Thank you, Marcus. I am to feel the thrill of being complimented by my own husband, I gather?"

"You may feel what you wish," he said. "The caustic tongue is new, Olivia."

"There is a great deal that is new," she said. "I am no longer a person you know, Marcus. It is fourteen years since I was your wife. I am *not* your wife, though in the eyes of church and state we are still married."

"Ah," he said. "So fornication comes lightly to you?"

"Not as lightly, perhaps, as adultery came to you once upon a time," she said.

"Touché." He watched her from cold, hooded eyes. And then his eyes strayed beyond her. "Sophia is watching us," he said, "and looking puzzled. This is the most wonderful night of her life, Olivia. That is what she said before dinner, is it not? I think we must defer our quarrel until a more private moment." He smiled suddenly and looked down into her eyes. "Did you have a glimmering of an understanding of all that it would mean to be a parent, Olivia? Did you know how smitten we both would be with love for our only daughter?"

"Enough that we would do this for her?" she asked, smiling back into his eyes. "No, I did not. Marcus, I would die for her. I know you will say that is pure melodrama, but it is true. I would."

"And smile at me for her," he said. "In some ways that is worse than dying, is it not, Olivia?"

"Don't invite me to quarrel again," she said.

"It is an art we never learned, is it not?" he said. "Five years and not one harsh word. We were the fairy-tale lovers, Olivia. The happily-ever-after lovers. Two children living in bliss together and together bringing a third into the world."

"Yes," she said. "Two children. But there is nothing wrong with childhood, Marcus. It is less painful than adulthood."

"Yes," he said. "But in real childhood, there is always someone who will kiss the hurt better and make all well. There was no one to do that for us, was there?"

"No."

His hand at her waist increased its pressure a little. "Let us separate that absurdly happy pair of children," he said. "Dance with your future son-in-law, Olivia. I want to dance with my daughter."

"Yes," she said, relieved and sorry. Relieved because they would no longer have to touch and look into each other's eyes and make conversation. Sorry for the same reasons.

"This ballroom is deuced hot," Lord Francis said to Sophia when they came together again later in the evening. "Hathaway was just saying how warm it still is outside. Warm, Soph, not stifling hot as it is in here. Shall we take a turn about the garden? I daresay we are expected to go slinking off together sometime during the evening, anyway."

"Like thieves in the night?" she said. "How foolish."

"Like lovers in the night," he said. "Those older ladies in a row over there—the ones who have not stopped nodding and simpering since they arrived—will be thrilled beyond words."

"The Misses Girten and Mrs. and Miss Macdonald?" she said. "They will more likely have a collective fit of the vapors, Francis."

"Fit of imagined ecstasy," he said. "Shall we go?"

"It *is* hot in here," she said. "I wish Mama and Papa would dance together again."

"It would not be right," he said. "They are the host and hostess, you know. And there is a prodigious number of unattached ladies that your papa must feel obliged to lead out."

"Do you think that is all?" she said, allowing him to take her out through the French windows onto the terrace at the west side of the house. "I could have sworn that they were quarreling just before they came to separate us during the first dance."

"I would say that is a promising sign, Soph," he said. "If they are quarreling, they are probably airing out their differences."

"Do you think so?" She looked doubtful. She followed his lead out onto the lawn, which led to the distant stable block. "But we always quarrel, Francis, yet we are not ironing out differences. We are merely quarreling."

"True enough," he said. "The terrace is black with people, Soph. I wonder they don't all run into one another at every turn. They have probably all poured out to catch a glimpse of me stealing a kiss from you."

"How absurd," she said. "As if people have nothing better to do with their time."

"There is nothing more romantic than a newly betrothed pair, though," he said. "Shall we satisfy them?"

"But Mama and Papa are not out here," she said. "And they are the only ones we are really trying to convince, Francis."

"True enough," he said. "But rumor will soon get back to them if we appear cool, and then they may never settle their own differences."

"Do you think so?" she said doubtfully. "Very well, then. We had better kiss. But don't do that with your tongue."

He sighed. "Your next beau or your next fiancé is going to think you a dreadful innocent if you don't know how to kiss, Soph," he said.

"I know how to kiss," she said indignantly.

"You know how to pucker your lips," he said. "That is child's stuff, Soph."

"Well!" she said, offended. "If you do not like my kisses, Francis, you do not have to kiss me, you know. It is all the same to me."

"Perhaps you had better learn while you have the chance," he said.

"From you?" she said. "From a rake?"

"Who better to learn from?" he asked.

Sophia could think of no suitable answer.

"You have to relax your mouth," he said, "and let me do the leading."

"Just as in dancing," she said.

"Just as in dancing," he agreed. "And never mind the puckers. They are not part of good kissing."

"Oh," she said.

He set a hand beneath her chin and raised it. "I have the feeling that it is a good thing it is dark out here," he said. "What color are you, Soph?"

"Is there a color brighter than scarlet?" she asked.

"Yes," he said. "The color of your face right now. Relax your mouth. And your teeth."

"But they are chattering," she said.

"Let me worry about that," he said and set his mouth to hers.

Sophia gripped his shoulders as if trying to inflict bruises as his lips teased hers apart and his tongue began to explore with exquisite lightness the soft flesh behind her lips and the warm cavity of her mouth beyond her teeth. He touched the tip of her tongue with his and circled her tongue slowly. Then he lifted his head away.

"You are a reasonably apt pupil," he said as her eyes fluttered open. "You can release your grip, Soph. I shall catch you if you fall."

"You flatter yourself," she said, her voice shaking. "You think I will fall merely because I have allowed myself to be kissed as a rake would kiss his . . . ? Well, as a rake would kiss?"

"I think there is a distinct possibility, Soph," he said. "Your knees are shaking."

"That is because it is cool out here," she said scornfully. "And I don't think that was proper kissing after all, Francis. I think it was improper. Oh, it is so hot out here."

"Somewhere in that last speech," he said, "there was a minor contradiction. But no matter. You will have some experience now to take to your next beau, Soph."

"I would never allow anyone to do that to me ever again," she said. "It was disgusting."

"Good enough to make the temperature soar, though, was it not?" he said. "We had better go back inside, Soph, before you decide you want more, and before you decide that perhaps you want a lifetime of it."

"Ohhh!" Sophia's bosom expanded with her indignation. "The very idea. Do you think yourself quite irresistible to women, Francis, just because you know how to kiss? Yes, obviously you do. I have never in my life known anyone so conceited. Why, I would rather . . ."

"The old familiar litany," he said. "The music has stopped, Soph, and it is supper time. I would hate to get back and find all the food gone. Let us walk."

"By all means," she said. "Let me not keep you from your supper, Francis. I would hate to be responsible for that cruelty."

"Thank you, Soph," he said. "You have a kind heart. But it is not quite elegant to snort, you know."

"I shall snort if I want to snort," Sophia said.

"Quite so," he said. "Go ahead then. Don't let me stop you."

"I happen not to feel like snorting again," she said, on her dignity.

9

OST OF THE EARL'S HOUSEGUESTS ANNOUNCED
their intention of leaving Clifton Court within a
few days after the ball in order to give their host more
freedom to prepare for the wedding. Everyone, though,
promised to return a few days prior to the event.

It was just as well, the duchess declared, since there
was so much still to do, and Olivia was going to town
for a few days with Sophia and Francis. She would like
nothing better than to go with them, she said, but how
could she leave Clifton Court at such a time? She sent
for her personal dressmaker to come to her there.

"You may avail yourself of her services, too, Olivia, if
you wish," she offered. "I am sure you would be pleased
with the results. And dear Sophia, too. There is nothing
Madame Blanchard loves more than the chance to dress
a bride."

But Olivia had her heart set on going away for a few
days. She must get away, she felt. She needed to think.
And so they were to leave three days after the ball.

Sophia was despondent. The idea she had had to bring
her parents together again seemed to have developed a
life of its own and taken itself somewhat beyond her
control. The preparations for her wedding seemed un-
stoppable, and now she was being taken to town to buy
bride clothes—all at her papa's expense.

She had been hopeful at first. After the first awkward meeting, her parents had seemed comfortable, almost happy in each other's company. And yet in the past few days, and especially since the ball, she had looked at them and wondered. Were they merely strangers being polite to each other? Would the approach of her wedding bring them closer? But how soon would that happen? How much longer could she wait before finding an excuse to end the betrothal?

And *had* they been quarreling during the ball? They had spent no time together at all after the opening waltz.

She was outdoors with Cynthia the afternoon before she was to leave for town with her mother and Francis. Cynthia, who lived only ten miles away, was also to return home the following day. Cynthia wanted to know when the charade was to end.

"It *is* to end, is it not, Sophia?" she asked. "You have not decided to marry Lord Francis after all?"

Sophia's answer included references to toads and snakes.

"But he is so very handsome and charming, Sophia," her friend said with a sigh. "Mr. Hathaway has been wondering, too. We both agreed that things have gone so far that they are well nigh impossible to stop."

Sophia grimaced. But the earl, who had been out riding with some of the gentlemen but had stayed in the stables longer than they after their return, was striding back to the house at that moment.

"There he is now, Cynth," Sophia said. "I am going to ask him if he and Mama have reconciled."

"Just right out like that?" Cynthia said. "Is it wise, Sophia?"

"But I must ask sometime," Sophia said. "They are unlikely to tell me what they decide or do not decide. Perhaps I will not know until after the wedding, Cynth. And yet when I say things like that to Francis, he almost has an apoplexy on the spot and either bellows 'What wedding?' in that obnoxious way of his or tells me I should be in Bedlam, which is not at all a complimentary thing to say to his betrothed, is it?"

"Except that you are not his betrothed," Cynthia reminded her.

"As he tells me ten times a day," Sophia said. "As if I could ever forget the fact. Who would want to be Francis's betrothed?"

"Just about every woman between the ages of eighteen and twenty-five who has laid eyes on him," Cynthia said.

"Don't let him hear you say that," Sophia said hastily. "He is too conceited for his own good as it is. I am going to talk with Papa. Do you mind?"

And she waved her arm to her father and tripped across the grass toward him as he slowed his stride and smiled at her.

"What?" he said. "No Francis in sight, love? Is this normal?" He lowered his cheek for her kiss.

"He is playing billiards," she said. "I came outside with Cynthia." She linked her arm through his.

"So tomorrow you are off to town for bride clothes," he said. "I suppose you intend to beggar me, Sophia."

"Oh, yes," she said, laughing, "but I daresay Mama will not allow me to, Papa. I wish things were not moving quite so fast."

He looked sharply down at her. "With the wedding?" he said. "You are not having second thoughts, are you?"

"Oh, no," she said. "I love Francis dreadfully, Papa, and three weeks still seems a frightfully long time to wait. But I just wish . . . Oh, I just wish we had longer to be with you and Mama. Always I was with one or the other of you but never with both. I can scarcely remember the time when we were all together. There must have been such times, weren't there, and many of them?"

"Yes," he said. "We spent a great deal of time together, Sophia, the three of us."

"And now only three more weeks," she said, "and I will be married and going away with Francis, and when we come back from our wedding journey, I will be living with him and not with you and Mama any longer. But when I do visit, Papa, will it be the two of you together, or will I have to make separate visits?"

"Sophia." He covered her hand with his. "You have been dreadfully hurt over the years, have you not? You have never said anything until now. I did not realize it, and neither did your mama. I am sorry, love. I am sorry more than anything that you have been the innocent sufferer."

"What happened?" she asked. Her father, she noticed, had changed his course so that they were no longer walking toward the house but toward the parterre gardens before it. "Why did you never come back? Why did you not send for Mama? Why did I always come alone when I visited you? What happened?"

"We just discovered that we could no longer live together," he said slowly.

"Papa," she said, "I am no longer a child. Something must have happened. Was it Lady Mornington?"

He looked at her sharply. "What do you know of Lady Mornington?" he asked.

"That she is your mistress," she said. "Though she is not one-tenth as lovely as Mama. Is *she* what happened?"

"No," he said. "I did not even meet the lady until six years ago, Sophia. And good Lord, she is my friend, not my mistress. Whatever gave you that idea?"

"It was someone else, then," she said. "Another woman. It was your fault, wasn't it, Papa? But how could you have wanted another woman when there was Mama? That is what men do, though, is it not? They marry and then they become bored with their wives and take mistresses. If Francis ever tries to do that, I will kill him. I will take the very largest book from our library and break his skull with it. I swear I will. But how could you have done it, Papa? I always looked up to you. You were my hero."

"I was your mother's hero, too," he said harshly. "I am human, Sophia. You say you are no longer a child. Well, learn that, then, that I am human. But it was not quite as you think. I did not take a mistress. Not until we were irrevocably apart, anyway. And I did not become bored with your mother. Never that. I loved her. I want you to know that. You were a child of our love and the two of you were my world."

"Then what *happened*?" she said rather petulantly considering her claim to be an adult. "If you loved her, you should have lived happily ever after. Why have you been estranged for most of my life?"

"Sophia," he said, and he gripped her hand very tightly as she fought to control her tears.

"Don't you love her any longer?" she asked. "Don't you, Papa? Are you merely being civil to each other because of the duke and duchess and the other guests? Is it all for show? Don't you love her?"

"I love her," he said. "I have never stopped, Sophia. Never for a single moment."

"Well, then," she said, brightening instantly and stopping in order to throw her arms up about his neck to half throttle him. "I will have the two of you to come back to after my wedding. My mama and papa together again. Oh, just wait until I tell Francis. Just wait until I do."

"But it is not as simple as that, Sophia," he said, taking her gently by the waist. "Life never is, love. What happened, happened. Fourteen years ago. It is a long time. We have both built and lived new lives since then. We are different from the people we used to be. There is no going back. There never is in life. Only forward. And love cannot bind two people who have lived apart for that long."

"Why not?" The tears were back in her eyes.

He shook his head. "It is hard to explain," he said. "Your mother was twenty-two, Sophia. Now she is thirty-six. I was twenty-six. Now I am forty. We cannot resume our relationship just as if those years had not passed."

"You could if you loved each other," she said. "I don't believe you, Papa. I don't believe you really love her after all. You just say you do because you are talking to me and it would seem wrong to tell your own daughter that you do not love your wife. Nothing is going to change, is it? This past week and a half had been for nothing, and nothing more will be accomplished in the remaining three. There will be Francis with his parents and his brothers and their wives. And then there will be me with you. And with Mama. And the two of you will be wonderfully civil to each other."

"Sophia," he said.

"No," she said, "don't say it. There is nothing more to say. You must be longing for this nuisance of a wedding to be over so that you can rush back to Lady Mornington. Your *friend*."

"Sophia," he said, and he took and held her hands very tightly. "I am sorry in my heart that you have conceived the wrong idea about Lady Mornington. But forget about her anyway. I shall not be returning to her even as a friend. I promise you. And I will tell you the reason why, too. Having seen your mama again, I know that I cannot return to a relationship that has been generally miscontrued—not just by you. Having seen your mama again, I know that she is the only woman I have ever loved or ever will." He squeezed her hands even more tightly. "But that does not necessarily mean that we will ever live together as man and wife again, love."

She dropped her head forward to look at their clasped hands.

"But there is one bond between us," he said. "A firm one that has never ever wavered. We both love you to distraction, Sophia. We both want your happiness more than anything else in life. For the next three weeks and for your wedding day we will not merely be practicing civility. We will be rejoicing together in your happiness. Together, love. And if it is important to you in the future to see us together, then I daresay we will come together occasionally. We love you that much. Both of us. Together, Sophia."

She raised her hand suddenly and set it against his cheek. "Papa," she said, and her voice was thin with suppressed tears, "I would do anything in the world to see you and Mama together again. Not just because of me, but because of each other. I would give up Francis if that could happen."

He laughed softly. "What?" he said. "Give up the love of your life, Sophia? For us?"

"Yes, I would," she said.

"Well," he said, releasing his other hand and stroking her hair, "that is quite an offer. You love him very much, don't you?"

"But I would give him up." She closed her eyes very tightly.

"You must marry him," he said, "and be very happy with him, Sophia. That is the very best thing you can do for Mama and me. And I will promise you that I will see what I can do about the rest of it. Do we have a deal?"

She jerked back her head and looked up at him with

shining eyes. "You are going to keep Mama here?" she asked. "You are going to be reconciled? You are? You promise?"

He frowned and shook his head. "Only that I will see what I can do, Sophia," he said. "I cannot make any promises about the outcome."

"Oh," she said, "but you always meant yes, Papa, when you used to say you would see what you could do. I always knew you meant yes, though I would pretend still to look anxious. Oh, I knew it would work. I knew all would be well. I am going to tell Francis. He will be so excited for me. I am going to find him now."

And the Earl of Clifton found himself with arms outstretched to the disappearing figure of his daughter, who was dashing down one diagonal path and across a flower bed toward the house with quite unladylike haste.

He bowed his head and set one hand over his eyes.

SOPHIA BURST INTO the billiard room just as Lord Francis was bent over his cue, fully concentrating on a difficult shot.

"Francis," she said, totally forgetful of the fact that ladies did not normally enter that particular room. "You must come. You are going to be so very pleased."

Lord Francis, unable to prevent the forward movement of his cue, hit by far the worst shot of anyone all afternoon. He straightened up, shaking his head ruefully.

The Duke of Weymouth chuckled. "Just in time, Sophia, my dear," he said. "Francis had not missed in ten minutes. The rest of us are feeling a trifle bored."

"Oh," she said as Lord Francis turned toward her, a resigned look on his face, "I am so sorry, Francis. I would have crept in had I known and waited until you had finished."

"Don't mention it, Soph," he said, smiling. "What better way is there of losing a game?" He took her hand on his arm and patted it. "You will excuse us, Papa? Gentlemen?"

"More than that," the duke said. "We will rejoice, lad, at your quitting the table." He laughed heartily.

"Well, Soph," Lord Francis said when they were outside the room, the door closed behind them, "this had better be worth losing a game over. You have told your father? And he now has all the embarrassment of breaking the news to mine? I had better go upstairs and make sure that all my things have been packed. I had better take myself off before my mother finds out and drowns me with her tears. If I were you, Soph, I would hide."

"Whatever are you talking about?" she said, frowning and leading him in the direction of the front doors.

"You have not ended our betrothal?" he asked.

"No, of course not," she said. "How absurd."

"But you said I would be so very pleased," he said.

She looked at him indignantly. "Oh," she said, "it is just like you, Francis, to remind me just how delighted you will be to be free of me. It will happen, never fear."

"But when, Soph?" he asked. "There are nineteen days to our wedding. Can a fellow be blamed for getting a trifle nervous?"

"I have heard that men always get nervous before their weddings," Sophia said kindly. "Women get excited and men nervous. It is quite natural that you should be feeling so."

"Soph," he said, "can I save time and just mention the word 'Bedlam'? Would you understand my meaning? And don't bother to answer. What will I be so very pleased about?"

"I am to marry you and live happily ever after," she said, drawing him down the steps outside the house onto the cobbled terrace. "And in the meantime, Papa will see what he can do about getting Mama to agree to stay with him. He just said so. We agreed on it." She beamed up at him. "You see? It is working after all and I need not have been burdening you with all my doubts in the past few days."

Lord Francis scratched his head with his free hand. "The one is not totally dependent on the other, by any chance, is it, Soph?" he said. "Am I to sacrifice my freedom just because you have an agreement with your papa?"

"Of course not, silly," she said. "But he told me that he loves her, you see, and he has agreed to see what he can do. That always means an undoubted yes when Papa says it. And he will work on it immediately, Francis, because there is not much time left. Within a week all their differences will be settled and they will be together again. You mark my words. And then we can announce that we have irreconcilable differences."

"Just to help them celebrate," he said.

"It will be quite a blow to them, of course," she said. "To all four of them. We will have to break the news gently."

"Is there a gentle way to break such news?" he said. "The trouble with us, Soph, is that we have no imagination. Neither of us. We did not picture it being quite like this, did we?"

"No," she said. She reached across and touched his hand with her free one. "And it will be worse for you, Francis, for you will be the jilted one. Would you prefer it to be the other way around? Shall we pretend that I still love you dreadfully and that you are the one with no heart?"

"Good Lord," he said. "There is not a stronger word in the English language than Bedlam, is there, Soph? If there is, you had better tell me what it is, because I am in dire need of it."

"I am merely trying to save you from some humiliation," she said. "I would take it on myself if I could, Francis. After all, I am the one to blame for all this."

"No, you are not," he said. "No one exactly stuck a dueling pistol to my head to make me do it. I thought it would be amusing. Amusing—ha!"

"I am sorry," she said. "Perhaps we can make it a mutual thing, Francis. We can go to Mama and Papa and your parents together, and tell them that we have discussed the situation quite rationally and in a perfectly amicable manner and have decided that after all, we would not suit. Then neither one will bear the blame or be humiliated. Shall we?"

He sighed. "We had better see how things develop after we return from London, Soph," he said. "But good Lord, you are going to be returning with five trunkfuls or so of bride clothes, aren't you?"

"Yes," she said. "Or perhaps not quite so much. You had better tell me where we are going for our wedding journey, Francis. There is a difference between the type of clothes I will want if we are going to Italy, and the type I will need if we are going to Scotland."

Lord Francis merely looked at her.

"But I have to know," she said. "You must tell me, Francis. Where would you take me if we really were about to be married, and if we really were going on a wedding trip?"

"To bed, probably," he said. "And you may well blush and look outraged, Soph. You could not expect any self-respecting male to resist that invitation, could you?"

"To bed," she said, both her cheeks and her eyes flaming. "With you, Francis? I would rather . . ."

"Austria and Italy," he said. "For the rest of the summer and probably the winter, too, Soph. We would dance in Vienna, and ride in a gondola in Venice, and lean with the Tower of Pisa, and get stiff necks in the Sistine Chapel, and shelter your complexion from the sun in Naples."

"And Rome?" she said eagerly. "Would we go to Rome, Francis?"

"Where do you think the Sistine Chapel is?" he asked. "The Outer Hebrides?"

"I forgot," she said. "You do not need to be quite so scornful, Francis. I am not a featherbrain, you know."

"Well," he said, "that is where I would take you, Soph—during the daytime. I suppose my first answer would still hold true for the nights. And don't get all puffed up again. We are talking only of where I would take you *if* we were getting married, the key emphasis being on the *if*. You will need light and pretty clothes."

"All right," she said. "But it is going to be dreadful to spend Papa's money on such a deception, is it not? And all the other expenses of the wedding. Oh, dear, I lay awake a whole hour last night just worrying about it all."

"Perhaps it will be worth the expense if we succeed in mending a broken marriage," he said, patting her hand again.

She looked up at him, suddenly happy again. "Even if by some chance it does not happen before the wedding," she said, "there is still hope. I have just remembered something Papa said. He said that if in future it is really important to us that we see both of them together, then they will come together. We will have other chances, you see, Francis—perhaps at Christmas or Easter or at a christening if one happens fairly soon."

Lord Francis continued to pat her hand and look down at her, an expression almost of amusement on his face.

"Oh," she said, her smile fading. "I forgot. No, that will not work, will it?"

"Perhaps they will come together the next time you are betrothed," he said. "Perhaps you could make a regular thing of this, Soph."

"Don't make fun," she said. "This is serious, Francis. And you don't think I would deliberately humiliate other gentlemen in this way, do you?"

"Only me?" he said.

"But you are different," she said, looking earnestly up into his face. "You are . . . Oh, I don't know. You are— Francis, that is all. I could not do this with anyone else. No one else would understand. I would not be able to talk like this with anyone else. And you do not have to say what you are about to say. Anyone else would have taken me straight off to Bedlam, I know."

"That is not what I was about to say," he said. "I was about to warn you again, Soph. You are not falling in love with me by any chance, are you? I don't altogether like this business of feeling comfortable with me and all that."

"In love with you?" she said, her eyes blazing to life again. "How stupid. What I meant was that I did not have to worry with you because you are just Francis and I really do not care if I hurt your feelings or not. Partly because you have no feelings, and partly because I have a whole lifetime of getting even with you to accomplish. Falling in love with you!" There was a world of scorn in her voice and on her face.

"Ah," he said, "that is all right, then. I was getting a little uncomfortable for a moment, Soph. Nineteen days. That means eighteen at the outside for being betrothed to each other. I suppose we can survive that long, can't we? And who knows? Perhaps it will be less than that. Perhaps your mama and papa will fall into each other's arms when we return from London. Perhaps they will have missed each other."

"Do you think so?" she said hopefully. "Oh, do you really think so, Francis?"

"I have to consider it at least a possibility," he said, "if I am to cling to my sanity."

10

*L*ORD FRANCIS MIGHT AS WELL BE SITTING INSIDE the carriage instead of riding his horse, Olivia thought. For much of the journey Sophia had had the window down, her betrothed riding alongside talking with her. It was a good thing that the day was glorious and the open window necessary for their very survival. Twice, Olivia had noted, Lord Francis reached across to touch Sophia's hand as it rested on the window. That was before she closed her eyes.

It made her heart turn over to see the love of those two for each other. She yearned to urge them to hold on to their love, not to let even the strongest tempest shake it. She wanted to warn them not to set each other on pedestals, not to expect perfection just because they were in love. She wanted to tell them to allow for human frailty. She was desperately afraid that they were too much in love.

"She is sleeping," Sophia said softly. "You do not need to keep on doing that, Francis, thank you very much."

"It is no trouble at all, Soph," he said cheerfully. "How do you keep your skin so soft?" And he chuckled for no apparent reason.

"Did you see?" Sophia's voice, still almost a whisper, sounded very eager. "Did you see them kiss?"

"Very promising," he said. "The footman holding the carriage door open almost swallowed his tongue. I'll wager it will be the *on dit* belowstairs today, Soph, and probably for the whole week."

"I could have swooned with happiness," she said.

"I'm glad you did not," he said. "I never know quite what to do with vaporish females. Does one douse them with water, slap their cheeks, rush all about the house yelling for vinaigrettes, or kiss them back to consciousness? I suppose that last would be strictly dependent upon the female involved, of course. I might have tried it on you, Soph."

There was a small silence. "I might wake her if I respond as I would like," Sophia said, and Lord Francis chuckled.

So it had worked, Olivia thought. Sophia had been delighted by it, and she would not be able to conclude that it had been done for the benefit of the guests. There had been no one else out on the terrace except a few servants and Sophia and Lord Francis. There had been no other witnesses.

She was reacting like a girl, she thought with some disgust at herself, retiring behind closed eyes so that she might relive a brief kiss.

"Remember to buy yourself some pretty clothes, Olivia," he had said, setting an arm about her shoulders after kissing their daughter farewell. "And don't let Sophia drive you to distraction." He had winked and grinned at their daughter. "I shall be watching for you in about a week's time."

And he had bent his head and kissed her—a firm kiss with closed mouth, neither too long nor too brief. A prearranged kiss, to reassure Sophia. The sort of kiss one might expect from a father or brother. Not one to dream about and live through over and over again in the mind just like a love-starved woman.

Which she supposed she was.

She had lain awake during the nights reliving every moment of their lovemaking in the hidden garden. Though lovemaking was hardly an appropriate term to describe what had happened. They had satisfied a voracious hunger and slaked a parching thirst. That was all. He had been away from the diversions of town and the arms of Lady Mornington for some weeks; she had been without a man for fourteen years. It had not been a lovemaking.

Yet she hugged to herself each night the memory of an uncontrollable passion that at the time she had mistaken for love. And had felt her body aroused anew by the remembered skill of his caresses. And had felt sick at the remembered evidence of his experience.

He had come to her dressing room the evening before, after she had finished dressing. He had opened the door from his own room after knocking, not waiting for an answer. She had flushed at the thought that she might have been undressed or even in her bath. Though doubtless he would have looked coolly at her and remarked that, after all, she was his wife.

"Have you further need of your maid?" he had asked.

"You may leave, Matilda, thank you," she had said, and the girl had left the room quietly.

They had scarcely spoken to each other since the ball, when they had quite alarmingly begun to quarrel in the middle of the dance floor. They had never quarreled. It was something new in their relationship, something she had no idea how to handle.

"Sophia is upset," he had said abruptly, his feet set slightly apart, his hands clasped behind his back. He had seemed to fill her very dainty dressing room. "She has seen through the facade of our amiability and believes it to have been adopted for the benefit of the other guests. And she has noticed the slipping of that amiability since the day of the ball. She was in tears when I talked with her this afternoon."

Olivia, sitting on the stool before her mirror, had twisted a brush in one hand. "Perhaps she will have to face the truth, Marcus," she had said at last. "Perhaps we can protect her no longer."

"No longer?" he had said. "Have we ever protected her, Olivia? If we had loved our daughter as we have claimed to do all her life, would we not have somehow patched up our differences and remained together for her sake?"

"Our differences," she had said, laying down the brush and looking up at him. "You were the one who decided that a whore's caresses were more exciting than mine, Marcus. You were the one who ruined life for Sophia."

"Oh, no," he said. "I am not going to carry the guilt of that indiscretion to my grave, Olivia. And I am certainly not going to add to the burden of my conscience the belief that I ruined our marriage and our daughter's happiness. There is such a quality as forgiveness, you know. Unfortunately it is something beyond your capabilities."

"I suppose," she had said, "you have been celibate from the time of that whore until a few afternoons ago, Marcus. I suppose I am to believe that of you."

"No," he had said. "I would not like to damage your impression of me as a depraved philanderer, Olivia. I have done too much other damage to your life, it seems. But I did not come here to quarrel with you."

"Did you not?" she had said. "Why did you come, then?"

"We had an agreement," he had said, "to make this month a very special one for Sophia. Can we not keep to it? We have been selfish enough for most of her life, Olivia. Must we also have her in tears as she prepares for what should be the happiest day of her life? It was the happiest of ours, was it not? Can we not at least do our part to see that it is so for Sophia, too?"

"And what about afterward?" she had asked. "Is it fair, Marcus, to allow her to believe that we have an affection for each other when immediately after her wedding she must know the truth?"

"She hopes that she can visit us together afterward," he had said. "Will it be too much to do for her, Olivia? To spend some time together with her once or twice a year? Must we be bitter enemies just because I once spent an hour with a whore and because you would not forgive the transgression? Do you find me so abhorrent?"

She had looked down at her hands.

"You did not find me abhorrent two afternoons ago," he had said.

She had looked up sharply at him. "That was the garden," she had said, "and the sunshine and warmth and . . ."

"And appetite," he had said. "It seems that we still find each other somewhat appetizing, Olivia."

"Yes." She had looked back at her hands.

"Well," he had said, "short of resuming a marriage that seems to have died many years ago, can we at least be mutual parents to the child who survived that marriage? You will be away for a week. By the time you return there will be less than two remaining before the wedding. Perhaps once or twice a year in the future we can force ourselves to spend a week or so in the same house. Can we do it?"

"I suppose so," she had said.

"She said she would give up Francis if only she could bring us back together again," he had told her. "Foolish child. But she meant it with all the earnestness of youth, Olivia."

She was twisting her hands hard in her lap, she had

realized suddenly. *Very well, then,* she had wanted to blurt out to him, *let us give her exactly what she wants, Marc. A marriage that is real.* But the words could not be spoken aloud. He had been standing stiffly before her, his manner businesslike, his voice abrupt and almost cold. He was trying to persuade her to agree to a workable proposition.

"We must try again, then," she had said. "We did well for the first week."

"This evening," he had said. "We must remain in the drawing room together. Tomorrow morning, when you leave, I must kiss you just as I will kiss Sophia."

"Yes," she had said.

He had stood there for a while not saying anything, as she examined the backs of her hands.

"I wish I could come with you," he had said. "I don't like to think of the two of you on the road with only young Sutton and my servants for protection. You will be all right, Olivia?"

"I came here alone," she had reminded him.

"You will have new clothes made?" he had said. "As many as you wish, Olivia, and have the bills sent to me with Sophia's?"

"You give me a generous enough allowance," she had said.

"My daughter is getting married," he had said. "At least allow me to buy my wife new clothes for the occasion. Will you?"

She had nodded.

"There are enough servants left at the house in town to see to your needs," he had said.

"Yes."

"Well." He had moved abruptly and set his hand on the knob of the door into his dressing room. "You have lived safely for fourteen years without my assistance. I daresay I need not worry about you now."

"No," she had said.

Come with us, she had wanted to beg him quite unreasonably. *Three weeks is all the time we have left.* And the memory caused a tickle in her throat now as she sat with closed eyes in the carriage and did not even hear the occasional chatter of Sophia and Lord Francis. They could not expect to return within a week at the very least. A week—seven whole days!

But there would be countless years without him again after Sophia's wedding, with perhaps the teaser of a week once or twice a year. She felt the desperate need to cry, but her daughter's presence in the carriage forced her to resist the urge.

How foolish—how indescribably foolish—she had been fourteen years ago. Imagining that she could no longer love him because he had fallen off his pedestal. She had loved him anyway all those years, but had deprived them both of the chance of a mended marriage. She had deprived all three of them of the chance for a happy family life.

She wished, and felt guilty at the wish, that Sophia had not met Lord Francis again and fallen in love with him. She wished she had not seen Marc again. For now, having seen him, she knew with a new pain all that she had missed in those empty years. And all through her own fault. Not Marc's, really. All people make mistakes and have the right to be forgiven—once at least. But she had refused to forgive. She had been afraid to forgive, afraid that their relationship would have changed. She had been too young and inexperienced to know that relationships are always changing, that they must change in order to grow and survive.

His lips had been warm on hers, his arm strong and sheltering. The side of her head was against the soft cushions of the carriage. She imagined that it was against his chest, his arm still about her, his cheek against the top of her head. She imagined herself falling asleep in the shelter of his arms, warm and relaxed and assured of his love.

IT FELT WONDERFUL to be in London again. She had always loved being there right from the moment of her arrival for her come-out Season. It was there she had first seen Marc and admired him from across the width of a ballroom for several hours before he had suddenly appeared at her side, their hostess with him to perform the introductions. She had fallen in love with him during the set of dances that had followed.

And had not fallen out of love since, though her love had brought her joy for only five years and misery and heartache for all the years since. And Sophia, of course. Her love had brought her Sophia.

She had never been given to extravagance. Even during that first year, when her mother had taken her to a fashionable modiste to have new clothes made that would be more suitable for town living than the ones she had brought with her, she had been horrified at the large number that had been deemed necessary. She had been afraid that she would make a beggar of her papa. In the years since, she had used the modest services of a local seamstress and had even made some of her own clothes.

She felt alternately hot and cold when she discovered just how much Sophia's bride clothes were going to cost. But Marcus had given her specific instructions to make sure that their daughter had all that was needed. Olivia supposed that her husband was a very wealthy man. He had had a comfortable fortune even before the death of his father. After that event, he had inherited a number of prosperous properties. He had also doubled her already generous allowance.

It was with only the greatest reluctance that she picked out patterns and fabrics for clothes for herself. But she would need some fashionable clothes for the week of the wedding, when Clifton would be overflowing with guests. Her own parents were even coming from the north of England.

Everything was to be made with the greatest haste, the dressmaker assured Olivia. She had received a letter from his lordship just a few days ago and had taken on extra seamstresses and deferred working on other orders so that Lady Clifton and Lady Sophia could take all their new clothes with them back to Clifton within a week.

And so they had four days to kill. Lord Francis took them to Kew Gardens and the Tower and St. Paul's and they spent a few evenings quietly at home. But news of their arrival in town was quick to spread and several hasty invitations were sent by hostesses eager to entertain the newly betrothed couple or curious to see again the long-absent Countess of Clifton.

They chose to attend a soirée at the home of Lady Methuen. Young Donald Methuen was a friend of Lord Francis. Olivia felt apprehensive about attending. It was so very long since she had been in town. She fully expected to be confronted with a roomful of strangers. It was a relief on their arrival to find that there were still some people who remembered her, and who made an effort to include her in a group and draw her into conversation. Sophia and Lord Francis had immediately been whisked away by a group of young people.

It was really quite pleasant, Olivia thought, after an hour had passed. It was good to be back. And she still seemed to have the social skills to cope with a large town gathering. Lord Benson, looking considerably more portly and florid of complexion than when she had known him as a rather handsome rake and gentleman about town, even tried to flirt with her. It was not altogether unpleasant to know that she was still young enough and was still in sufficient good looks to invite flirtation.

If she could only have left after the hour, she thought afterward, she would have been thoroughly charmed by the evening. As it happened, she did not leave, and the evening gave her a sleepless night.

A lady joined the group with which Olivia was currently conversing. Another lady, Mrs. Joanna Shackleton, a friend of Olivia's during that long-ago Season when they had both made their come-out, took her arm firmly and would have drawn her away. But Olivia merely smiled at her and resisted the pressure on her arm. She was listening to a story being told by Colonel Jenkins.

"Good evening, Mary," the colonel said when his story was at an end. "You are feeling better?"

"Oh, yes, I thank you," the lady said. "It was just a slight chill, you know. Nothing to keep me at home for more than a couple of days."

"James and I were wondering if your literary evening would have to be cancelled," a lady to Olivia's left said. "I do hope your recovered health will make that unnecessary, Lady Mornington."

"Oh, absolutely." The lady smiled. "I would not cancel those plans for all the chills of a cold winter. It promises to be an interesting evening. Mr. Nicholson is to be there."

Olivia felt the pressure on her arm being renewed, but she ignored it. The lady was quite different from what she had expected. What had she expected? A tall, voluptuous woman with flaming red hair, she supposed, and scarlet lips. A woman whom one would only have to glance at to know her as a harlot.

In fact Lady Mornington was petite with short dark

hair and a refined, quiet manner. She was not at all pretty, and it was not just spite that forced her to such a conclusion, Olivia decided. She was not pretty, though she did have fine intelligent gray eyes.

"Have you all received your invitations?" the lady asked, looking about the group. "If not, it is a dreadful oversight for which you must forgive me." Her eyes stopped on Olivia even as the pressure on the latter's arm intensified.

"Olivia," Joanna said, "there is someone . . ."

"But I am sorry," Lady Mornington said, smiling. "I am afraid you are a stranger to me."

"Oh, the devil!" Colonel Jenkins said. "I just realized."

"Olivia Bryant," Olivia said.

"Bryant?" Lady Mornington's eyebrows rose. "Oh. You are the Countess of Clifton."

"Yes."

"Mary," the Colonel said, "what are you drinking? Let me take you to find a tray."

"Olivia," Joanna said, "there is someone . . ."

"You are here alone?" Lady Mornington asked.

"With my daughter," Olivia said. "We have come to have her bride clothes made. My husband stayed at Clifton Court."

"Ah, yes," the lady said. "I read the notice of the betrothal in the *Morning Post*. The wedding is to be soon?"

"In a little over two weeks' time," Olivia said, "at Clifton. We will be returning there the day after tomorrow."

Lady Mornington smiled. "This must be an exciting time for you," she said. "Your daughter is a pretty and charming young lady and took well earlier in the Season, I heard. And Lord Francis Sutton is a gentleman with a good sense of humor. I like him."

"Yes," Olivia said. "Marcus and I are pleased with her choice."

Lady Mornington smiled again and turned back to the colonel. "By all means," she said, taking his arm, "let us find this tray, Colonel. I am as dry as the Sahara Desert."

"Olivia, I am so sorry, my dear," Joanna said, leading her away in the opposite direction. "I tried to save you from that embarrassment. You do know, I assume?"

"That Lady Mornington is Marcus's mistress?" Olivia said. "Yes."

"But I would not be worried," Joanna said. "You are many times lovelier than she is, Olivia, and certainly no older. But men seem to find it necessary to have a *chère amie* as well as a wife. They are all the same."

That was another thing she had expected, Olivia thought. She had expected Lady Mornington to be a very young woman.

But the facts did not console her, she found when she was alone that night, tossing and turning on her bed, trying to sleep. If Marc's mistress had been more as she had expected, she would have been less concerned. The woman would have been obviously nothing more than an object for physical pleasure. But Marc could not have chosen Lady Mornington merely for his bed. There must be far more to their relationship than the physical.

She did not know why the thought should disturb her. Or rather, she pretended not to know. And she pretended not to be disturbed. It did not matter to her, she told herself, what his mistress looked like. Indeed, there was probably a dozen other women with whom he slept but who were not dignified by the title *mistress*. She did not care.

But the not caring kept her as wide awake as caring would have done. And it was somehow different, she found, imagining what the woman looked like, and actually seeing her and talking with her. That woman, she told herself, picturing Lady Mornington as she had appeared in the Methuen drawing room, had been with Marc for about six years. He had kissed those lips and touched the body countless times. He had slept in her bed probably more times than he had slept in his wife's.

It did not matter. She did not care.

But at some time before dawn, she got up hastily from bed and vomited into the close stool, retching until her stomach was empty and hurting. And then she lay shivering and crying in bed, telling herself over and over again that she did not care, that it did not matter.

And that it was all her own fault anyway.

THE DAY AFTER Olivia, Sophia, and Lord Francis had left for London, Clifton was empty of all guests except the duke and duchess. *Very empty,* the earl thought as he rode out late in the morning to pay a promised call on one of his tenants.

He was missing her—them. Somehow, though he had not fully realized it until she left, she had taken charge of most of the wedding preparations. He had thought that his housekeeper and cook were doing the bulk of the planning, but it seemed that Olivia had been guiding them, and without her to run to, they were running to him. And so was Rose, with a hundred different concerns that he supposed she had taken to his wife in the previous week and a half.

He was missing seeing her and hearing her voice. And he was becoming thoroughly annoyed with himself. He had got over her years before, although he had never stopped loving her. He had even been happy, or comfortable at least. He had found the perfect woman in Mary—one who accepted his need for conversation and companionship but did not press other claims on him.

There had been a time—one evening—when their relationship might have developed into something more intimate. But they had both agreed, rather shamefaced, when they were already in her bedchamber, that it would be impossible. She still mourned a dearly beloved officer husband killed in Spain; he still loved a wife from whom he was estranged. After that they had been content with a warm friendship, unusual between a man and a woman. And of course it became the common belief that they were lovers. They had always scorned to try to put an end to the rumors.

Mary was the perfect woman for him. He did not need Olivia any longer.

Except that missing her was like a gnawing toothache.

And except that he had meant what he had said to Sophia, that he would not go back to Mary, having seen Olivia again, and having loved her again, though he had not, of course, said that to Sophia.

She was gone for ten days, three longer than any of them had expected when they left. But it had been ambitious to have expected all those clothes to be made within a week, he supposed. In the meantime, early wedding guests began to arrive, mostly family. The duke's three older sons arrived with their wives and children. The earl's mother came with her sister from Cornwall and Olivia's parents from the north of England. Clarence Wickham came, escorting Emma Burnett. Each time a carriage appeared, he expected it to be his own returning from London. Each time he hastened out onto the terrace only to find himself greeting other guests.

But finally they came, late one afternoon when it was raining. He knew this time as soon as he got outside that it really was his carriage. And he felt as if butterflies were dancing in his stomach.

"Hello, sir," Lord Francis said cheerfully, vaulting out of the carriage as soon as it came to a stop and the door had been opened. "A pea-soup day, would you not agree? But the roads are good hereabouts. No over-turned carriages and shrieking ladies or any drama like that."

The earl shook his hand and turned to hand Sophia out. But young love proved too fast for him. Lord Francis turned and lifted her by the waist.

"Ugh," she said. "It has not stopped raining all day. Papa, how wonderful to see you. We were afraid that we would not get home today, after all. Is the rain not dreadful? Wait until you see all the clothes I have bought. You will have ten fits. Francis, put me down, do. I shall have bruises at my waist."

"I thought you might not like to get your feet wet," he said.

"Better wet feet," she said, "than have you carry me like this into the hall and be the laughingstock among the footmen. Put me down."

"As you wish, Soph," he said, setting her feet on the wet cobbles.

The earl had turned to the carriage, feeling as eager and as timid as a schoolboy. She was wearing a blue dress and pelisse and a straw bonnet decorated with bright flowers. She looked like a little piece of summertime caught in all the gloom of the rain. He smiled at her.

She smiled back and set a hand in his.

"Welcome home, Olivia," he said. And then he released her hand and imitated his future son-in-law. He took her by the waist and lifted her carefully to the wet ground. "I have missed you."

"And I you," she said. "We were away far longer than we had planned. One of the new seamstresses proved not worth her hire, I am afraid, and all sorts of alterations had to be made."

"No matter," he said. "You are home and safe now." And he kissed her warmly on her parted lips.

He was glad that Sophia and Francis were still outside and watching them. She could not realize how deeply from the heart his words had been spoken or how eager he had been for that kiss.

"Yes." She smiled up at him and took his offered arm. "It feels like heaven to be home again. Does it not, Sophia?"

11

THE DISMAY AT HAVING SO GIVEN HERSELF AWAY AS to glow at him as soon as she set eyes on him; to set her hands eagerly on his shoulders to be lifted to the ground instead of extending one cool hand; to assure him that she had missed him, too; and to raise her face for his kiss—the dismay soon faded. After all, Sophia had been standing there watching them eagerly and for her sake they had agreed to show each other affection.

Besides, as soon as they had all hurried inside out of the rain, noise and near chaos greeted them. Guests had begun to arrive, it seemed, and soon Olivia was in her mother's arms, and then her father's. And Marc's mother was nodding rather stiffly to her from a little distance away. Emma and Clarence were there in the background—the former waiting to hug her, the latter to squeeze her hand and kiss her cheek.

Sophia and Lord Francis were being besieged by his brothers and their wives and by grandparents and even two children inexplicably escaped from the nursery. There was a great deal of laughter and noisy banter.

"So you finally ran him to earth, Sophia," the duke's eldest son, Albert, Viscount Melville, said, setting an arm about her shoulders. "We all thought he might keep running from you all his life. But the more fool he if he had. And we might have known you would be more persistent than to allow that."

"She finally stuck out a slippered foot and brought him down actually, Bertie," Claude said. "At least that is what I heard. Is it true, Sophia?"

"I heard it a little differently," Richard said. "I heard that Frank waited until your foot was reaching out to take a step, Sophia, and then deliberately tripped over it."

There was loud merriment from everyone gathered in the hall.

"Unfair, unfair," Sophia protested, her cheeks bright with color. "He made me a very pretty offer, did you not, Francis?"

"On one knee," he said. "It was a great shame to waste such an affecting scene on an empty room, wasn't it, Soph?"

Olivia felt a hand at her waist. "Emma and Clarence have been impatiently awaiting your return, Olivia," her husband said, smiling at her friends. "As have I. But we have had a chance to get reacquainted since yesterday afternoon."

"Is that when you arrived?" Olivia asked, looking at them. "We were away three days longer than we expected. It was very frustrating when we longed to be back home. There is so much yet to do," she added hastily.

"You must call on me for assistance," Emma said. "You know that I am never happier than when I am busy, Olivia."

"I want to hear all about London, Olivia," Clarence said. "Most especially if it is still in the same place as it used to be. It is an age since I was there last."

The hand at Olivia's waist tightened slightly. "If you will excuse us," he said to her friends. "Have you said hello to Mama and Aunt Clara, Olivia? They arrived the day before yesterday."

"No," she said. "Not yet." And she turned in dread to speak to the dowager Countess of Clifton. They had used to be on friendly terms.

"Well, Mama," the earl said, "they arrived home safely despite all our worries." His arm drew his wife closer against his side. "Olivia kept the youngsters in line, it seems." He looked down and smiled at her.

Olivia was grateful. "How are you, Mother?" she said uncertainly and reached out rather jerkily to kiss her mother-in-law on the cheek. "Aunt Clara? Did you have a good journey? I am sorry I was not here to greet you." And she was sorry she had spoken the last words. She had not been there to greet them for fourteen years. And indeed fourteen years before, Clifton had not even belonged to Marc.

"I am well, thank you, Olivia," the dowager said.

"You are in good looks, dear," Aunt Clara said, kissing Olivia, too. "The years have been kind to you."

"Thank you," Olivia said and was thankful when the arm at her waist turned her again.

"Do you remember Francis's brothers?" the earl asked her. "They have done some growing up since you saw them last."

"Indeed they have," she said. "Bertie still has his smile and Claude his cleft chin. You must be Richard. I would never have known you." She smiled at the tall sandy-haired young man with the small girl in his arms.

"And you look not a day older, ma'am," Claude said gallantly. "I can remember those times when you were constantly pleading with Papa not to be too harsh on Frank. It was understandable that an active young boy would find entertaining your daughter something of a burden, you used to say."

"And yet his hand never felt one mite the lighter than

it did on those occasions when you were not there to intercede for me," Lord Francis said. "You caused me a great deal of pain in those days, Soph."

"You have not met our wives, ma'am," the viscount said. "Allow me to make the introductions."

Sophia caught her mother's eye and then looked to her father. She looked entirely happy, Olivia thought.

"I don't know why we are all standing down here," the earl said, raising his voice after the introductions had been made, and the two children, one of the viscount's and one Richard's, had been identified. "I believe tea was about to be served in the drawing room when we were distracted by the sound of the carriage. Shall we go up?"

"A cup of tea will be most welcome," Aunt Clara said.

The earl kept an arm loosely about his wife's waist as they ascended the stairs. "We can release you from your duties at the tea tray this afternoon, Mama," he said, "now that my wife is home."

"Olivia will doubtless wish to freshen up after her journey," the dowager said. "It will be no trouble, Marcus."

"Then we will wait for her," he said. "Olivia is never long about these things. Sophia, you had better go up with your mama, too."

Oh, goodness, Olivia thought, there was a seductive warmth about the atmosphere of Clifton Court—a family atmosphere. And her husband had thrown himself wholeheartedly into the role they had both agreed to before her departure for London. *My wife is home.* Her feet felt heavy on the second flight of stairs.

"Mama," Sophia said. "I am frightened. I am so frightened."

Olivia looked in surprise at her daughter, whose face was suddenly chalky white.

"What have I done?" Sophia said. "All these people, Mama!"

Olivia took her arm. "Oh, Sophia," she said, "it is overwhelming, is it not? When you first think of marriage, you imagine that it involves only you and your partner. And then you realize that so much more is involved. It seems to get beyond your control, does it not? Almost as if you could not stop it, even if you wished to do so."

"And there are many more people yet to come," Sophia said.

Her mother squeezed her arm. "You don't want to stop it, do you?" she asked.

Sophia turned at the top of the stairs in the direction of her room. She gulped. "I am just terrified," she said. "They are all so very happy, Mama."

"It can be stopped, of course," Olivia said. "You must never be in any doubt about that, Sophia. You will not be irrevocably married until the ceremony has been performed and the register signed. You must not feel as if all your freedom has been taken from you. But neither should you give in to panic for its own sake."

Sophia drew in a ragged breath. "I did not know it would be like this," she said. "And Mama, there are two trunkfuls of clothes."

"Papa would have been disappointed if you had brought home less," Olivia said. "Sit down, Sophia, before you fall down. Now, tell me." She took her daughter's hands in a firm clasp. "Everything else aside—the clothes, the guests, all the preparations that have been made—do you still love Francis? Do you want to spend your life with him as his wife?"

Her daughter's eyes filled with tears.

"Do you, Sophia? Those are the only two questions that matter. The only ones."

One tear spilled over. "But you did not spend all your life with Papa," she said. "Only a few years."

"Is that what you are afraid of?" Olivia asked. "That your marriage will not last? Your papa and I have been very foolish, Sophia. We threw away something very precious. You must learn from our mistake. You must learn not to love blindly, not to expect perfection from each other. You must not be alarmed if you occasionally quarrel. You must learn that your life together is more important than anything else."

"Will you stay together now?" Sophia asked, withdrawing one hand from her mother's in order to wipe away a tear. "You really are happy to be home, Mama, aren't you? And Papa was happy to see you. You will stay together and love each other again?"

"We have discovered at least," Olivia said, "that there is joy in being together with you again, Sophia. Your betrothal has accomplished that. Now that we are about to lose you to a husband, you see, we realize how important those times together can be." She smiled. "Your marriage will bring us together at least occasionally. Neither of us will be able to resist seeing you whenever possible, and if that means seeing you together, then together we will be. Will that make you happy?"

"At Christmastime?" Sophia said. "And at christenings?"

"And for other occasions, too, I daresay," Olivia said.

"If I marry," Sophia said.

"If you marry." Olivia smiled. "Have you recovered from some of your terror? There is some color back in your cheeks. Do you love Francis, Sophia? Do you want to be his wife?"

Her daughter stared back at her and licked her lips. "Of course I love Francis," she said. "I always have, even though he used to be so horrid to me." There were tears in her eyes again. "I have always, *always* loved him, Mama. I wish I had realized that sooner. I would not have been so foolish."

Olivia smoothed a lock of hair back from her daughter's face. "Yes," she said. "Love is terrifying sometimes, isn't it? Sometimes it seems safer to run from it rather than face all the joys and heartaches it might bring. Don't run, Sophia, if you truly love. You will always be sorry, believe me. Do you feel better now that you have answered the essential question? We must be going down. I am supposed to be pouring the tea."

"Yes." Sophia got to her feet. "I will wash my hands."

FOR THE REST of the afternoon and most of the evening Lord Francis was called upon to give a full accounting of his days in London to his father, to listen to a detailed description by his mother of all the wedding preparations that had been made in his absence, to allow himself to be quizzed by his sisters-in-law about his courtship of Sophia, and to be teased by his brothers about his betrothal to the very girl he had named the Prize Pest as a child.

Sophia was faring no better, with two grandmothers and a grandfather to fuss over her, a great-aunt to kiss her and pat her hand, all her future sisters-in-law to want an exhaustive description of her bride clothes, and her future brothers-in-law to tease her.

"It is still raining," Lord Francis said, staring gloomily from a drawing-room window late in the evening.

"The gardens are not very romantic at night when rain is dripping down your neck, or so I have heard, Frank," Claude said. There was a general chuckle.

"And it is tricky to hold an umbrella and one's betrothed at the same time," Richard added.

"I am just remembering why I have envied Soph's

being an only child," Lord Francis said, not turning away from the window.

"When it rains, Frank," the viscount said, "one has to improvise. The gallery is still where it used to be, Lord Clifton?"

"In the very same place," the earl said, "complete with all the family portraits."

"There you are, then," Bertie said. "Problem solved, Frank."

"Just remember that all of Sophia's ancestors will have an eye on you," Claude said.

"Don't do anything to upset them," Richard added. "Or anything I wouldn't do, Frank."

"And if he tries to hide from you, Sophia," Claude said, "come and tell me and I shall tell Papa, and Frank can discover if his hand is as heavy as it used to be."

"London was remarkably peaceful, was it not?" Lord Francis said, turning from the window. "No brothers to set up a predictably idiotic chorus. Did you spend all day yesterday rehearsing while we were still away, the three of you? Come on, Soph. Let's go and stroll in the gallery. There will be no peace for us here if we do not."

"Just make sure you keep him strolling, Sophia," Richard said.

"Supper will be in half an hour's time," the earl said. "You will have her back down by then, Francis?"

"Yes, sir," Lord Francis said, and ushered his betrothed out through the door and up the stairs to the long gallery on the top floor.

They walked side by side up the stairs after Lord Francis had picked up a candlestick with a lighted candle from a hall table. They did not touch or exchange a word.

"We have to keep up appearances," he said when they reached the gallery, using his candle to light two set in wall sconces and setting his own down on a table. "We could hardly have said we did not want to be alone after such brotherly concern, could we, Soph? We have hardly had a chance to exchange a word all evening."

Sophia was examining a portrait next to one of the wall sconces.

"Oh, Lord," he said, sinking down onto a cushioned bench against one wall, "what are we going to do next?"

"Mama and Papa like being together with me," Sophia said. "Mama said so. After we are married, they will come together occasionally just to spend time with us. It is better than nothing, I suppose, but I don't think they will ever live together again, Francis. Too much time has passed. Almost my whole lifetime."

"After we are married," he said.

"Yes." She turned to look at him. "We ought to have thought more carefully, ought we not?"

"That sounds rather like the understatement of the century," he said. "Lordy, Soph, a family gathering and all in their best wedding humor. And not a suspicion among the lot of them or a single expression of uneasiness about our possible incompatibility considering our childhood relationship. I am beginning to know what a trapped animal must feel like."

"We have to end it now," she said, her voice shaking. "Tonight, Francis. Right now. We have to go down and tell them all that we have had a dreadful quarrel and have put an end to our betrothal. In a few days' time there will be many more people. It will be harder then."

"Do you want me to slap you around a bit first?" he asked. "Do you want me to stand still while you rake your fingernails down one of my cheeks?"

"Don't make a joke of it," she said. "This is deadly serious, Francis."

"A joke?" he said. "Have you ever had fingernails down your cheek, Soph, and the blood dripping onto your cravat?"

"We have to do it now," she said.

"I can't see your person very clearly in this light," he said. "But if your body is shaking as badly as your voice, Soph, you had better come and sit down. I have told you of my difficulty with vaporish females before."

"I am not vaporish," she said, coming to sit beside him. "Just terrified. We had better do it without further delay, Francis. Let us not think about it longer or talk about it, either. Let us go and do it."

"We have not had enough time for such a nasty quarrel," he said.

She looked at him in incomprehension.

"If we go down now, two minutes after coming up here," he said, "we can hardly expect them all to believe that we have quarreled so violently as to have called off the whole wedding."

"Then we shall say we quarreled this afternoon," she said. "Or yesterday."

"Soph!" he said. "Why would we have waited until this evening, and smiled and received everyone's congratulations in the meantime, if that had happened? Have some sense."

"Then we must wait awhile," she said. "How long? Five minutes? Ten? My courage will have given out by then."

He took her hand in his. "Perhaps we should wait a few days," he said. "Imagine how it would be, Soph. Carriages emptying themselves of smiling, festive guests every hour for the next several days. And we would have to greet each carriageful with the same story."

She gulped noisily.

"It does not bear thinking of, does it?" he asked.

"Oh, Francis," she said, "what are we going to do?"

"The very question I asked you a few moments ago," he said. "Though I might have saved my breath. You have just thrown it right back in my teeth. And if you gave an answer, it would probably be something cork-brained like suggesting that we stand up at the front of the church, the rector behind us, and make the announcement there."

"Don't be horrid!" she said. "I am the one who wanted to go down immediately and put an end to it."

"Or you will be suggesting that it will be easier for all concerned if we get married anyway," he said.

"Oh," she said, jumping to her feet and standing before him, her hands on her hips, "I don't know why I agreed to this stupid scheme in the first place, Francis. The scheme itself is bad enough. But I must really have had feathers in my brain to have agreed to do it with you of all people. Do you imagine that I am still running after you just because I was always stupid enough to do it when we were children?"

"The thought had crossed my mind, I must confess," he said. "You aren't wearing stays by any chance, are you, Soph? You are about to burst them if you are."

"You toad!" she said. "You eel! You . . ."

"Snake?" he suggested.

"Rat! You conceited rat!"

"Quite so," he said. "We'll wait until everyone has arrived, Soph, and then make one grand announcement. Maybe by that time, your mama and papa will have decided that they cannot live without each other after all."

"It is just not going to happen," she said. "I was foolish to think it would. It was stupid to think I could bring them together when they have lived apart forever. This whole business has been stupid."

"If we are to wait a few days," he said, "we had better look when we go down as if we have been doing what everyone thinks we are doing."

"Making love?" she said scornfully.

"Er, I think your papa might be up here with the proverbial horsewhip if he thought that, Soph," he said. "Kissing is what everyone is imagining us doing."

"Well, there is no one to observe us," she said, "so we do not need to feel obliged."

"But there is definitely a just-kissed look," he said. "Everyone will be looking for it when we return, especially my esteemed older brothers. For the sake of my self-respect, Soph, I can't take you back down looking totally unkissed, you know."

"How foolish," she said. "Is this how rakes get ladies to kiss them, Francis? The ladies must be very stupid, I must say."

"Rakes don't usually kiss ladies," he said, "unless they happen to be their betrotheds, and a roomful of brothers belowstairs are waiting to see that they have done their job thoroughly."

Sophia clucked her tongue and took a step backward.

"We are fortunate, too," he said. "There was a time, you know, Soph, when people used to do it on wedding nights. Flock into the bridal chamber after a decent time, I mean, to view the evidence that the groom had done his job."

"Oh!" Sophia said. "They never did. You are making that up just to shock me. Papa would not like it at all if I told him that you had just told me that."

"By Jove, no," he said, getting to his feet. "He wouldn't, would he? You had better not tell him, Soph. He might forbid the marriage or something like that."

"I don't think you ought to kiss me," she said. "We are not really betrothed, after all."

"But your papa granted us all of half an hour," he said. "I think I had better, Soph."

She tilted her face up resolutely and waited.

"You are still puckering." He looked down at her critically. "Ah, that's better," he said when she opened her mouth to make some sharp retort. "Mm."

Sophia never did make the retort.

"You aren't still shaking, are you, Soph?" he said against her ear a few minutes later. He had both arms wrapped about her.

"Of course I am not," she said breathlessly. "Why would I be shaking?"

"I don't know," he said. "But your arms are so tight about my neck that I thought you were afraid of falling."

"Oh," she said, trying to remove her arms but finding herself too closely held to have anywhere else to put them. "No. But what else am I to do with them?"

"Put them back," he advised. "Some poor devil is going to thank me one of these days, you know, Soph."

"What?" she said. He was distracting her full concentration by nibbling on her earlobe.

"For teaching you how to kiss," he said. "I must say you are an apt pupil. This is becoming almost as much pleasure as duty."

She bent her arms back at the elbows and shoved hard at his shoulders. "Please do me no favors," she said hotly. "It is certainly no pleasure to me. And if I do not look just kissed to your brothers now, Francis, I never will. Besides, I am going to be embarrassed. And besides again, I don't like kissing and don't intend to do it with anyone else ever again. I want to go back downstairs."

"Some poor devil will never know what he has missed, then," Lord Francis said, strolling across the gallery to extinguish the two candles he had lit earlier, and picking up the candlestick again. "I hate to tell you this, Soph, but any decent lady would not allow herself to be touched anywhere but on the closed lips before her wedding night. I suppose that is some consolation for you, though. You will be spared some shock when your wedding night finally does come along."

"I didn't ask you to put your arms about me and pull

me so close," she said, on her dignity, descending the stairs beside him, a foot of space between them. "And I certainly did not invite you to do that with your tongue. You ought not have started to kiss me when my mouth was open to speak."

"Ah, Soph," he said, "you should have kept it firmly shut when I was so close."

"And I certainly did not give you permission to do that to my ear," she said severely.

12

APART FROM THE FACT THAT HE HAD BEEN MISSING his wife and despising himself for doing so, the few days before her return had been pleasant ones for the Earl of Clifton. There was a good feeling to be had from the approach of a daughter's wedding, he found. He enjoyed the noisy cheerfulness of the duke's family, and it was good to see his mother and aunt and even Olivia's parents. Pleased for their granddaughter's happiness, they had greeted him with warmth and none of the frowns and recriminations he had half expected.

It was good, too, to see Emma and Clarence and be reminded of the good years of his marriage at Rushton. Clarence had been his friend before he became Olivia's— the two men had gone to school and university together. But they had not seen each other in ten years.

Clarence, in fact, was the one guest who somewhat clouded his general feeling of well-being. He had put on some weight about the middle and his blond hair had thinned, though he was by no means bald. But he still had the pleasant good looks that had drawn flirtatious glances from the barmaids of Oxford and more refined glances from the ladies in the London ballrooms. He had seemed impervious to the charms of them all. He was keeping himself for his future bride, he had always said laughingly when teased by his friends.

Clarence had been Olivia's friend even before the breakup of the marriage. He had been her close friend since. Her letters occasionally mentioned him, and Sophia frequently referred to him when talking of home.

And Olivia, he remembered from a certain afternoon in the hidden garden, had become a passionate and experienced lover at some time during the past fourteen years.

The earl tried not to pursue such thoughts. But the thoughts and imaginings pursued him, it seemed, and were not to be resisted during the evening on her return. She had sat with her parents and Emma at tea before mingling more freely with the other guests, and ended up standing alone with Clarence beside the tea tray for all of fifteen minutes. At dinner, she sat with the duke and her father. And in the drawing room afterward, she talked with the duchess and Richard and his wife. He joined her there himself and sat beside her until she was called away to help Claude's wife find some music to play on the pianoforte.

And then she sat on a sofa close to the pianoforte with Clarence and Emma, and stayed there even when Emma got up to play while Claude's wife sang. The two of them were deep in smiling conversation, turned toward each other so that they appeared to have eyes for no one else.

The earl strolled toward the two of them. They both looked up and smiled at him.

"We are reminiscing, Marcus," Clarence said. "It seems only yesterday that Sophia was a child and now she is only a little more than a week from marrying. And looking very happy about it, too."

"Yes," the earl said. "She should know what she is about. They have known each other all their lives." Reminiscing about Sophia's childhood and girlhood was something he could not participate in.

"Do you remember the first time they met?" his wife asked, smiling up at him in some amusement. "It was at Rushton when she was just a toddler. All the boys had new balls and three of them would have cheerfully indulged Sophia by sharing with her. But it was Francis's ball she wanted and Francis she wanted to play with."

Clarence chuckled. "I was there at the time," he said. "The first notice he took of his future bride was to pull a gargoyle face and poke out his tongue at her, if I remember correctly."

"A short while before shoving her backward into a patch of only half-dried mud," the earl said. "Her dress was white, was it not, Olivia?"

"Oh, yes," she said, "so it was."

"And poor Francis was turned over William's knee for his first spanking concerning Sophia," the earl said.

The other two looked at each other and laughed.

The earl turned away when the noise level rose in the room as Francis and Sophia came back, Sophia looking quite unmistakably rosy about the mouth.

His little girl, the earl thought, as the three brothers went into their usual teasing act and Francis pursed his lips and assured them that jealousy would accomplish nothing and Sophia blushed. She was too young to be mauled about by young Francis. But in nine days' time, she was going to be his bride.

Oh, Sophia, he thought, *all the lost years.* Years when he had seen her for only brief weeks two or three times a year, though Olivia had never denied her to him when he had asked. Years when he might have watched her growing up and stored away a wealth of memories for his old age and for telling his grandchildren.

His eyes strayed back to his wife, who was laughing with Clarence over something Bertie had just said.

Later that night, he found himself restless as he undressed and made ready for bed. He was unable to think of lying down and addressing himself to sleep. He was not tired. He wandered to the window of his bedchamber and drummed his fingers on the sill. It appeared to have stopped raining outside. Perhaps he could take an early morning ride. But there was a night to live through first.

He thought of going downstairs to the library to find a book. But he did not feel like reading. He would not be able to concentrate.

His wife was in the next room, he thought, stopping abruptly the pacing he had begun. He had felt the emptiness of the room during the previous ten nights, though he had never been into her bedchamber since her arrival at Clifton. But he had felt its emptiness nonetheless. And now she was there again. He could feel her closeness.

Her closeness made him restless. He wanted to talk with her. Only to talk. He wanted her companionship. That was surely what he had missed most through the years. They had been very close friends. They had been each other's second half. He had not been whole in all the years without her.

He wandered through to his dressing room. She was probably asleep already. And even if she were not, she would be outraged if he went into her room. She was at least entitled to the privacy of her bedchamber. But she was his wife and all he wanted to do was talk. She was probably asleep.

He turned the handle of the door between their dressing rooms quietly, not at all decided whether he would open the door. But he did, slowly and indecisively, and stepped into her dressing room. It smelled faintly of her perfume. Olivia's dressing room had always smelled this way. The door into the bedchamber was open. There was a candle burning in there.

She was reclining against her pillows, he saw when he stood in the doorway, a book open in her hands. But she was not reading it; she was looking at him and closing the book and setting it down on the table beside her, next to the candle.

Foolishly, now that he was there and she was not after all asleep, he could think of nothing to say. He stood and looked at her and she looked quietly back, not helping him out by saying anything or ordering him from her room.

"Can Sophia survive the next week?" he asked at last. "She seems excited enough to burst."

"She almost gave in to a fit of terror this afternoon just after our arrival," she said. "Seeing so many family members already gathered here has brought home the reality of it all to her. She had the feeling of being swept helplessly along by events."

"She is not having second thoughts, is she?" he asked. "It can still be stopped, all of it."

"I assured her of that," she said. "I told her that all that matters ultimately are her feelings for Francis and her wish to spend the rest of her life with him. She realized then, of course, that she has loved him all her life. I think she has, too, Marcus, though how she could have done so through their childhood, I do not know. At least she knows that he is not perfect."

There was a silence in the room for several moments. He moved beyond the doorway and came to stand beside her bed. She was wearing no dressing gown, only a thin cotton nightgown, quite low at the bosom. Her hair was shining and loose over her shoulders.

"Yes," he said. "It is important that she knows that. Have we done the right thing, Olivia, in allowing her to marry? I have been feeling something close to panic myself."

"Yes, we have," she said. "I believe they truly love each other, Marcus, and are truly good friends. They have made the decision to marry and we must respect that. She is of marriageable age, after all, though she is young. We cannot live her life for her or ever know if everything we have ever done for her was the right thing. We can only ever do our best. The rest is up to her."

"We deprived her of a family life," he said, seating himself on the edge of the bed.

"Yes," she said. "But we can do nothing to amend what is past, Marcus. And had we remained together just for her sake, perhaps we would have grown to hate each other. Perhaps we would have bickered and quarreled constantly. Would that have been better for her?"

"I suppose not," he said. "Would it have been like that between us?"

"We can never know," she said. "We have exchanged some angry words since my coming here."

"You don't regret your decision, Olivia?" he asked her.

"There is no point in regrets," she said.

"Hm," he said, and he reached out and took a lock of her hair in his hand and spread it over one finger. "Sophia told me that you went to a soirée at Lady Methuen's. Did you enjoy it?"

"I was surprised to find that I knew some people," she said, "even after all this time. Joanna Shackleton was there."

"Ah, yes," he said. "She lives most of the year in town. Her husband is in the government, you know."

"I liked being in London again," she said.

"Did you?" He looked broodingly down at her. "You always did like the excitement of a few weeks there, did you not? You might have gone there over the years, Olivia. I always told you that. I would have stayed away."

"There was always Sophia," she said. "The country was better for her. Besides, I never had any great wish to go. Rushton has always offered enough social activity for me."

"I hope you had plenty of new clothes made," he said. "Did you?"

"Far more than I need," she said. "I did not realize that you had written to the dressmaker, Marcus. I suppose you needed to, since the order was to be so large and so hurried. But you need not have given her such strict instructions about what I needed."

"If I had not," he said, "I would have been fortunate to have found you returning with more than two new frocks and one bonnet. The straw you were wearing this afternoon is very pretty, by the way. It is new?"

"I would neither find nor dream of wearing such a frivolity at Rushton," she said. "But Sophia would not let me out of the milliner's without it and Francis, when goaded by her, assured me that I looked very handsome in it."

"I would rather say that it looks very handsome on you," he said.

"I was not allowed to pay any of the dressmaker's bill," she said. "I intended to pay at least part, but it seemed you had sent strict instructions about that, too."

"I must be allowed to dress my women for a family wedding, Olivia," he said.

"Is that what I am?" she said, watching his thumb stroke over the lock of hair across his finger. "One of your women?"

"My daughter's mother," he said.

He watched her swallow, and he lowered his head and kissed the pulse at her throat. She was still watching his hand and her hair across his finger when he raised his head again. He waited for her to say something, to become angry, to order him to leave. She said nothing.

With his free hand he smoothed the hair back from the side of her face and cupped her cheek in his palm.

He traced the line of her eyebrow with a light thumb. She closed her eyes and he kissed one and her cheek and her chin. He kissed her mouth, and it trembled beneath the light pressure of his.

He lifted his head and looked down into her open eyes. He could see no anger there, no repugnance, no fear—only a calm acceptance of the moment.

He got slowly to his feet, pulled loose the sash of his dressing gown, and shrugged out of it. He watched her, giving her plenty of time to send him away. Her eyes were on his. He lifted his nightshirt over his head, dropping it beside the dressing gown. Her eyes roamed over him as he watched her. She still had not told him to go away.

She lifted her eyes to his as he drew back the bed-clothes and grasped her nightgown at the hem and slid it up over her body. She raised her arms when she realized that he was not going to stop at her waist. He dropped her nightgown on top of his own garments.

It was strange, he thought, that in five years of a perfect marriage they had never been naked together. He had never seen her as he was seeing her now. With his hands and his body he had known her to be beautiful and desirable, and his eyes had confirmed the evidence of his other senses when she was clothed. But their married years had been very decorous. Very close. Very, very loving. But lacking somewhat in physical passion.

She was beautiful beyond description, his thirty-six-year-old estranged wife. His daughter's mother. Livy. She moved over on the bed as he lay down beside her. He did not extinguish the candle.

She was Livy. His eyes told him that in the candlelight, and his hands and his body, too. And yet she was a woman he did not know. His hand at her waist and his mouth on hers told him that she was instantly on fire, that there need be no slow, painstaking efforts to arouse her. She turned onto her side and her palm pushed its way up from his waist to his shoulder. She sucked on his tongue and arched her hips against his. He heard her moaning, as a certain shock in him gave way to instant response.

Livy. My God, Livy.

His hand confirmed his expectation that she was hot and wet. Desperate for release. Too aroused for foreplay. He held her with one arm and stroked her with light and knowing fingers until she shattered against him. And he held her, crooning to her, unaware of what words, if any, he spoke, as her shudderings gave place to relaxation.

He held her for a few minutes longer before turning her onto her back and coming on top of her, spreading her legs with his knees, and mounting her while she came awake again.

She was warm, wet, languorous. To be enjoyed at his leisure. He wanted to take her slowly. He wanted always to be where he was at that moment. He wanted it to last forever. There never had been anyone but Livy. There never could be.

He loved her with a slow, deep rhythm, his face in her hair, breathing in the scent of it, his body knowing her again as he had known her as a young man, as a young husband. She was warm and relaxed and comfortable as she had been then. Loving her was an emotional and a physical experience intertwined, inseparable. Loving was the perfect word for what they had always done together in her bed and for what they were doing together now.

And yet he was not in the past after all. He was in the present. And she was different. After a few minutes she was no longer passive. Her hips picked up the rhythm of his loving, circling to his movements, and she lifted her legs from the bed to twine about his. Her shoulders were pressing into the mattress, her breasts lifting to press more intimately against his chest. She was breathing in gasps.

He lifted his head and looked down at her, and she looked back, her lips parted, her eyes heavy with passion. His woman? Yes, his woman to stroke into, to pleasure, to love. His woman to bury himself in, to bring him release. To bring him peace. And love.

Her eyes closed as he changed his rhythm, deepening his penetration of her body. And she could no longer keep the rhythm, but pushed up against him, taut with need.

He watched her, felt her body's response with his own, waited for that indefinable moment when he knew that she would come to him, and lowered his head into her hair again, coming to her at the same moment. And he allowed pure physical reaction to take him beyond the moment and into the world of semiconsciousness beyond the climax. Her body was soft and comfortable beneath his own.

SHE DID NOT regret it. She *could* not regret it. She had longed for him ever since that afternoon in the hidden garden. She had discovered then how close to starvation she had been for fourteen long years. She might have kept her sexuality unexpressed for the rest of her life, but once having had him again, her hunger gnawed at her like a physical pain, like a warning of imminent death.

She had ached for even a sight of him while in London. She had even cried for him. And she had been unable to sleep earlier, or to read, either, though she had been trying to lose herself in a book. She had been too aware of his presence in the very next room, probably asleep. Her need for him had been a throbbing deep in her womb.

She had thought first of all when she had turned her head for surely the twentieth time in an hour and seen him standing silently in the doorway to her dressing room that he must be a product of an over-fertile imagination.

She had wanted him with a sick yearning while they talked and when he sat down on the side of her bed and took a lock of her hair between his fingers.

She did not regret what had happened. Or if she did, it was only the fact that she had been so uncontrolled, so unable the first time to wait even for him to come inside her. She supposed she would feel embarrassed at that memory once the night was over. And he would perhaps laugh at the evidence she had given him of just how much she had missed him.

But the other loving, the one just finished, had been wonderful beyond imagining. He had often used to like to be in her for a long time. He liked the feeling of being physically one with her as well as one in every other way, he had used to tell her. "One body, Liv. It feels good, does it not? Tell me it feels good."

It had always felt good because he was Marc and she loved him and she was doing what a wife does to show her husband that she loves him. Sometimes there had been the beginnings of active pleasure, occasionally even the near completion of pleasure, though always with something just eluding her.

That something was no longer eluding her. And she wondered if he always experienced that pleasure. If so, she could understand why he had liked to be intimate with her so often and why he had always slept so deeply afterward.

It was wonderful. She did not believe her body had ever felt so drained of energy and so relaxed. His weight was heavy on her. Her legs, which she had untwined from his, were spread wide on either side of his. She felt too wonderful to sleep. She would not be able to lift an arm to save her life, she thought with a smile.

And what next? her mind asked, refusing to be stilled as the rest of her body was still. *What tomorrow? And what next week—after Sophia's wedding?* She tried not to think beyond the wedding.

What would she say if he asked her to stay?

What would she do if he did not?

She tried not to think.

He woke with a start and then lay still again. She waited for him to move. She hoped he would not. She hoped that he would fall back asleep or else lift his head and kiss her.

Marc. Marc. She tried to talk to him with her mind. She was afraid to speak. She did not know what to say. Did what had happened change anything? Everything? Nothing?

He lifted himself off her without looking at her and sat on the edge of the bed, his back to her. Then he got to his feet and crossed the room to look out of the window. The candle had burned itself out.

"You have had a good teacher, Olivia," he said.

"What?" She was not sure she had heard what he had said.

He looked back over his shoulder. The room seemed curiously light. "He has taught you well, whoever it is," he said. "And has obviously given you many lessons."

She reached down for the blankets and pulled them slowly up over herself. She was still not quite sure that she understood.

"Clarence, I suppose?" he said.

Clarence? He was accusing her of having had a lover? And Clarence? Did he not know? Marc and he had been friends for years. But then Clarence had said that she was the only one he had ever told and that he had never done anything to make anyone suspicious.

"You must not be afraid of me, you know, Olivia," he had said to her one evening when he was escorting her home across the park from Emma's.

She had never before thought of being afraid of him. But one gossip of the village had regaled them all quite improperly for part of the evening with tales of an unknown rapist in a town no more than ten miles distant. And she had not really been afraid, of course, only more conscious of the darkness and loneliness of the park.

"Perhaps you wonder why I have never tried to make love to you since Marcus left," he had said. "I suppose you realize that there has been some gossip about us in the village since we do spend a great deal of time together."

"I care nothing for gossip," she had assured him.

"I must tell you something," he had said. "Something I have never told anyone, Olivia, and never thought to tell. But you need to know that you must never fear me. I do not care for women in that way, you see."

She had been stunned. "Do you mean . . . ?"

"Yes, I do," he had said. "And unfortunately it is something one cannot change by a mere effort of will. I am as I am. But no woman or man knows except you. For willpower does enable one to be chaste, you know. I have chosen chastity over the other choice. Are you totally disgusted?"

She had been. Nauseated, too. But he had been her dear friend for several years at that time.

"I am sorry," she had said, "I cannot respond so soon, Clarence. I want not to be shocked. Certainly I want not to be disgusted. I think life must have been hard for you."

"Life is never easy, is it?" he had said. "You know that better than anyone, Olivia. I shall call on you in a few days' time and you shall tell me quite honestly if you can continue to be my friend. And you must not lie to me. I shall know, you see."

No, she supposed Marc did not know.

"You need not think that I am waiting for an answer," he said. "I am not accusing you, Olivia. It would be rather ridiculous to start acting the outraged husband at this late date, would it not? I am glad, in fact, to find that you have been having some pleasure out of life. I imagine that he has been good to you?"

"He is my friend," she said. "My dear friend."

"Ah," he said.

"Lady Mornington was at Lady Methuen's soirée," she said.

"Ah, was she?" he said. "I hope you avoided the embarrassment of coming face-to-face with her."

"No," she said. "We spoke. She seems a refined lady."

"You expected a vulgar whore?" he said. "She is not. She is my friend." There was a pause. "My dear friend."

She said nothing.

He crossed the bedchamber and stooped down to pick up his nightshirt. He pulled it on and drew his dressing gown over it.

"Well," he said, "must we feel guilt at this night of infidelity to our dear friends, Olivia? I think not, do you? We are, after all, still married in the eyes of church and state. And sentiment always attaches itself to such occasions as family weddings. I think we can forgive ourselves."

"Yes," she said.

He laughed softly. "At least you can forgive yourself," he said, "even if you are unable to forgive others. Good night, Olivia. Sleep well."

"Yes," she said. "Good night, Marcus."

After he had gone, she got out of bed, drew on her

nightgown, and sat on the window seat against which he had stood a few minutes before. A little later she returned to the bed to fetch a blanket to wrap about herself. And she stared out of the window into the darkness until she finally fell asleep a little before dawn.

13

THEY CAME SEEMINGLY BY THE DOZENS DURING
the next week, the wedding guests. There were
family—the duke's brother and sister and the former's
wife; their children with their spouses and children; two
cousins of the earl's and one of the countess's, with their
families; and friends of everyone, including the bride
and groom.

"I had not realized there were so many rooms at Clifton, Papa," Sophia said to him one afternoon after they
had greeted cousins of two generations and a few infants of the third.

"If any more people arrive," he said, putting an arm
about her shoulders, "we may have to sweep the cob-
webs out of the attics, Sophia, and even set up tents on
the parapets. The next time you decide to marry, my
girl, remember all that comes along with a wedding, will
you?"

The next time you marry. His eyes were twinkling
down at her. He was teasing, of course. But she silently
resolved that there would never be a next time. She
could not do this to Papa again. Besides, she would have
no wish to marry once this betrothal was safely in the
past.

"Everyone has arrived," she told Francis that evening
when several of the younger people had strolled outside.

"And so they have," he said. "I'll wager your papa is glad there are only three more days of this, Soph. One trips over guests wherever one turns. Are you cold?"

"No," she said through chattering teeth. "We cannot wait any longer, Francis. It is going to have to be done tonight. Is it to be by violent quarrel or amicable mutual consent? Either way it must be mutual, I think. I do not want you to seem thoroughly jilted."

"You think we should have a few servants round everyone up and send them to the drawing room?" he said. "There is going to be an almighty squash in there, Soph. And who is to make the announcement? It can hardly be me since honor does not allow me to break a betrothal. You?"

"Me?" Her voice came out a squeak.

"Or perhaps there should be a private meeting with our parents first," he said. "Perhaps your papa will make the announcement."

"Oh," she said and unconsciously took a death grip on his arm. "He will be so humiliated. It does not seem fair that the task should be his, does it?"

"And yet it was for his happiness that we undertook this whole charade," he said.

"Yes," she said doubtfully.

"It looks hopeful, Soph," he said. "They have been acting like a couple since we returned from London. They are always together to greet people, and there has been enough of that in the last few days, heaven knows."

"Yes," she said, "but I cannot help thinking that they are doing it just for my sake since I told Papa how I felt, Francis." She pulled on his arm. "We must not keep strolling like this, putting it off. We must go back to the house now and ask Mama and Papa and your parents to come to the library."

"Oh, Lord," he said, "I do believe Great-uncle Aubrey and cousins Julius and Bradley and Lord Wheatley have taken possession of the library, Soph, with a brandy decanter and a bottle or three of port."

"To the blue salon, then," she said.

"Aunt Hester and Aunt Leah are exchanging a year's worth of *on dits* in there," he said, "with your great-aunt Clara and cousin Dorothea and half a dozen other ladies as audience."

"The morning room, then," she said.

"The older children have been allowed to spill out of the nursery and into there for the evening, if you remember," he said.

"Well, somewhere," she said. "There has to be an empty room somewhere, Francis."

"I have my doubts," he said. "But if we summon them to the middle of the hall, I daresay no one will hear what is being said."

"Francis!" she said.

"I'll tell you what, Soph," he said, patting her hand. "This evening is entirely the wrong time to do it. Half the men are into their cups and the ladies are into their gossip and a few people out here have stolen into the shadows for a private *tête-à-tête* and a dozen or so people arrived only today and would not take kindly to having to pack their half-unpacked bags to leave again at dawn. I think perhaps we should leave everyone to an evening's entertainment and tell them tomorrow in the light of day."

"In the light of day," she said. "Oh, heaven forbid. Francis, it has to be done soon. If we go on like this much longer, we are going to be married."

"The devil, yes," he said. "We cannot have that, can we? Tomorrow it must be, then, Soph, and not a moment later. Married, by Jove. I cannot think of any fate more dreadful, can you?"

"None," she said tartly. "Especially marriage to you. I could think of better ways to be comfortable in hell."

"Oh, come now," he said, "there is no need for spite, is there, Soph?"

"Well," she said, "you are always saying things about dreadful fates and all that. Do you think our marrying would be any better a fate for me? Do you think I am secretly panting for you? Do you think I am secretly hoping that there will be no way out of this betrothal after all? If the time does not seem right to you tomorrow, Francis, I shall go up on the roof and yell the news out to the whole countryside. How do you like that?"

"I like it very well," he said. "I shall summon everyone out onto the lawn for you, shall I, Soph? The mental image of your standing up there, arms extended, hair streaming in the breeze, is enormously stimulating. I think you would need a larger bosom to carry it off to effect, though."

"Oh," she said, "so now my bosom is too small, is it?"

"Are you sure you will feel up to discussing such a topic with me once the first flush of your ire has cooled?" he asked. "I think perhaps it is time I kissed you and took you inside, Soph."

"Don't you come near me," she said.

"A strange command," he said, "when you are clinging to my arm."

She released it.

"Will you be very glad to be rid of me, Soph?" he asked, cupping her face in his hands.

"Yes, very," she said. "Very, very glad."

"You will have no one to quarrel with," he said.

"And no one to insult me," she said.

"And no one to whom to release your venom."

"I won't need to with you gone," she said.

"You are going to miss me," he said.

"True," she said. "Just as I miss the surgeon who pulled one of my teeth last year. Just as I miss the pair of shoes I threw out early this spring because they gave me blisters on all ten toes. Just as . . ."

"Well," he said, "at least we share mutual feelings about being rid of each other. I was afraid that you might miss me in earnest."

"Conceited—mm," she said as he kissed her.

"Mm, yes," he said after a considerable interval of silence. "We share that sentiment, too, Soph. Let's do it one more time, shall we? By this time tomorrow, all will be over."

"It cannot be too soon for me," she said. "Mmm."

"Mmm," he said a while later. "I am in total agreement with you, Soph. Shall we go inside before this mood of rare amity is broken by another quarrel?"

"I don't know why you are kissing me anyway," she said. "We do not have to deceive anyone any longer, do we?"

"Sometimes, Soph," he said, "one has to do something purely for oneself."

She looked up at him.

"I could see that you were longing to be kissed," he said. "Ah, that's better. You suddenly look much more yourself."

"You toad!" she said.

THEY HAD SPENT a great deal of time together since her return from London. But apart from that one night with its bitter ending, they had not been alone together. He had not been to her room again although she had lain awake at night watching the door to her dressing room, expecting him and knowing that he would not come, longing for him and dreading that he would appear.

There were three more days to Sophia's wedding, she told herself on the evening after the last of the guests had arrived. Easy days since there was so much to be done and so many guests to entertain and relatives and friends to spend time with. There would be no chance for them to be alone with each other, and he had shown that he had no further wish to come to her at night. She did not know why he had come that one night. He was missing his mistress, perhaps?

Emma and Clarence were planning to leave the day after the wedding. It was enough that Lord Clifton had entertained such large numbers during the week and more leading up to the nuptials, Emma said. The least they could do was take themselves off without delay once the festivities were over.

"And you will be glad of some peace and quiet and relaxation, Olivia," she said, "after all this excitement."

Yes, she would. But she would not find those things at Clifton. When her friends returned to Rushton, she had decided, she would go with them. There she would begin her battle for inner peace all over again.

She was sitting beside her husband on a sofa in the drawing room, their shoulders almost touching. They were in a group with her parents and the Biddefords and Emma and Clarence. Several guests were in other rooms of the house. Most of the young people had gone outside for a stroll, the rain having finally ceased the day before.

"Yes," her father was saying, continuing a conversation that had been in progress for several minutes. "What you say is quite right, Miss Burnett. One does not need a large number of close family members to achieve contentment in life. We have only one daughter and one granddaughter, though we wished for more of each, did we not, Bridget? But we have each other and our circle of good friends and we live a blessedly contented life."

"Friends are the key to contentment," Emma said.

"One can choose one's friends, you see, whereas one cannot choose one's family."

"Except one's spouse," the earl said.

"But friendship consists in freedom," Emma said, launching on her favorite theme, "the freedom to give or to withhold affection. That freedom instantly vanishes in marriage. Once one is compelled to friendship, then it no longer is friendship but forced amity. Freedom is killed. Love is killed."

"Not necessarily," Olivia's father said, leaning forward in his chair.

"Olivia," Clarence said with a smile, "I am going to take myself off for a turn about the terrace. If I stay any longer, I will not know who are my friends and who are not or even what friendship is. Would you care to join me?"

She got gratefully to her feet. "That sounds wonderful," she said.

"Would anyone else care for a stroll?" he asked, looking about the group. But everyone else seemed engrossed in the discussion.

Olivia met her husband's eyes and half smiled. "Excuse me?" she said.

"Of course." He inclined his head.

It was a beautiful evening, fresh after the days of rain and cool, too, but not cool enough to necessitate running upstairs for a shawl.

"Emma is in her element," she said, taking Clarence's arm as they stepped out onto the terrace. "She has a totally new audience on whom to unleash her theories."

"I know," he said, grinning. "But I am the old audience and thought it time to come outside for fresh air."

"Ah," she said, breathing in the freshness, "it does feel good."

"Things are going well for you, Olivia?" he asked. "I half expected to find the two of you at daggers drawn when I arrived. Instead, I was witness to all of Marcus's impatience to have you home from London, and the sight of the two of you after your return looking like a pair of reunited lovers."

"He was eager to have Sophia back home," she said. "He has not seen enough of her over the years, Clarence. I always knew from his letters that he loved her. I did not realize until I came here that his love for her equals my own."

"Will you be staying?" he asked. "You know my opinion about that old quarrel and about your long and unnecessary separation."

"It was not a quarrel," she said, "and it was not unnecessary. I am going to come home with you and Emma."

"The day after the wedding? Are you sure, Olivia?"

"I can scarcely wait," she said. "I feel as if I cannot breathe here, Clarence. I want to be home in my own world with my own friends and activities."

"With Emma and me and the Povises and the Richardsons and everyone else?" he said. "Are we worthy substitutes for Marcus, Olivia? Has he said he wants you to go?"

"He has not said that he wants me to stay, either," she said. "It is intolerable being here, Clarence. When I first came, as you know, I thought it would be merely to spend a few days discussing Sophia's future and rejecting Lord Francis's offer. There seemed to be no question of our allowing her to marry. In fact, of course, it was not as simple as that. You warned me, did you not? Neither of us had faced the fact that she is grown up and of marriageable age and that Francis is a perfectly eligible partner for her, even if he has been a little wild since coming down from university. If I had known that this was to happen, I would have written to Marcus telling him that any decision of his would have my support. I would not have come."

"But you would have come for her wedding," he said.

"Oh," she said. "Yes, I suppose I would have. And we have more or less agreed, Clarence, to come together occasionally after Sophia is married, to visit her or be visited by her. I wish it did not have to be. I am already dreading the next few weeks."

"Because you will have to go through again what you went through years ago when Marcus first left?" he asked.

"How will I survive it?" she asked.

"By being proud and stubborn and as strong as any ten other women put together," he said. "And as foolish as twenty."

"What am I to do, then?" she asked. "Go down on my knees to him and beg him to take me back?"

"Perhaps allow him to do that same thing," he said.

She laughed. "I met Lady Mornington in London," she said. "She is not at all lovely, Clarence. And I know that sounds tabbyish, but I do not mean it that way. She seemed like a perfectly sensible, amiable, intelligent woman. She looked like the kind of woman a man would become attached to. They have been together for six years, I believe—longer than he and I were together. I told him I had met her, and he did not deny a thing or try to justify himself. He merely said that she was his dear friend."

"He did not leave you from choice, Olivia," he said. "And fourteen years is a very long time, you know."

"Oh, yes," she said. "I know, Clarence. Believe me, I know." She added on a rush, "We have been together again."

"Have you?" he asked quietly. "Are you sure you should be saying this to me, Olivia?"

"But I have to talk to someone," she said. "I feel so

very alone. I cannot talk to Mama. She would only advise me as she has always done to do my duty, whatever that might mean. And I cannot talk to Emma. She would only advise me as she always does to forget about all men and thereby relieve my mind of all stresses and negative emotions."

"And you do not want that advice?" he asked.

"Clarence," she said, "you are my very best friend. Oh, yes, you are. You know you are and have been since Marcus left. I can talk to you about anything on earth and know that you will listen with a sympathetic ear. You will, won't you? We have been together—twice. And it was wonderful and dreadful."

"Dreadful?" he said.

"Afterward," she said, "both times, when I expected tender words, he had only coldness to offer. As if he had been merely using me, putting me in my place, reminding me that I am still his wife to be so used if he chooses."

"Did you give him tender words?" he asked.

"But he must have known my feelings," she said. "I did nothing to hide them."

"Did you know his feelings?" he asked. "Before he spoke, I mean?"

"But I was wrong," she said. "When he spoke, I knew I had misunderstood entirely. We have been apart too long, Clarence. I do not know him any longer. He is a stranger to me. I think Marc must have died many years ago."

"Perhaps you need to talk to him, Olivia," he said. "Just talk as you are talking to me now. You used to talk to each other constantly, did you not? I used to come upon you out riding or walking together, and you were always so deep in conversation that you both would look thoroughly startled when I hailed you. It happened so many times that it was a private joke I had with myself."

"I would not know how to begin," she said.

"Then begin anywhere," he said. "Begin with the weather. Ideas often flow once the tongue has been set in motion."

"It sounds too simple," she said. "I don't think it could work, Clarence."

"You will not know unless you try," he said. "Why not invite him outside now? We seem to be the last ones out here and it seems to me that we have been outside far longer than I intended to keep you. We will be fortunate not to run into search parties."

"It is late," she said. "Perhaps tomorrow."

"Never put off until tomorrow what can be done today," he said, grinning. "My mother used to say that so often to us children that we used to mouth the words with her if we could just get sufficiently far behind her not to be observed."

She sighed. "You always make life sound so uncomplicated, Clarence," she said. "Perhaps I will do as you suggest. I shall see if he is busy with someone."

The Earl of Clifton was not busy with anyone, it seemed. He came striding across the hall to meet them as they stepped inside the house, his eyes passing from Clarence to his wife.

"I need to have a word with you, Olivia," he said, taking her arm.

She looked at Clarence and he gave her an encouraging smile.

"I shall see if there is any tea left in the drawing room," he said.

Her husband's hand was firm on her arm. He led her without a word across the hall and opened the door into his private study.

"What is it?" she asked him. "Is something wrong? Sophia?"

There was no light in the study. He closed the door

firmly behind them and plunged them into darkness. And he swung her around quite ungently so that she collided hard with his chest, and found her mouth with his own.

The urgency of the kiss had nothing to do with passion or need or love, she realized after the first moment of shock and latent joy. It was a kiss designed to bruise her lips and cut the flesh behind them against her teeth. It was a kiss intended to hurt and insult. She pushed against his shoulders, was wrestled even closer to him, and finally went limp in his arms.

"You will keep away from him while you are in my home," he said at last, his voice tight with fury, "whatever you do at Rushton. My home is full of guests come to celebrate a wedding. Your daughter's and mine. The proprieties will be observed. Strictly observed. Do you understand me?"

She could not see him at all. Her eyes had not even begun to accustom themselves to the darkness.

"Clearly," she said.

"Where were you?" He had her by the wrists.

"Outside."

"Where outside?"

"Outside."

He shook her wrists. "When your mother asked Sophia if you were coming in, Sophia said she had not seen you," he said. "Where were you? In the garden? In the hidden garden?"

She said nothing.

"Answer me." He shook her more roughly.

"I will not," she said.

"You were in the hidden garden," he said and his hold on her wrists loosened. "I'll not have it, Olivia. Not on this property or during this week." The fury had gone from his voice, leaving it flat and expressionless. "At least I did not invite Mary here."

"Lady Mornington?" she said.

"At least I did not invite her here, Olivia," he said. "I think you might have done as much."

"Clarence is my friend," she said.

"Yes," he said, "and Mary is mine."

"Well," she said, "you can be back with her within a week. The guests will doubtless all leave within a day or two of the wedding. I shall be returning home with Clarence and Emma. You need not delay your departure for London."

"I have known peace of mind with her," he said. "She accepts me for who I am."

"Then you are fortunate," she said. "There are not many women who would accept any such thing."

"Olivia," he said. "Stay away from him."

"Why?" she asked. "Are you jealous, Marcus?"

"Envious," he said and there was an edge of anger to his voice again. "I don't have Mary here to dally with."

"I suppose, then," she said, "that I am more fortunate than you. May I leave now?"

He released her wrists and opened the door in silence. She went past him into the hallway and he closed the door quietly behind her, remaining inside the room.

SHE PROBABLY WOULD have told herself the next morning that she had had a sleepless night. Certainly she had tossed and turned for a long, long time and punched her pillows and rearranged the bedclothes and thought of getting up and dressing and going downstairs in search of something to eat or outside in search of air.

But she must have fallen asleep eventually. Otherwise, she would have heard him coming into her dressing room, and seen him coming into her bedchamber and crossing the room to her bed. She would have seen him pulling off his clothes. As it was, she was aware of him only as the bed beside her dipped with his weight.

And then one arm came beneath her and turned her onto her side and his free hand came along her jaw and over her ear and his mouth found hers and explored it warmly and gently. She came fully awake.

He said nothing, only kissed her slowly, almost lazily, touching just her face, her nightgown separating their bodies.

"Easy," he murmured to her when desire surged and she arched herself against him. "Easy."

And she imposed relaxation on her body and allowed him to lead the way by slow, deliberate, erotic stages until he finally stripped away her nightgown and came onto her and into her and she knew only the frenzy of wanting him, of needing what he was giving her. She pressed her knees to his waist and urged him on to that newly discovered world beyond passion.

"Yes," she told him as it happened. "Yes."

He sighed against her ear.

She did not try to hold him as he disengaged himself from her and removed his weight from her. She only kept her eyes closed and willed him not to leave her. There was a far worse desolation in being alone after love than in being always alone. She had discovered that on two recent occasions.

Please don't go, she begged him silently. And he slid his arm beneath her neck again and drew her close and pulled the blankets up about them.

"He has taught you passion," he said, his voice low against her ear, "but not control. I'll teach you control and the greater wonder that follows it."

She thought he would leave then. And she expected to feel fury and the need to order him out of her bed and her room. But she was too tired for anger and too warm and comfortable to want him gone. She willed him not to leave. She burrowed her head into the warm hollow between his shoulder and neck.

Fourteen years without you have taught me passion, she told him silently as she slipped into sleep. *Not Clarence or any other nameless he. Just your long absence from my life, Marc.*

He woke her again in the night and loved her slowly and thoroughly. And remembering his words, she began to learn to hold her desire in check, so that all the meandering paths to glory might be explored and enjoyed, and the glory itself might be the more shatteringly wonderful.

Even then he did not go back to his own room.

14

SOPHIA SLEPT FITFULLY THROUGH THE NIGHT. SHE did not know quite how she was to face the day and the announcement that would have to be made. She wished she had insisted that they do it the evening before despite the reasonableness of Francis's objections. Really, there was no right time to do such a thing. And she wished that she had been blessed with an imagination. She had never thought of what a betrothal and planned wedding would involve beyond bringing her parents together. She had not thought of anything beyond the hope that once together, they would realize that they could not be apart again.

She got up very early and dressed herself and brushed her hair without the services of a maid, intending to go downstairs and outside even though there were heavy clouds that made it look chilly outside.

But she would not do so, she decided suddenly. She would not wait any longer. She *could* not. And why should Francis bear all the embarrassment of confronting both sets of parents when really none of this whole situation was his fault? She would go to her mother, she decided, as she had often gone whenever she was burdened with a problem. She had always liked to go in the early morning, when she could climb into bed beside Mama and curl into her warmth and feel that all the burdens of the world had been lifted off her shoulders and onto Mama's sensible and capable ones.

She could no longer do that, of course. But she would go anyway. Mama would know how best to break the news to Papa and to the duke and duchess. And Mama would be able to advise her on how and when they should make the announcement to all their gathered friends and relatives.

It was not going to be that simple, of course. It was a dreadful thing she had done, despite the purity of her motive, and the consequences were going to be equally dreadful. Indeed, they did not bear thinking of. And it was the effort of not thinking of them that had kept her awake through much of the night, waking from dreams and fighting to remain awake.

But she would go anyway. If there was anyone who could help her it was her mother. Besides, Mama should be the first to know. And perhaps Papa, too, but she did not care to think what Papa would say to her or what he would do. Though it was a baseless fear—Papa had never struck her even when she was a child.

Perhaps she should wait for a more civilized hour, she thought as she stepped outside her room into a deserted corridor and closed the door behind her. Mama was going to be fast asleep. Perhaps she should wait an hour longer. But even an hour was too long to wait—her wedding was supposed to take place two days hence. She walked resolutely and with thumping heart and shaking knees in the direction of her mother's room.

She tapped lightly on the door and opened it slowly and quietly as if afraid to disturb the mother she had come to waken.

"Mama?" she whispered, stepping inside and looking across to the bed from which the curtains were looped back.

And then she stopped abruptly as she found herself

staring into her father's eyes. She could not afterward explain to herself how she had the presence of mind to notice details, but she did. Her father's bare arms were about her mother, her head cradled on his arm, her face against his bare chest. Her long fair hair was tousled and covering his arm. Her back was bare. Her father's free hand drew the blankets up about her sleeping mother.

He frowned at Sophia and formed a "Sh!" with his mouth though he made no sound. She backed up until she felt the door handle behind her and then she fled through the door, closing it as quietly as her shaking hands could accomplish. She stood outside the door gulping in air, feeling such a welling of excitement inside that she thought she would surely burst if she had to keep it all to herself.

Cynthia? Cynthia had always been one of her closest friends. But she did not spare Cynthia more than a glancing thought. Her hasty footsteps and overflowing heart took her to another door and she rapped on it a little less lightly than she had tapped on her mother's. Even so she had to repeat the knock.

Lord Francis was wearing breeches when he opened the door. They were all he was wearing. His hair was still disheveled from his pillow. Sophia noticed none of those details.

"What the devil?" he said. "Go away this instant, Soph. Are you mad?"

"Francis," she said, her hands clasped to her bosom, her eyes shining, "guess what? We did it. We did it."

Lord Francis took a step forward, looked to right and left along the still-deserted corridor, grabbed Sophia by one wrist, and hauled her inside his bedchamber. He shut the door firmly.

"We certainly did," he said. "We backed ourselves into a corner. Don't you realize what would happen if you were seen knocking on my door at this hour of the morning, Soph? Your reputation would be in shreds even if you really were within two days of your wedding. There would certainly be no question of calling off the wedding. In one moment I am going to stick my head out there again to make sure there are no watchers at the doors and then you are going to tiptoe all the way back to your room again. Are you this desperate for my body?"

She chuckled and threw her arms about his neck. "They are in bed together and he has his arms about her and she is sleeping with her face against his chest," she said. "We did it, Francis! We did it." And she kissed him smackingly on the cheek.

"Soph, Soph," he said, trying to put her from him, "if there is any attacking to be done, I would prefer to be the instigator, if you don't mind too much. *Who* are in bed together? Oh, your mama and papa, I suppose. And you went walking in on them. Then you can be very thankful that she *was* asleep, my girl. You might just have acquired a permanent blush."

"Do you think they . . . ?" she asked.

"I have no doubt that they . . ." he said. "It usually happens when a man and woman get into bed together, you know, Soph. And I would feel a great deal more comfortable if you were not quite so close to mine, especially in my present state of, ah, dishabille. I am lamentably human, you know."

"Oh," she said, and she jumped away from him and appeared to notice for the first time his naked upper body and his bare feet. She flushed slowly.

"What you see is going to be all yours in two days' time, Soph, if you don't get out of here unnoticed," he said. "In which case it is to be hoped that those blushes mean you like what you see. So they spent the night together, did they?"

"Yes." She clasped her hands before her, and her eyes shone again. "It has worked, Francis. It was all worthwhile after all. Now I will not mind all the embarrassment facing us today. I shall not mind at all, at least for my sake. I shall mind for yours, for you have done me a great kindness and I shall never forget it for all that we quarrel dreadfully whenever we are alone together for longer than two minutes. I shall mind the embarrassment to you."

"Look, Soph," he said, "we need to talk a few things over before getting together with our parents. But not here and now, thank you very much. There are limits to my better nature. I'll meet you outside in half an hour. By the fountain. Agreed?"

"Yes," she said. "But I will take all the blame, Francis. It will be worth it now that I know they are together again forever and ever. Oh, you are wonderful."

"You won't think so for much longer if you keep standing there looking like that," he said, striding resolutely back to the door and opening it gingerly. "It is still deserted. Good Lord, I'll wager even the servants are not up yet. Out you go. Now!"

Sophia went, favoring him with a wide and radiant smile as she passed him. Lord Francis in his turn favored the ceiling with an exasperated grimace.

HE TRIED TO draw his arm out from beneath her without disturbing her. God, but she looked beautiful, flushed and disheveled with sleep. And even more beautiful when she opened her eyes and stared upward at him, at first blankly and then with recognition.

"I had better go," he said.

She said nothing.

"I had no right to question the propriety of your behavior last night," he said. "I, of all people. I don't really believe that you would carry on an affair here under the very nose of your mother and mine and a host of other relatives and guests. I'm sorry."

She still said nothing.

"You should understand the way I felt, though," he said. "It is something of a shock to come actually face-to-face with one's spouse's lover. Not that I blame you, Olivia. It is just strange seeing you again, that is all. My wife and not my wife. Someone I used to know who now has a life I know nothing about. I am sorry about this, too. It is in poor taste, I suppose, even if it is the most lawful bedding that either of us has indulged in in fourteen years."

He smiled when she remained silent, and sat up on the edge of the bed to pull on his nightshirt.

"But it was never your way to forgive, was it?" he said, and he left the room without looking back at her.

He wished this dratted wedding was at an end already and everyone gone home. Including Olivia. He did not doubt that she would leave with Clarence, her friend Emma with them to lend propriety to the journey. He wished she were gone already. He wished that he never need see her again.

His love for her had become a quiet thing over the years, locked away deep inside him, no longer disturbing his day to day living. Now that love had become a pain again, worse even perhaps than it had been at the start. For at the start there had been a great deal of hope—hope that she would forgive him, that she would realize that she could not live without him, that she would see that it was not worth throwing away a life of potential happiness for the sake of one transgression, however bad.

Now there was no hope. Although her manner toward him in the daytime was amiable, there was a reason for it, an agreement they had come to. And although

she had allowed him into her bed and even greeted him
there with a passion she had not shown before, her mind
was not in accord with her body. She would not speak
with him or respond to him or forgive him when passion
was satiated.

There was no point in going to bed, he thought when
he reached his own dressing room. It must be infernally
early, but there was no more sleep to be had. He rang for
his valet and peeled off his nightshirt.

And what the devil had Sophia wanted with Livy at
this hour of the morning? Some other crisis concerning
her wedding, no doubt. They would all be fortunate if
the girl did not fall into hysterics long before the ceremony was safely over.

OLIVIA LAY STILL after pulling the blankets up over her
breasts. She stared upward at the canopy.

How he had changed, she thought. She had always
been the focus of his world, she, and Sophia after her
birth. And Rushton. He had never wanted anyone or
anything else. He had often groaned when she had reminded him of some assembly that they were to attend.
He had not wanted to attend that Lowry wedding without her. She had urged him to go, thinking that it would
be good for him to see his friends again.

And yet now he could lie in her bed, propped on one
elbow, and talk about her supposed lover and the taste-
lessness of their making love together just as if it were
the most normal thing in the world for a husband and
wife to behave so. And the sickening thing was that she
knew it was quite normal. Marc had become part of his
social world. She had not.

Why had she not denied an involvement with Clarence more vehemently? she wondered. She had told him
the night before that Clarence was her friend, but he had

misunderstood or else disbelieved her. She had left it at that. She had felt too upset and too weary to protest something that he should have known without any question at all. If he knew her as she had thought he knew her, he could not even have wondered about her and Clarence.

But Marc belonged to the real world. She was the strange one. What other woman would have urged her man to go alone to London for a wedding and all the parties and drinking and rioting that would be an inevitable part of it? Only a totally credulous innocent.

She longed to be at home. She longed to be away from this and back in the peace of her own home. Except that she knew that that peace would no longer be waiting there for her, but would have to be fought for all over again.

And perhaps never found. For the previous fight had been made possible by the fact that she had considered herself right. What he had done was unforgivable. And though she had forgiven him nonetheless in her heart, she had truly believed that they could never live together again, never restore the trust and the friendship that had bound them so closely together.

She knew now—too late—that she had been wrong in every way. What he had done was not unforgivable. It had been human and everything human was forgivable. And she knew that if only she had had the courage to try, they could have built an even stronger relationship than before, because it would have been based on reality. They would have suffered together and been strengthened together.

She had given away the chance to have her marriage grow. And it was too late now. Oh, it was true that he was treating her with kindness and deference during the daytime, but that was all a charade they had agreed to. And it was true that he had made love to her four

times—on three separate occasions—and that they had
been wonderful together, far more wonderful than they
had ever been during the years of their marriage. But it
had been a physical thing only. Sex only.

He had talked about Clarence as if he did not mind if
he were her lover. And he had talked about Lady Mornington as if she were an accepted part of his life. Making
love with his wife was what had made him feel guilty,
not the fact of the existence of a mistress.

He had changed too much and she had changed too
little. The gap between them after fourteen years was
insurmountable. Only one thing remained unchanged.
She still loved him. And her love had become a pain
again and would remain so for many weary months. She
knew that from experience.

Olivia turned over onto her stomach and buried her
face in the pillow where his head had lain.

"How can you be ten minutes late," Lord Francis said,
"when you were dressed already, Soph, and all you had
to do was come downstairs and out through the door?"

"I went back to my room," she said, "and had a fit of
the panics. I thought for a while that I was going to
vomit, and I did not want to vomit all over you, Francis.
I have the feeling under control now."

"Are you sure?" he asked. "There are two benches
here, Soph. We can sit on separate ones if you like."

"And then I was halfway down the stairs," she said,
"and remembered that I did not have my cloak and it
looked cloudy and raw outside. Actually it is quite
warm, is it not?"

"Sit down here," he said. "We have to talk before
other people start getting up and wandering out here."

"Yes," she said. "Shall we have breakfast first, Francis, and then ask Mama and Papa and your parents to

come to the library? Or shall it be the other way around? Either way, I am sure I shall not be able to eat a bite. I keep thinking of kidneys. Oh, I wish I could think of some other food." Her teeth were chattering.

"Soph," he said, "you don't really think we can do this, do you?"

"I don't want to talk about it," she said. "I just want to do it. I shall have that feeling again if I think."

"The guests are all here," he said, "and the neighbors stirred up to fever pitch. The rector is puffed up with importance and the cook and your father's chef from London are considering giving up sleep for the next two nights in order to get all the baking done. The wedding cake is made and the flowers have been chosen for cutting tomorrow. Your dress is made and your mama's and my clothes. And . . . well, I could go on forever, couldn't I?"

Sophia licked her lips nervously. "You see what I mean?" she said. "We must not think, Francis, or we are going to end up married to each other. We have to do. No one can force us to marry, after all."

"I think we had better all the same," he said.

She stared at him.

"It would save an awful lot of trouble," he said.

Her jaw dropped inelegantly.

"You would be able to enjoy your breakfast after all, Soph," he said. "And even perhaps have some kidneys."

"Are you mad?" she said. "Have you gone totally insane? Are we to put up with each other for a lifetime just in order to avoid a little trouble now?"

"In short, yes," he said.

"Francis." She stretched out her hands to him until he took them, and set her head to one side. "I cannot let you do it. Really I cannot. Oh, you are very wonderful. But you would never be able to face life with me. You know that—you spent all of your boyhood fleeing from me. I will take all the blame. Truly, I will. I will make sure that there is not even a whisper of blame put on you. It will be all right, Francis. It will be forgotten. Perhaps you can go away for a year or so until the embarrassment has passed. It will eventually, you know. Perhaps you can go to Italy and see the Sistine Chapel—in Rome."

Lord Francis sighed. "I had hoped to avoid this," he said. "But I think it is time for a little confession, Soph. Or perhaps not so little, either. I have trapped you."

"No," she said. "I have trapped you, Francis, by my thoughtlessness. But I shall put all right, you will see."

"Soph," he said, "I knew from the very start exactly how it would be. I knew that all this would happen—a blind man would have known it. I knew we would find ourselves within a couple of days of this wedding and no reasonable way out of going ahead with it."

"But you did it anyway," she said, "for Mama's and Papa's sake. How wonderful you are, Francis."

"I did it to trap you into marriage," he said.

Sophia laughed and then looked at him in incomprehension.

"When I saw you again this spring," he said, "I just couldn't believe that I had done so much running from you when we were younger, Soph. You had changed. By Jove, you had changed. And yet you stuck up your nose whenever I came close and you started to drop all sorts of nasty remarks about rakes and suchlike until I did not know how I was going to get you to take me seriously."

"Nonsense," she said. "You are making this all up just so that I will believe you and you can laugh at me. This is most unkind, you know, especially on this of all mornings. Don't you know that I . . ."

"Then some ass—was it Hathaway?—suggested this most corkbrained of corkbrained schemes," he said, "and I saw immediately where it could lead. I thought that perhaps my agreeing to it would give you time to realize that I was not the wild libertine you took me for."

"Francis," she said, "be serious, do."

"Well, take it or leave it," he said. "I thought I had better confess, Soph. But however it is, we had better get married. All hell will break loose here if we don't. You have to think no further than my mother."

"I don't want to think at all," she said.

"And your parents are going to start blaming themselves," he said. "They will wonder where they went wrong with you, Soph, and before you know it they will be at each other's throats and leaving each other for the rest of two lifetimes."

"Don't," she said. "I don't want to think."

"Don't, then," he said. "Just marry me."

"I don't want to marry you," she said. "I would rather marry . . ."

"A toad," he said. "I love you, Soph."

"Oh, you do not," she said indignantly. "You are a brazen liar."

"I love you."

"You do not."

"Love you."

"Do not."

"Do."

"Don't. You horrid man. I hate you. I do. I hope you go away this very morning after I have made the announcement, and I hope I never ever see you again."

"You don't, Soph," he said.

"I do."

"Don't."

"Do."

"Do."

"Don—. I hate you, Francis. I hate you. Take your hand away from my face."

"It feels so soft, Soph," he said. "So much softer than my hand."

"I don't want you touching me," she said.

"Don't you?" He moved closer to her on the bench and lowered his head to feather a kiss across her lips.

"Or kissing me," she said.

"Don't you?"

"No."

"It feels so good, though, does it not?" he said. "Like this, Soph? And this? Shall I tell you what I wanted to do with you when you came to my room earlier?"

"No."

"I wanted to do this," he said, kissing her again and running his tongue along her closed lips. "And this." He slid a hand beneath her cloak and cupped one breast lightly in his hand.

"Don't," she said.

"I shan't tell you the rest of what I wanted to do," he said. "I'll show you on our wedding night, Soph. Not tonight or tomorrow night. The next night."

"You are saying that to frighten me," she said. "Don't touch me there, Francis." She set a hand over his, the fabric of her cloak between them. "It makes me feel funny. And don't do that with your tongue. Please."

"Don't you think that perhaps you want me, Soph?" he asked.

"Want you?" she said. "*Want* you? You would just love for me to say yes, would you not, so that you can ridicule me. Don't, Francis. Don't do that." He was rubbing a thumb over her nipple.

"Marry me," he said. "Tell me you love me, Soph, and that you will marry me. And then on our wedding night you can tell me all the things to stop doing so that I can keep on doing them."

"Francis," she said. "Please. Do you think I don't remember all the times you deceived me years ago?"

"I love you," he said.

She sighed. "Well," she said, "you always won every contest, did you not, Francis? You always made me believe you and then you called me idiot for being so gullible. Why should anything have changed? Why not this time, too? All right, then. I do love you and I will marry you. And now it will serve you right if I do not release you from our betrothal but marry you and plague you for the rest of our lives."

"Plague me, Soph," he said. "And stop pulling away like a frightened rabbit. Let me kiss you properly."

"Frightened?" she said. "Of you? Who do you think you are?"

"Your betrothed," he said. "The man who loves you. The man you love. Let me kiss you properly."

"Francis," she said, setting one hand over his mouth and looking wistfully into his eyes, "do you mean it? Tell me now if you do not. Please? I will not be able to bear it if you kiss me and tell me those things again and then laugh at me and run away from me."

"If I don't mean it, I am playing a pretty dangerous game, aren't I?" he said. "Parson's mousetrap waiting to snap its jaws?"

"Do you really love me, then?" she asked.

"I really do, Soph," he said.

"Really and truly?"

"And that, too," he said.

She pulled herself away from his hold suddenly and jumped to her feet. She looked at him with shining eyes.

"I have to go back to the house," she said. "I have to find Mama and Papa. I have to tell them that we are betrothed."

"Soph." He scratched his head. "If I were to whisper the word 'Bedlam,' you would not start ripping up at me, would you?"

She looked blankly at him and then chuckled. "We

have this moment become betrothed," she said, "and no one knows."

"It will be our secret," he said. "Sit down here and let me kiss you properly."

She sat. "Will we have to stop quarreling now?" she asked.

"And lead a dull respectable life forever after?" he said, horrified. "Heaven forbid. Let me see now, where was my hand? It was somewhere warm and comfortable. Here?"

"Did you mean it when you said it was small?" she asked as his hand covered her breast again.

"I have seen many larger," he said. "And, ah, touched a few, too."

"Have you?" she said tartly. "Am I to be compared to your—to your pieces of muslin for the rest of my life?"

"Only when I want to start a quarrel," he said. "My hand feels good there, though, does it not? Admit it, Soph."

"You would love me to do just that, would you not?" she said. "You conceited . . ."

He kissed her.

". . . toad," she said.

"Hush, Soph," he said. "I have waited long enough. And you are the loveliest kisser, my love, that it has ever been my privilege to kiss."

"Oh," she said. "Mm."

"And you have the loveliest bosom, too," he said without removing his mouth from hers. "No answer needed or allowed."

"Mmm," she said.

15

"THIS CRAVAT IS TOO TIGHT," LORD FRANCIS complained to Claude, pulling at the offending garment and twisting his head from side to side.

"It is your usual size?" his brother asked.

"Of course," Lord Francis said.

"My guess is that it is a quite normal wedding cravat, then," Claude said.

"Eh?"

"Made exactly the same size as all your other cravats," his brother said, "instead of a couple of inches larger to accommodate the swelling of the throat that comes with wedding days. Your shoes are probably going to be too tight, as well. Now, are they?"

"Ah, I see how it is," Lord Francis said. "I am to be the butt of everyone's wit on the very day when I cannot think up one witticism to hurl in return."

"The cook always puts a dose of poison in the breakfast, too," Claude said. "Just the groom's, of course, not anyone else's. Is your stomach feeling queasy, Frank?"

Lord Francis smoothed the lace at his wrists over the backs of his hands and took one final look at himself in the mirror.

"If I could plan this all over again," he said, "I would choose an unmarried man for my best man, Claude, just as any sensible groom would do. The chances are, he would not be standing there cackling at me. I did not crack one stupid jest when I was your best man."

"You were too busy wondering how long it would take Henrietta's cousin Marianne to fall under your spell during the wedding breakfast," Claude said. "I have been told that she fell under it when we were all still at the church, though I did not notice myself, my attention being otherwise occupied."

"She was too plump for my taste as it turned out," Lord Francis said.

"She was too *eligible* for your tastes," his brother said. "That was the problem, Frank. Her papa all but asked you your intentions, did he not?"

"By Jove," Lord Francis said, "that was it, too. It was never safe to flirt with a girl of reputation, was it?"

The two of them were in the dressing room adjoining the bedchamber where Lord Francis had spent the night. It was at the home of a neighbor of the earl's, it not being at all the thing for bride and bridegroom to spend the night before the wedding beneath the same roof or to set eyes on each other before they met at the altar. Claude had ridden over early.

"I am glad you use past tense," Claude said. "You are crying off all women except Sophia for the future, Frank?"

"Good Lord, yes," Lord Francis said. "She would make a road map of my face with her fingernails if I should take it into my head to start looking about me."

"For no other reason?" his brother asked.

Lord Francis thought a moment. "I intend to start setting up my nursery," he said. "It would be too confusing to be setting up more than one. And far too expensive."

"The same old Frank," his brother said. "One never gets a straight answer out of you. It's not that Sophia kept on pursuing you and you just got tired of running?

Bertie and Dick and I were talking last night. We were a little worried."

"The chase continued until quite recently," Lord Francis said, pulling on his shoes and wincing. "Until two days ago, in fact. But the direction changed. Have you ever watched a cat deciding in the middle of a wild flight from a dog to stop and face the battle? Almost inevitably the dog takes fright and flees with the cat in hot pursuit. Let us say that I am the cat of the story. Devil take it, but these shoes must be a size too small."

His brother laughed. "Time to go, Frank," he said. "It would not do to keep the bride waiting, you know."

"Soph?" Lord Francis said. "Oh, Lord, no. I would never hear the end of it. We would quarrel over it all the way to Italy. I would far prefer to quarrel over something I knew myself in the right over."

"You aren't intending to spend your married life quarreling, I hope?" Claude said, frowning as his brother passed a hand nervously through his hair and turned to the door.

"I intend to be happy," Lord Francis said. "I shall see to it that I quarrel with Soph every day of our lives, Claude. What was that you said about cooks poisoning breakfasts? Were you serious? I hope my stomach is not going to continue this gurgling when I have it inside the church. It could be a trifle mortifying, don't you agree?"

"The poison loses its effect as soon as you clap eyes on your bride," his brother said.

"Ah." Lord Francis opened the door.

"HOLD STILL ONE more minute, Sophia," Olivia said, down on her knees in the middle of her daughter's dressing room. "There, it is perfect." She sat back on her heels and looked up. "Oh, you look so very beautiful."

Sophia's wedding dress was of a very pale blue muslin;

the silk sash and the embroidery at the neck, short puffed sleeves, and scalloped hem white. The housekeeper, with the assistance of one of the gardeners, had woven a posy of flowers for her hair and a smaller one to wear at her wrist. Altogether she looked exactly what she was—a young and innocent bride.

"Mama," Sophia said, her eyes wide and frightened. "Oh, Mama."

Olivia got to her feet, smiling. "We talked yesterday, Sophia," she said, "for an hour or more. You know exactly what is facing you and appeared very eager—yesterday. But a wedding day, of course, is different. There are so many conflicting emotions to be dealt with, are there not?"

"He says he loves me," Sophia said, her eyes large with tears suddenly. "He has said so over and over again in the past two days. Do you suppose he means it, Mama? One never quite knows with Francis. He always has that annoying twinkle in his eye."

"He must have been saying so for far longer than two days, Sophia," Olivia said. "And of course he must mean it. Why else would he be marrying you? He has been under no pressure, as far as I know, to find himself a bride."

"Maybe there are other reasons," Sophia said. "Maybe he felt himself trapped and decided to be gallant about the whole thing. Though it is quite unlike Francis to be gallant. Oh, Mama, what if he does not love me?"

Olivia took her hands and squeezed them. "Before you panic, Sophia," she said, "look inside yourself. Deep inside. That is where you know the truth. You know whether he loves you or not. Does he?"

Sophia looked down at their hands. "Yes," she said at last. "He does. Mama, he does." She looked up again, her eyes shining. "He loves me and I did not even suspect it until two days ago. I thought he hated me. He always used to say the most lowering things about me and about the possibility of being trapped into marrying me. But he was doing it just to have fun with me, just to goad me. He likes to see me angry. He likes to quarrel with me. He says we are going to quarrel every day for the rest of our lives. He loves me. Oh, Mama, he loves me."

"Sophia?" Olivia smiled and frowned simultaneously at this strange speech. But there was a firm tap on the dressing room door and it opened before she could say more.

"Ah," the Earl of Clifton said, "my two ladies. A haven of sanity in the middle of a madhouse. Rose is weeping already; half the children have escaped from the nursery and are playing some sort of spirited game that necessitates a great deal of running and shouting on the stairs; Claude's wife is trying to herd the children back to the nursery; Wheatley has inexplicably lost his coat; there have been no fewer than three inquiries from the stables about the exact time we want the barouche brought around; and Cynthia is reputedly having the hysterics because as bridesmaid she should be with the bride but instead has to stand still to have her hem turned up because it is too long after all. Need I continue?" He grinned.

"Papa," Sophia said. "Oh, Papa, I am so frightened."

"Well," he said, "perhaps a very little haven of sanity. What is it, Sophia?"

"It has all been so sudden," she said. "Everything has happened so fast. And now it is my wedding day before I have had a chance to think."

"The month has gone fast, has it not?" he said. "But both you and Francis were adamant that it not be delayed any longer, Sophia. Has it not been long enough?"

"But we decided to get married only two days ago," she said.

The earl and his wife exchanged glances.

"It was a pretend betrothal," Sophia said. "A counterfeit passion, Francis called it. To bring the two of you together, to give you a chance to patch up your differences. We were to put an end to everything once we had succeeded. And it worked, did it not? I will never be sorry that we did it because it worked. I was not quite sure until two mornings ago when I went into Mama's room and saw you . . ." She blushed. "Then I was finally sure. But then when I told Francis that we must call everyone together to tell them that there would be no wedding, he said that yes, we must marry because it would be too troublesome to stop all the preparations at such a late date."

"Sophia!" the earl said.

The countess merely looked at her, aghast.

"And he said he loved me," Sophia said quickly. "He said that he had planned it all from the start, that he had known all along how it would be, and that he had always planned to marry me no matter what happened with you. He said he loved me and so we decided to marry after all."

"Sophia!" the earl said again.

"And I love him, too," she continued, the color high in her cheeks. "I always worshiped him when we were younger, but I did not know that I still did so until I started to wake up at nights with my cheeks wet because I had been dreaming of our betrothal ending and of never seeing him again." She was breathless with the speed of her confession. "I would die if I never saw him again."

The earl passed a hand across the back of his neck. "Perhaps no haven of sanity after all," he said. "I am speechless. I do not know what to say." He looked to his wife for help.

But Sophia had darted between them and had taken

an arm of each, being careful not to squash the flowers at the wrist she had passed through her father's arm. "It is all like a fairy tale, is it not?" she said, looking at first one and then the other, her face alight with love and happiness. "You are together again as I have always dreamed of your being and I am about to marry the man I have loved for as far back as I can remember. And he loves me. And we are to marry in the very church where you married. And the sun is shining after all the unsettled weather of the past week or so. And . . . oh, and, and, and." She laughed excitedly.

"Yes, the three of us together again," the earl said, covering her hand with his own. "You are right, Sophia. It is a wonderful day—despite the most hair-raising scheme I have ever heard, you little minx. We are going to be having Francis pacing at the altar if we do not get moving, you know. I have a little gift for you before we leave the room."

She looked up at him expectantly.

"I had them sent especially from London," he said, "since a young lady should graduate from pearls on her wedding day."

He drew a delicate necklet of diamonds from a pocket and clasped it about her neck.

"Happy wedding day, sweetheart," he said, turning her and kissing her on the cheek.

"Oh, Papa," she said, tears in her eyes. "In many ways you will always be my very favorite man."

"You had better say your favorite *father*," he said. "That way you will not create any misunderstandings. And a small gift for you, too, Olivia." He turned his eyes to his wife. "I twisted the arm of your maid and discovered that you would be wearing green today." He looked appreciatively at the rich green of her silk dress and drew an emerald necklace from another pocket. "Do you want to wear that silver chain, too?"

She looked at him mutely before fumbling with the catch of her silver chain and removing it. He replaced it with the emeralds while she bit her lip and leaned her head forward.

"A gift for our daughter's wedding," he said, turning her by the shoulders as he had done with Sophia and kissing her on the lips while their daughter looked on, her eyes shining.

"Thank you." Olivia looked up into his eyes and fingered the emeralds at her throat. "Thank you, Marcus."

The door burst open suddenly without even the courtesy of a knock.

"Sophia," Cynthia said, her eyes as round as saucers, her dark blue dress now indisputably the perfect length. "Everyone else has left and the barouche is at the door and I could have died when I tried on my dress and found that I tripped over the hem whenever I moved and you have managed without me anyway and look even more lovely than I expected and Lord Francis is going to burst with pride when he sees you and . . ."

"And we had better not keep the horses waiting any longer," the earl said firmly. "Or the groom, either."

"Oh, Cynthia," Sophia said, taking her father's arm to be led down the stairs, "I have told them. And I am so happy I could burst. And my legs feel like two columns of jelly. I do believe I am going to be sick."

THE CHURCH WAS full. Olivia saw that as the Viscount Melville escorted her down the aisle to her seat at the front. It was also looking at its most beautiful, the sunlight glowing through the stained-glass windows, the floral decorations bringing the summertime inside. She was not sure how the church had looked at her own wedding. She had had eyes for nothing and no one except her bridegroom.

Lord Francis, looking very slim and very young and very anxious, was standing with his brother and glancing back to the doorway where Sophia would appear soon with Marc.

Sophia. She felt like crying. Her daughter was about to be married. The sole person she had had to live for for fourteen years. She was to be married. For love. Despite that strange, bizarre story she had told less than an hour before, she was marrying for love.

As she, Olivia, had married for love nineteen years before. In the same church. And suddenly the years rolled back and it was Marc standing there looking pale and nervous and then fixing his eyes on her as she approached with her father. And it was she approaching, feeling that her legs would surely not carry her one inch farther, and then focusing her eyes on the man waiting for her at the altar. Marc. The man she loved. The man she was going to spend the rest of her life loving.

Lord Francis's eyes stilled and lit up suddenly and there was a stir in the church. Olivia, getting to her feet, found herself fighting an ache in her throat and blinking her eyes. And there they were, long before she had won the fight, Sophia's face bright and glowing, seeing no one but Lord Francis. And Marc, looking broad-shouldered and calm and capable. The organ was filling the church with sound.

He sat beside her after giving away their daughter to the man who was about to become her husband. His shoulder touched hers. And she thought quite vividly, distracted from the wedding service for a moment, of what Sophia had told them in her dressing room. She had done it for them. She had betrothed herself to Francis so that they would come together and sort out their differences. And she had seen them together in bed—three mornings before, the last time they had been together—and had concluded with joy that her scheme had worked. Dear naive Sophia.

"I will," Lord Francis said.

Olivia's hand was taken suddenly in a strong clasp, and he placed their joined hands on his thigh.

"I will," Sophia said.

They squeezed each other's hand almost to the breaking point. She pressed her shoulder against his arm. Someone was sniveling—doubtless Rose.

"What God has joined together," the rector was saying, "let no man put asunder."

He squeezed her hand even more tightly, if that were possible, looked down into her face, and then laid a large linen handkerchief in her free hand. She dabbed at her eyes with it.

What God has joined together, . . . She clung to his hand . . . *let no man put asunder.*

He had kissed her at the altar—she could remember the heat in her cheeks at his kissing her in full view of a churchful of people. He had checked her steps as they walked down the aisle together, preventing her from running with the exuberance of the moment. He had forced her to smile at all their relatives and friends beaming back at them from the pews. And then they had stood on the steps outside the church, shaking hands and being kissed, shaking hands and being kissed, on and on for what had seemed like an eternity. She could remember the bells pealing.

And then he had taken her hand and raced with her along the twisting path of the churchyard to the waiting carriage before anyone else could get there. And he had drawn the curtains across the windows of the carriage and taken her into his arms and kissed and kissed her until the carriage had stopped outside Clifton and the coachman was coughing outside the closed door.

Nineteen years ago. And fourteen of the years since lived apart.

There was a stir and a murmur in the church. A smattering of laughter. Lord Francis had his hands at Sophia's waist and she had her face turned up eagerly for his kiss.

Olivia's hand was raised to her husband's lips and held there for a long moment.

And then somehow they were all outside the church and Sophia launched herself into first her mother's and then her father's arms, looking so eager and so happy that Olivia ached for her innocence. And then Francis was hugging her and calling her Mama and laughing. The duchess was weeping into a large handkerchief and uttering incoherencies about her baby. It was the happiest day of her life, she told anyone who cared to listen— all her babies were happily settled.

The church bells pealed out their glad tidings.

And then Olivia's hand was being shaken and her cheek kissed by a whole host of relatives and houseguests and neighbors. She and her husband were being congratulated on having produced such a beautiful bride. She realized that he had one arm tight about her shoulders and she one arm about his waist only when she found that she was shaking people's hands with her left hand.

"Yes," Marc was saying, "we are the most fortunate of parents. Aren't we, Olivia?"

"She has been the joy of our life," she said.

But suddenly there was no one else to greet, though there was still a great deal of noise and laughter and milling about.

"Francis is not as wise as I was," the earl said, looking down at his wife, his eyes twinkling. He still had an arm about her shoulders. He nodded to the roadway beyond the churchyard. "It could take them ten minutes to get away."

Francis and Sophia were in their carriage, but the door was being held open by laughing guests and flowers were being pelted inside and Richard and Claude were actually trying to unharness the horses while their brother's attention was distracted. But Francis had been to a few weddings in his time and participated in active mischief. He poked his head out of the doorway, his face wreathed in a grin, and yelled at the coachman to start and run the rascals down. He closed the door when the carriage was already in motion.

"Ah," the earl said as a hand inside the carriage pulled the curtains across the windows. He turned and smiled down at his wife.

"Oh, Marcus," she said, "can she really be all grown up, then? Is it all over already?"

SOPHIA WAS WAVING tearfully from the window of the carriage later the same afternoon. But there was no one to be seen any longer. The carriage had turned a bend and the house was out of sight. Her husband, she saw when she turned to look, had already settled back against the cushions. He was smiling at her.

"Tears, Soph?" he said. "You are sorry to be leaving your mama and papa?"

"We will not see them for months and months, Francis," she said, blowing her nose and putting her handkerchief away resolutely. "Perhaps not until Christmas."

"Perhaps you should stay with them," he said, "while I go to Italy alone. I can tell you all about it when I return. I'll even tell you if the Sistine Chapel is still in Rome."

She looked at him a little uncertainly. "Perhaps you would prefer to go alone," she said.

He grinned and stretched out a hand to her. "Don't make it this easy for me," he said. "And what are you doing all the way over there? Trying to create a bulge in the side of the carriage? You aren't afraid of me by any chance, are you?"

"Afraid of you?" she said. "Pooh, why should I be afraid of you?"

"Because I am your new husband, perhaps," he said. "Because we are right in the very middle of a wedding."

"We are not," she said. "The wedding is all over. And we are on our way on our wedding journey at last."

"Only the ceremony and the breakfast are over, Soph," he said, lacing his fingers with hers and trying to draw her toward him. "The rest of the wedding—the most important part—is still to come. We are not married until that part is completed, you know."

Her cheeks flamed, and she resisted the pull of his hand.

"Are you afraid?" he asked.

"Afraid?" she said with a brave attempt at scorn. "Of course not, Francis. The very idea."

"Shall I tell you what I am going to do to you tonight?" he said. "Would it make it easier if you knew what was in store?"

"I know," she said quickly. "And I don't want you to say a word. You want to do it only to embarrass me."

"Not a word?" he said. "This sounds distinctly promising. Shall I show you, then, Soph? A sort of rehearsal in the carriage?"

"Don't touch me!" she said.

"Er," he said, "why are you clinging to my hand, Soph, if I am not to touch you?"

"Francis," she said, "don't do this. Let us quarrel tomorrow, shall we? But not today. Today I do not feel up to it."

He chuckled and leaned across the carriage, taking her by surprise by scooping her up into his arms and depositing her on his lap.

"Admit that you are afraid," he said, "and I will have mercy on you, Soph."

"Never," she said. "I have never been afraid of you even when you made me climb that tree because there were wild dogs loose and then went for help so that you could hide in the bushes and bark. I was not afraid."

"Soph," he said, tucking her comfortably against him, "did I do that to you?"

"Yes, you did," she said, burrowing her head against his shoulder. "But I was not afraid, Francis. And I am not afraid now."

"I can't tease you any longer, then," he said. "What a dull journey this is going to be."

"But is it not dreadfully embarrassing?" she said, hiding her face against him. "I think it must be. I shall die of embarrassment."

"Not before I will," he said. "In fact, Soph, I can hardly contain my trembles even now." He shook, convulsively. "I shall be sure to extinguish every light tonight and draw every curtain, including the ones around the bed so that you will not see my blushes. It is the most embarrassing thing ever imagined. We might both not survive it. Indeed . . ."

Sophia punched him sharply on his free shoulder. "Don't make fun of me," she said. "You have no sensibility at all. You are quite horrid and I hate you."

"This is better," he said. "Perhaps I am going to enjoy the journey after all."

"You have done nothing but laugh at me ever since we drove off," she said. "I wish I had not let you talk me into this three days ago. I wish I had held firm. You are horrid, Francis, and I wish heartily I had not married you."

"Kiss me," he said.

"I am not going to kiss you," she said. "Ever. I hate

you. I would rather kiss a toad. I would rather kiss a . . ."

"Snake," he said. "Kiss me."

". . . rat. No."

"Kiss me, Soph," he said softly. "Kiss me, my wife."

"I am, aren't I?" she said.

"Almost, yes." He rubbed his nose against hers. "Kiss me."

She kissed him.

16

AFTER THE NEWLYWEDS HAD BEEN WAVED ON their way late in the afternoon, the guests from the neighborhood began to order their carriages brought around and took their leave. The duke and duchess withdrew to their private apartments with their family for an hour's breather, as the duke put it, before dinner and the informal dancing that was to follow it in the drawing room. The other houseguests, too, withdrew to some private and quiet activity, all the excitement of the wedding breakfast at an end.

Olivia abandoned everyone and fled to the hidden garden. It had been such a turmoil of a day, she thought, closing the wooden door gratefully behind her. She desperately needed some peace. And it was there waiting for her, the air inside the rose-draped walls and the surrounding trees of the wood still and heavy with summer, the only sounds the chirping of birds and the droning of unseen insects.

She felt heavy with desolation. Sophia was gone and would be gone for several months. And even when she returned, she would no longer be living at Rushton but in the home of her new husband. There would be only the occasional visit to look forward to.

She sat on her favorite stone in one of the rock gardens and feasted her eyes on the flowers all about her.

She breathed in their scents. She felt guilty about being depressed on Sophia's wedding day. Despite the girl's confession of the morning, she had been brilliantly happy and very obviously was deeply in love with Francis. And he with her. They would be happy together. She hoped. Oh, she hoped. It made her nervous to see a bride and groom too deeply in love, especially when the bride was her own daughter.

But it was for herself she felt depressed, Olivia realized. Everything seemed at an end. Her marriage had ended long ago. Now Sophia was gone. And there was Marc to leave all over again the next day. Endings. All endings. No beginnings. And yet she was only thirty-six years old.

No beginnings. Unless . . . But it could not be. Not now. Not at her age. Not when they had tried without success for all those years after Sophia was born until they separated. It would be too ironic. And too bizarre. She had a married daughter who might herself expect to be a mother within a year.

And yet, she thought, clasping her knees and noticing the daisies dotting the lawns, despite a mower's frequent care, it was not impossible. They had been together four times on three different occasions. And she was several days late. She was never late.

She set her forehead on her knees and closed her eyes. She must not begin to panic. It would be foolish when there was no way yet of being in any way certain. Nor must she begin to hope. It would be foolish to invite all the corresponding disappointment when she discovered— as she surely would within the next few days—that it was not so.

She must not begin to hope, she told herself. She must not begin to hope that there would, after all, be something—*someone*—to fill the emptiness. Some part of him to keep close to herself for a while longer.

She was in the same position, drowsy, almost sleeping when he came. She had been expecting him, she realized when she heard the latch of the door. He would have known where she had come, and he would have come there himself to say good-bye. Tomorrow's farewell would be public. Not that it would not have been better to keep it so, of course, but she had known he would come.

"Olivia," he said when she lifted her head from her knees. He was walking toward her. "They were happy, were they not? We did the right thing not to try to persuade her to cry off after she had told us the truth this morning?"

"They were happy," she said. "I don't believe there can be any doubt of that, Marcus. She glowed. And he was looking at her with every bit as much pride as we were. And with every bit as much love, too, I am sure."

"It hurts to lose a daughter, doesn't it?" he said. "Almost as if we really have lost her."

"Rushton will never be her home again," she said. "Or Clifton, either."

"And yet," he said, "it feels wrong to be dejected."

"Yes."

"She is happy and all we have ever wanted for her is happiness."

"Yes."

"Olivia," he said, "she did it for us. To bring us together."

"Yes."

"And young Francis saw his chance and agreed to the foolish scheme," he said.

She laid her forehead back against her knees. She felt rather than saw that he came closer and set one foot up on a stone close to her, as he had done on a previous occasion.

"She thought she had succeeded," he said. "She saw

us together. She had come into your room for something but only I was awake. She drew what seemed to her the only conclusion."

"Poor Sophia."

"You are still planning to leave with Emma and Clarence tomorrow?" he asked.

"Yes," she said. "I have a craving to get my life back to normal again."

"You would not like to stay awhile?" he asked. "To relax here?"

"I cannot relax here, Marcus," she said.

He said nothing for a while. "Do you have any regrets, Olivia?" he asked. "If you could go back, would you do anything differently? Would you perhaps forgive me—if you could go back?"

She looked up after a long silence. "I forgave you long before you stopped asking," she said. "I knew that you had given in to a momentary weakness and that you were truly sorry. But I could not just continue on as if nothing had happened, Marcus. I did not believe I could love you as dearly as I always had or trust you as implicitly or be as close a friend to you. Everything was spoiled and I did not see how it was to be put right again."

"And now it is very much too late," he said. "We have grown whole worlds apart with only some appetite and perhaps a little affection left for each other. You have Clarence. It is too late, Olivia. Isn't it?"

She put her head back down again. And he had his Mary. "Yes," she said. "Fourteen years too late. We both made a dreadful mistake, and now it is too late."

She thought of Lady Mornington, the small rather plain woman who had been his mistress for six years. The woman who had looked sensible and intelligent, an altogether suitable companion for Marc. Yes, it was too late. She had voluntarily given up her rights as his wife and now had no right even to try to burden him with a dilemma. He had known peace with his Mary, he had said.

"Yes, it is too late," she said again.

"He is a good man," he said. "Almost worthy of you, I think. I always wondered why he showed no particular inclination to marry. I did not see that he loved you, too. But his devotion has been rewarded. You are happy with him, Olivia?"

She swallowed, tried to frame an answer, and said nothing. He would feel guilty, perhaps, if he knew the truth, guilty about his own liaison. And she no longer wanted him to feel guilt. She had burdened him with more than his fair share years before.

His hand touched the back of her head lightly and briefly. "I wish I could set you free for him, Olivia," he said. "But there would be too much scandal, for the fault would have to appear to be yours."

"I would not want Sophia to be the daughter of divorced parents," she said.

"No." He lifted his hand. "And I do not want any more bitterness between us, Olivia. There has been enough. We will spend Christmas together, if Sophia and Francis are home from Italy?"

"Perhaps they will go to William and Rose," she said, looking up once again.

"Sophia will want to be with us," he said.

"We must wait and see," she said. "But yes, if she wishes it, Marcus."

He smiled and touched her cheek with the back of his fingers. "Perhaps we will be grandparents before a year has passed," he said.

"Yes." She swallowed.

"I would like that," he said. "To have a child in the family again. It does not seem long since Sophia was a baby, does it?"

"People used to laugh at us and think us very eccentric," she said, smiling, "because we would never leave her in the nursery with her nurse but spent almost all our days with her."

"And nights, too," he said. "The little rascal would never sleep, do you remember? I think I wore a hole in the carpet of the nursery, walking back and forth with her for hours on end."

"You were always good with her," she said. "My energy used to give out and you used to order me off to bed."

"And Nurse was snoring in her bed," he said with a laugh.

"Oh, Marcus," she said, "they were good times."

"Yes," he said, "they were. Perhaps we will be able to recapture some of the pleasure with our grandchildren, Olivia. Though the thought is absurd. You a grandmother? You are only thirty-six years old and look years younger."

She smiled fleetingly.

"Well," he said, "that is all in the future. Perhaps far in the future. Tomorrow you have a long and tedious journey to face. Do you have everything you need, Olivia?"

"I will have Emma and Clarence to keep me company," she said.

"Yes, of course," he said. "And at Rushton? You are comfortable there? Should I increase your allowance?"

"No," she said. "It is already over-generous."

"Well, then," he said. "Everything seems to be settled."

"Yes." She smiled at him. "Almost everyone is leaving tomorrow, Marcus? And William and Rose the next day? You will be glad of quietness again."

"I shall leave for London without delay," he said.

Ah, yes. Lady Mornington. Olivia found herself fighting tears.

"It will be time for me, too, to get my life back to normal," he said.

Yes. She held her smile.

He set one hand on her shoulder and squeezed it tightly enough to hurt. "I am sorry for what has happened here between us, Olivia," he said. "Sorry if you found it distressing or distasteful. I ought not to have forced myself on you merely because you are still legally my wife."

"You did not use force," she said. "But I am sorry, too. It feels almost like being unfaithful, does it not?"

He squeezed her shoulder again and turned to walk back across the small garden. She watched him go. He stopped with his hand on the latch of the door and looked back over his shoulder.

"Olivia," he said, "I did love you, you know."

Did. *I did love you.* She stared at the door long after he had gone and long after tears had blurred her vision.

Did. Past tense. All over and gone. All endings. It was too late for them now. Very much too late. It was what he had said and what she had agreed to. Doors closing everywhere. None opening.

She dared not hope for the one glorious beginning that might yet compensate for all the other endings.

She dared not hope.

And yet she could not stop herself from hoping.

HE HAD AVOIDED Clarence as much as he possibly could during his stay. They had once been the best of friends. And he could still not see any reason for not liking the man. He was amiable, courteous, always willing to fall in with whatever activity suited other people. But how could they still be friends?

Was it possible, the Earl of Clifton wondered, to be friendly with the lover of the wife one still loved? And yet he could not blame either her for taking a lover or him for loving her. She had chosen wisely and well. Clarence had always been devoted to her. He could see that now, looking back. And faithful, too. They had been friends for longer than the fourteen years. And lovers for probably many years. He did not know for sure. They must always have been very discreet. He had never heard a whisper of scandal concerning them.

He had been avoiding Clarence. But seeing him strolling alone from the direction of the stables, he paused and then redirected his steps so that they would meet.

"You have been out riding?" he asked.

"No, no," Clarence said. "Just checking for myself to see that my horses will be ready for the journey tomorrow. Most of the people at the house seem to be resting."

"It was good of you to come so far," the earl said. "I appreciate it, Clarence."

"How could I resist an invitation to Sophia's wedding?" Clarence said. "I have always thought of her as a type of niece."

"It has been good for Olivia to have you and Emma here," the earl said. "And it will make my mind easier to know that she will have your company for the return journey."

"We will be making an early start," Clarence said.

"Clarence." The earl spoke impulsively. They both stopped walking. "Look after her."

"I shall fight off any highwaymen with two guns blazing," Clarence said with a grin. "And Emma will send them fleeing with her tongue. Have no fear."

"That is not what I meant," the earl said. "I meant look after her for the rest of your life."

Clarence's eyebrows rose. "What?" he said.

"I don't think we need to keep up this civilized pretense," the earl said. "I may not have lived with her for many years, Clarence, and I may have had other women while she has had another man, but I still care for her, you know. I want her to be happy."

Clarence pursed his lips. "This other man being me?" he asked. "Is that what Olivia has told you, Marcus?"

"I am sorry I mentioned it," the earl said, "since I seem to have caused you some embarrassment. I suppose it is difficult to discuss openly such a matter with the husband of your mistress and your former friend to boot. I just . . . Well, never mind."

"What has she told you?" Clarence asked. "How long we have been lovers? How frequently we indulge our amours? Where? What degree of satisfaction . . ."

Lord Clifton's fist caught him a left hook to the chin at that moment and he fell awkwardly. The earl stood, feet apart, his fists clenched, waiting for the fight he fully expected. Clarence propped himself on one elbow and felt his jaw gingerly.

"I don't believe it is quite dislocated," he said. "You might have warned me to defend myself, Marcus."

The earl's shoulders slumped suddenly and he reached down a hand to help his former friend to his feet.

"Devil take it, Clarence," he said. "Forgive me, will you?"

"You are a fool," Clarence said, accepting the offered hand and getting to his feet, still feeling his jaw. "You still love her, don't you? And yet you are going to let her go home tomorrow—with me."

"I'll not impose myself where I am not wanted," the earl said. "I never did, Clarence, and I have not changed. I will not interfere with her freedom, either, despite that facer I just planted you. I just want to make sure that you will be good to her. But then there is nothing I can do to ensure that, is there?"

"Olivia is very dear to me," Clarence said, "and I will do all in my power to be good to her, as you put it, Marcus. More than that I cannot say. I don't know what she has said to you. But you are a fool for all that. If I had ever had the sort of happy and secure relationship that the two of you used to have, I would have fought heaven and earth to keep it. And public opinion and the law of the land, too, if necessary," he added quietly.

"Well," the earl said, "we had better return to the house. My guests are going to have regained their energy soon and will be ready to resume the festivities. Do you think my daughter made a good match? Olivia and I are pleased despite early misgivings. Young Sutton has been something of a hellion since coming down from university. But he appears to care for Sophia."

They walked back to the house together.

CLAUDE AND RICHARD and their wives and children were also leaving early the following morning. The terrace before the house seemed crowded with carriages and even more crowded with people. There was noise and laughter and the shrieks of children. And tears.

"Olivia, my dear," the duchess said, folding her friend in her arms when she was able to tear herself away from her children and grandchildren for a moment, "how wonderful to have seen you again and to have this connection of marriage between our two families. We must not let it go so long again. Perhaps within nine months we will share a grandchild."

Olivia hugged her in return while the duke was shaking Emma heartily by the hand and assuring her that he had been charmed to have had a chance to converse with such a sensible lady. Clarence and Marcus were taking their leave of Francis's brothers and their families.

And there were her mother and father to hug and kiss, and more tears to be shed.

The horses were snorting and stamping in the chill morning air. The coachmen were stamping their feet and were very obviously eager to be on their way. Servants and trunks were already loaded into the accompanying carriages.

The duke hugged Olivia. "It has been wonderful to see you again and in such good looks, Olivia," he said. "I hope it will not be so long until the next time, my dear."

The children were inside the carriages with Richard's wife. Claude was handing in his own wife. Emma was already seated in their carriage, and Clarence waiting beside the door. Marcus was shaking Richard's hand.

Olivia felt panic clutch at her stomach. She turned hastily and reached out a hand for Clarence's.

"Olivia," a voice said from behind her and she turned back again. "Have a good journey."

His hand closed about hers, warm and firm. Such a strange formal gesture. Such formal words. She had expected him all the night before, although she had known it would have made no sense at all for him to come. Not after their words in the hidden garden. But she had expected him. She had wanted him desperately. She had even got out of bed at some time during the night, determined to go to him herself. But she had got no farther than the door into her dressing room. As soon as all his guests had left, including herself, he was to return to London. To Lady Mornington.

"Yes," she said. "Thank you."

"Good-bye, then," he said.

"Good-bye, Marcus."

There was a moment when perhaps they swayed a little toward each other. Perhaps not. Perhaps it had been in her imagination. And then his hold on her hand shifted so that he could help her into the carriage. Clarence came in behind her and seated himself opposite.

Both he and Emma studied the formal garden beyond the far window.

"Good-bye," he said again, and he stood back so that a footman could close the door firmly.

The coachman must already have been in his place. The carriage began to move almost immediately. She looked at Marcus once through the window and felt panic grab at her again. She clenched her hands hard in her lap so that she would not throw the door open and hurl herself from the carriage.

Good-bye, Marc. She leaned back against the cushions, closed her eyes, and fought the sharp pain in her throat.

"Olivia," Emma said. "Why are you being so foolish? For a lady of remarkable good sense, you have always been most foolish in your marriage. What on earth are you doing here with Clarence and me?"

"Not now, Emma," Clarence said. "Your timing is disastrous. Change places with me, if you please?"

A few moments later Olivia found her hand in her friend's reassuring large one.

"I hope that it is not your favorite coat, Clarence," she said, her voice ominously calm. "It is going to be soaked."

"I shall squeeze out the excess moisture when you are finished," he said, "and it will be as good as new again."

She laughed shakily. And then she turned her head, buried her face against his sleeve, and cried and cried.

"Oh, dear," Emma said. "Is there nothing we can do, Clarence? Would it help if we turned back? I always feel so helpless when it comes to affairs of the heart."

"We could converse about the weather," he said. "That would help, I believe, Emma. That topic invariably leads on to others."

* * *

THE DUKE AND Duchess of Weymouth left early the following morning. The Earl of Clifton was on the road for London just one hour later. He could not have stayed longer at Clifton if his life had depended upon it, he thought.

He had gone to the hidden garden after she had left the day before, and sat for an hour or more on the stone where she had always liked to sit. But although the sun shone and the birds sang and the flowers bloomed, there was no peace to be had there. She was gone. Her absence from the garden—and from his life—was like a tangible thing.

He had been horribly reminded of what his life had been like for a year and more after he had left her.

During the night, unable to sleep, he had wandered into her bedchamber, sat down on her side of the bed, and laid a hand on her pillow. But she was gone. Irrevocably gone. He had counted the months to Christmas—almost five. An eternity. Would Sophia and Francis be back by then or would they extend their travels on the Continent? And would she come even if they were home? Would there perhaps be some excuse for not coming? Winter weather? Bad roads?

He had wondered if he would ever see her again.

And finally and foolishly, he had lain down on her bed, his head on her pillow, and slept.

He was going to spend the rest of the summer and the autumn and winter in London, he had decided. Perhaps he would go to Brighton for a week or two if the weather remained warm. It did not matter where he went as long as he did not have to remain in Clifton.

He had a visit to make in London, one that he would really rather not have made at all. But it had been no casual acquaintance. It had lasted for six years. And Mary was his friend. No more than that, in fact. But he had to end the whole relationship. Because she had been such a close friend, somehow the relationship now seemed adulterous to him.

Perhaps it was foolish to end a good friendship when he might possibly never even see Olivia again. End it he must, though. But he could not just drop her without a word. He had to explain to her. She would understand. She knew that he loved Olivia, just as he knew that she still grieved for her dead husband.

Life might be altogether less complicated, he thought, if he loved Mary instead of his wife. If she really were his mistress.

17

*H*E HAD THREE LETTERS FROM HER BEFORE HE SAW her again.

The first came two weeks after his arrival in London. It had been to Clifton Court first. It was a short, strange letter, and left him wondering what her motive had been in writing it. Why had she not simply told him face-to-face?

"I want you to know," she had written, "that Clarence is not my lover and never has been. I have never had any lover but you. Clarence is my friend, as you have always known and as I told you. He is my friend. There has never been even a suggestion of anything else between us."

That was all, apart from a polite inquiry after his health and the expressed hope that they would hear from Sophia soon.

Was it true? the earl asked himself. But of course it was true if Livy said it. There could be no doubt about that.

Did she want him back? Was she trying to clear the path for his return? Was that why she had written? It was his immediate and first hope. Or perhaps it was just that Clarence had complained to her and embarrassed her and she thought it time to clear up the misunderstanding.

Or perhaps she wished to remind him once more that the responsibility for the breakup of their marriage was entirely his. She had remained faithful, if unforgiving.

But not entirely unforgiving. She had told him that she had forgiven him even before he had stopped asking. But she had considered it impossible to continue with their marriage. All had been spoiled, she had said. And it was far too late for them anyway to try to pick up the threads of a relationship that had lapsed fourteen years before. She had said that, too.

No, there was no room for hope. No point in writing back to her to tell the truth of his relationship with Mary. For though he had never lain with Mary, he had lain with other women. He put the letter away with all the other letters he had received from her over the years, most of them concerning some problem with Sophia or some estate business. Never anything personal. But he had kept them all anyway.

The second letter came soon before Christmas. Sophia and Francis had still not returned from Italy. They were to spend the holiday in Naples, they had written. They expected to be home by spring. The earl had written to his wife that he hoped she would accept the invitation to spend Christmas with William and Rose and their family. He could assure her that Rose was particularly eager to see her now that there was the connection of marriage between their families.

She wrote back to say that she would be unable to go. She had already made her excuses to Rose, she had said. She was recovering from a chill and did not feel it wise to travel. Besides, she had other commitments for the holiday. She wished him a happy Christmas.

He wrote again, asking about her health, but she did not reply. He considered going to her but did not do so. She had made it plain as she possibly could without being openly offensive that she did not wish to see him again and would do so only when it became necessary for the sake of their daughter's happiness. She would not thank him for arriving on her doorstep to express his anxiety over a long-cured chill.

He spent Christmas with the duke and duchess's family and several other houseguests and felt lonelier than he had ever felt in his life.

The third letter came early in April, just after Sophia and Francis had returned from the Continent and taken up temporary residence in London. Sophia had known, of course, from letters that had reached her from home, that they were still living apart, but it was evident that she had not given up hope. Perhaps Mama would come to London for part of the Season, she had suggested. She could even stay with them if she wished, instead of with Papa. The four of them could go about together.

She had written to persuade her mother to come. And he had written to tell her that Sophia was glowing with health and happiness and young Francis was still doting on her. But it would mean a great deal, he had written, if she would consent to spend a few weeks in town so that they could all be together on a few occasions.

She could not come, she wrote back. He let the letter fall into his lap and read no more for a while. So much for a hope that he had always known to be unreasonable. And so much for a promise she had made to spend some time with him when Sophia should return.

She was made of marble, he thought with a wave of unaccustomed anger against her. She was quite implacable in her contempt of him and what he stood for. She would not come. So. He would never see her again. He might as well drown himself in liquor and go on a tour of all of London's whorehouses that night. He might as well . . . He picked up the letter wearily and read on.

"It is not a recurrence of the chill," she wrote. "There never was a chill. I could not bring myself to tell you the real reason. I find it difficult now. But you have a right to know. I should have told you a long time ago. I will be delivering a child sometime this month. Of course, a journey to London is out of the question.

"I would like to see Sophia if she would care to come here and miss the beginning of the Season. Will she be embarrassed to have a sister or brother so much younger than herself, I wonder? You need not feel obliged to come, Marcus. Nor need you feel guilty. I want this child more than I have wanted anything for a long, long while. And I have been in good health. I shall inform you of the event as soon as my confinement is over."

The Earl of Clifton got to his feet with such haste that his chair crashed to the floor behind him.

THE AIR FELT good. After three days of rain, the sun was shining again and there was the smell of fresh vegetation. Spring had come late. There were still some daffodils blooming, and the tulips and the other late-spring flowers were coming into their own. The trees had all budded into new leaf.

It felt good to be strolling outside in her favorite part of the garden beside the house. It had always been called the rose arbor, though at present it was filled with spring flowers. The roses would not bloom until later.

She sat down slowly on a wrought-iron seat. She felt as if she had just walked five miles instead of the short distance from the house. The baby had dropped, although there were still two weeks to the expected birth date. It was a little easier to breathe, but it was difficult to walk. And difficult to sit, too, she thought ruefully.

Indeed, she had been feeling quite out of sorts all day. Hot and restless with alternating spells of listlessness and nervous energy. She could not recall having felt quite so huge and heavy with Sophia. But of course, that had been almost nineteen years before. It was not surprising that she did not remember. And she was also nineteen years older than she had been then.

Would Sophia come? she wondered. And perhaps Francis, too? She hoped so. She wanted to see them. She wanted to assure herself that what Marc had written about them was true. And she wanted Sophia close to her again. She had been almost nine months without any family. An unborn baby, she thought, spreading one hand over her bulk, did not quite qualify as family capable of keeping her company.

It was going to be a boy, Mrs. Oliver, the housekeeper had predicted. She could always tell from the way it carried. And she claimed she was almost always right.

Olivia hoped Sophia would come.

And she hoped that Marc would not come. She could not bear to see him. Not now. She needed tranquility in her life for the next few weeks. She hoped he would not feel obliged to come.

She could hear the sound of horses far down the drive. It sounded like more than one. Clarence usually rode over. Perhaps it was Emma, she thought, or the rector's wife. She had promised to call one afternoon during the week. Perhaps it was Sophia. But no. Her letter would not have reached London more than a day or two before. There would have been no time for Sophia to come.

It was a curricle, she saw as the vehicle came into sight. She stood up to watch it. Whom did she know with a curricle? There was no one in the neighborhood. It must be someone come from a distance.

Marc?

But no, it could not be Marc. There would not have been the time for arrangements to be made for a journey and the journey accomplished.

She drew her shawl closer about her shoulders and spread both hands protectively over her unborn baby.

It was Marc. She knew it long before she could see the driver clearly and despite the improbability that it was he. Her thudding heart and the blood pounding at her temples told her that it was he. But she could neither run to him nor away from him. She stood quite still.

It was Marc. And he had seen her. He was signaling to a couple of grooms who had appeared at the gateway of the stableyard to see who was approaching. He jumped down from the high seat, leaving both curricle and horses to their care.

It was Marc. Her baby moved violently inside her. He had flung his hat onto the seat of the curricle. She had forgotten his silvering hair. She had forgotten how attractive it looked.

She was standing in the middle of the rose arbor, a woolen shawl drawn over a flimsy, loose-fitting dress. She was enormous with child and quite pale and quite impossibly beautiful. He did not even look behind him to see if the two grooms he had signaled were coming to take his horses. He strode toward her.

"Livy," he said, reaching out his hands to take the hands she had stretched out to him. "My God. Oh, my God." Her hands were cold. He squeezed them tightly.

"Marc," she said, "why did you come? Oh, why? I have been hoping and hoping that you would not."

"Have you?" he said, and he could feel his jaw tightening. "You did not think I would be interested in the birth of my own child? You did not think I would consider it important enough that I need be informed before now?"

"Yes," she said, "I knew you would be interested. It might be a son. Perhaps you will have an heir long after you must have given up all hope of having one."

"And perhaps it will be a daughter," he said. "Either way it will be a child of my own body. And of yours. You had no right to keep it from me this long. No right at all." All the shock and anxiety and love that had sustained him on his journey were converted suddenly and unexpectedly to anger. He had committed one wrong long ago in the past, and ever since she had made him into a monster of depravity and insensitivity.

She withdrew her hands. He had come because of the baby. Of course. It would be his only reason for coming. She had known that. It was why she had not wanted him to come. And yes, it had been spiteful to make those remarks about a son and heir. He would love the child if it were a girl, just as he had loved Sophia. He would want to share the child as he had shared Sophia. But it was her child. This time she had done all the suffering alone.

"This is my child," she said. "All mine. You shall have no part of this child. You have not been here."

"I was there at the start," he said harshly. "I will not satisfy you, you see, by suspecting you with someone else. No child can be yours alone, Livy. The child is ours. And I would have been here ever since the start if you had only said the word. You know that."

"No, I do not," she cried. "You could not wait to return to London and your whore."

"Mary is not a whore," he said, "and never was my mistress, either. And you know you are being unfair. I wanted you to stay longer, if you will recall. Or have you forgotten that detail? Does it not fit your image of me as a compulsive womanizer and therefore must be suppressed from your memory?"

"I don't want to argue with you," she said, turning away from him. "I don't want you here."

"What is it?" he asked when she stopped abruptly.

"Nothing," she said, taking a deep breath. "The baby moved. It is low and awkward."

He reached out and touched her shoulder. She was heavy and awkward with his child. He felt an ache at the back of his throat. "How have you been, Livy?" he asked. "Has it been a difficult confinement?"

"Because I am thirty-seven years old?" she asked him. "No, I am still capable of bearing, Marcus. I must return to the house. I need to sit down in a proper chair."

She was being deliberately nasty and spiteful. She realized that, but she could not seem to help herself. It was either that or cast herself into his arms weeping. She would not show him that she needed him, that she had longed for him every moment of every day and night since she had returned from Clifton the summer before. He had come because of the baby. He had left Lady Mornington so that he might have a new child to go back and boast about. Had he told the truth about her? She frowned.

"Let me help you," he said.

His arm was so much firmer than Clarence's. So much easier to lean on. But the distance to the house suddenly seemed a formidable one.

"What is it?" he asked when she stopped.

"More movement," she said. "I need to get back to the house. I have not been feeling well today."

"And you have no one to insist that you stay indoors when you are feeling so?" he asked. "You will have me from now on."

"There are two weeks to go," she said. "Sophia was late. Perhaps this child will be, too. It could be a month. You will miss part of the Season if you stay. There will be no need to do so. I shall let you know immediately."

"You might as well save your breath for the walk," he said. "This is my home, too, if you will remember, Livy. This is where I plan to be living for some time to come."

"I don't want you here," she said.

"Don't you?" he said. "Too bad."

"I was hoping that Sophia would come," she said.

"I sent a note around," he said, "but I did not wait

long enough for a reply. I had the sudden and strange urge to visit my wife. For all I know they may be on my heels. What is it?" She had stopped walking again and was drawing a deep breath instead of setting a foot on the bottom step leading up to the house.

"I think," she said, "that this baby is not going to wait another two weeks. I think it is going to be born much sooner than that."

There were more servants than usual in the hall, all of them curious to see the master they had either never seen or not seen for many years. The front doors were open. There were certainly enough servants present to answer the earl's roar for attention. Soon one was scurrying for My Lady's maid, another for Mrs. Oliver, and a third for the doctor. The remaining ones gawked as My Lord swept his very pregnant wife up into his arms as if she weighed no more than a feather and half ran up the stairs with her.

SHE COULD NOT lie down. The pains were more severe and more frightening when she tried to lie down and rest between times. She should try to lie on her side, her maid told her. She should bring her knees up to cushion the pain, Mrs. Oliver advised. She should pile the pillows beneath her head so that she was not so flat, the doctor said.

They might all go hang, the earl said, and leave his wife to do what was most comfortable for her. And no, damn it, he would not leave the room. His wife was about to have his child and he would damned well stay in the room if he damned well pleased.

He apologized to the ladies for his language when his wife relaxed after a particularly lengthy contraction, but refused to change his mind.

"Lean against me, Livy," he said, "when the pain comes again. Perhaps it will help."

And so when her indrawn breath signaled the onslaught of another bout of pain, he got behind her at the side of the bed and stood firm while she pressed back against him and arched her head back onto his shoulder.

"It helps?" he asked when she relaxed again.

"Yes," she said.

Her maid had disappeared. The doctor and Mrs. Oliver were deep in low conversation at the other side of the room—probably some conspiracy to get rid of him, the earl thought.

"Livy," he said. "I came because of you, you know. Not because of the baby."

She was sitting upright again, her head dropped forward. Her eyes were closed.

"The child was begotten in love," he said. "At least on my part. I love you. I always have and I always will. About that at least, I have always remained steadfast."

She lifted her head and drew a deep breath and he took her against him again and stood firm as she grappled with her pain. She stayed against him when it had passed.

"I have never been as much of a womanizer as you seem to think," he said. "There was someone for a year after you made it clear that there could be no reconciliation between us. And a few since for brief spells. And there was Mary for six years—my friend, as Clarence has been yours, Livy. But I broke off with her immediately after Sophia's wedding, nevertheless. I knew there could be no one but you, even if you would never have me back."

"Marc," she said, "you do not need to say these things."

"Yes, I do," he said. "I know you have a low opinion of me, Livy. But you must have consoled yourself while

Sophia grew up with the knowledge that my fall from grace came several years after her conception and birth. I think you need to know that this child, too, is not the child of a total degenerate."

"Marc," she said. But she drew in a sharp breath and pressed her head back into his shoulder. "Oh," she said when it was finally over. "It hurts. It hurts, Marc."

"Oh, God," he said. "If only I could do this for you."

She laughed softly.

"I love you, Livy," he said. "For the child's sake I want you to know that. I have always loved you. And I have been faithful to you since its conception. It broke my heart when you left last summer and I have longed for you every day since. I want you to know that for the child's sake, not to make you feel uncomfortable."

"Uncomfortable," she said. "It is so hot in here. Open a window, Marc."

"They are all open," he said. He raised his voice. "A cool cloth, Mrs. Oliver. Hand it to me. Her ladyship is feeling uncomfortably warm."

It was a long labor. The doctor took himself off to sleep in another room in the house some time after dark. Some time after midnight, the countess's maid replaced Mrs. Oliver at her vigil. The earl refused to leave. If he moved from the bedside in order to wet the cloth afresh or sip some water, his wife would cry out in panic for him when another wave of pain assaulted her. She had become dependent upon the warmth and firmness of his body at her back.

Daylight came before she finally felt the urge to push and her maid went flying off to rouse the doctor.

"Take my strength, Livy," her husband murmured against her hot temple during an ever-shortening interval between pains. "I wish I could give it all to you, darling."

"Marc," she said. "Marc. Ahhh!"

He held her by the shoulders, willing his strength to flow into her.

He had paced belowstairs during the long hours of her delivery of Sophia. The time had been endless, and he had seen in her face afterward that the birthing had not been easy for her. But he had had no idea of what a woman must suffer to bring a man's child into the world. He would have died for her if he could, to save her one more moment of pain. But he could do nothing for her but stand and hold her and bathe her face between pains and remember the pleasure it had given him to plunge his seed into her.

Even after the doctor came back to the bedchamber and persuaded her to lie down at last and position herself for the birthing, it was not over and not easy. It terrified Marc to see her use more energy, at the end of hours and hours of the weakening pains than he had ever used during a hard day's work.

My God, he thought, as he helped Mrs. Oliver for surely the dozenth time to lift her shoulders from the bed as she bore down to release herself of her burden. *My God!*

Both the housekeeper and the doctor had given up long before trying to make him leave as any proper husband would do. He had been an improper husband for long enough, he thought. Why change now?

And then she bore down and did not stop, only letting out her breath with a whoosh two or three times before gasping it in again. And he watched in wonder and awe as his son was born. He was sobbing, he realized as he lowered his wife back to her pillows, and he did not care who saw it.

"We have a son, Livy," he said. "A son."

And the baby was crying and being set, all blood streaked, on his mother's breast as Mrs. Oliver wiped at his back with a cloth.

"Oh," Olivia said. "Oh." She touched him, smoothed a hand over his head, touched his cheek with light fingers. "Look at him, Marc. Oh, look at him."

And then Mrs. Oliver was taking the baby away to clean him and the doctor was coughing and suggesting that his lordship leave the room while he finished with her ladyship.

The earl straightened up and dried his eyes with a handkerchief. But she turned her head and smiled radiantly up at him before he could turn away.

"We have a son, Marc," she said, reaching up one weak hand, which he took in a firm grasp. "We have a son."

He raised her hand to his lips and laid it against his cheek. "Thank you, Livy," he said. "I love you."

The doctor coughed again.

18

EVERYTHING LOOKED REMARKABLY THE SAME AFTER almost fifteen years. It was true that downstairs she had made some changes. The draperies and carpets and some of the furniture had been changed. He remembered her writing for permission and funds to make the changes. But the park he was looking at through a window was much the same. There had never been formal gardens at Rushton; only the kitchen gardens and the greenhouses behind the house and the rose arbor to the west. The room behind him, his bedchamber, had not been changed at all. Some of the belongings he had left behind were still in the drawers.

He had slept for five hours and bathed and shaved and felt much refreshed, though he was still feeling somewhat light-headed at the knowledge that he had a son. Just three days before, he had not even known that Livy was with child. And now he had a son. And he was at Rushton again, looking out at the familiar park, his wife and child in the next room, presumably asleep since he had left instructions that he was to be called when she awoke.

Had she named the child yet? he wondered. What would she name him? Jonathan? That was the name they had picked for a boy before Sophia had been born. But that was a long time ago. It was still nearly impossible to believe that he was almost forty-one, Livy thirty-seven, that they had been estranged for close to fifteen years, had been together briefly the summer before, and now had a newborn son. A son born that very morning.

He had been absently watching the approach of a vehicle along the driveway. It gradually revealed itself to be a traveling carriage belonging to Lord Francis Sutton. They had had his note, he thought with some relief, turning away from the window and hurrying to the door. And they had traveled at a pace almost as furious as his.

He met them outside the house. Francis, vaulting out of the carriage even before the steps were lowered, flashed him a grin over his shoulder.

"Here she comes," he said as Sophia hurried into his arms, was lowered to the ground, and raced toward her father. "If I had allowed her to run instead of riding in the carriage, she would have run. Wouldn't you, Soph?"

"Papa," she cried, her face flushed and anxious. "Is it true? I could not believe it, though Francis said that there could be no doubt about it since you have such neat handwriting and the words were as clear as day. Is Mama with child? *Is* she? And *where* is she?"

"It's true, Sophia," he said. And he folded her tightly in his arms and felt his tears flowing again quite unexpectedly. "You have a brother, born this morning. I was with her."

She went very still in his arms. "I have a brother," she said. "I have a brother?" She tore herself from his arms, whirled about and launched herself at her husband. "Francis, I have a *brother*."

"I heard you the first time, Soph," he said, swinging her once around. "But it bears repeating twice more, I must confess. A little less volume, though, sweetheart."

"I have a brother," she said once more, releasing her death grip on his neck and beaming first at him and then at her father. "And Mama? Is she well? Where is she? I want to see her. And I want to see the baby."

"Congratulations, sir," Francis said, extending his right hand. "If I did not have enough brothers to plague me, now I have a brother-in-law, too. But at least this one is younger than I."

"What is his name?" Sophia asked, linking one arm through her husband's and one through her father's and drawing them up the steps to the house. "I can't wait to see him. And Mama."

"He is still nameless, I believe," the earl said. "And as for seeing them, Sophia, they are possibly still asleep and I would not want them woken. Your mother had a hard time. Go upstairs to freshen up and I shall have refreshments sent to the morning room. In the meantime, I will go up and see and come for you in ten minutes' time if they are awake—or if your mother is, at least. Good enough?"

"Not nearly," she said. "But I know that tone of voice too well to try to defy it, and I know Francis will take your part if I try to insist on seeing Mama without further delay. He has developed into a tyrant, Papa. I am a mere shadow of my former self."

"Which is about as great a bouncer as you have ever told, Soph," her husband said, taking her firmly by the hand and leading her up the stairs. "If you are a shadow of your former self, I would hate to have met the original. I have never found Amazonian wenches very appealing. Ten minutes it will be, sir."

OLIVIA WAS AWAKE, the baby asleep beside her, a fist curled beneath one fat cheek. He had his father's dark hair. She felt deliciously lethargic after a sleep of several hours. She stretched her toes and felt her almost flat stomach with satisfaction.

She wondered when he would come. She could send for him, but she wanted him to come without being summoned. She wanted him to come because he wanted to come. To see his son, she thought. To see his heir. He would come to see the baby.

But no, she would not indulge in thoughts even tinged with bitterness. He had said wonderful things to her the night before, things she had longed to hear the previous summer, things that she wanted to hear again. Perhaps he had said them to comfort her during her labor. But she had believed them then, and she wished to believe them now.

She wished he would come. She turned her head to the door and it opened as if in answer to her thoughts. She watched him come inside and close the door quietly behind him. He was wearing clean clothes and he had shaved. His hair had that soft look it always had when freshly washed.

"You may leave us, Matilda, if you please," she told her maid.

"Livy," he said, leaning across their son to kiss her cheek. She noticed that his eyes looked only at her, not at the baby. "Have you slept? Are you feeling better?"

"I feel wonderful," she said. "I have never felt better in my life."

"Liar." He smiled at her.

And then he looked down at their child and the look of tenderness on his face made her want to cry.

"Is he not beautiful?" she said.

"No," he said, smiling. "We will have to add a new word to the dictionary, Livy. There is no adequate word that I can think of. What have you named him?"

"*We* have named him Jonathan," she said. "Unless you have changed your mind since last we thought we might have a son."

"Jonathan," he said, touching one knuckle to his son's soft cheek.

"I was listening to you last night," she said, "although I could not respond a great deal. I heard everything, Marc."

"Good," he said. "Then I need not repeat it all."

"Would you?" she said. "If I had not heard? It was not just that I was in pain and needed comforting?"

"Shall I start now?" he asked. "With I love you? I can talk on that theme for an hour or so, if you wish." He sat on the edge of the bed, careful not to disturb the baby, and turned to look down at her.

"Marc." She lifted a hand and laid it on his arm. He covered it with his own hand. "I was dreadfully wrong, was I not? Only things can be spoiled beyond repair. Not relationships. We could have repaired ours, couldn't we? It could have been as strong as ever. We could have been happy again, couldn't we?"

"Only if we had both been committed to being so," he said.

"And I was not," she said. "I would not allow for your humanity, Marc. I wanted you perfect or not at all. And so I emptied my life of all that might have given it meaning—except for Sophia. I did a dreadful thing. I destroyed the rare chance of a life of happiness. And I did terrible things to you, too. You have not been entirely happy through the years, have you?"

"Don't kill yourself with remorse, Livy," he said. "Guilt can eat away at you and destroy the future as well as the past. I know. I lived with guilt for years until someone persuaded me that divine forgiveness has to be accompanied by forgiveness of self. You told me last summer that you had forgiven me. Have you?"

"Yes," she said.

"Then forgive yourself, too," he said. "Mine was the greater sin, Livy."

"All the lost years," she said sadly, tears in her eyes.

"We have lived through them," he said. "And they are gone. All we really have is the present and as much of the future as has been allotted us. And at present, I am with my wife and my son and I am feeling almost entirely happy. I will be totally happy if my wife can assure me that the three of us will be together for the future, too."

"Marc," she said, "I never for a moment stopped loving you. I never did. And last summer—I loved you so very much. When you said he had taught me passion, it was of yourself you spoke. I had never got over missing you or wanting you."

"Don't upset yourself," he said, drying a spilled-over tear with his thumb. "We were both living under a misunderstanding last summer, and both nobly freeing the other for what we thought a deeper attachment. But last summer, we loved, Livy. Whichever of those lovings started Jonathan was a loving indeed."

"It was the one in the hidden garden," she said. "The first one. I already suspected the truth before I left Clifton."

He smiled. "I am glad it was that one," he said.

"You cannot know," she said, "how I hoped and hoped and tried not to hope at all."

"Livy," he said, "tell me in words what I think I am hearing but am too afraid to be quite sure of. Are we together again? Are you taking me back? Are we going to bring up Jonathan together? Are we going to piece together an old spoiled relationship and make something perfect of it again?"

She took his hand, which had been stroking the hair from her face, and brought his palm against her mouth. She felt hot tears squeeze their way past her closed eyelids.

"I have wasted so many weary years," she said. "I

don't want to waste another moment, Marc. Stay with me forever."

"And ever," he said, leaning carefully over her and kissing her mouth. "Is our son and heir trying to break up a tender moment?"

The baby was fussing and squirming. He suddenly contorted his face, opened his mouth wide, and yelled out his need for food and attention.

"My other man needs me," she said, turning and slipping her hands beneath the baby and lifting him. His crying did not abate. "He needs a dry nappy and my breast in that order. Marc?"

He laughed down at her.

"It is either you or Matilda," she said. "I don't think I have the strength yet." She laughed back at him.

"I don't think male hands were made for this task," he said, crossing the room to fetch a clean nappy. "You never made me do this for Sophia, Livy."

"Then it is high time you learned," she said. "I must say I am rather out of practice myself. Let us see what we can accomplish together."

They had done a great deal of laughing and cooing, and the baby a great deal of crying before the clean nappy was successfully, if somewhat inexpertly, in place and Olivia, propped against a bank of pillows, stopped the crying with her breast.

"Oh," she said, looking down in wonder at her baby and smoothing one hand over the soft down of his dark hair, "I remember this feeling. Oh, Marc, I am a mother again when I thought only to have the comfort of being a grandmother. How wonderful!"

"Oh, Lord," he said, "I am not much of a father, am I? Sophia is here, Livy, and Francis. She was all ready to come roaring in here, bringing all the dust of travel with her, but I ordered her to freshen up and have some tea and Francis hauled her away. I promised to be back for her within ten minutes. That must be well over half an hour ago."

"Sophia is here?" she said. "Oh, what a glorious day this is turning into. I shall see her, as soon as this hungry little babe has finished sucking. Will you go and tell her that, Marc?"

"Yes," he said, taking his seat on the bed again close to his newfound family and gazing down at them as if he would never have his fill. "In just a moment, Livy. How I envy my son."

She looked up at him and laughed softly. "Your turn will come," she said, "if you will but give me a couple of months."

"I'll wait," he said. "But my love does not depend on just that for nourishment, Liv. I have what I want most in the world right now at this moment—my wife with our son at the breast right before my eyes, and our daughter under the same roof. What greater happiness could there possibly be?"

She smiled at him the dreamy smile of a woman suckling a baby.

SOPHIA CLOSED THE door to her mother's bedchamber a little more hastily than she had opened it. She turned a blushing face to her husband.

"We cannot go in," she said, "and I am very glad that it was I who peeped and not you, Francis."

"Good Lord," he said, "what is going on in there? She has just given birth, has she not?"

"She is nursing the baby," she said. "And Papa is sitting on the bed watching. And neither of them looked embarrassed." Her color flamed even higher.

He placed one hand beneath her chin and raised it. "What a strange combination of boldness and prudery you are, Soph," he said. "What is she supposed to do—

hide away in the darkest corner of the nursery and blindfold the baby?"

"No," she said, "but I would have thought she would at least be embarrassed."

He tutted. "All those things we do in the dark," he said, "and that draw such satisfying sounds of pleasure from you, Soph, would cover you with confusion if I could just persuade you to leave a candle burning one of these times, would they not? And yet nothing different would be happening. I could describe your body to you in the minutest detail, you know. Do you think your father does not know what your mother's breasts look like—and feel like and taste like for that matter?"

"Don't," she said. "You are trying to make me uncomfortable, as usual. He has dark hair, Francis."

"The baby?" he said. "Nice change of subject, Soph."

"And Papa was sitting close," she said. "And they were smiling at each other. Not at the baby, but at each other. What do you think that means, Francis?"

"It means that they were smiling at each other, I suppose," he said. "But you are fit to bursting with some other interpretation, I can see. You tell me, then."

"They are together again, that is what," she said. "And how could they not be? You see, it must have happened last year, Francis. It must have, if she has had a child. But they were too stubborn then to admit that they could not live without each other. But now the baby has brought them together and they will stay together and live happily ever after. That is the way it is, I will wager."

"Wagering is not ladylike, Soph," he said, "and I would not wager against such a theory anyway. It sounds altogether likely. We had better find something to amuse ourselves with while we wait for the heir to Clifton to finish his port and cigars. Could I interest you in a little sport in our rooms? That inn bed last night must be where the spare coals for the fire are stored."

"Francis!" she said.

"I know," he said, sighing, "it is broad daylight. But we can pretend we are in China, Soph. I imagine it must be dark down there."

"I would blush all the way to my toes," she said.

"I know," he said. "That is what I want to see. Well, if it is not to be that, we must go off somewhere and have our daily quarrel. We have not had it today and the day has been dreadfully dull."

"It has not!" she said indignantly. "Do you call arriving in Rushton and seeing Papa again and finding that his note really meant what it said and discovering that Mama had already had the baby and that I am a sister and you a brother-in-law—do you call that all dull?"

Lord Francis yawned loudly, steering his wife in the direction of their rooms.

"I see how it is," she said hotly. "My family means nothing at all to you. You have always had brothers, and now you have sisters-in-law and nephews and nieces. You do not know what it is like to grow up alone, with even one's parents living apart. You do not know what it is like to long and long for a brother or a sister. You think all this is dull?"

"It begins to get more interesting," he said, closing the door of their sitting room behind them.

"And now it seems that at last Mama and Papa are back together again," she said, "something I have dreamed of for years and years and something we schemed to bring about last year. Now it has happened, and you call it dull, Francis? Or beginning to get more interesting?"

"Very much more interesting," he said, taking her face between his hands and running his thumbs across her lips.

"And don't think you can kiss me now and all will be well," she said. "You have done that every day of our married life and I have always been foolish enough to give in to you. But this is my family you are calling dull. My mama and papa and brother. It is me you are calling dull. Stop it!"

He was feathering kisses on her mouth.

"This is all very, very, very interesting," he said.

"Stop it!"

"Fascinating."

"Don't."

"Indescribably gloriously wonderful."

"Don't start doing that with your tongue," she said.

"Why not?"

"Because it always weakens me," she said severely. "I want an apology from you."

"You have it," he said. "Abject, servile, groveling apologies, Soph."

"You make a mockery of everything," she said, her arms creeping up about his neck.

"No, I don't," he said. "One thing I don't make a mockery of, Soph. Two. My feelings for you and what is inside you. We had better not break the news right away, by the way."

"Why not?" she said. "I cannot wait."

"They might find it a little bewildering," he said. "All on the same day becoming parents and learning that in six months' time they are to be grandparents. We had better wait a day or two at least."

"My brother is going to be an uncle in six months' time," she said. "I wonder what his name is, Francis."

"Do you think you could wonder in a supine position?" he asked. "I think you are going to have to get over this maidenly aversion to daylight, you know, Soph. And I'll tell you why. I have every intention of doing what your papa is doing now, when you are doing what your mama is doing now."

"You would not," she said. "I would die of mortification."

"'Here lies Lady Sophia Sutton,'" he said, "'who passed from this life, at the age of nineteen years, of mortification when her husband gazed at her naked breast with an infant attached.' Do you think it would make a suitably affecting epitaph? Churchyard viewers would weep pailfuls when they passed by it, don't you think?"

Sophia giggled.

"Ooh," he said. "Not good. Not good at all, Soph. You are supposed to be clawing at my eyes by now so that you would not notice that I have walked you through to your bedchamber and am laying you back on your bed. Let me think of something quickly to revive this quarrel."

"You do not really mean to, do you?" she asked as her head touched the pillow.

"Look at your naked breast in naked daylight, or make love to you at a time when I don't first have to search for you in the darkness?" he said. "Both, actually, Soph."

"Just kiss me," she said, stretching up her arms to him. "That will be enough for now, Francis. Doubtless Papa will be coming for us soon."

"Don't worry about it," he said. "I have locked all the doors. We can tiptoe along to your mother's room again in half an hour's time and nobody will be any the wiser about what we have been up to. Now, let's see if I have been making love to a woman all these months or to a crocodile or worse."

"Don't be horrid," she said. "Don't look!"

"Mm," he said. "It is all woman so far. Of course, one never knows what the next inch of fabric removed might reveal. This is most interesting. I am sorry I ever called the day dull, Soph."

"Oh," she said. "I shall die. Don't look so deliberately, Francis, and with that odious twinkle in your eye. I would like to blacken it for you. I really would. You are the most horrid man I have ever known. I should never have married you. I should have married a toad before considering marrying you. I should have . . ."

"Eels, snakes, rats, buffaloes, elephants," he said. "I would not advise elephants, though, Soph. Too heavy. Especially when you start swelling as you will soon. Mmm. All woman after all, my love. And sure enough, blushing all the way down to the toenails. I love every rosy inch of you, you know, and shall proceed without further ado to prove it to you."

"I hate you," she said. "I really do."

He grinned at her. "Enough quarreling for one day," he said. "Time to kiss and make up, Soph. Tell me that you love me." And he lowered his head to hers.

"Mm," she told him.

"Good enough," he said.

The Notorious Rake

1

THE THUNDERSTORM WAS ENTIRELY TO BLAME. Without it, all the problems that developed later just would not have happened. Without it she would never in a million years have taken him for a lover.

But the thunderstorm did happen and it raged with great ferocity for all of two hours, seeming to circle London instead of moving across it and away. And so all the problems developed.

Because she had spent the night with him.

Because of the thunderstorm.

She had never been afraid of storms as a child. While her elder sister had gone racing into the comforting arms of their nurse at the first distant flash of lightning, she had always raced for the nearest window and flattened her nose against it to enjoy the show until the storm got closer and she had been warned away from her perch. And then she had sat in the middle of the room, waiting in eager anticipation for the next bright flash and counting the seconds until the crash of thunder told her just how close the storm was.

It had never occurred to her to fear storms until she was in Spain with her husband during the Peninsular Wars, camped out in wet and muddy misery with the rest of his division. Lightning had struck so close to their tent that it had killed the four soldiers in the very next one to theirs. She had screamed and screamed in Lawrence's arms, returning to sanity only when shouting voices beyond their canvas shelter had indicated that tragedy had struck with the lightning, though miraculously it had missed them.

She had been calm then in the face of death. But ever after that, storms had paralyzed her with terror. And Lawrence was no longer there to comfort her. He had been killed more than seven years before.

Mary Gregg, Lady Mornington, had accepted an invitation from her friend Penelope Hubbard to make up a party of eight to Vauxhall Gardens to listen to a concert and to enjoy the beauty of the pleasure gardens. The party had been organized by the new wife of one of Mr. Hubbard's friends, and the lady had found herself with an uneven party of seven at the last moment. She needed another lady, whom Penelope had promised to provide.

Mary really ought to come, Penelope had said. She had been down lately and was in danger of becoming a hermit. A rather ridiculous fear in Mary's estimation, since she still held her almost weekly literary evenings and never refused an invitation to an entertainment that promised stimulating conversation.

But she *had* been down. Dreadfully down. Marcus had met his wife again after a fourteen-year separation and had fallen in love with her again—not that he had ever stopped loving her. Mary had always known that. He had never made a secret of the fact. Just as she had never made a secret of the fact that she had loved Lawrence and still grieved for him.

But she and Marcus had been close friends for six years. They had not been lovers, though it seemed to be the general belief that they must have been. But now they could no longer be friends, just because they were of different genders and he was hoping for a reconciliation with his wife. Mary was finding the emptiness in her life hard to bear. She had not realized quite how much he had meant to her until he was gone.

Yes, she was very down. And so she accepted Penelope's invitation even though the prospect of an evening at Vauxhall did not appeal to her a great deal. It appealed even less when she discovered who one of the other guests was. Lord Edmond Waite! She could not understand why Mrs. Rutherford would have invited such a man.

Lord Edmond Waite, youngest son of the Duke of Brookfield, was everything that Mary most despised. He was a libertine and a gamester and a drunkard—and a jilt. She did not know the man, of course, and she was willing to concede that rumor and gossip were not always reliable sources of information. But not everything she had ever heard of him could be untrue, she thought. And she had never heard any good of him. None. It was said that he had been all but betrothed to Lady Dorothea Page, that they had been intended for each other since her infancy. And yet he had gone running off with Lady Felicity Wren, if rumor was correct, and had in his turn been jilted when she had married Mr. Thomas Russell. Lord Edmond was not held in high repute by the *ton*. Only his wealth and rank ensured that he was still received at all. And not everyone received him even so.

Mary did not relish the thought of spending an evening with a party that included Lord Edmond in its number. But she had no choice except to make a scene and go home. Good manners prevented her from doing that. She set herself to avoiding him and conversing with the other members of the party.

"I believe it is going to storm," she remarked to Mr. Collins before the concert came to an end. The air was still and heavy. Ominously so.

"I do concede you may be right, ma'am," he said, looking up at the sky, dark and invisible beyond the light of the colored lanterns that lit the boxes and hung from the trees. "We will have to hope that it does not break before we return home."

"Yes," she said. Rachel would have to sleep in her room with her. It would be some comfort to have her maid there, though not nearly as satisfactory as a man's arms. Marcus had always come when there was a storm brewing, and he had always stayed with her until it was safely past. She returned her attention to the music of Mr. Handel.

It was very obvious to her that a storm was approaching, though no one else seemed at all concerned about it. Rather, everyone appeared to be enjoying the unusual warmth and stillness of the evening. And Mary did not know whether to be impatient to be gone and home to the relative safety of her house or to be glad that she was in company with seven other people and surrounded by dozens of others. But then, of course, she had been surrounded by many thousands of other people in Spain. Numbers did not ensure safety against lightning.

Penelope and her husband got to their feet when the concert was over and suggested a stroll along the lantern-lit paths of the gardens.

"It is such a beautifully warm evening," Penelope said.

"It is going to storm," Mary said.

"Do you think so?" Penelope, too, looked up to the invisible sky.

"Good," Mr. Hubbard said. "A storm will clear the air. It has been very hot and muggy for two days now."

"But let it wait another hour or two yet," Mr. Collins said, also getting to his feet and offering his arm to Mrs. Rutherford on his other side.

The four of them went off walking. Mary glanced at the other three occupants of the box. They were arguing with great animation over something, and Miss Wetherald was doing a great deal of laughing. Without at all

meaning to, Mary caught Lord Edmond's eye and he got
to his feet.

"Ma'am?" he said, reaching out a hand for hers.
"Would you care for a stroll?"

She certainly did not care for any such thing. Not with
him, at any rate. But how could she refuse without
seeming thoroughly rag-mannered? She could not.

"Thank you," she said, smiling and taking his hand so
that he might help her to her feet.

He was a handsome man in a way, she supposed. He
was tall, perhaps a trifle too thin, though he had an ath-
letic body for a man who must be in his mid-thirties. His
dark hair was thick, not thinning at all, his face narrow
with a prominent aquiline nose, rather thin lips, and
eyes of a curious pale blue. Many women would find
him attractive and undoubtedly did. She did not. She
took his offered arm.

"Tell me how you enjoyed the concert," he said. It
seemed more command than question.

"Very well," she said.

"You like Handel's music, then?" he asked. "I prefer
Bach myself."

"Do you?" she said. "Each has his merits, I suppose."

They lapsed into silence. It was not a very promising
beginning, the brief conversation they had had having
been anything but profound and neither seeming willing
to defend a preference.

"You still have all those literary gatherings at your
house?" he asked. "Brough attends most of them, does
he not? He likes that sort of thing. He tells me that your
salon always attracts the best talent."

"That is very obliging of him," she said. "Yes, Mr.
Brough is a regular visitor to my salon. I have a gathering there most weeks."

"Poets and such?" he said.

"Yes," she said, "and artists and politicians and people who just simply enjoy an intelligent conversation."

"Ah," he said, and they lapsed into silence again.

Goodness, Mary thought, she was strolling in Vauxhall Gardens with Lord Edmond Waite. She could not quite believe that she had sunk so low. She wished that they would catch up to Penelope and the others, but they must have taken a different path. There was no sign of her friends ahead of them.

"It is going to storm," she said. There was a breeze swaying the upper branches of the trees, making a swishing sound. On the ground the air was still very close.

"Probably," he said. "It will not be a bad thing. It will clear the air."

"Yes," she said.

She wanted to be back at the boxes, where there was the deceptive safety of numbers. She wanted to be at home, where she could hide beneath the relative safety of her blankets, Rachel sleeping in a truckle bed close by. She wanted to be mistaken about the storm. Perhaps it would just rain.

"Perhaps there will just be a good rain," she said.

"Perhaps." He looked up to the sky, still invisible beyond the lantern light. "Though I doubt it. I believe we will have a good fireworks display before morning. But not yet, I think."

It seemed to Mary that she was the only person at Vauxhall concerned about the approach of the storm. But perhaps not. As they walked on, they met fewer and fewer people. Was it just because they were moving away from the crowded area around the boxes? Or were other people being wiser and leaving while there was still time?

"Perhaps it would be wise to turn back," she said. "It would not be pleasant to be caught in a storm."

He smiled down at her. "Could it be that you are

afraid of storms, Lady Mornington?" he asked. "Or is it my person that makes you uneasy? You may relax, ma'am. I do not make a practice of ravishing unwilling females."

Mary set her teeth together. She would not answer such words. Oh, she would not so demean herself. How dare he! He was more vulgar even than she had expected.

"If you wish to turn back," he said, "we will do so."

The path was deserted suddenly. There was no one else either ahead of them or behind them. And the trees were rustling in the growing wind. Of course they must turn back. Some heavenly fury was about to be unleashed, even though there had been no distant flashes to warn of an approaching storm.

"I am quite happy to walk on," she said. She would be damned before she would admit fear of any sort to the likes of Lord Edmond Waite.

He chuckled. "I fear you are right, though," he said. "The storm is much closer than estimated. It is these lanterns. They make it impossible to see if the sky is clear or cloudy. I believe we had better return. We seem not to have a great deal in common conversationally anyway, do we?"

Mary turned back with an inward sigh of relief. But as she did so, a large spot of rain splattered on her nose and then another against one eye.

"Damnation," her companion said. "The heavens are about to open. We are going to get soaked."

"We will have to run," she said as two cold spots landed on her shoulders and then more continued to come at her, too numerous to count. The wind was suddenly sweeping through the trees.

"Not back to the boxes," he said, releasing her arm and taking her firmly by the hand. "This way."

And he drew her at a run along one of the darker, narrower paths through the trees, the wind moaning through the branches, the rain lashing down on them, until they reached one of the rustic shelters that were dispersed at intervals through the gardens. He pulled her inside.

"Blast!" he said, shaking rain from his hair and brushing ineffectually at his damp coat. "We will probably be stuck here for an hour or more. I hope we can find some topic of mutual interest on which to converse."

Mary dried her arms with her hands. She felt uncomfortably chilly suddenly. "I think perhaps I was right about one thing at least," she said. "It is just going to be a good rain. There will be no storm."

"I would not count on it," he said, turning to push the wooden table against the inner wall so that they would have more protection from the rain. The shelter was walled on only three sides. Fortunately the wind was blowing against the back wall, so that almost no rain was coming in at them.

And sure enough, even as he spoke, the first flash lit up the sky. Mary sat carefully on the wooden bench that was attached to the table. She folded her hands in her lap. The thunder came a long time after. Perhaps it would not come close, she thought. Perhaps they were just on the fringe of the storm.

"Now, then," he said, seating himself beside her, "what shall we talk about? Your late husband was a colonel with the cavalry, was he not? And you were in the Peninsula with him? Tell me about it. What was the life like? Or does it pain you to talk about it?"

"It was a long time ago," she said. "The pain has dulled."

"You were fond of him?" he asked.

"I loved him."

"Ah," he said. "Love."

There was another flash, brighter and longer than the

first. The rain was sheeting down beyond the shelter. The wind was howling around them.

"The autumn rains were the worst," she said. "Or perhaps the heat of summer. When it was hot and dry, we longed for the rains, and then when it rained, we wished and wished that we could have the heat and sunshine back."

The crash of thunder was a little louder and more prolonged.

"I have heard," he said, "that conditions were quite intolerable, that men died of the heat and died facedown in the mud. It amazes me that Colonel Lord Mornington would have voluntarily taken a woman there."

"It was not voluntary," she said. "I insisted on going. And I am glad I did. Our two years there were the only time we had together. I would not be without those two years."

"Love indeed," he said.

"It *was* love," she said quietly, "despite your tone of sarcasm. There is such an emotion, such a commitment, my lord, even though many poor people choose to heap scorn on the very idea."

"Ah," he said, "I detect a setdown. I am one of your 'poor people,' Lady Mornington?"

"Yes," she said. "I would guess that you have never known love."

He chuckled. "And so you comforted your grieving heart after your colonel's demise with Clifton," he said.

With Marcus. The Earl of Clifton. Lord Edmond's tone made her relationship with him sound sordid. It had not been sordid, though for six years she had been the close friend of a married man. It had not been sordid. But she would be damned before she would justify herself to anyone, least of all to her present companion.

"That is my own affair, my lord," she said, and then

she was furious with herself for her choice of word as he chuckled again.

Lord Edmund Waite clearly had a sordid mind.

And then suddenly and quite unexpectedly the storm was close. They could actually see the lightning fork above the trees, and the thunder crashed only moments afterward.

"And they said there would be no fireworks at Vauxhall tonight," Lord Edmond said.

Mary clasped her hands very tightly in her lap, tried to impose calm on her mind, and failed miserably. At the very next flash she launched herself against her companion's shoulder, wailing horribly. Her terrified mind could form no words.

"What is it?" He laughed and set one arm about her shoulders. "It was not my person after all, then? You *are* afraid of storms? It is a good thing you had no children, Lady Mornington. Who would comfort whom?"

The thunder rocked their shelter. Mary clawed at his shoulders and burrowed her head against his chest, wailing out her hysteria.

"Hey," he said, the amusement gone from his voice. "Hey." She was almost unaware of the fact that he slid one arm beneath her knees and lifted her onto his lap. He opened his coat and wrapped it about her as best he could. "By Jove, you really are frightened, aren't you?"

"Hold me," she babbled at him as the storm reached a rapid crescendo. "Hold me."

"I have you close." His voice was quiet and quite serious now. His arms were tight about her, his cheek against the top of her head. "I have you safe, Mary. It *is* Mary, is it not?"

But she could not get close enough to him. She wanted to crawl inside his clothes, inside his body. They were so very exposed, in an open shelter and among trees. And the storm was directly overhead.

"Hold me!" she commanded him, her face hidden against his neck. "Oh, God. Please. Oh, please."

She resisted as one hand lifted her head away from its hiding place. She clawed at his wrist. And then her face was hidden again—against his. His mouth was warm and wide over hers.

"You will be quite safe," he murmured into her mouth. "I have you safe, Mary."

She clung to him for the next several minutes as he alternately kissed her and murmured to her. There was some comfort. If only she could have him closer. Her back felt so very exposed to danger despite the strength of his arms about her. But there was some comfort. She opened her mouth to his tongue, which came warm and firm right into her mouth and stroked her own tongue.

"I have you safe," he told her as he laid her head against his shoulder eventually and held it there with a warm and steady hand as the storm receded somewhat. The rain, too, had eased a little, though it was still falling far too heavily to permit them to venture out in it.

Some sanity began to return. She knew that she was on Lord Edmond Waite's lap, her head cradled on his shoulder, held there with one hand that played gently with her short curls. His other arm was protectively about her. She knew that he had been kissing her and putting his tongue into her mouth—something Lawrence had never done. It was perhaps what one might expect of a libertine. She closed her eyes and relaxed. The storm would be over soon.

"Have you always been like this?" he asked her.

"Four men from my husband's regiment were killed by lightning one night in the very next tent to ours," she said. She swallowed. "There was the smell of scorched flesh."

"Ah," he said. "You have every right to be afraid, then. It is almost over."

"Yes," she said. But she did not move. She felt safe where she was. "Thank you."

He chuckled. "No need, ma'am," he said. "There are compensations for offering comfort to a frightened lady."

Such ungentlemanly and ungallant words should have infuriated her. But if she were furious, she would have to lift her head and remove herself from his lap. It was safer and more comfortable to let the words pass.

And then it was obvious that the storm was coming back.

"Oh, no," she moaned, and her head burrowed against his neck again. His hand stroked over her head and shoulder.

"It will pass again," he said.

"Please," she said as the thunder cracked only moments after the lightning. "Oh, please."

After that the sounds she made became less coherent. She was unaware of the fact that he shrugged awkwardly out of his coat and wrapped it about her. She burrowed inside it. There was a little more warmth at her back, but still terror was there. She expected at any moment the unknown pain that lightning would bring as it struck. She tried again to climb inside him.

And then he stood up with her in his arms and turned so that his own back was to the open side of the shelter rather than hers. The tabletop was hard against her back, but enormously comforting. She reached for him blindly while he raised her gown to her waist and loosened his own clothing.

And then the blessed comfort of his weight was on her, the hardness of the table beneath, and she felt shielded from the terror. Her mouth found his and opened to it. And then he was between her thighs and pushing up inside her, hard and warm, and he came reassuringly deep. She felt almost safe.

"Hush," he said against her mouth, and she realized that she was still wailing and obeyed his command.

The simultaneous flash of lightning and crack of thunder shook the earth, or so it seemed. But he was moving in her with slow deep strokes and his weight was so heavy on her and the wooden top of the table so unyielding that she could scarcely draw breath. She felt as if she had finally succeeded in crawling inside him, and she felt almost safe. She heard someone whimpering and forced herself to be quiet again.

"It will be all right, Mary," he said against her mouth. "It will pass again."

"Yes," she said. Yes, it was going to be all right. There was an ache—an ache that made her clench inner muscles and that rose into her throat so that breathing became even more difficult. Yes, it would be all right. He was going to take her into himself, and she would be safe. "Oh, please," she pleaded into his mouth.

"God!" he said suddenly. "Oh, God, woman."

And he drove into her, bringing her an agony of pain as he pounded her against the hard wooden surface, a glory of ecstasy. She cried out, and he thrust once more very deeply into her and relaxed his weight on her.

The storm moved gradually off again.

The removal of his weight woke her. The air was chill. His coat was spread beneath her, her thin evening gown bunched above her waist. She pushed it down as he stood with his back to her, adjusting his clothing while he stared out into the rain.

"Will it come back again?" she asked.

"Your guess is as good as mine," he said. "I have not had much luck in predicting this night's events."

She sat up on the edge of the table and wondered when embarrassment and horror—all the normal feelings—would return. At that moment all she could feel was gratitude. Gratitude that Lord Edmond Waite had taken possession of her body!

"How long has it been?" she asked. "An hour?"

"About that, I suppose," he said. "I wonder how many other people ignored all the signs as we did and are trapped somewhere about the gardens."

"I don't know," she said.

He laughed. "All sorts of interesting things might have been happening hereabouts," he said. "This is far more exciting than the usual fireworks display, is it not?"

There it was again—his vulgarity. She wished he had said nothing, had merely stood silent while staring out into the darkness. She did not want to be reminded just yet of exactly whom she had been stranded with and what she had forced him into doing. And not in her wildest imaginings would she ever be able to persuade herself that she had been the victim and he the aggressor.

"It is coming back," she said after a few minutes, her voice shaking. "It can't be, can it?"

"But it is," he said.

He stood with his back to her until the storm came close again, and then he stepped over the bench, lifted her from the table, and sat with her, his back to the open side of the shelter.

But this time she was less mindlessly terrified. She was tired, with the pleasant ache inside that came from a good loving. She did not think such thoughts, only felt such feelings. He held her head against his shoulder, and she closed her eyes and drifted into a state that approximated sleep—as far as one could sleep in a crashing thunderstorm.

It stayed overhead for a long time, but when it moved off this time, it went to stay. And eventually the rain stopped, too.

"Well," he said, looking down at her light slippers, "the paths are going to be rather muddy, but at least we can move out of our prison house. I profoundly hope that my carriage is still waiting for me."

He carried her along the narrower and muddier path despite her protests, and they walked side by side, not touching, along the main path. She needed her hands to hold his coat in place about her shoulders. He had insisted that she wear it, though he must be cold in his shirtsleeves, she thought.

His carriage was still waiting, one of three. It seemed that they had not been the only ones trapped by the storm. He helped her inside, gave some instructions to his coachman, and then climbed in to take his seat beside her.

2

THE CARRIAGE HAD TRAPPED THE EARLIER HEAT OF the evening and not lost it during the storm. Lord Edmond Waite settled gratefully into the seat beside Mary. It was chilly outside in only shirtsleeves—and a somewhat damp shirt at that.

He looked across at her. Huddled inside his evening coat, she looked even smaller than she was. He felt all the unreality of the moment. Lady Mornington, of all people. And not only was she seated in his carriage, alone with him, his coat about her shoulders, but she had cuddled on his lap and given passionate kiss for kiss. And she had made love to him on the table as fiercely as he had made love to her.

Lady Mornington! He felt rather like laughing—at the whole bizarre situation, perhaps. At himself.

Lady Mornington was everything he had always most shunned in a woman. She was independent and proud and dignified—not that she had any reason to think herself above people like himself. It was common knowledge that she had been Clifton's mistress for years until he had dropped her quite recently. Or until she had dropped him—in all fairness, he did not know who had put an end to the liaison.

And she was an intelligent woman, one who liked to surround herself with artists and brilliant conversationalists. Her literary salons were highly regarded. The woman was a bluestocking, a breed he despised. He liked his women feminine and a little mindless. He liked his women for his bed.

He had always looked on Lady Mornington with some aversion. Not that he knew the woman, he had to admit. But he had had no desire to know her. She was not even physically desirable. She was smaller and more slender than he liked his women to be. There were no pronounced curves to set his eyes to roving and his hands to itching. And she was not pretty. Her dark hair was short and curled—he liked hair to be set loose about his arms, to twine his hands in, to spread over ample breasts. She had fine gray eyes. That had to be admitted. But they were intelligent eyes, eyes bright with an interest in the world and its affairs. He far preferred bedroom eyes. And then, the woman must be thirty if she was a day.

He had not been pleased to discover that Lady Mornington was one of Mrs. Rutherford's party to Vauxhall. Or the Hubbards, for that matter. He had not expected any fellow guests of high *ton*. He was still smarting from the *ton*'s censure over his jilting of Dorothea—the iceberg. Not that they had been officially engaged, of course. But everyone had been expecting it, and the obligation had been there. He could not deny that.

And he was still nursing a broken heart over Felicity's desertion. Beautiful golden-haired Felicity Wren, whom he had wanted for years, even before she was widowed, and who he had assumed was his earlier in the year, though she had teased him with a pretended preference for her faithful hound, Tom Russell.

She would not be his mistress. Finally he had had to realize that she really would not be. But by that time he had been too deeply infatuated with her to give her up. Instead he had jilted Dorothea and gone off to elope with Felicity. For her sake he had been willing to behave in a manner that even for him was dastardly.

But she had sent Tom Russell to the place where she had agreed to meet him. Tom Russell to announce that she was to marry him within the week—from choice. It was to be a love match. And Russell had looked at him with all the contempt of a man who has never given in to any of the excesses of life, and had offered to fight him if he were not satisfied.

He had declined the honor, and had returned to London to lick his wounds, to face the collective scorn of the *ton*, to drink himself into oblivion. And to find himself a new mistress, someone to help him forget all that he had lost in Felicity.

"You are warm enough?" he asked Lady Mornington, looking down at her.

"Yes, thank you," she said. "Would you like your coat back?"

"No," he said. "Keep it about your shoulders."

He had always wondered what Clifton had seen in Lady Mornington, since it was as clear as day that Clifton could have had just about any female he had cared to cast his sights on. But he had chosen the plain bluestocking Lady Mornington and had remained with her for what must have been five or six years.

He had his answer now. Beneath the plain and demure image she presented to the world, Lady Mornington hid a wild and earthy sexuality that had taken him totally by surprise earlier and had all but robbed him of control despite the extreme discomfort of the tabletop, which had not been quite long enough to accommodate their legs.

Of course, he thought, the woman had been quite distraught with fear of the storm. He had never seen anyone so beside herself with terror. Perhaps her behavior had been atypical. Perhaps her usual performances in bed were as passive and as decorous as he would have expected of her. He looked at her again and thought with some unease of the instructions he had given his coachman.

"Is that thunder again?" she asked, her knuckles tightening against the edge of his coat.

"It is very distant," he said. "I don't believe it will come over again. Though of course I have been known to be wrong before."

She looked up at him, and her eyes lingered on him before being lowered again. Was she looking at him with as much amazement as he was looking at her? He still could not quite believe the reality of what was happening. Devil take it, he had taken her walking only because their eyes had accidentally met when she was sitting a little apart in the box and he had felt that it would be unmannerly to leave her sitting there.

He did not like the woman, or she him, without a doubt. They had nothing whatsoever in common. They had not even been able to sustain a polite conversation during their walk. They had nothing to say to each other now.

The carriage drew to a halt and the coachman opened the door and set down the steps.

"Where are we?" she asked as he vaulted out onto the pavement without the aid of the steps and turned to hand her out.

"At my house," he said. The words were true, strictly speaking, though it was not his home. It was the house where he lodged his mistresses, when he had one in keeping, and where he brought his casual amours when he did not. It was in a quite respectable part of London and the staff he kept there were above reproach and were paid well to keep their mouths shut.

He was ready to sneer and climb back into the carriage with her if she protested. But after a moment's hesitation she took his hand and descended to the pavement and looked up in some curiosity at the house. He blessed a very distant flash of lightning.

He led her up the stone steps and through the door, which a manservant was already holding open for them, and into the tiled hallway. He took the coat from about her shoulders and handed it to the servant. She looked quietly about her.

"You would like some refreshments?" he asked her.

She brought her eyes to him and they rested on him for a long moment. "Tea, please," she said.

Lord Edmond nodded to his servant, took her arm, and led her upstairs, deciding to forgo the formality of leading her into a salon first. He had done that once with Felicity and had never got her beyond the salon.

"You will wish to refresh yourself," he said, taking her into the bedchamber and across it to the door leading into the dressing room, which was decked out with all the conveniences a woman could need. "Your tea will be brought to you here. Come back out when you are ready."

"Thank you," she said, stepping inside the dressing room and allowing him to close the door behind her.

He expelled his breath. She could not possibly have mistaken his intent. An imbecile would have understood it, and Lady Mornington was no imbecile. And yet she had made no resistance at all.

Was she still caught up in leftover fright from the storm? Did she need a man to help her live through the night? Or was she missing Clifton as he was missing Felicity? Or did she feel perhaps that she owed him some debt of gratitude for the comfort he had undoubtedly brought her at Vauxhall? Or did she fancy him—did she derive some sort of sexual thrill out of consorting with a rake?

He stripped off his shirt and pulled off his boots. After some consideration he left his pantaloons where they were.

And as for himself, why had he brought her here? Lady Mornington was as out-of-place in this house as an angel would be in hell. He smiled grimly at the simile and glanced about him. All the hangings of the room were red. For the first time he rather regretted the vulgarity. He glanced up at the scarlet draperies beneath the canopy of the bed.

Why had he brought her here? To find out if the passion would still be there now that the storm had gone? To console himself for Felicity? To revenge himself on a scornful society with one of its most respected hostesses—respected despite the fact of her amour with Clifton? To punish himself with the scorn he had expected from her when the carriage drew to a halt outside?

He did not know.

She was still fully clothed when she stepped out of the dressing room and closed the door quietly behind her. Her hair had been freshly brushed. Her cheeks were flushed. She looked very small and slender and respectable in this room. Her eyes looked curiously about the room and then came to rest on him. She looked him up and down, though there was no notable contempt in her eyes.

"Your tea was brought up?" he asked.

"Yes, thank you," she said.

Come here, he was about to say to her. But he swallowed the command and crossed the room to her. She watched him come. An opportune and distant flash of lightning lit the room for a moment.

"It is far away," he said.

"Yes."

He set his arms loosely about her, found the buttons at the back of her gown, and began to undo them. She stood still, her eyes on his chest. When he had finished his task, he lifted the gown off her shoulders with the straps of her chemise, and down her arms. Both rustled to the floor, and he stooped down on one knee to roll down her silk stockings. She lifted her feet one at a time while he removed them with her slippers. And she took a step away from her clothes.

She was pleasingly proportioned even if she was not voluptuous. Her breasts were small, but firm and prettily shaped. Her waist was small, her hips wider, her legs slim and well-shaped, though they were not long. He cupped her breasts in his hands and set his thumbs over her nipples. He kept them there until they hardened, and then stroked them. She raised her chin sharply and closed her eyes.

He lifted her up and carried her to the bed. He stripped off his remaining clothes before joining her there.

He explored her mouth with his tongue, and she surprised him by responding with her own so that he was able to entice it into his own mouth and suck inward on it.

"Mm," he said. "How do you like it, Mary? Do you have any special preferences?"

She opened her eyes and regarded him as if she was thinking carefully of her answer.

"Slow," she said eventually. "I like it slow."

He kissed her openmouthed again. "With lots of slow foreplay?" he asked without lifting his mouth from hers. "Or is it the main event you like to be slow and long?"

Again the pause before her answer. "Both," she said.

He gave her both, imposing an iron control on his body. It was not easy. After the first couple of minutes, once his hands had gone to work on her as well as his mouth, she gave herself with a wild abandon. But she gave herself not only to be loved, but to love. Her hands moved on him, and her mouth and legs and body, with as much eroticism as his on her. Except that she had the luxury of two separate climaxes, one before he mounted her and one after, before the final shared cresting as he spilled his seed in her.

Well, he thought, removing himself from her after a minute or two of total exhaustion and settling her in the crook of his arm as he drew the blankets up over them, he would never again be able to look at Lady Mornington and see her body as sexually unappealing. And he would never look at her again and be a little afraid of her as an intelligent woman somewhat beyond his touch. Intelligent she might be. But she was also an all passionate, uninhibited, feminine woman.

Strange, he thought. He had been in search of a new mistress for several weeks. And finally he had found her where he had least expected. Lady Mornington! It was almost laughable.

He followed her into sleep.

She woke him twice during the night, once when the storm moved briefly overhead again, and he turned her over onto her back once more and mounted her without foreplay and loved her swiftly while she held him close. And again when dawn was beginning to light the room. She was standing beside the bed, touching his arm. She was dressed.

"My lord," she said, "I wish to go home if you please."

"Edmond," he said, laughing.

She turned her back on him and walked unhurriedly to the window as he threw aside the blankets and stepped naked out onto the carpet.

She was unwilling for him to accompany her home. "I would be obliged for the use of your carriage," she told him, "but there is no need for you to come, too, my lord."

But he insisted, of course, and they sat silently side by side during the drive to Portman Place, not quite touching, looking out at the early-morning streets, still partly wet from the downpour of the night before.

"At least no one will be complaining of dust for a day or two," he said.

"No," she agreed. "It will be the mud."

That was the extent of their conversation.

He stepped down from the carriage at Portman Place and handed her out as his coachman rang the doorbell.

"Thank you," she said, looking up at him. If she was embarrassed by the appearance of a curious servant in the doorway to her house, she did not show it. "Good day to you, my lord."

He held her hand for a moment longer. "I shall do myself the honor of calling on you this afternoon," he said.

She hesitated for a moment, looking down at their hands. "Yes," she said at last, looking up into his eyes again. "I shall be at home."

He raised her hand to his lips before releasing it.

MARY WAS USUALLY an early riser. The morning was too exhilarating a part of the day to be wasted in sleep, she always told anyone who was startled to discover that she frequently walked in the park at a time of the morning when only tradesmen and maids exercising the family dogs were abroad. But it was mid-morning when she awoke on the day following Vauxhall. And even then, when she opened her eyes and saw her cup of chocolate looking cold and unappetizing on the table beside her bed, she would have gone back to sleep if she could.

But she could not. She lay on her stomach, her face

buried in her pillow, and remembered. And felt quite physically sick. She wished it could all be written off as a dream—as a strange, bizarre nightmare. But she knew that it could not. There was that unmistakable, almost pleasant aching in the passage where he had been and worked. There was the tenderness of her breasts, which he had touched and fondled and sucked and bitten. There were the dryness and slight soreness of her lips. And somehow there was the smell of him on her arms and in her hair, and the taste of him in her mouth.

No, it had been no dream. Vauxhall had been real. The storm had been real. And he had been real.

She sat up and reached over to the bell rope to summon her maid. She had to have a bath and wash her hair. If only it were as easy to wash him out of her memory and out of her life, she thought as she swung her legs over the side of the bed.

She cursed the thunderstorm for the first time. Without it she would have arrived safely back at the box, having had a quite horrid time walking with him, and she would have been able to part from him with the fervent hope that she would never have to be in company with him again.

But the storm *had* happened, and it had come at just the worst possible moment. The memory of it had her gripping the edge of the bed in blank terror for a moment. Never since that dreadful night in Spain had she been forced to live through a storm out-of-doors—or as near outdoors as to make no difference.

"A bath, please," she said when her maid appeared in the room. "And some tea, Rachel. No, no more chocolate, thank you." Her stomach revolted at the very thought.

Dear Lord, there had been no one to cling to but him. And she had clung, desperately and mindlessly. And she had been so intent on climbing right inside him that eventually he had climbed right inside her—with her full consent and cooperation. Indeed, she was very much afraid that she had given him little choice.

With Lord Edmond Waite! He had been inside her body. She spread one palm over her mouth and closed her eyes. Dear God, inside her body. Where only Lawrence had been before. And no one for seven years. And now him.

When her bathwater had arrived, she sent Rachel back down to the kitchen to fetch a brush. And she scrubbed at her skin with it until the soapsuds were almost overflowing onto the floor and her skin looked rather like that of a lobster. But he had been inside her. She could not scrub him away.

He had said he would call on her during the afternoon. But she did not want him inside her house. Perhaps he would not come, she thought. But perhaps he would feel obliged to come. Perhaps he would feel obliged to offer for her. Would a libertine and a jilt feel obligated to offer marriage to the woman who had seduced him during a thunderstorm? The thought of marrying Lord Edmond Waite made Mary laugh most hysterically as she stood up and wrapped a towel about her shoulders.

Or perhaps he felt he owed her some apology. Did such a man ever apologize? Perhaps he would not come. She hoped and hoped that he would not come. Ever. She hoped she would never have to face the embarrassment of coming face-to-face with him again.

And it could not be avoided any longer, could it? she thought, wiping the suds angrily from one foot and losing her balance and hopping around on the other. There had not been only that encounter at Vauxhall, for which perhaps she could forgive herself. There had been that horridly sordid house, which was obviously his love nest, and that sickeningly vulgar room with its scarlet velvet hangings and wide soft bed. And her almost inexplicable lack of resistance to being taken there.

With how many other women had he lain in that bed? she wondered, and felt again as if she must vomit. It had been a certain gratitude, perhaps, a certain embarrassment that had taken her there unresisting. He had done her an enormous favor at Vauxhall. There could be no arguing about that, sordid as their encounter there had been. Dear Lord, on a tabletop . . . She shook her head clear of the thought. And there had been some leftover terror, the need to cling, the fear of being alone. And a certain lassitude left over from that first encounter. A certain curiosity, perhaps? She shuddered. For whatever reason, she had found it impossible to refuse him.

And you enjoyed what you got there. The inner voice was almost audible in the room. *You enjoyed every moment of it.* Mary shook her head again, but the voice could not be hushed.

She had always been something of a passive lover, though she had always given herself with willingness and tenderness. Certainly Lawrence had never complained or accused her of coldness. And men, she had always thought, liked to do the loving. Women, she had thought, were the receptacles for their pleasure. Not that she had ever lacked pleasure herself. Lawrence had pleased her.

She had not been passive the night before. Her frenzy was understandable at Vauxhall when the storm was raging. But there had been no storm that first time in the scarlet room. And yet . . . And yet . . . Oh, God.

You enjoyed every moment of it. And you gave every bit as good as you got.

She closed her eyes very tightly. She could not have. She could not. The man repulsed her. He was everything she found most repulsive.

And most attractive, the voice said, unbidden.

Surely he would not come that afternoon, she thought.

Surely, like her, he would wake up that morning appalled by what had happened between them the night before. But he had said he would come. She would not be there, she decided. She would go out. But she had told him she would be at home. She could not go out.

She dressed herself with shaking hands and brushed through her damp curls. She could still feel where he had been inside her. Well, she had asked for it to be slow, and slow it had been. The resulting soreness was inevitable. It had been seven years.

She rang for the bathwater to be removed.

THE BOTTOM FELT rather as if it had dropped out of Mary's stomach when the doorbell rang during the afternoon and she waited in the downstairs salon for her visitor to be announced. But when the door opened, she found with enormous relief that it was Penelope who was following the butler into the room, not Lord Edmond Waite.

"Mary," Penelope said, reaching out her hands to take her friend's, and kissing her on the cheek. "What a relief to find you at home. I was half afraid that you were still wallowing in some mud at Vauxhall. What on earth happened to you? Adrian had to almost drag me home. There was no point in our waiting around for you, he said, when doubtless you had taken shelter somewhere and were not alone anyway. But, Mary . . ." Her eyes grew saucer wide. "You were not alone! You were with Lord Edmond Waite, of all people. Do tell all."

"We waited out the storm, and then he brought me home in his carriage," Mary said, and hoped she was not blushing.

"I am so very sorry," Penelope said. "That you were subjected to his company at all, I mean. I feel very responsible, since I invited you. It never occurred to me that some of the Rutherfords' guests would not be respectable. She is new to town, you know. He did not ravish you or anything unthinkable like that, did he?" She stifled a giggle.

"Nothing like that, I do assure you," Mary said firmly. "We found shelter from the rain and passed the time in conversation."

"Conversation?" Penelope said. "From all I have heard, the man is capable of only one kind of converse with women. But then, I daresay he stands somewhat in awe of you, Mary. Many men do because you dare to be openly intelligent. That is what Adrian tells me, anyway. Did you know that he killed his brother?"

"Adrian?" Mary frowned.

"Lord Edmond, silly," Penelope said with a laugh. "Ages and ages ago. He was jealous of him, apparently, and killed him. And killed his mother indirectly, too. She died of a broken heart. I am surprised you had not heard."

"People do not die of broken hearts," Mary said. "And surely it did not happen quite as cold-bloodedly as you make it sound, Penny. No, I had not heard."

"Well," Penelope said, "it is ancient news and I do not know any of the details of it. I am glad you arrived home unravished." She laughed. "But you have a terror of storms, do you not? Did he offer you comfort, Mary? Oh, I should not laugh, should I? It must have been quite dreadful for you, and I am sorry. I came to drag you out for a walk."

"I cannot," Mary said, and this time she knew that she had not avoided blushing. "I am expecting someone."

"Oh, bother," Penelope said. "But I will forgive you if he is tall, dark, and handsome. Who is he?"

"I did not say it was a he," Mary said.

But the door opened again at that moment and the butler announced Lord Edmond Waite.

Mary noticed only her friend's eyebrows disappearing up into her hair before turning to greet her visitor.

3

$\mathcal{H}$E TOOK HER HAND IN A FIRM CLASP. HE DID NOT, Mary was relieved to find, raise it to his lips.

"Lady Mornington?" he said. "Mrs. Hubbard? I came to satisfy myself that neither of you took a chill or any other harm from last night's storm."

"None whatsoever, I thank you, sir," Penelope said, looking curiously from him to Mary as he took the seat indicated. "But then, Adrian had the foresight to get us back to our carriage before the rain started. Was it not a dreadful storm? I cannot remember one that lasted so long."

He was again Lord Edmond Waite, Mary thought, looking at him appalled. A stranger, elegantly attired, tall, rather too thin—no, "lean" was the better word, memory told her treacherously—with a harsh, thin-lipped face and strangely pale blue eyes. He was a man with a reputation that had always made him best avoided. A man to despise. A man who was not in any way a part of her world.

A man with whom she had spent a night of wild and abandoned passion. She shuddered.

"Nor I," she said, and his eyes turned on her and burned their blue ice into her. "I am quite well, thank you, my lord."

"I blame myself," he said, "for having ignored the

signs until it was too late. I did not know about Spain, of course, but even so, the experience of a severe thunderstorm with only a frail shelter for comfort is not a pleasant one for a lady."

"But at least Mary had you for company, my lord," Penelope said.

"Yes," he agreed. "At least she had that." He turned back to Mary. "Would you care for a drive in the park later, Lady Mornington?"

How could she refuse? It would be churlish to do so, especially with Penelope sitting there, listening with interest.

"Thank you," she said. But she really did not want to go. How could she spend an hour or more in company with him, when they had nothing whatsoever in common? How could she let herself be seen driving in the park with Lord Edmond Waite? She would be ashamed to be seen with him.

"I shall ring for refreshments," she said, getting abruptly to her feet. But he put up a staying hand and got to his feet.

"I shall not interrupt your visit with Mrs. Hubbard, ma'am," he said. "I have business that needs to be attended to. I shall return for you at half-past four?"

"I shall be ready," she said. "Thank you."

And he bowed to both ladies and took his leave.

"Well," Penelope said, looking closely at her friend's flaming cheeks after the door had closed. "Mary?"

"How could I have refused him?" Mary asked. "Could I have refused him, Penny?"

"You could have been expecting other visitors," Penelope said. "You could have had another appointment. You could have been indisposed, though of course you had just said that you took no harm last night. You could have simply said no."

"But he showed me a kindness last night," Mary said.

"Did he, indeed?" Penelope said. "What exactly did happen last night, if I may be so bold as to ask?"

"Nothing," Mary said. "Nothing happened."

"Nothing." Her friend looked at her curiously again. "And yet you blush more scarlet than scarlet and feel obliged to take a public drive with London's most notorious rake. Mary!"

"And that will be the end of it," Mary said. "I shall thank him for staying close to me and talking to me all through the storm, and he will be satisfied that indeed I took no harm. And then this whole nasty situation will be at an end."

"He is an attractive man," Penelope said. "I know that many women find him so. And to many his reputation is just an added attraction. You are in a vulnerable position at the moment, with the Earl of Clifton gone. You were very fond of him, I know. I think you were perhaps in love with him, though you would never admit as much. I insisted you come to Vauxhall last evening mainly because you were in low spirits. You will not turn to Lord Edmond, will you? Oh, anyone but him, Mary. There must be any number of perfectly respectable gentlemen who would be only too pleased to befriend and even court you. You are only thirty years old."

"Turn to Lord Edmond Waite? Penny, please!" Mary looked expressively at her friend. "The very thought of him makes me shudder."

"We are talking about his person, not the thought of him," Penelope said. "I am more sorry than ever about not asking Mrs. Rutherford who her other guests were to be last evening and about the unfortunate chance that put you in Lord Edmond's company just when the storm began. But I do believe that like everyone else, he could have predicted its start and hurried you back to our carriage. It was just like the man to trap a lady into a forced *tête-à-tête*. He did not try anything, Mary?"

"No," Mary said firmly. "He did not try anything, Penny. Do you think I would have allowed it?"

"No," Penelope said without hesitation. "Of course you would not. And among all the bad I have heard of the man, ravishment has never been part of the list. Enough of that unpleasant subject. Who is coming to your salon the evening after tomorrow? Anyone of special interest?"

Mary was relieved at the change of subject, relieved not to have to be telling more and more lies. *What would Penny say if she knew the full truth?* she wondered. The full truth did not bear thinking of. The more her mind touched on it, the more incredible it all seemed. It could not have happened, surely.

But it had.

Penelope stayed for half an hour before rising to take her leave.

"I shall look forward to the evening," she said. "I always enjoy listening to Mr. Beasley's theories on reform and to all the animated argument that his radical views inevitably arouse. If Sir Alvin Margrove does put in an appearance, there are sure to be sparks flying. It was courageous of you to invite them both on the same evening, Mary."

"When a person holds such extreme views," Mary said, "it is always desirable to have someone who holds the opposite, just so that the rest of us ordinary mortals can form a balanced opinion ourselves."

"Well," Penelope said, "I must be going. Shopping tomorrow? Can we possibly persuade ourselves that we need new bonnets or silk stockings or cream cakes?"

Mary laughed. "Definitely not cream cakes," she said. "But I am sure we can find some purchase that we cannot possibly live without. My carriage or yours?"

And then she was alone again, with an hour and a half to kill before Lord Edmond Waite was to return for her. An hour and a half in which to develop pneumonia or typhoid or something equally indisputable. If only she could put the clock back twenty-four hours, she thought, closing her eyes briefly, and find an excuse—any excuse—not to go to Vauxhall. If only she could.

But she could not. And that was that.

LORD EDMOND WAITE had not gone back to bed after taking Mary home. He had gone to his own home, saddled his horse, and gone for a brisk gallop in the park, there being no one else there at that time of the morning to object to his speed. Not that a few objections would have slowed him anyway. And then he had gone to Jackson's Boxing Saloon and sparred for a few rounds.

He would normally have gone to Tattersall's or the races in the afternoon, and then sought out a decent card game at Watier's. Dinner at White's and a visit to the theater or opera house to see what new talent if any had arrived fresh from the country—there had been a dearth of good talent lately. A look-in at some *ton* entertainment if there were no interesting prospects to pursue at the opera house. A perusal of all the young things at the Marriage Mart and a sneer at all their mamas, who would inevitably note his arrival and his raised quizzing glass with some alarm.

As if he were interested in bidding at the Market for a gauche and innocent little virgin.

The life sometimes became a trifle tedious. But then, there was no other that he knew of. He might have been happy with Felicity—he *would* have been happy. He would have taken her all about Europe and the British Isles. He would have wanted to show her off to the world. He would have wanted to give her the world.

Well, he wished her joy of her country swain. She would doubtless settle down with him to a life of dull respectability and half a dozen children and never know what she had missed with the man she had jilted.

But devil take it, he missed her and the chance at happiness he had glimpsed for the merest moment. He might have been happy. But he would not have been. It was not in his nature, not in his fate, to be happy.

One fact about his planned elopement with Felicity he would never regret, anyway. It had enabled him to get rid of Dorothea. Ignobly, it was true. His reputation would probably never recover from the blot he had put there by abandoning her. The note he had sent her had been very stark and to the point. He had not let her down gently.

Well, he thought as he climbed to the driver's seat of his curricle late in the afternoon, at least he was about to embark on a new adventure in his life. It would brighten the dullness for a while at least. Lady Mornington! Who would have thought it? If anyone had told him twenty-four hours before that by this time today she would be his mistress and that he would be more than eager to repeat his bedding of her, he would have laughed with the loudest scorn. Lady Mornington?

But he had seen her with new eyes when he had called upon her briefly earlier in the afternoon. Her small, slender figure had looked pleasing to him because he knew what she looked like without the clothes and what she felt like beneath him on a bed, her legs twined about his. And her eyes had looked lovelier because he had known what they looked like when she was making love. Her hair had looked pretty because he knew how softly the warm curls twined about his fingers. Long hair would not suit such a small lady.

And he had no longer been afraid of her—had he really been afraid? She might be a bluestocking, she might be intelligent. But she was also a woman—his woman.

Lady Mornington—looking as dignified and prim as ever, and looking totally different than she had ever looked to him before. He had almost laughed aloud, and probably would have if her friend Penelope Hubbard had not been with her. It was a shame, that. He had been looking forward to being alone with her.

She was coming down the stairs when he was admitted to the hall of her house. She wore a spring-green dress with a matching pelisse and an unadorned straw bonnet. She would, of course, be outshone by a hundred ladies on fashionable Rotten Row. But it did not matter. He had been infatuated with Felicity because she was the loveliest woman he had ever known. Perhaps he was ready now for the opposite. Though not quite the opposite, either.

She smiled at him. "Some fresh air will feel good," she said.

"You have not been out today?" he asked her. "I suppose you slept the morning away."

She did not answer, but concentrated on drawing on her gloves, and waited for her manservant to open the front door.

Outside, he helped her up to the high seat of his curricle. "I hope you would not have preferred a carriage or barouche," he said. "But I always believe that during a drive in the park one must both see and be seen. It is the nature of the game, is it not?"

She smiled again. "This conveyance is fine," she said. "Is it new?"

They conversed so politely on the way to the park that Lord Edmond almost laughed. They were behaving like strangers. Who would have thought that only a matter of hours ago they had been in steamy embrace in his scarlet room? He could hardly believe it. He could hardly believe that she was the same woman.

"You slept well this morning?" he asked her.

She stiffened.

"I am afraid I did not allow you much sleep before you returned home," he said.

"I would prefer not to talk about that," she said.

"Would you?" he said. "Do the memories embarrass you? They need not. You were magnificent."

"Last night was a strange out-of-time experience," she said. "The storm made me lose my mind. I am grateful for the comfort you offered. I just wish it might have taken a different form."

"But there was no storm," he said, laughing, "when you told me that you liked it slow, that you liked both the foreplay and the main event slow. And you proved to me more than amply that you had not lied. You did indeed like it—as I did."

Her jaw hardened, he saw, and she gazed very rigidly ahead of her. "If you are a gentleman," she said, "you will forget last night, or at least keep your memories strictly to yourself. But of course, you are not a gentleman, are you?"

His eyebrows shot up. "You do not mince words, do you, Mary?" he said. "That was a blistering setdown."

"I am Mary only to my intimates," she said.

"Then I am glad I did not call you Lady Mornington," he said. "I am nothing if not your intimate, Mary."

"Hush," she said. "May we please change the subject?"

He had turned his horses' heads between the gateposts leading into Hyde Park, and almost instantly they were among other carriages and horses and pedestrians. It was right on the fashionable hour.

He considered her in silence for a moment. She was rigid with anger or embarrassment or something. He supposed that he might have guessed she would not accept the situation as easily as he had. She was doubtless embarrassed to know that she had revealed her passionate nature so early in their relationship.

"I hope you do not expect me to discuss Virgil or the Elgin Marbles or any such thing," he said. "Shall we discuss bonnets? What do you think of Miss Hodgeson's— she is the lady in blue with the sharp-nosed dragon seated beside her."

"It is elegant," Mary said.

"Do you think so?" He set his head to one side and stared at the bonnet. "If all the fruit is real, I suppose there is practical value to it. She and the dragon can have some tea without having to go home for it. If it is not real, then I would have to say that she is imposing a great deal of unnecessary weight on her neck and it is in danger of disappearing into her shoulders. Wouldn't you agree?"

"I am sure the fruit weighs nothing at all," Mary said.

He chuckled. "You have no sense of the absurd, Mary," he said. "Do you ever laugh?"

"When something is truly funny, of course," she said.

"Ah." He winced. "Another setdown. Do you specialize in them?"

She did not have a chance to reply. Colonel Hyde, one of her acquaintances, signaled to his coachman to stop his barouche alongside the curricle. Clearly he intended to talk. Lord Edmond inclined his head to the man and touched his hat to Mrs. Hyde, who sat hatchet-faced at her husband's side.

"Ah, Mary, my dear," the colonel said. "So you are taking the air, too, are you? Waite?"

"Hello, Mary, dear," Mrs. Hyde said. "Are you quite safe up there?"

"I am taking good care of her, ma'am," Lord Edmond said.

But the colonel's good lady chose to ignore his very

existence. Just as if Mary had decided to take a ride in the park in the passenger seat of a curricle with only the horses for company.

"Quite, thank you," Mary said. "Have you recovered from your cold?"

"Who is to be at your salon the evening after tomorrow, eh?" the colonel asked. "Dorothy wants to go listen to that Madame Paganini or whatever her name is at Rossford's, but the woman screeches. I would prefer to enjoy some intelligent conversation at your house. Who is it to be?"

"Mr. Beasley for certain," Mary said. "And Sir Alvin Margrove has said he will look in if he can."

"Ha." The colonel barked with laughter. "I would not miss it for worlds, dear. There will be a duel at dawn the following day, for sure. I'll have to bring Freeman with me. He will shoot himself if he finds out later that he has missed such fun. Will you be there, Waite?"

"Beasley and Margrove?" Lord Edmond said. "They can set the House on a roar, I have heard. They may just be too much for Lady Mornington's salon. I shall be there to protect her if it should come to fisticuffs."

"Marvin," Mrs. Hyde said frostily, "we are blocking the thoroughfare. We must drive on."

The colonel touched his hat and gave his coachman the signal to drive on.

There was a short silence in the curricle.

"Your literary—or political—evenings are not invitational?" Lord Edmond asked. "You hold open house?"

"Anyone is welcome," she said, her voice stiff.

"Then I shall be there," he said. "If you have no objection, of course."

"I am not sure the entertainment will be quite to your taste," she said.

"Ah," he said. "Your meaning being that there will be

no gaming tables and no deep drinking and no willing barmaids, I suppose."

"The words are yours, my lord," she said, "not mine."

"Sometimes," he said. "Not always, I must admit, but sometimes I can live without those things. Perhaps for one evening out of seven. I am not utterly depraved, you see, Mary, only almost so."

"I wish you would not talk so," she said. "It is not seemly."

"But then, you yourself said that I am no gentleman," he said. Two of his acquaintances, he saw, had been about to bring their horses up alongside his curricle. But both looked askance at Mary, raised their eyebrows at him and rode on.

And yes, he thought, it would seem strange to them that he was taking her of all people for an afternoon drive. But then, they did not know. He felt as if he were hugging a precious secret to himself. He drew his curricle away from the most frequented part of the park.

"It is strange," he said, "how people can be quite different from what we expect them to be. You are very different."

"You do not know me at all, my lord," she said.

"On the contrary," he said, "I think I know you very well indeed in the biblical sense, Mary. I think it unlikely that there is one inch of your body, inside or out, that I did not explore to my great pleasure last night."

She looked away to the trees beside the path.

"I would have expected you to be cold," he said, "or at least only decorously warm. I have known many women, Mary, but none as passionate and as uninhibited as you."

Her teeth were white and even, he noticed as they bit down into her lower lip.

"You are different from what I would have expected," he said. "Wonderfully different."

"You do not know me at all," she said again.

"Was it your husband who taught you?" he asked. "I did not know Lord Mornington, I regret to say."

"This is insufferable," she said.

"Or was it Clifton?" he asked. "I must confess that I used to wonder what he saw in you, Mary. Now I know. And I know why he kept you for so long. I think I might want to keep you longer."

Her eyes blazed at him when she turned her head, and he saw yet another facet of Lady Mornington's character.

"This is intolerable!" she said. "Set me down at once."

He raised his eyebrows. "Alone in the middle of the park?" he said. "I am enough of a gentleman not to do that, Mary."

"Gentleman!" she said. "You do not know the meaning of the word. Let me be very clear, my lord. Despite what happened at Vauxhall, I was and am grateful to you. I believe I might well have gone out of my mind if you had not taken it upon yourself to comfort me. What happened afterward happened because it was a strange night and because the storm lingered in the distance and because . . . oh, because everything was strange. I do not blame you for anything that happened. I was as much to blame as you—more so, perhaps. But what happened was over when you took me home last night. I wish to have no further acquaintance with you. None whatsoever. Do I make myself clear?"

"Mary," he said, "you enjoyed it as much as I."

"It brought me comfort," she said. "Enjoyment was no part of it."

"You are a liar," he said. "Next time, Mary, I shall force you to admit to your enjoyment before I allow you release. You will tell me in words as well as with your body."

"If you will not set me down," she said, "then take me

home, please. I thought when I awoke this morning that I had awoken from some nightmare. But it is still with me. I want it to end the moment you set me down outside my own door. It is to end."

He turned his horses in the direction of the gates. Yes, he should have expected it, he thought. A woman of Lady Mornington's pride could not be expected to give in unprotesting to her physical nature. Doubtless she was a Puritan and considered physical passion to be sinful. She had been married for a number of years—he did not know how many. And she had been Clifton's woman for five or six years. She had probably not had any other men except him the night before. Having been bedded by three separate men—and only one her husband— would doubtless seem sinful to someone like her.

Well, he would have to teach her. Slowly. Lady Mornington must learn as she loved—slowly.

"It will not end," he said quietly to her. "You know it as well as I, Mary. Something began last night, and it is very far from its end. Very far. But I can wait." He laughed. "I am named suitably. I can wait for you to accept the inevitable, as I have. We will be lovers. You will be my mistress. Perhaps for longer than you were Clifton's. I cannot imagine growing quickly tired of what we shared last night. But I can wait—for a while. I am not by nature a patient man, but I can patiently await something I really want."

"Then you had better be prepared to wait until your dying day," she said.

"Perhaps," he said. "But I think not. I think it will be sooner than that."

He was content to be silent for the rest of the distance to Portman Place. And he was glad when he got there that he had brought his curricle. Had she not been perched so high above the road, he did not believe she would have allowed him to assist her to the ground. As it was, he lifted her by the waist and slid her down his body. He felt her shudder.

"I shall attend your salon two evenings from this," he said.

"I wish you would not." She raised her eyes to his.

"But you said yourself that you hold open house," he said. "You would not turn me away, Mary, or have me thrown out?"

"Please do not come," she said.

"You will be ashamed to have me seen there?" he asked. And he smiled at her, although he found it a little difficult to do so.

"Yes," she said fiercely. "If you will force me to be so ill-mannered, yes. I will be ashamed."

"Ah," he said, his eyes glittering down at her, "but no one will know that we have lain together, Mary, unless you choose to make the announcement yourself. Or that we will lie together again more times than you can count."

She turned sharply away from him and rapped the knocker on her door before he could do so himself.

He watched her straight and rigid back until the door opened and she disappeared inside without another word or a backward glance. He smiled and climbed back into the seat of his curricle.

But he was not amused. Felicity, too, had fought him, and he had refused to believe that she did not mean to have him eventually. He had even offered her marriage in the end because it had seemed to him that there was no other way of having her. Was he being just as blind and just as foolish with Mary? Was he inviting rejection just as surely?

But he had never had Felicity. He had had Mary, and she had wanted him then. No other woman had wanted him as she had wanted him the night before. No other woman had loved him as she had loved him.

It could not be the end. That could not have been both

a beginning and an ending. There was a feeling of near-panic at the very thought.

Devil take it, but he would have her. And she would like it, too. He would make her tell him so the very next time he had her beneath him and mounted. He would keep her writhing with unfulfillment until she had told him that she enjoyed it. And that she loved him.

He would make her tell him that she loved him. By God, he would. And she would mean it, too.

4

*M*ARY'S ENTERTAINMENTS WERE KNOWN TO MOST people as literary evenings, though that was not, strictly speaking, a true description of them. Sometimes she did have poets or playwrights in attendance, but very often it was politicians or artists or musicians. Occasionally there was no special guest at all, but just those who liked to gather for an evening of good conversation without the distraction of dancing or card playing.

She was proud of her literary evenings and of the class of people who attended them.

She had told no one that Lord Edmond Waite planned to attend this particular one—not even Penelope. Perhaps he would not come, she thought. Surely he would not, on mature consideration. He would be vastly out-of-place. And she must have made quite clear to him that she had no wish or intention of furthering their acquaintance.

But she looked forward to the evening with a trepidation she did not normally feel. Normally she would have been excited at the prospect of having Mr. Beasley and Sir Alvin Margrove in a room together—in her salon. She knew that the gathering of guests would be larger than usual as a result, though it was by no means certain that Sir Alvin would be able to find the time to come.

Even Mr. Beasley alone would draw people to her house, however.

But her eagerness was tempered by anxiety. She wished she could be back to the old days, when Marcus would be coming, as like as not, and staying afterward, too, when everyone else had gone home. He had stayed just so that they might talk and relax cozily together. It had not been discreet of them, perhaps. Inevitably there had been some gossip. And that gossip might have had foundation. There had been one occasion early in their acquaintance when he had embraced her and she had responded. She had even led him to her bedchamber, but once there she had faced him with outer embarrassment and inner shame, and he had laughed, breaking the tension, and agreed that, no, such a relationship was not possible between them. She had joined in his laughter, relieved and a little shamefaced.

After that, surprisingly perhaps, they had developed a deep and warm friendship. She wished she could have those days back. But she could not.

And Lord Edmond wanted her to be his mistress, had confidently predicted that it would be so. It would be laughable if it were not so annoying—so infuriating in the extreme.

She dressed with greater care than usual, wearing an apricot-colored gown more suitable for a concert or the theater, perhaps, than for a literary evening. And she washed and fluffed her hair so that the curls were softer and glossier than usual. She did it to boost her confidence, to enable her to feel good about herself.

There was an anxious hour when her salon filled with familiar and a few less-familiar faces, while neither of the main guests appeared. But Mr. Beasley arrived finally and apologized for being somewhat late. Mary breathed a sigh of relief. If he was somewhat late, then so was Lord Edmond, and probably that meant that he would not come at all.

Young Mr. Pipkin had arrived unfashionably dressed, long hair unkempt, one pocket bulging with copies of his latest poetry. Mary built a group about him and stayed there herself, listening to his theatrical readings of very mediocre poetry, and was pleased to find that most listeners were able to give positive and tactful criticisms of the poems. Perhaps he should try writing in the more modern vein instead of feeling himself confined to the heroic couplet, Lord Livermere suggested. He would find more rein for his talents.

Mary began to relax and enjoy herself. Although there was no sign of Sir Alvin Margrove, the group about Mr. Beasley was large.

And then she saw him—Lord Edmond Waite, that was. He was standing in the doorway of her salon, a quizzing glass in one hand, dressed with exquisite elegance in black evening clothes. He looked rather satanic, Mary thought, anger warring with dismay as she moved away from Mr. Pipkin's side. He was looking about him with a supercilious expression, as if he had walked in upon a colony of worms.

"Ah, Lady Mornington," he said as she approached him, "I am sorry to be so late. You must have been afraid that I was not coming at all."

He reached out an elegant lace-covered hand, and she was aware as she placed her own unwillingly in it that his arrival was attracting a considerable amount of covert though well-bred attention. She felt she would surely die when he bowed over her hand and raised it to his lips.

"Not afraid," she said, appalled at her own lack of manners. "Hoping, my lord."

"Well," he said, and he still retained her hand in his. He even covered it with his other hand. "Sometimes,

Mary, one feels the compulsion to see how the other half lives. Your literary evenings are quite famous."

"Thank you," she said. "May I direct you to a tray of drinks?"

"On the assumption that I cannot live without a glass in my hand?" he said. "Perhaps you should give direction that a tray of drinks be placed at my personal disposal. And you do not need to direct me. I can see with my naked eye three trays with servants attached to them. To which one shall I escort you?"

"I do not like to drink," she said. "And I must return to Mr. Pipkin's group, if you will excuse me. He is reading his poetry and will perhaps be hurt if I desert him so soon."

"And I will not?" he said. "Pipkin? The one who likes to look and live the part of a poet but has a lamentable lack of talent to go along with the image?"

"His work is interesting," she said.

"If I were an aspiring poet," he said, "and you called my work interesting in that best hostess voice of yours, Mary, I should drown both it and myself in the nearest duck pond. Go, then. I shall see to my own entertainment."

Mary returned gratefully to the group she had just left, and felt all the bad manners of her behavior and hated him for having forced her into it. It was inexcusable of her to abandon a late guest without first of all seeing to it personally that he had a drink in his hand and had been introduced into some group.

She hesitated, as there was a flurry of polite applause to herald the end of one of Mr. Pipkin's longer and more impassioned pieces. Perhaps she should return to Lord Edmond? Even considering who he was, she would have treated him with the proper courtesy if those events surrounding Vauxhall had not happened. Of course, her salon would be the last place on earth he would be if it had not been for Vauxhall.

She was relieved to find when she looked behind her that he was half hidden among the large group about Mr. Beasley. The look on his face had changed to one of amusement. *How dare he?* she thought, giving in to a wave of anger. *How dare he find one of the country's most prominent and progressive politicians amusing?* How dare he find her entertainment amusing! Doubtless he would be far more comfortable and serious if she had a few half-naked dancers cavorting on the tables.

"Mary!" Penelope Hubbard tapped her on the arm and drew her to one side. Their mutual friend Hannah Barrat was with her. "Whatever is this?"

"Lord Edmond Waite?" Mary did not pretend to misunderstand. "He said that he has a curiosity to know how the other half lives."

"I could have died when he walked into the room," Hannah said. "Julian will not like it above half when I tell him, though Julian is a thoroughly dry old stick, of course, and I never pay him any mind. The whole idea of women being interested in politics and matters of the mind shocks him. But Lord Edmond Waite, Mary. He is somewhat beyond the pale, is he not? Poor Lady Dorothea Page."

"I told you about Vauxhall," Penelope said.

"So you did," Hannah said. "I think I would have developed smallpox and returned home when I saw that he was one of the party, Penny. And you were caught in the rain with him, Mary? That was most unfortunate. But could you not discourage him from coming here this evening?"

"My guests come not by invitation only," Mary said. "I would not turn away a guest. Besides, he is behaving with perfect propriety." For some reason her anger was suddenly directed against Hannah.

"Mary," Penelope said, "Vauxhall less than a week ago; a drive in the park the day before yesterday; here this evening. The man is not conceiving a *tendre* for you, is he?"

"How ridiculous!" Mary said. "Of course he is not."

"He must be sent about his business without further ado, Mary," Hannah said. "It will do your reputation no good to be seen consorting with him, you know."

"Oh, come, Hannah," Penelope said crossly, "sometimes you can be as stuffy as that husband of yours. And yes, of course I apologize for the insult. But friends can be excused for some plain speaking. Is he bothering you, Mary? Do you want me to be sure to be the last guest to leave?"

Mary hesitated. What if he really did as Marcus had always done and lingered after the other guests had taken their leave? Except that Marcus had always done it with her consent, of course.

"Yes, please, Penny," she said. "I would be grateful."

Penelope gave her friend a penetrating look. "He is being troublesome, then," she said.

"I must go and see if the refreshments are ready in the dining room yet," Mary said, and she smiled and turned away from her friends.

"A wonderful evening, Mary," Colonel Hyde told her at supper. "It is a shame that Margrove was unable to come, and a shame perhaps that most of us are in such awe of Beasley that we put up no argument against his theories. But one must confess that they are interesting theories. And as usual you have attracted the cream of London society here."

"Thank you," she said.

He leaned a little closer to her. "Waite is the one who puzzles me," he said. "What on earth is he doing here, Mary? The man does not have two serious thoughts to rub together, does he?" He chuckled. "Dorothy was put out that I stopped in the park the other day. People would talk about our showing civility to such a man, she said. But how could I ignore our little Mary, I asked her."

Mary's smile was a bit forced. "I hold open house," she said. "Anyone is welcome to come, provided he is appropriately dressed and well-behaved, of course."

"Of course," he said, patting her hand. "I did not mean any criticism, Mary. It is a thoroughly pleasant evening, as usual."

Provided he is well-behaved. The words echoed in Mary's mind less than an hour later. They were back in her salon, in three groups this time. Mr. Pipkin was surrounded by a new group of the curious or of those who felt that good manners dictated that he not be left in isolation. Mary had maneuvered some people into his group herself. A second group had gathered spontaneously to discuss the play at the Drury Lane they had seen the night before. The third and largest, of course, was about Mr. Beasley.

Mary joined the third group, despite the fact that Lord Edmond Waite was still part of it and still a silent and amused spectator. Or so he was for a while, at least. Mr. Beasley had been delivering a lengthy monologue in which he was expounding some of his most radical theories. He gazed about at his gathered disciples with condescension and satisfaction. There were several murmurs of surprise and disapproval, even of shock, but no one spoke up against him as Sir Alvin Margrove would surely have done. Not until Lord Edmond spoke up, that was, his voice bored and quite, quite distinct.

"Beasley," he said when the great man paused for breath, "you are an ass."

Everyone, including Mr. Beasley, froze. But the politician had not been a member of the House for several years for nothing. He recovered himself almost immediately.

"I beg your pardon, sir?" he said in a tone that boded ill for his critic.

"You are an ass," Lord Edmond repeated, and Mary closed her eyes, white with fury. "I cannot imagine how so many apparently intelligent people can stand here and listen politely to such utter drivel."

"My lord." Mary stepped forward. She was using her best hostess voice, she realized, instinct having taken over, though she had no idea how she was going to smooth over the moment.

But Mr. Beasley held up a large staying hand. "Don't distress yourself, pray, ma'am," he said. "Doubtless the gentleman will explain himself."

"Redistributing wealth equally will make everyone equal in value and happiness," Lord Edmond said. "Utopia will have been arrived at. Heaven will be on earth. It is an idea as old and as asinine as the proverbial hills."

"Of course," Mr. Beasley said, looking about him for approval, "the speaker is one of the wealthy and privileged. One who would have much to lose under the new order. The same would apply to most of us in this room. Most of us, however, have a spirit of humanity and justice."

"Spirit of cow dung," Lord Edmond said. "If you seriously believe that by artificially making everyone equal, Beasley, you will make them content to remain equal and to live happily ever after, then obviously you have a pea for a brain."

"I have ever found," Mr. Beasley said, inhaling deeply so that he appeared to swell to twice his size, "that those people of dull mind and brain invariably attribute like intellectual powers to those they cannot understand."

"And I have ever found," Lord Edmond said, "that

asses consider themselves to be intellectual giants. If you are to bring justice to the poor, Beasley, you do not abolish all property rights and title and position. Do you seriously think that by setting a gin addict and pickpocket down on a few acres of land and stuffing a wad of money into his hand you are enabling him to live a happy and productive existence for the rest of his life? He will spend the money on gin and sell the land for more and steal from his neighbor to secure yet more for his future."

"A liquor addict." Mr. Beasley pursed his lips. "From one who knows, sir? I would have no experience of such matters myself."

"And have sealed your own doom and confirmed me in my estimation of you by admitting as much," Lord Edmond said. "If you do not understand people, Beasley, then you cannot concoct theories for their happiness. Have you learned nothing from the Revolution in France and from the career of Napoleon Bonaparte? A wonderful exercise in univeral liberty and equality, would you not agree?"

He turned away from the interested group as Mary squirmed with embarrassment and impotent fury. How dare he? Oh, how dare he!

"I must be leaving, Lady Mornington," he said. "I wish I could stay and converse longer, but I believe I have made my point, and I would not wish to monopolize the conversation."

She could have let him go. She could have stayed to smooth over the situation as best she could. There was no compulsion on her to see him to the door. But she turned and preceded him from the room.

"A delightful evening, Mary," he said, closing the salon door behind him.

She rounded on him, her eyes blazing.

"How could you!" she said. "How could you so have embarrassed me and ruined the evening?"

He raised his eyebrows. "As I understand it," he said, "these evenings are meant for conversation, not for the delivery of monologues. I seem to remember that Colonel Hyde was looking forward to the evening because a few sparks would fly if Margrove had come. Well, Mary, I rescued the evening from dullness for you. I believe I stirred up a few sparks, did I not?"

"You called him an . . ." She drew in her breath sharply.

"Ass?" he said. "And so he is, too. A horse's ass, to be more precise. How can you listen to him spouting such poppycock without shouting with laughter, Mary? Politeness must be very deeply bred into you."

"And perhaps it is as well," she said, her voice tight with fury. "Or I would tell you precisely what I think of you."

"I wish you would anyway," he said, smiling at her and flicking her cheek with one long finger.

"You are unspeakably vulgar," she said. "Your language belongs in the gutter."

He considered. "In the farmyard, I believe," he said. "Asses and cow dung are to be found there, Mary. Duck ponds, too. Have you never been into the country?"

"I believe you were leaving," she said with icy courtesy.

"I must take you there sometime," he said, looking down to her lips. "It would be an education for you, Mary. You would not believe, for example, the number of uses there can be for a haystack. I will show you at least one of them."

"Please leave," she told him.

"When will I see you again?" he asked. "Will you come to Kew Gardens with me tomorrow? There are no duck ponds there, or haystacks, either. Nothing to shock your sensibilities. Will you come?"

"No," she said, "thank you."

"Because I called Beasley an ass to his face and a horse's ass to yours?" he said. "My apologies, Mary. I was angry with the man. Forgive me?"

"Please leave," she said.

"You will not come to Kew?"

"No."

"No without the thank-you this time," he said with a sigh. "You must mean it, then. But I shall see you sometime soon, Mary. I do not like this primness. It is what I have always disliked in you. I like the other Mary—the real Mary. Good night."

He took her hand in his, and she steeled herself to having it kissed again. Instead he leaned forward and kissed her firmly and briefly—and openmouthed—on the lips.

"Get out!" she whispered fiercely. One of her servants was at the door, just out of earshot, waiting to open it for him. The man must have seen. "If I never see you again, it will be too soon."

"A cliché unworthy of you, Mary," he said, his pale blue eyes boring into her for a brief moment before he released her hand and turned to leave the house without a backward glance.

If she were any more furious, Mary thought, she would surely explode into a thousand fragments. She was . . . furious! Feeling had shivered downward from her mouth, just as if it were a physical reality, past her throat, through her breasts, down into her womb, and lower, leaving an uncomfortable throbbing between her legs. They felt rather as if they might collapse beneath her.

And she remembered again all that she had remembered with great and physical clarity each night since

Vauxhall. She turned quickly and hurried back into the salon.

HE DID NOT know quite why he was pursuing her with such determination. She seemed seriously to want to have nothing to do with him, and her world was not his. He could not understand how she could take people like Pipkin and Beasley seriously. He had always found the deliberate pursuit of intellectuality either amusing or tedious. Could she not see that it was all hogwash?

He had been sent down from Oxford once upon a time for saying as much to a don—though his language had been rather more colorful on that occasion and had strayed somewhat from the farmyard. And he had bloodied the man's nose. Mary would have had ten fits of the vapors—though perhaps not. She had followed the drum for a few years with her husband, had she not? She must have heard it all, and more, then.

The Oxford episode had been atypical of him at that time, of course, happening as it had a scant month after Dick's death and at a time when his mother's life had hung by a thread. Lord Edmond's mouth formed almost a snarl as his mind skirted the memories. The don had been fortunate not to have had his neck wrung. Sanctimonious fool!

Why was he pursuing Mary? For the sheer challenge of overcoming such obvious resistance? Perhaps. He had pursued Felicity for similar reasons. So that he might degrade her and show his contempt for her world? No, not that. He felt no hatred for her, only a certain amusement at the fact that he might be the only man in existence, with the possible exception of Clifton, who knew that a more worldly and more earthy—and damned more interesting—Mary lurked below the demure surface.

Because her performance in bed had left him aching for more? Yes, definitely that. Women, in his experience, did not enjoy sex. Either they lay still and limp as fish, submitting to having their legs thrust wide and their bodies penetrated, and smiling like sweet martyrs afterward—that type he rarely bedded twice. Or else they twisted and gyrated and panted and shouted out with ecstasy and then adjusted their hair and held out a palm for payment. At least such women worked hard for a living, and often they knew how to give exquisite pleasure. He occasionally returned to them for more. Twice he had employed one of them as his mistress, one for a year and a half, the other for longer than two.

Mary fell into neither category. She was the only woman he had had who had quite openly and honestly enjoyed having sexual intercourse. And so she was the only woman with whom his own pleasure had been un-marred. Just the memory of that first bedding in the scarlet room could make his breathing quicken and his temperature soar—the time when she had asked for it slow and had been given it slow.

Yes, that was the reason. There could be no other. He wanted her. But not as an occasional bedfellow, someone with whom to while away the tedious hours of a useless existence. More than that. As a long-term mistress—very long-term if her performances continued to match those of that night. He wanted to have her to start his days and as dessert to his luncheon, as a mid-afternoon exercise, as an appetizer before whatever entertainment the evening had to offer, and as a nighttime lullaby and a middle-of-the-night drug.

He wanted to teach her more—much more. And he wanted to learn all she had to teach.

He wanted her. And by God, she must want him, too. As far as he knew, she had had no one since Clifton. And a woman of such passion and appetite could not possibly find fulfillment from abstention. She was just too prim and too respectable for her own good—despite Clifton. Doubtless his reputation bothered her. Many ladies had avoided him even before he had dumped Dorothea. After that, many had totally shunned him—like Mrs. Hyde in the park the other day. The old fool! As if he cared.

Perhaps Mary had heard about Dick. It was a fifteen-year-old scandal, dead almost as long as Dick himself. But perhaps she had heard about it.

She must be made to realize that reputations and labels do not make a man. The man she saw and thought she knew was no more the real person than she was the woman he saw. The two people who had met and loved during all the frenzy of a bad storm were not the two people that the *ton* knew and the two people they had thought each other until that night. He could see that clearly. She must come to see it, too.

And if she did not, well, then, by God, he would make her see it. He wanted her. And he needed her. And he would have her, too.

And so he set about discovering where he might meet her within the following week. She would be at the theater with the Barretts and a few more of their friends two evenings after her literary evening, he discovered by devious means, which were second nature to him. And she had accepted an invitation to the Menzies ball three nights after that. He had not himself received an invitation, but he would not allow that to deter him from going. They were scarcely likely to make a scene by turning him away. And if they did, well, then, it would give the tabbies something else to gossip about for a few days until another scandal came along to amuse them.

Lady Mornington had not seen the last of him by any means.

5

SHE HALF EXPECTED HIM TO CALL ON HER THE NEXT day to try to insist on taking her to Kew. It was an enormous relief when he did not. He did not appear all day, or all the next day. He had finally taken the hint, she thought, though the words she had used to him could hardly be classified as a hint. He had finally accepted the fact that she wished to have no further dealings with him.

Life settled back to normal. No one, she had found, seemed to blame her for Lord Edmond's dreadful breach of good manners to Mr. Beasley. Indeed, several people had commented when she returned to the salon that the brief argument had livened the evening. Colonel and Mrs. Hyde made no mention of the incident when she called on them the following day, and when she dined with Penelope, Mr. Hubbard being from home, her friend remarked only that actually it had been rather funny.

"And though I may quarrel somewhat with his choice of words, Mary," she said, "I could not help agreeing with the sentiment. It seems he was the only person present willing to cross swords with Mr. Beasley."

She would put the whole ghastly episode behind her, Mary thought as she prepared for the evening at the theater. There would be dinner at Hannah's first and then on to the Drury Lane, one of a party of six. Hannah had invited the Viscount Goodrich as her escort. Mary had known him for several years and had always liked his quiet good manners and sensible conversation. He was about ten years her senior, about the same age as Marcus, in fact. Hannah had confided in her that he had shown definite interest in learning that her "friendship" with Marcus was at an end, and had asked his friend, Hannah's husband, to pair them up for some occasion.

"He has been a widower for eight years, Mary," Hannah said, "and is ready to make another match, if Julian has understood the matter right. It would be splendid for you."

Mary tended to agree. She had not really thought of marriage since Lawrence's death. She had grieved for a long time. And then there had been her new life to set up in London, and her long friendship with Marcus had satisfied her need for masculine companionship—while it had lasted. But she was thirty years old and childless. And she had needs—needs that had lain dormant in her since Lawrence's death, but that had recently flared again.

She quelled a vivid and unwilling memory of just how well those needs had been satisfied during the notorious Vauxhall night. But she needed more than physical contact with a man; she needed a relationship. Perhaps she could have both with the viscount. Perhaps she could have another marriage. It was too early to plan yet, of course. But the possibility was enough to add some pleasurable anticipation to her preparations for the evening. She wore her new rose-pink silk.

Dinner was everything she could have hoped for. The food was superior—the Barretts' cook had had several covert offers from other households but had remained loyal to her employers. The company was good—the Waddingtons were the other couple—and the conversation stimulating. And the Viscount Goodrich was flat-teringly attentive without being embarrassingly so.

"You should always wear such vivid colors, Lady Mornington," he had said in the drawing room when she had first arrived. He had looked at her apprecia-tively. "They become you."

She had felt good about the evening from that mo-ment on.

The play that evening was to be *The Tempest*, by Wil-liam Shakespeare. It was not one of his more entertain-ing plays, Lord Goodrich gave as his opinion during dinner, though it was one of his most thought-provoking. And of course it could be a visually pleasing play, pro-vided it was produced well. Did not Lady Mornington consider Caliban one of Shakespeare's most villainous characters?

"I must confess that I have always felt a little sorry for the man—for the creature," Mary said. "But it happens in great literature, does it not? The most satanic charac-ters can be so well-developed that one cannot help but identify with them. Satan himself in *Paradise Lost*, for example. Perhaps there is the realization through such creatures that there but for the grace of God go we."

"And unfortunately," Mrs. Waddington added, "evil aways has a rather fatal attraction for us."

The discussion became lively when Mr. Barrett stepped in to disagree with the ladies.

Mary looked forward to watching that particular play. But she discovered as always on their arrival at the theater that just the place itself, just the atmosphere, was enough to arouse excitement in her. Had life only been a little different for her, she often thought, perhaps she would have been an actress.

"Mary," Hannah whispered, leaning toward her just before the play began, "that dreadful man has just arrived and is staring at our box—at you, I would imagine—through his quizzing glass."

"Where?" Mary had no doubt who "that dreadful man" was.

"First tier of boxes," Hannah said. "Almost opposite. Ah, he has lowered the glass. He has not pestered you since that dreadfully vulgar display he made in your salon? You showed great fortitude, I must confess, in not swooning quite away. I am sure I would have, had it happened in my home."

Mary did not look immediately. But she leaned a little closer to the viscount, who was waiting to make some comment to her, and she smiled warmly back at him and continued the conversation. She felt self-conscious and angry, though it was unfair to do so. Lord Edmond Waite had as much right to be at the theater as she, she supposed.

She looked finally just as the play was beginning. Her eyes went immediately to the right box. He was alone. He did not have his quizzing glass to his eye, but he was looking directly across the theater at her, just as if there were nothing of interest to see on the stage. Mary turned her head sharply away to watch the action, and leaned another fraction of an inch closer to the viscount. Their shoulders almost touched.

She found herself wishing over the next hour that it were one of Shakespeare's simpler plays. She was finding it difficult to concentrate.

The Waddingtons left the box during the interval to call upon acquaintances in another box, and Hannah and her husband stepped into the hallway to stretch their legs. The viscount asked Mary her opinion of the production of the play and proceeded to give his. She wished that she had paid it more attention.

When the door to the box opened, she turned her head, expecting to see Hannah return. She froze.

"Ah," Lord Edmond Waite said, "my eyes did not deceive me. Good evening, Mary. Goodrich?"

Mary? She bit her lower lip.

"Waite?" The viscount's voice dripped with ice.

"Good evening, my lord," she said. And when he reached out a hand to her, she felt obliged to set her own in it. And inevitably he raised it to his lips.

"Your salon was well-attended two evenings ago," he said. "You must have been gratified. Of course, you provided your guests with stimulating company, Mary, as always. I came to thank you for an interesting evening and to apologize for having had to leave early."

"I understand," she said. "You had another appointment."

"You were not there, Goodrich," Lord Edmond said, and only then did he release her hand. "You missed a splendid evening. But then, Mary's literary evenings are quite famous. I daresay next week's will be just as stimulating. Perhaps I will be able to stay later next time."

His pale blue eyes were openly caressing her. Mary was rigid with fury. What was he implying for Lord Goodrich's benefit? That they had some sort of relationship? Some sort of intimacy? How dare he call her Mary in someone else's hearing? Or even when there was no one else to hear, for that matter.

"I have always intended to sample one of Lady Mornington's entertainments," the viscount said, his voice stiff and cold. "Perhaps I shall do so next week."

"And how are you enjoying the play, Mary?" Lord Edmond asked. "A little dry, would you say?"

"By no means," she said. "I find it quite stimulating to the mind." Her words sounded pompous even to her own ears. And they were quite untrue.

"Prospero likes the sound of his own voice too much," he said. "He should be content to allow the Bard's words to speak for themselves."

"But is not the whole point of performed drama to breathe life into words that are dead on a page?" the viscount asked, not even trying to hide his contempt.

Lord Edmond considered. "I have never found words on a page particularly dead," he said. "Only perhaps the mind that reads them."

It was a masterly setdown. But quite unnecessary. And very unmannerly under the circumstances. And who was he to talk of dead minds? And to the Viscount Goodrich, of all people?

The viscount shrugged and turned away. The insult was beneath his notice, it seemed.

"Don't you admire Caliban, Mary?" Lord Edmond asked. "And don't you wish that he could rise up and sock all the other sanctimonious characters between the eyes? I would have made a hero of him if I had been Shakespeare." He laughed. "Perhaps it is as well I was not."

"Perhaps," she said. But she could not comment on Caliban in the viscount's hearing. How could she condemn him when she had spoken up in his defense at the dinner table?

"You are not to be drawn," Lord Edmond said. "I think you must secretly like him, Mary. I believe women sometimes do admire what seems ugly and brutish. Beauty and the beast and all that."

"That would seem to imply that women crave brutality and abuse," she said. "It does not show a great respect for either women themselves or their minds."

"Ah," he said, "you become too deep for me, Mary. I do not believe I mentioned abuse. It seems that I am interrupting a *tête-à-tête* here. I came merely to pay my compliments. I shall see you again, my dear."

My dear? Mary's eyes widened.

"Good night," he said. "Goodrich?"

But the viscount, who was gazing down into the pit,

did not reply. Lord Edmond looked back to Mary, winked at her, and left the box. She could hear herself exhaling.

"Lady Mornington," the viscount said, "I did not know you were acquainted with Lord Edmond Waite. Are you sure it is wise?"

She looked at him in some surprise. "I have only the slightest acquaintance with him," she said.

"And yet he calls you by your given name?" he said.

"I have never given him leave to so do," she said. "He was being impertinent."

"The man has an unsavory reputation," he said, "especially since he humiliated Lady Dorothea Page so unpardonably. You have heard about that?"

"Yes," she said. "I do not like the man, I do assure you."

"I am relieved to hear it," he said. "If you had only given me the slightest signal, ma'am, I would have requested in no uncertain terms that he leave the box immediately. I do not like the fact that his visit here was made under the eye of half the *ton*."

For your sake or mine? she wanted to ask him, looking at him curiously. But he did not supply the answer to her question.

When the last stragglers had returned to their boxes, she noticed later, Lord Edmond Waite's box remained empty. He did not reappear for the rest of the evening.

Viscount Goodrich's carriage conveyed the Waddingtons home before Mary, though her house was closer to the theater. She sat alone beside him during the short ride home.

"You are to attend the Menzies ball?" he asked her.

"Yes." She smiled. "I am looking forward to it. I like to dance occasionally."

"We are all entitled to some frivolous enjoyment in life," he said. "Will you do me the honor of dancing the opening set with me, ma'am, and perhaps a waltz later in the evening?"

"Thank you," she said. "I shall look forward to it."

"But that is all of three days in the future," he said. "May I take you for a drive—tomorrow? Perhaps as far as Kew?"

Kew. She remembered another invitation to drive there.

"That would be pleasant," she said. "I always enjoy a stroll in Kew Gardens."

"Then I shall come for you after luncheon," he said.

He helped her down to the pavement when his carriage stopped outside her house, and squeezed her hand before releasing it.

Inside the house, Mary handed her evening cloak to her manservant and ran lightly up the stairs, well pleased with the evening if she blocked from her mind the one discordant episode. The viscount was a pleasant, intelligent companion. And he seemed eager to see her again—Kew the next day and two sets with him at the Menzies ball.

It would be good, she thought, to have a beau again, to have someone interested exclusively in her. It would be good to have a man to dream of. To have a possible marriage to hope for. She was ready for marriage again, she thought, for the assurance that her man would always come home to her at night. She was ready for children. It was not too late, surely. She was only thirty years old.

She pictured the viscount in her mind with his pleasant features and slightly receding fair hair. And she saw Lord Edmond Waite's pale blue eyes intent on hers.

Well, at least, she thought, a new man in her life would help her banish the memories. And in future, if Lord Edmond tried to intrude himself into her company while

Lord Goodrich was near, he would be told in no uncertain terms to take himself off.

Mary thought of his saying that words were not dead on a page, only the mind that read them. And she smiled despite herself.

So MARY AND Goodrich were about to become an item, were they? Lord Edmond Waite thought, viewing the two of them waltzing together. His hand was spread across her back in a proprietary manner and she was smiling up at him. He himself was late. He had had no wish to run the gauntlet of a receiving line when he had received no invitation. But as he had suspected, no one had impeded his progress into the ballroom. And only a few matrons appeared to have noticed him and frowned possessively at their young charges lest they rush at him and elope to Gretna with him without further ado.

Ah. She had seen him. And had jerked her head away and was smiling even more determinedly up at Goodrich. It was a promising sign. At least she was not indifferent to him. She was damned hostile, but that was better than indifference.

Goodrich. He did nothing to keep the sneer from his face as he raised his quizzing glass to his eye and surveyed them through it. She could hardly have chosen anyone duller or more respectable if she had tried. A pillar of respectability. The man had had the same mistress in keeping since several years before the death of his first wife, and was rumored to have been faithful to her—apart from some beddings of his wife while she had still lived, presumably. The mistress was now plump and matronly herself, and the mother of five offspring.

But Goodrich was a respectable soul. If he felt himself in need of another wife, he would certainly not dream of marrying the woman who had given him all for years without benefit of clergy and presented him with a whole brood of bastard children. No, he would marry Lady Mornington, who curiously had preserved her reputation for respectability despite her lengthy liaison with a married man.

Lord Edmond's lips thinned into an arctic smile. He wondered how eager Goodrich would be to lay even the tip of one finger on Mary if he knew just how eagerly and lasciviously she had given herself little more than a week before to a certain gentleman currently out of favor with the *ton*.

The waltz was ending. Lord Edmond inclined his head to Lady Menzies, who had just caught sight of him from a short distance away and was staring at him, somewhat startled. He strolled in the direction in which Goodrich was leading Mary. They had joined the Hubbards and the Barretts before he came up to them. He made his bow to the group.

"A grand squeeze," he said, "for so late in the Season."

"Yes, indeed," Penelope Hubbard said. "We were just saying so ourselves."

Lord Edmond turned his gaze upon Mary. "May I?" he asked, touching the card at her wrist.

"That dance is mine, Waite," the viscount said stiffly. Lord Edmond raised his eyebrows. "Which?" he asked.

"Whichever one you were planning to claim." The viscount fixed him with a hard stare.

The devil, Lord Edmond thought, there could be a duel at dawn if he was not careful. That would do wonders for his reputation. Especially if he put a bullet between Goodrich's eyes, as he would be sorely tempted to do. Five bastards might have to face the morrow as orphans.

"Indeed," he said, lifting the card from Mary's unresisting wrist and opening it. His eyes glanced through it. "Ah, but you forgot to write your name, Goodrich. And

I believe it is just as well. Mary's card tells me that you have already danced two sets with her. Would you sully her reputation by claiming a third?"

They were one step closer to that duel, he saw when he glanced up.

"Her card is full," the viscount said slowly and distinctly, as if he were talking to an imbecile. "There is no dance free for you, Waite."

The other two ladies were shifting uncomfortably, Lord Edmond was aware. Mr. Hubbard was clearing his throat.

"Perhaps that is for the lady to say," he said. "Mary?"

"Lady Mornington to you," the viscount said. "And you will let go of that card if you know what is good for you, Waite."

A few other people close by were beginning to look at their group.

"Oh, please," Mary said. "I will be happy to dance one set with you, my lord."

"Ma'am, there is really no need to give in to coercion, I do assure you," the viscount said.

But Lord Edmond ignored him. He looked through the card. "A waltz?" he said. "The second set after supper?"

"Yes," she said, her voice breathless.

He scribbled his name in the space next to that particular set, made his bow to her, and withdrew to the card room, where luck was with him and he won three hands in succession.

He wandered alone in the ballroom and anterooms and out onto the balcony during supper and returned to the card room when the dancing resumed, a spectator rather than a player. He was listening to the music, waiting for the first set to end.

She was not with her friends this time. She was alone, walking purposefully along one side of the ballroom as if she were on her way somewhere definite. But he knew that she had merely chosen not to be embarrassed again in front of her friends. His lips curled.

"Mary?" he said, touching her on the arm. "My dance, I believe?"

"Yes." Her face was pale, her jaw set. "I have never given you leave to address me by my given name."

"Mary," he said softly, drawing her into his arms as the musicians prepared to play. "I have made love to you. Three times. And you to me. Am I to address you formally?"

She looked up into his eyes. "You will never let me forget that, will you?" she said.

He wondered yet again why he was pursuing her so relentlessly. She was so much older and plainer than most of the other dancers. At least he thought she must be. He could no longer remember if she was pretty or plain, old or young. She was Mary.

"Do you mean that you would forget it if I were not here to remind you?" he said. "I think not. I think that you remember every moment of every day. I think you relive those encounters every single night. You cannot deny it, can you?"

The music began, and he moved with her, noting again how small she was—she reached barely to his shoulder—and how slender. She was light on her feet and responded well to his lead. She was a good dancer.

"I like this gown," he said, looking down to the pale green silk at her shoulder, "as I liked the apricot-colored one you wore at your salon. Pale colors suit you. You have a strong enough character that you do not need to hide behind vivid shades—like the pink you wore at the theater."

She stared at his shoulder. She was not going to answer him, it seemed.

"Had you given Goodrich permission to send me

away?" he asked. "I found his attitude most obnoxious."

"Yes," she said, her face animated with anger again. "I had. But you have no conception of what good manners demand, do you? There would have been a nasty scene if I had not agreed to dance with you. I chose not to make a scene."

"I am glad," he said. "I would hate to have had to punch him in the nose, Mary, or direct a pistol at him tomorrow morning."

She drew in her breath. "You would have done either or both, would you not," she said, "without a thought to the distress you would have caused to a number of people? Without a thought to my reputation?"

"I do not like to have watchdogs set on me, Mary," he said. "Perhaps you should know that now. I would hate to have to harm Goodrich or anyone else. Argue with me face-to-face. Or do you not have the courage to do so?"

"I do not wish to argue with you," she hissed at him, "or to converse with you or to have any dealings whatsoever with you. I want you out of my life. Completely and immediately and forever. But you will not believe that, will you?"

"No," he said. "Or I will not accept it, at least. I want you in my life, you see, Mary. Completely and immediately—and yes, perhaps forever, too. I believe this conversation is becoming rather too intense for the scrutiny of all these eyes. It needs a little more privacy."

He danced her out through the French windows onto the stone balcony. It was rather a chilly night. There was only one other couple out there, and they were on their way back inside.

Lord Edmond Waite and Mary danced alone. And in silence. She did not immediately resume their quarrel, and he would not. She closed her eyes, he noticed. And he drew her fractionally closer and breathed in the scent of her.

It was eight days ago. The storm must have been in progress already at this particular time of night. He must have been holding her. Kissing her. Perhaps he had been in the process of laying her down on the table. Perhaps he had already been inside her.

If it were eight days ago, he would have the rest of that night to look forward to. God, if it were just possible to put back the clock. If it were just eight days ago.

Mary!

He looked down at her and knew in some shock that he was falling in love with her.

Had fallen.

6

$\mathcal{T}$HE AIR WAS COOL ON THE BALCONY. BLESSEDLY cool—she had become overheated in the ballroom. The music was lovely, the sort of music one could hardly resist moving to. The waltz must be the most wonderful dance in the world. Mary kept her eyes determinedly closed. She willed her partner to keep quiet. She wanted to believe that she was waltzing with any good partner anywhere.

"Mary." His voice was low and caressing.

She held her breath, but he said no more. She kept her eyes closed and they danced on. Until he twirled her about and stopped. There was something hard and cold at her back—the stone balustrade. Something brushed her cheek—the leaves of one of the large potted plants that stood at intervals along the balcony. She opened her eyes. They must be more than half hidden behind the plant. He was standing very close to her, his arm still about her waist, his other hand holding hers. He was looking at her intently.

"Mary," he said.

"I have danced with you," she said, anger rising again. "I have even made an effort to be polite to you and to stop quarreling with you. But this is more than enough. I am going to return to the ballroom now—alone. And I would ask you, my lord, to leave me alone in the future.

Strictly alone. I do not wish ever to speak with you again."

For answer he lowered his head and kissed her.

Her one hand was not free—he was gripping it tightly. With the other she pushed at his shoulder and slapped at his face, twisting her own away from it. They struggled in silence until he had her two wrists imprisoned. He set her hands against his chest and held them there until the fight went out of her.

"Do you wish me to scream?" she asked him. "Is that what you want? Yet another scandal? You will get nothing else from me, my lord, without a very loud scene, I promise you. Let me go, if you please."

"Mary," he said, making no move to release her, "we were good together. More than good. The best. We could be so again—and again and again."

"You make me sick," she said. "Physically sick. Nauseated. Are you so perverted that you like to pursue women who can vomit just at the thought of you?"

"You did not vomit last week," he said. "You gave every bit as good as you got. You enjoyed every moment." He looked at her in silence for a long while. "Is it my reputation? Is it that you know I have had many women and have recently jilted one lady in order to run off with another? Is it all the rumors of excesses and reckless living? Is that it?"

"Yes," she said, tight-lipped. "That is precisely it. Strange, is it not, that a woman would shun such a man? And one who killed his brother and his mother, too, if all the stories one hears are to be believed."

She wished that anger had not caused her to add those last accusations. She knew nothing with any certainty. And usually she scorned unsubstantiated gossip. His lips thinned and twisted into a sneer. His nostrils flared, and his eyes bored into hers.

"Ah, so you *have* heard that one, have you?" he said.

"Well, it is true, Mary. I killed them. Are you afraid I will kill you, too? Put my hands about your neck, perhaps, and squeeze?" He suited action to words, except that he did not squeeze. "It would be a new method for me. That is not how I killed them. Are you frightened?"

"No," she said, holding her voice steady. "I am not afraid of you, my lord." But she lied. She was, she realized, mortally afraid of him. Not afraid that he would kill her. Not there and then, anyway. But afraid that, say what she would, he would not leave her alone. Afraid that she would never be free of him. And a little afraid of herself, perhaps.

"Liar," he said. "Mary, has it ever occurred to you that all the stories you have heard, all the labels that have been put on me, do not make up the complete man? Do you not think that perhaps there is a great deal more to be known?"

"You would try to deny it all, then?" she said. "You would have me believe that you are a worthy and upright citizen?"

"Hardly that," he said. "No, it is all true, Mary, what you have heard, and a great deal more that you have not heard, I do not doubt. But even so, there is a large part of myself—a very large part—that is not accounted for by such a public image. Do you feel no curiosity to get to know what you do not yet know?"

"No," she said. "None whatsoever."

"Mary Gregg, Lady Mornington," he said, "widow of Colonel Lord Mornington of the Guards, former mistress of the Earl of Clifton, bluestocking, hostess of one of the most respected literary salons in London. Is that all of it? Is that who Mary Gregg is?"

"Of course not," she said. "Those details do not tell you who I am, only what I am or have been. And not all of those are true even. You do not know me at all, my lord."

"Touché," he said.

Her hands were still spread on his chest, she saw, though he no longer held them prisoner there. His own hands were now at her waist.

"I do not want to be having this discussion with you," she said. "I believe this waltz is almost at an end. I have promised the next dance to someone else."

"If it were not dark out here," he said, "I should open your card to find out if you tell the truth, Mary. But no matter. The waltz has not quite ended. Kiss me."

She stared at one of her hands. "Please," she said. "Let me go. I do not want to have to scream."

"Kiss me," he said, and he lowered his head to kiss her neck below one ear.

She closed her eyes and swallowed.

"Kiss me." He whispered the words an inch from her mouth.

"Please," she said.

"Mary," he whispered against her mouth. "Mary."

"Please," she said. And one hand was on his shoulder and moving up behind his neck, and her head tipped to one side, and her lips trembled against the light pressure of his.

"Mary," he said. "Kiss me."

She kissed him, her hand bringing his head forward, her mouth opening as his tongue came to meet it. And the ache was there again, intensified a hundredfold, and she knew that he could satisfy it. That he would satisfy it. One of his hands had slid down her back and brought her against his swelling groin. She pressed herself closer.

And then both her hands were against his shoulders, pushing firmly, and she turned her head to one side.

"Now be satisfied," she said. "Now have done and go away. Please!"

"You were humoring me?" he asked.

"How else can I be rid of you?" she said.

"Mary," he said, "you lie through your teeth. Your body is far more honest than you. Your body admits that it wants me, that it is fated to be mine. Why will you not admit it, too?"

She turned her head back to look at him. "The physical is the only aspect of life that matters to you, is it not?" she said. "If I were to admit that, yes, I am attracted to you at the basest physical level, you would exult, would you not, and feel that that was all-sufficient? It would not matter to you that I do not like you, that I do not respect you, and that I would despise myself for the rest of my life for giving rein to my basest instincts."

"You would deny the body, then?" he asked. "It is an unhappy thing to do, Mary. We have to live inside our bodies for the rest of our lives."

"Some of us," she said, "also have minds to live with. And consciences, too."

His smile was somewhat twisted. "Ah," he said, "it was obliging of you to explain that. I have often wondered what can give meaning to the lives of those who do not indulge their bodies as I do."

She swallowed.

"I want you, Mary," he said, "and I mean to have you. Not just from selfish whim, but because I know that you want me, too, and because I hold the strange belief that we can find a measure of happiness together. Stop fighting me. It is a useless struggle, I do assure you." He dropped his hands to his sides and took one step back from her. "But enough for tonight. It is time for me to find a few bottles from which to drink deep, and a few wealthy and foolish young bucks to separate from their fortunes at the tables, and a willing whore with whom to enjoy what remains of the night."

"I can live without having the details spelled out to me," she said coldly.

"Well," he said, "that is what you expect of me, is it

not, Mary? Is it not better to know for sure than merely to imagine? If I did not tell you, you might fear that you were doing me an injustice in your imagination."

She frowned. "You hate yourself, don't you?" she said.

He sneered and drew breath to speak. But the words were never uttered.

"Lady Mornington," the voice of Viscount Goodrich said from just beyond the potted plant, "may I escort you back into the ballroom, ma'am? Or would you like me to throw out your, ah, dancing partner first?"

One side of Lord Edmond's mouth lifted in a smile. He stood quite still and looked into Mary's eyes.

"We have been conversing," she said. "But the waltz is at an end, I hear. I would be thankful for your escort, my lord."

Although she looked at Lord Edmond, she was speaking to the viscount. She stepped to one side and around the former. He did not move, either to help or to impede her progress.

"Good night, Mary," he said softly. "Thank you for the dance and for the conversation."

"Good night, my lord," she said, and she set her hand on the viscount's sleeve.

HE DID NOT believe in love. Love brought only pain and bitterness. Love ruined lives, deprived them of all meaning and direction. He believed only in lust, only in the satisfaction of the body's cravings. And yes, she had been right. Only the physical mattered. Nothing else. Not mind. Not conscience. What did he care for conscience? Conscience had tormented him once upon a time, until it had seemed to be a toss-up whether he would end up in Bedlam or in hell, dead by his own hand. Somehow he had steered clear of Bedlam, and his hand had shaken like an autumn leaf when he had set the dueling pistol first against his temple and then inside his mouth. He had been too much the coward to pull the trigger.

Yes, he believed only in lust. She was damned good in bed, better than anyone else he had ever had, and so that was why he craved more. It was her body he craved. He cared nothing for her mind or her feelings or for all those other elements that were a part of her in addition to her body. He wanted her body. Lust was all.

He did not believe in love.

And yet in the two days following the Menzies ball, liquor seemed to have lost its power to make him drunk and gaming to amuse him and whoring to give his body ease. And so he gave them up, hurling a full decanter of brandy into his fireplace late on the second night—the night of her literary salon, which he had stayed away from—having already thrown in a winning hand at Watier's before the game was quite won so that players and spectators alike had gaped at him in disbelief.

And before going home and smashing the decanter, he had taken a delicious little whore into his scarlet room, sat down to watch her undress, and then ordered her to dress again while he stalked from the room to summon his carriage. He had paid her twice her usual fee—merely for undressing in his sight and dressing again out of it.

Her body had been twice as luscious as Mary's.

On the third day he called at Mary's house and sent up his card. He repeated the call for the following six days. Each time she was from home and he left without disputing the message. Once he saw her driving in the park in Goodrich's barouche. He deliberately redirected his horse so that he would pass her, and he raised his hat and gazed steadily at her until she flushed and acknowledged him with a nod. Then he rode on without even attempting to engage her in conversation.

The word was out that Goodrich was courting her in earnest.

He made no move to discover where she was likely to be during the week. He wanted her body, not her. There were a thousand women in London alone with bodies more attractive than Mary's, and many of them willing bodies, too. He would choose another woman and teach her to perform as Mary had performed for him, and better. She did not want him. Well, then, he would forget her. She did not matter to him. He believed only in lust, not in love.

But he sat in his dressing room late one night, staring at his boots and remembering that she had kissed him at the Menzies ball and that for a few moments she had been hot and willing in his arms, his for the taking. And he woke more than one night aroused for her and remembering her at the ball pressing herself against his groin, wanting him inside her.

He cursed her and damned her. He conjured up a mental image of her and ruthlessly criticized every aspect of her appearance. Her legs were too short, her hips too narrow, her breasts too small, her whole body too dumpy, her hair too unfeminine, her face too plain, her eyes too . . . He shook his head. Well, she had one good feature. One! And she was too old and too prim and too everything else he did not like.

It was almost laughable that he, who had always been considered something of a connoisseur of women, could not shake from his memory a woman whom no one in his hearing had ever called pretty or lovely or attractive or bedworthy. He would be the laughingstock if it were known—as it well might be if he did not forget her soon—that he had determinedly pursued the very plain and ordinary Lady Mornington and been rejected. People already knew such a thing of Felicity Wren, but at least Felicity was breathtakingly beautiful.

But Mary! His lips curled with contempt—contempt for his own reactions to her.

On the night of her next literary evening—she had a lady novelist and a more reputable poet than Pipkin on her guest list, he had heard—he arrived at her house again. But he did not take advantage of the fact that she held open house. He sent in his card with a note scribbled on the back. And he waited for her reply, wondering what he would do if she ignored it or sent a message that she was not at home.

He stood in the hall of her house and bowed to Sir Henry and Lady Blaize as they entered and handed their outdoor garments to the butler before making their way to the salon. He smiled arctically when Lady Blaize openly ignored him and Sir Henry merely frowned and bobbed his head in what might have been a greeting.

Old fools! Did they think he cared?

The outside door opened again to admit the Viscount Goodrich at almost the same moment that Mary stepped out of the salon, Lord Edmond's card in one hand.

"Ma'am?" The viscount made his best bow to her before noticing either her frown or the fact that Lord Edmond Waite stood silently in the shadows.

"Ah," Lord Edmond said. "The eternal triangle."

The viscount turned sharply in his direction, and his eyes narrowed. "Lady Mornington," he said, "is Lord Edmond Waite an invited guest?"

"I send out no invitations for these evenings," she said.

"Do you want him here?" he asked.

She did not reply.

"Waite," the viscount said, "you may leave under your own power or you may choose to be thrown out. It is all the same to me, though I think perhaps I would prefer the latter. Which is it to be?"

"The second, if you wish to have your nose flattened

in line with the rest of your face," Lord Edmond said coolly. "I was unaware that this is your house, Good-rich. I wish for a word with Lady Mornington. I am awaiting her answer."

"Her answer is no," the viscount said. "You have five seconds to take yourself off."

"Mary?" Lord Edmond spoke quietly and unhurriedly.

"I shall talk with him for a minute, my lord," she said. "I thank you for your concern, but I am in my own house and quite safe." She looked at Lord Edmond all the while she spoke.

"Perhaps I should stay with you to make sure of that," the viscount said, and Lord Edmond smiled into Mary's eyes.

"Thank you," she said, "but that will not be necessary."

"Scurry out of range of my fists while you still may," Lord Edmond said.

"And that will not be necessary, either," she said firmly. "There will be no violence or talk of violence in my home, gentlemen. Lord Goodrich, you will find several people gathered in the salon already. Lord Edmond, will you step this way, please?"

She led him across the hallway and into what must be a morning room. There was an escritoire against one window, its surface strewn with papers, several books carelessly scattered on tables, and an embroidery frame with a mound of many-colored silks on the arm of the chair before which it stood. It was clearly a room that was lived in. A feminine and cozy room.

She turned to face him as he closed the door quietly behind his back. "What is the meaning of this?" She held up his card in one hand.

"That if you were from home this time I would be obliged to kidnap you?" he said. "I hoped that it would provoke exactly what it has provoked. I hoped that you would admit me."

"To my salon?" she said. "You know you need no invitation there, my lord. You would not have been turned away. Though of course you would have been unwelcome."

"Mary," he said, "you do not know how you wound me. I am human. I have feelings."

She laughed shortly. "Well, bless my soul," she said, "and so do I."

"I have given up gaming and drinking and whoring," he said. "They have had no attraction for me in the past week. I took a girl to the room where I took you, Mary, and could do nothing with her except send her home with a handsome fee clutched in her hand. I could not lay her on the bed where you had lain and do with her the things I did with you."

She flushed. He watched her swallow. "The great reformation," she said. "Thirty years or more of debauchery wiped out in one week of abstemious living, and now you are worthy to take me as a mistress. Am I to fall into your arms?"

"If you wish," he said. "I would be surprised, but I would close them about you fast enough."

She laughed again. "Get out," she said, "and stop wasting my time. I have guests to entertain."

"Not quite thirty years," he said. "But a goodly number, I will admit. A week has been more than an eternity. More than a week. Will you give me a chance, Mary?"

"A chance?" She laughed incredulously. "A chance for what?"

He shrugged. "A chance to show you that you will not have a drunken womanizer for a lover," he said. "A chance to show you that there is more to me than you know?"

She closed her eyes. "I cannot believe this is happening," she said. "You try to convince me that a miraculous transformation has happened in your life, and yet you can scribble on the back of your card that you will kidnap me if I will not speak with you, and you threaten Lord Goodrich, who would protect me, with violence?"

"He was the first to offer to throw me out," he said.

"Because he knew you were uninvited and unwelcome," she said. "Because he cares for me."

"You are sleeping with him?" he asked.

Her eyes widened and her flush returned. "Get out of here," she hissed at him.

"I will kill him if you are," he said.

She clamped her teeth together, grasped one side of her gown, and moved sharply around him toward the door. But he set one hand on her arm and whirled her around to face him. And he set his mouth to hers, releasing his hold on her for a moment—a moment during which she might have broken away but did not—in order to encircle her with his arms and draw her against him.

She kissed him back with fierce passion for a few seconds and then gradually went limp in his arms. She was crying when he lifted his head, and shaking with sobs.

"I hate you," she said when she could. "And I am so afraid of you. I no longer know what to do, I am so afraid."

He drew her against him and held her there with arms like steel bands.

"Why?" he asked. "Because I want you? Because I have killed? Because you want me?"

"Because you will not take no for an answer," she said. "Because nothing I say or do will persuade you that I want nothing to do with you. Because I am afraid I will never be free of you."

"And because part of you does not want to be?" he said. "Give in to it, Mary. Come to bed with me. Be my mistress. Let me prove to you that I am no monster and that what happened between us less than three weeks ago was merely the prelude to a glorious liaison."

"You see what I mean?" she said, and she was crying noisily again against his cravat.

He held her to him, rocking her until she was quiet.

"Give me one small chance," he said. "Come out with me tomorrow. There is a garden party at Richmond. Lady Eleanor Varley's—my aunt. There is no one more respectable in England. The only less-than-respectable thing she ever did was continue to associate with me when . . . well, after I had killed my brother and mother. She was the only one—the only one." He set his cheek against the top of her head and inhaled deeply. "Come with me there, Mary."

She did not answer for a long while. But finally she lifted her head and looked up at him with reddened eyes. "Yes, I will," she said so that his arms tightened about her again. "On one condition."

"What?" he said.

"That after tomorrow," she said, "if I still feel as I do now—and I warn you that nothing on this earth can change my mind—you will accept my rejection and leave me alone."

He considered. "I don't think I can do that, Mary," he said.

"Then I will not come," she said.

He stared into her eyes for a long moment. "Very well," he said at last. "I promise."

He watched her eyes light up in triumph and swallowed against what felt like a lump in his throat.

"I shall come for you soon after luncheon," he said.

"Yes." She smiled at him. "I shall be ready."

"And eager for the end of the day and the end of an affair that was never quite an affair," he said.

"Yes." She continued to smile.

He dropped his arms to his sides. He felt rather as if every part of his body was made of lead. Including his heart. What had he promised? What had he done? He set one hand on the knob of the door and paused to look back at her.

"I would bathe my eyes with cold water before returning to the salon if I were you," he said.

She was still smiling. "Yes," she said.

"Good night, Mary," he said.

"Good night, my lord."

He left the room, leaving the door open behind him.

7

IT WAS A BEAUTIFUL DAY. OF COURSE, MARY thought, it would have to be. It was just too much to hope that anything would happen to put a stop to Lady Eleanor Varley's garden party. The sun was shining from a cloudless sky. And it was hot without being oppressively so, she discovered during a late-morning visit to the library.

She would really rather be doing anything today but what she was preparing to do, but she cheered herself with the thought that it was for the last time. Once the day was over, then so would be all the unpleasant train of events that had begun with the thunderstorm at Vauxhall—if he was anything at all of a gentleman, of course. If he kept his promise. Strangely, the night before she had not considered that perhaps he had promised only because promises meant nothing to him. She had believed him.

Penelope had been disturbed. Lord Goodrich must have told her that Lord Edmond had come to the house and that she was talking privately with him.

"Mary," she had said, "he has a *tendre* for you. Are you quite sure you do not return his regard? Oh, please say that you do not. You can only end up being hurt."

"I have no *tendre* for him," Mary had said firmly.

"And he has promised, Penny, that after tomorrow he will leave me alone."

But her friend had looked unconvinced. "It would be better to call on Lord Goodrich's protection," she had said. "Or better still, to betroth yourself to him. Lord Edmond Waite would not be able to argue with that. Though, of course, betrothals mean very little to him, either."

But she could not betroth herself to a man who had not asked her, Mary thought.

The viscount had been vexed. "You should give me leave to give the man a good horsewhipping, Lady Mornington," he had said when she had finally returned to the salon after a lengthy visit to her room to bathe her eyes. "He does not deserve the dignity of a challenge to a duel. And you need not have allowed him to bully you into a private *tête-à-tête*."

"Thank you," she had said, "but I was not bullied."

"You have *what*?" he had said when she told him about the garden party. "You have agreed to allow him to escort you? I can only express my deepest disapproval, ma'am."

But her chin had gone up at that. "I would remind you, my lord," she had said, "that I am free to do as I wish."

He had taken her hand in his then, regardless of the groups of guests gathered in the salon. "My apologies," he had said. "I speak only out of concern for you, ma'am. I can see that Waite has been pressing his attentions on you and that as a lady you have found it difficult to discourage him in a manner that would convince him. Allow me to protect you. Send word that you have a prior engagement with me for tomorrow that you had forgotten about. And let me stay with you tonight in case he comes back."

Oh, no. Not that. Was that all Viscount Goodrich

wanted of her, too? She must seem fair game both to him and to Lord Edmond Waite—and perhaps to others, she supposed. She was a widow and a woman who had apparently taken a lover for several years after her husband's death. For the first time she was feeling sorry that she and Marcus had done nothing to dispel the rumors about them, but had chosen to laugh at them instead. But she was not a woman of easy virtue. They would have to realize that—all of them. And yet, she had thought uneasily, she was a woman who had spent a night in the vulgar love nest of a notorious libertine— with no coercion at all.

"Thank you," she had said, "but I have accepted Lord Edmond's invitation, and I have no fears for my safety."

He had released her hand and they had both turned to mingle with the guests.

Mary had chosen a bright yellow dress for the garden party. She had even had her maid take it out of her wardrobe and iron it. But she changed her mind at the last moment and dressed in her blue sprigged muslin. He had said that she looked better in pale colors, she thought unwillingly. That had nothing to do with her change of heart, of course. It was just that she had always wondered if yellow was her color. She had a suspicion that perhaps it made her complexion look sallow.

He came earlier than she had expected, though she was ready. The afternoon had scarcely begun. She slid her feet into her blue slippers, tied the blue ribbons of her straw bonnet with the cornflower-trimmed brim, and drew on her gloves. She was pleased with the effect when she glanced at herself in the mirror.

He seemed pleased, too. His eyes moved over her in open appraisal as she descended the stairs. It was not a gentlemanly thing to do, but she no longer expected him to behave like a gentleman.

"You look lovely, Mary," he said, reaching out a hand

for hers as she stepped down onto the bottom stair. "Like a delicate flower."

"Thank you," she said, placing her hand in his. They looked rather as if they had coordinated their appearances, she thought. He wore a coat of blue superfine over buff-colored pantaloons and shining white-topped Hessians. She felt almost like returning the compliment. Despite his rather narrow face, with its prominent nose and thin lips, he was a handsome man. And his blue eyes, though too pale, were a distinguishing feature. They were compelling.

"You are ready?" he said. "I feared perhaps I was early. But I thought we might arrive before the masses so that you may talk with my aunt at some leisure. Do you know her? I believe you will deal famously together."

"I know her by sight," she said. "We have never met."

Lady Eleanor Varley was a high stickler, known for her strong opinions and forthright manner. Mary had not known that she was Lord Edmond's aunt—and one who had not cut him from her acquaintance despite anything. Perhaps she was not such a high stickler after all.

He had brought an open barouche. It was perfect for the weather. It was also very public. She was to be displayed to view, it seemed, as she had been in the park more than two weeks before.

"It is a beautiful day," she said as the barouche moved away from Portman Place.

"Yes, it is," he said. "My aunt doubtless put in a special order for just this weather. But if I have only one day with you, Mary—half a day—I do not intend to spend it talking about the weather."

She looked at him suspiciously. Where was he taking her?

He seemed to read her thoughts. "And no, I do not mean that I am intending to tumble you in some conveniently secluded spot," he said. "I do not believe my aunt sports such places on her grounds. And I have not given clandestine orders to my coachman to take us to my, ah, second residence."

"It is as well," she said. "I would create a very loud scene."

"And it would not serve my purpose anyway," he said. "I have half a day in which to persuade you that perhaps I am worth getting to know after all."

She turned her head away and watched the buildings on the opposite side of the street.

"Tell me about yourself," he said. "Was your marriage to Mornington really a love match? Why did you decide to follow the drum? Why were there no children? Am I being impertinent?"

Of course he was. But at least he had made it possible for the long drive to Richmond to be made with comparative ease. It would have been a difficult task to fill up the time with small talk.

"It was a love match," she said, "although he was twelve years older than I. I went with him to Spain because I was a realist, I suppose. I was not an adventurer and I hate discomfort, both of which facts make it strange that I went. But I knew and accepted that he was likely to be killed before the wars ended, perhaps well before. And I was unwilling to marry him, enjoy a brief honeymoon with him, and then see him go, knowing that perhaps I would never see him again. So I went. And I am glad I did. We had only two years together. But they were good years despite the discomforts."

"But there were no children," he said.

"If I had been with child," she said, "Lawrence would have sent me home. As it was, he felt guilty about the life I was subjected to. He wanted children. We both did. But I would not have any until the wars ended. Afterward I was sorry." She looked down at her gloved hands. "There was a spell after his death—six weeks—when I thought that, after all, perhaps I was to have his child. But it was not so. I really knew him to be dead then. I knew it was the end."

"I am sorry," he said.

"Why should you be?" She raised her head. "You were not responsible for either his death or my false hopes."

"I am sorry that you suffered," he said. "Suffering can kill. Not always physically. But it can kill dreams and it can deaden hope and the will to live."

She looked up at him in some surprise. He described it so well, just as if he knew.

"You have never wanted to marry and have children since?" he asked.

The conversation was becoming very personal. She could hardly believe that she was talking thus with Lord Edmond Waite of all people. But then, why not with him? No other gentleman of her acquaintance would be so unmannerly as to ask her such questions.

"Not for a long time," she said. "It somehow seemed disloyal to Lawrence to think of marrying someone else—as if I had not cared. And I began another life and made new friends. I have had little chance to be lonely."

She could feel him looking at her. He sat relaxed across one corner of the seat, one foot propped on the seat opposite.

"I suppose I should tell you something about my life in return," he said. "The trouble is that there is very little to tell, Mary. Very little that would impress you, anyway. I had a happy childhood."

"Did you?" She turned her head to look fully at him. It was hard to picture him as an innocent child. He was smiling at her rather mockingly.

"We were three boys," he said. "How could we not have been happy? Of course, I was the youngest and might have been at the mercy of the other two. But Dick—he was the middle one, the one I killed—was so sweet-natured that I was never harassed. He would shame Wallace out of bothering me just by looking reproachfully at him. Dick was everyone's favorite, and no one ever resented him for it."

Mary swallowed and looked down at her gloves again.

"Ask it," he said softly.

"You killed him?" She looked up at him. "Surely you cannot mean it."

"Oh, but I do," he said. "I did. And you see? I cannot even talk about my childhood and have you see me as a person worthy of knowing. You want to know what happened."

"Yes." She bit her lip.

"It was the day after my birthday," he said. "My twenty-first. I had been drinking all day and all night and decided to clear my head with a brisk gallop. Dick tried to dissuade me—said I was still foxed and would do myself some harm." He laughed. "When I insisted, he came with me. He had not taken one drop beyond the glass with which he had toasted me at dinner, of course. I cleared a gate that should have been unclearable—at full gallop. I was watching and laughing when Dick came over after me. He broke his neck."

Mary tasted blood.

"They would not have allowed me to attend the funeral," he said. He laughed. "Not that I was around to attend it anyway. I took myself off from there as fast as I could, and never went back."

It was horrible. She did not know what to say. And yet it was not as bad as she had imagined. It had not been a cold-blooded murder. But it was also worse than she had imagined. How he must have suffered.

"And then there was my mother," he said. "You will want to know about that, too."

"Not if it is painful," she said.

He laughed. "She died of consumption a little more than a month after Dick," he said. "My father had taken her to Italy for a winter, and they were both convinced when they returned that she had recovered. She seemed better, too, I must admit. But she outlasted Dick by less than five weeks. He was her favorite, you see, as he was everyone else's. So I killed her, too."

"You say it almost with pride," she said. "As if you really wish people to see you as a murderer. Strictly speaking, you are not."

"Ah, but I am," he said, "in the popular estimation. And why fight public opinion, Mary? The truth of the matter is that Dick would be alive now if it had not been for me. And perhaps my mother, too. Fifteen years they have missed because of me."

"And yet you behave as if you do not care," she said. "For fifteen years you have behaved as if you do not care. *Do* you?"

He was grinning at her, she saw. And yet the mockery was still in his eyes. "I have a quarrel with learned and intelligent people," he said. "You like to read and to exercise your mind, do you not? You like to converse with other people like yourself. And you pride yourself on your wisdom. Or perhaps I do you an injustice there. Perhaps you do not even pretend to be wise. Wisdom does not come from books, Mary."

"Has the subject been changed?" she asked.

"By no means," he said. "I am merely saying that you would not have asked your question if you had any of the wisdom that perhaps you imagine you have."

"But you have not given up drinking," she said, "or any of the other excesses that must have led to that accident. I would have thought you would have given it all up out of remorse. You might have shown your family your sorrow. Perhaps by now you would have been reconciled with them."

He laughed at her.

"It does not matter to you, does it?" she said. "Nothing matters."

"I remained true to one thing, at least, for many years," he said. "I remained true to my obligation to Dorothea."

"Perhaps it would have been better if you had not," she said.

"Undoubtedly," he said. "I would not have had to escort an iceberg about London several times."

"You are not even sorry about that," she said indignantly. "And yet you say that you wish me to see you as a worthy companion? I can see nothing worthy at all, my lord."

"No." He spread one arm along the side of the barouche and the other along the back of the seat, almost touching her shoulder with his fingers. "There appears to be nothing there to see, does there? Perhaps we should have confined our conversation to the weather after all."

"Yes," she said. "Or perhaps you should see that any interest you may have in me is ridiculous. Perhaps there are some women who would admire your lack of conscience and see something manly in it."

"There are plenty of women who admire the fatness of my purse," he said, "and are willing to perform for a portion of its contents."

She flushed and turned her head away.

"But none of them has ever been as good in bed as you, Mary," he said. "I cannot forget that. I want you there again. I want to make love to you."

She turned her head sharply to look at him in anger. "Perhaps you should offer me payment, too, then," she said. "Only, more than you have ever offered before, to match my superior performance."

"Would you come to bed with me for money?" he asked her, his eyes glinting beneath narrowed lids. "You could name your price, Mary. Would you be my whore?"

"No," she said. "Not your whore or anything else. I think you should take me back home, my lord. We are going to do nothing but wrangle all afternoon."

"But you have promised me the whole of it," he said. "And you see what you have done to me, Mary? I set out to impress you, to convince you that really I am not so bad once you get to know me. And yet somehow once again you have maneuvered me into acting deliberately to shock you. How do you do it?"

"Perhaps by holding up a mirror to you," she said, "so that you can see yourself as you really are."

He stared at her through narrowed lids for a long moment.

"You are vastly accomplished at giving setdowns," he said. "Do you ever consider the pain you give with them, Mary?"

"I never seem to feel obliged to set down anyone but you," she said. "And I think you are incapable of feeling pain."

"Another one," he said, "hot on the heels of the last. Are you going to marry Goodrich?"

"That is none of your concern," she said.

"Ah, yes, it is," he said. "I would not be willing to share you with a husband, Mary. No, don't say it." He held up a staying hand. "Are you going to marry him?"

"He has not asked me," she said.

"He will," he said. "You are respectable enough to be married, despite the lapse with Clifton. And I believe the man is on the lookout for a leg shackle. Don't marry him."

"Why not?" She could not resist the question.

"No passion," he said. "The man would not be good in bed."

"Is that all that matters?" she asked scornfully. "Do you think that is the all-important thing in marriage?"

He considered. "No," he said. "I suppose if I were considering marriage—as you probably know I was, not so long ago—I would consider looks and breeding capability. And I would be careful not to choose a shrew or a giggler or someone who has to drag about a large canvas bag full of hartshorn and lavender water and whatnot. And I would not want a timid little thing without a tongue in her head. Or someone who gazed at me reproachfully whenever I arrived home after midnight. But bedworthiness is important, too, Mary, despite your scorn for the physical. I could not stomach making love to a cold fish for the rest of my life—or even to a warm fish. She would have to be like you."

"But I would never marry you," she said.

"Certainly you would not," he said, "because I would never ask you. You see how well I learn from you, Mary? That was a setdown almost worthy of you, was it not?"

She smiled despite herself.

"You are pretty when you smile," he said.

"And am not when I do not?" she asked.

"No," he said.

She raised her eyebrows.

He laughed. "You will never get the expected answers out of me, Mary," he said. "I am not a gentleman, remember? You are not pretty. At least, I have never thought you so. I had never thought you attractive or worthy of a second glance until almost three weeks ago. It is strange how one's perceptions can change. Actually, you have looked remarkably pretty to me in the last three weeks, though I know with my mind that you are not. Now, which would you prefer? Mind, which you so value? Or intuition, which you scorn?"

"Your opinion does not matter at all to me," she said. "I do not care how you see me."

"Very well, then," he said. "You are too short and too flat-bosomed and remarkably plain of features. Let us have some plain speaking."

"And you are no gentleman," she said, stung, glaring at him, "at the risk of repeating myself."

"But, Mary," he said calmly, "you do not care what I think of you."

"That's true enough," she said crossly, turning to stare rigidly forward to the horses' heads. She stiffened when she felt the backs of two of his fingers caress her cheek briefly.

"You look lovely to me even when you do not smile," he said softly. "And if your body has imperfections, then I certainly did not notice them three weeks ago. Nor did they mar my great pleasure in you."

She closed her eyes. It did not matter, she told herself determinedly. His opinion did not matter. Whether he found her beautiful or whether he found her ugly—it was all the same to her. She had been hurt only because the words had been brutal and unmannerly. And it did not matter how well he had been pleased by what had once happened between them. *My great pleasure in you.* It did not matter. She did not care. She wanted only to forget.

He sat up suddenly so that his shoulder almost touched hers, and he took her hand in a firm clasp and held it on the seat between them.

"We are almost there," he said. "Time is slipping fast already. Too fast for me. Too slow for you. Right?"

"Right," she said.

For some reason she was remembering sitting beside him during the storm, trying to control herself, trying not to show him her fear. She was remembering trying to climb into him when her control snapped. And the way he had scooped her up onto his lap and proceeded to comfort her in any and all possible ways. A woman he had never considered either pretty or attractive. Just someone who needed comforting.

Was he the sort of man to do something merely to comfort another person?

She was about to ask him, but she was a little afraid of his answer.

LADY ELEANOR VARLEY'S house was set in extensive grounds in Richmond. Long lawns interspersed with flower beds and shrubberies sloped gently to the banks of the River Thames. Long tables set with crisp white cloths had been set out on the upper lawn just below the terrace. Servants were carrying out trays of food and large bowls of drink. Four early arrivals were strolling down beside the river. Four others were playing croquet on the lawn beside the house.

Lord Edmond handed Mary from the barouche but did not lead her immediately to the garden. He took her indoors to where his aunt was standing in the middle of a morning room, its French windows onto the terrace thrown wide, giving orders to a harassed pair of servants.

"I might as well do it all myself and save myself the cost of servants," she said, shaking her head. And then she spotted her nephew. "Ah, Edmond, dear, there you are. I was not looking for you for at least another three hours. You are always notoriously late."

"Your usual exuberant welcome, Aunt," he said, setting his hands on her shoulders and kissing her cheek. "I am on my best behavior today. I have Lady Mornington with me."

"Ah." Lady Eleanor held out her hand. "Lady Mornington. Welcome. I have been wanting to meet you this age. I keep meaning to attend one of your literary evenings, since the Clements are always full of enthusiasm about them. But I never seem to get around to it. I have seen you somewhere before."

"We have occasionally been in attendance at the same ball or assembly," Mary said, shaking hands with her hostess.

"And since when are you back with the literary set, Edmond?" his aunt asked. "It is about time, I must say."

"I am not with any set," Lord Edmond said. "I am with Lady Mornington, Aunt. I coerced her into accompanying me here today."

"Coerced?" Lady Eleanor chuckled. "That is probably true, too, dear. Any lady takes her reputation in her own hands when she is seen with you. I take it you know about the Lady Dorothea Page and the Lady Wren episodes, Lady Mornington? Shocking businesses, both. Though as for Dorothea, I must say Edmond is well rid of her. The girl will rule the man who finally takes her to the altar. And these marriages that are arranged from the cradle are ridiculous affairs, in my estimation. No chance of success at all. What do you think, my dear?"

"I am very glad that no marriage was ever arranged for me," Mary said. "I do not believe I could marry where my feelings were not engaged and where I did not feel liking and respect."

"Very sensible," Lady Eleanor said. "Now, take my arm, my dear, and we shall step outside, where I should have been this past hour. Tell me who has been at your salon for the past few weeks. Whom have I been missing? And who is to be there next? Tempt me. Perhaps I shall look in on you."

"And what am I to do, Aunt?" Lord Edmond asked. "Trot along behind like a faithful lapdog?"

"You may run along and bully the servants, Edmond," she said. "They should have had all the tables set long before now. Growl at them, dear. You are so very good at growling. It will be far more effective than my nagging. When I nag at my servants, they invariably proceed to do exactly what they were doing before, which is not a great deal. Do you have any trouble managing your servants, Lady Mornington?"

The two ladies walked arm in arm out to the terrace, and Lord Edmond was left in the middle of the morning room, scratching his head.

8

*I*T WAS NOT WORKING WELL AT ALL. SHE WAS THE only woman he had ever really wanted to impress, and it was impossible to impress her. Oh, he had wooed other women, but he had always done so with confidence, playing by the rules of the seduction game that he had learned over the years. Only once had he failed—with Felicity. But then, he could not recall wanting to impress Felicity. He had only wanted to lure her to his bed, and had been willing to do so even at the price of a leg shackle. He wanted to impress Mary, to make her like him, respect him, think him worth knowing and perhaps loving.

But it was not working. There was nothing to impress her with, he was realizing. There was nothing likable or worthy of respect about him. Was there really nothing? Had his life been so utterly worthless? Had he so hated himself that he had wasted fifteen years of his life—all his young manhood? He remembered with a jolt that she had commented on the fact that he hated himself.

He had nothing to offer her beyond a certain expertise in bed. It had always been enough with women—enough to please them and enough to satisfy himself. It had pleased Mary, too, but she was not the type of woman to wish to build a whole relationship on that alone. And she was right. No relationship could thrive on just sex.

But did he want a relationship? he asked himself, and laughed inwardly. He was incapable of having a relationship.

After half an hour he managed to detach her from his aunt's side. He had thought the two of them would get along famously, but he had not expected that they would leap into such instant friendship. He took her walking down by the river, and when there was a boat free, he rowed her out onto the water. By his request she told him about Spain, and he listened, fascinated, to her accounts of various campaigns and the endless marches to and fro across the Peninsula. He had heard some of the stories before, but never from a woman's point of view.

But it was a one-sided conversation. He had nothing to tell her. Nothing beyond his twenty-first year, and before that time his life had been so wrapped up with family that it was difficult to tell any story that did not involve Dick. And as soon as he mentioned Dick, she would be reminded of how he had killed him as a result of a drunken debauch.

He looked at himself through her eyes and saw a worthless fellow, someone who had done nothing that he might lay with pride at the feet of his chosen woman. Chosen? For what? For his mistress? That was what he had wanted. She attracted him and had proved to him already that she could satisfy him more fully than any other woman he had had.

Had wanted? Was that no longer enough? No, it was not, he realized with numbing shock. It would not be enough to have Mary only in bed, to take her to his house once or twice a week, to stay at hers once or twice more. Not nearly enough. He wanted her in his life, an integral part of it. A part of him. He wanted her as his wife.

"Shall we stroll up to the house?" he suggested when he handed her out of the boat. "You are probably ready for some tea. Perhaps there will be another couple who will wish to join us in a game of croquet."

He no longer wanted to be alone with her. Knowing what he now knew, he realized even more the impossibility of the whole situation. His wife! He would see the scorn in her eyes if he so much as hinted at such a thing. And it would be like the lash of a whip. He would be quite defenseless against it.

"Yes," she said, taking his arm. "That would be pleasant."

The poke of her bonnet reached barely to his chin. She was light and dainty, like one of the delicate flowers on her bonnet. The thought amazed him. If someone had told him a little more than two weeks before that he would ever look at Lady Mornington and compare her to a delicate flower, he would have chuckled with vast amusement. It was hard to remember how he had used to view her.

"Are you enjoying yourself?" he asked, and then wished he had not done so. Why invite one of the setdowns she was so good at?

"It is very pleasant," she said. "The surroundings are lovely and the weather perfect. Your aunt is very amiable. I am pleased to have made her acquaintance at last."

She was also good at diplomacy.

"Ah," he said. "So I have done something that meets with your approval, Mary. I have effected a meeting between the two of you."

"Yes," she said. "Thank you."

She had said not one cross or scornful word to him since their arrival. It was as if she had decided that since this was the last day she would have to spend with him, she would be pleasant. She had been scrupulously polite. She seemed to have surrounded herself with an impregnable armor. And there was so little of the day left.

But it was just as well, he thought. It would be as well

when the day was over and he could return to normal living again. There was a new actress at the Drury Lane, a tall brunette who played some of the more minor roles. He had heard that Crompton had taken her under his protection already. But he would oust the opposition with no trouble at all—Crompton was nothing but a gauche boy with a fortune too large for his own good—and enjoy the girl for a few days, or a few weeks if she pleased him.

It would be a relief to return to normal life. He would feel safe again.

They were not alone again for the rest of the afternoon. They played croquet in company with several other couples and then had tea on the upper lawn with the same people. They were all very merry. No one in the group noticeably shunned him. He supposed they would not feel it appropriate to do so, considering his relationship to their hostess.

A few people were already taking their leave. He would have to order around the barouche soon, he thought with mingled regret and relief. The day was all but over. And nothing whatsoever had happened in it to make her want to repeat the experience. Quite the contrary, in fact.

They strolled up to the terrace with two couples with whom they had been having tea, and waved their carriage on its way.

"So, Mary," he said, "the day nears its end."

"Yes," she said.

But before either of them could say more, his aunt stepped between them and took an arm of each.

"I do believe the party has been a success," she said, "for which I have the weather and your growls to be thankful for, Edmond. The servants actually behaved like real servants."

Actually, Lord Edmond thought, pursing his lips, his

aunt's servants probably found it far easier to perform their duties when she was not constantly hovering in their vicinity giving confusing and contradictory orders. All he had done earlier in the afternoon was stroll up to her butler and say quietly, "Growl. Now I have followed her ladyship's instructions, Soames, and you may go about your business without further interruption."

The butler had grinned at him for a moment before remembering that he was a butler and pokering up quite as if he had never in his life been taught to smile. "Yes, my lord," he said. "Thank you, my lord."

"But I shan't be sorry to see everyone on the way and to be quiet again," Lady Eleanor said. "I have scarcely had a chance to exchange a dozen words with either Lady Mornington or you, dear."

"I shall summon the barouche without a moment's delay," Lord Edmond said. "Never let it be said that I cannot take a hint, Aunt."

"Oh." She laughed merrily. "I would not be so rag-mannered, dear. I merely meant that I shall be glad to have the two of you to myself for a few hours. You will, of course, be staying for dinner."

Sweet, seductive idea. "I invited Lady Mornington for the afternoon," he said. "Perhaps she has other plans for dinner and the evening."

"There is one easy way of finding out," she said, turning to smile at Mary. "Do you have another engagement, my dear? I do hope not, as I have looked forward all afternoon to having a pleasant conversation with you over dinner. Do please stay. *Do* you have other plans?"

Her eyes met his across his aunt for a moment. She thought he had arranged this, he thought. She thought he was not playing fair.

"I have the barouche with me, Aunt," he said. "It is not very suitable for night travel."

"Then you shall take one of my carriages," she said,

"and return it to make the exchange some other day. Do not make difficulties where there are none, Edmond. Lady Mornington?"

"I would be pleased to accept your invitation, ma'am," she said.

His heart leapt with gladness—at a mere delay of the inevitable. He smiled at her, and then thought that the smile would convince her even more that he had arranged it all.

And so after everyone had left, the three of them strolled again down by the river before Lady Eleanor retired to her room to change for dinner and had Mary directed to a guest room to freshen up. And they sat down to dinner together, a long leisurely meal followed by coffee in the drawing room. Conversation did not flag for a single moment.

"You are remarkably quiet, Edmond," his aunt said at one point during dinner. "I can remember the time when your papa used to have to frown at you and warn you *sotto voce* not to monopolize the conversation when it was on topics to your liking."

He smiled. "I am enjoying listening to you and Mary exchange views, Aunt," he said. "I like it when people do not always feel obliged to agree with each other."

"Oh, I believe Lady Mornington and I respect each other's minds too much to do anything so silly," she said. "Is that not right, my dear?"

"And how dull conversation would be," Mary said, "if people always agreed with each other."

"Beasley and the crowd gathered about him at your salon," he could not resist saying.

"What was that, dear?" Lady Eleanor asked, and he was obliged to explain to her what had happened at Mary's house.

"I called the man an ass when I could stand it no longer," he said. "Mary was forced to take me aside and scold me roundly."

"Mr. Beasley?" his aunt said. "He *is* one, dear, but you should never have said so in quite that way. And in the hearing of ladies? I wonder Lady Mornington did not have you thrown out. Edmond hates humbug, my dear, and sometimes is not too careful about how he shows it. It is hard to believe, is it not, that he was in a fair way to becoming one himself once upon a time?"

"A humbug?" he said. "Surely someone would have done me the kindness to shoot me. Instead I did myself the favor of having myself tossed out of Oxford on my ear. Did you know that unsavory fact about me, Mary?"

"There were extenuating circumstances," his aunt said, but he was smiling at Mary. One more nail in the coffin of his faded hopes.

"No, I did not," she said.

But his aunt did not pursue the topic, he was thankful to find. The conversation resumed where it had left off, in a discussion of Wordworth's poetry, which Mary loved and his aunt considered sentimental drivel.

It was late dusk already when they finally took their leave. Too late and too chill for the barouche. Lady Eleanor's traveling carriage was brought around, and she insisted on lending Mary a warm woolen shawl and on having some heavy rugs put inside the carriage to cover her lap.

"Nights can be quite chilly after such warm days," she said, "when there is no cloud cover to keep in the heat. I have enjoyed the latter part of the day more than I can say, dears. You must have Edmond bring you again, Lady Mornington. This has been too pleasant an evening not to be repeated."

"I have enjoyed it, too," Mary said, submitting to having her cheek kissed by Lady Eleanor.

"I did not know you had enough sense left to escort

someone of Lady Mornington's caliber, dear," his aunt said, turning to Lord Edmond to give him a matching kiss. "I am so glad. It is time my favorite nephew came back from the unpromised land where he has exiled himself altogether too long."

"It was a mere garden party, Aunt," he said.

But she patted one of his cheeks and smiled at him.

The carriage was plushly upholstered inside with green and gold velvet.

"You are warm enough?" he asked Mary as he took a seat beside her. "Do you want one of the rugs over you?"

"No," she said. "The shawl is enough, thank you."

The carriage jolted into motion and they both turned to wave to his aunt, who had come out onto the terrace with them.

And suddenly the interior of the carriage seemed very confined. And very quiet.

SHE HAD NOT bargained on the intimacy of a return home in darkness and inside a closed carriage. She was embarrassed and not at all sure that there was anything else left to talk about.

"Was this all your idea?" she asked.

"No, it was not," he said. "It might have been, I must confess. I have been known to maneuver as deviously. But it was not."

"Oh," she said.

They lapsed into silence.

Just the long drive back into town, she thought. It was almost at an end. And surely he would keep his word. Surely he would. He must have realized during the course of the afternoon that they had nothing in common. And he had been quite unable to participate in the conversation at dinner and in the drawing room afterward. Indeed, much as she had liked Lady Eleanor, she had thought that perhaps their hostess had been rather ill-mannered to choose topics of conversation about which he seemed to know nothing.

She wished it were at an end already. She wished they had not stayed for dinner. By now she would have been at home, all her associations with Lord Edmond Waite just a bad dream.

And then his hand reached across and took hers in a warm clasp.

"A penny for them, Mary," he said.

"Nothing," she said. "I was thinking back over the day, that was all. I like your aunt."

"And she you," he said. "She will wish to continue the acquaintance."

"She will be welcome to attend one of my literary evenings," she said quickly. "I believe I will send her an invitation."

"She wants me to take you there again," he said, and she could see in the near-darkness that he looked at her and smiled.

Oh, no, she thought. She had not seriously considered what she would do if he turned out to be a totally dishonorable man. What if, after all, he continued to pursue her? She turned her head away and dared not ask him. How would she know if he spoke the truth anyway?

They rode for some minutes in silence, until he released her hand and put his arm about her shoulders.

"Please don't," she said, keeping her head turned away from him.

"The day is almost at an end," he said. "Perhaps there is half an hour or a little more left. It is almost over."

"Yes," she said.

"You will be glad?"

"Yes."

His free hand came beneath her chin and turned her

face toward him. She could hardly see him in the darkness. Except that his face was very close to hers.

"Don't." She could hear that her voice was trembling.

"So little time, Mary," he said. "Half an hour. How many years do I have left, do you suppose? Twenty? Thirty? Forty? Even if it is only ten or five—or one— half an hour is such a little time to have left before all the emptiness."

"Don't talk like that," she said crossly. "Am I to believe that you have conceived a grand passion for me? Am I to feel sorry for you? You want to bed me. That is all. And I will not be bedded."

"Mary." His hand pulled loose the ribbons of her bonnet and tossed it aside before she realized what he was about. "Give me that half-hour of your time. That is all I ask. I will not bed you here, though the conditions are tempting. I promise. Just give me that half-hour."

Sometimes she tired of fighting. It would be such a relief not to have to fight any longer—after the next half-hour was over. But first there was the half-hour. She let her head relax sideways against his arm and closed her eyes as his hand lightly caressed her cheek and her ear. His thumb feathered across her closed eye, across her eyebrow. Across her mouth.

"Mary."

There was a lump in her throat. She tried to swallow it. She wanted to fight when his mouth took the place of his thumb, first against her eyelid, and then lightly, and closed, against her own mouth.

"Mary."

And she wanted just to stay still and let it happen. It was hard to believe that she had allowed so much at Vauxhall and afterward. She could no longer remember quite why she had done so or quite how pleasurable it had been. When it was dark, as it was now, and when she closed her eyes and her mind to the identity of her companion, when she allowed herself only to feel and not to think at all, she could feel the urge to give in to his caresses.

His tongue was tracing the outline of her lips, sending sensation sizzling through her. It was too raw a feeling. She parted her lips to imprison his tongue between, and opened her mouth to suck it inside. He moaned.

It was so good sometimes just to feel, not to think or to reason. So very good to feel a man's strong arm about her, to feel his other hand stroking over the side of her head and down over her shoulder to her breast, lifting to slide inside her dress, warm and slightly rough over her soft skin. To feel his thumb rubbing over her nipple until that raw ache began again. It was good to feel a man's mouth wide on hers, his tongue exploring and caressing inside.

It felt good to want and know oneself wanted. Good to feel totally and merely woman.

"Mary," he was saying into her ear. "Oh, my God, Mary."

And she knew again who he was. It was impossible to block thought for more than a few brief minutes. But she did not much care, she thought, lifting her hand from his shoulder and running her fingers lightly through his hair.

"I will not bed you against your will," he said. He was running one hand hard up and down her arm. Her shawl seemed to have disappeared. "Tell me you do not want it."

"I do not want it," she lied.

He pressed her head into his shoulder and held it there with one firm hand. His arm about her held her like a vise. They rode thus the rest of the way home. And he held her so for a few moments after the carriage had come to a halt, while the coachman opened the door, set down the steps, and discreetly withdrew.

She did not know whether he had had her conveyed to her own home or to his love nest. She did not much care.

"Mary." He released his hold on her head so that she tipped it back to look up at him. She could see his face dimly in the light from the street—her street. "I must ask you now, though I know the answer. Will you see me again?"

She swallowed and heard an embarrassing gurgle in her throat. She shook her head and watched his jaw harden.

"There is nothing else but this," she said. "I cannot explain this, my lord, but it is all there is. There is nothing else. This is not enough."

"No, it is not," he said unexpectedly. "If you can find nothing else in me to want but my lovemaking, Mary, then I do not want to see you again, either. I have a life to get on with."

She looked at him rather uncertainly and made to move away from him, but the arm about her shoulders tightened.

"I wanted you to want me," he said fiercely. "*Me*, Mary, despite everything. But it was a foolish wish, was it not? And now I reap the final harvest of that night of drunkenness. The final punishment. The final hell. If I could go back and change things, I would do it, you know. Do you think I would not change things if I could? For Dick, Mary? And for you. I would change the last fifteen years for you if I could, relive them, put something of some worth into them. But I cannot. And so I have nothing whatsoever to offer you except the ability to give you pleasure, learned appropriately enough in the beds of countless whores. I want to offer you all the precious things the world has to offer, and all I can give you is that." He laughed harshly.

She stared at him, dumbfounded.

"You did not suspect that a man like me was capable of love, did you?" he said. "It will work to your advantage, though, Mary. I will stay away from you. I will keep my promise to you because I love you. You have nothing more to fear from me, you see."

He lifted his arm clumsily away from her and jumped out of the carriage. He turned to lift her down, not waiting for her to set her feet on the steps. The front door of the house was already open.

"Go, then," he said, sliding his hands hard down her arms and gripping both hands hard enough to hurt. "And be happy, Mary. That is all I want for you. Please, be happy."

He squeezed her hands even more tightly and raised one of them rather jerkily to his lips before releasing both and jumping back inside the carriage without even waiting for her to disappear into the house.

THE CARRIAGE TOOK him to Watier's, as instructed. He sat inside, still and silent, for five whole minutes after the coachman had opened the door and stood politely to one side, waiting for him to descend.

"Take me home," he said at last.

He did not want to be alone. But he certainly did not want to be in company. And it seemed there were no other choices.

"Bring the brandy decanter to my dressing room," he told his butler as he passed him in the hallway of his home and began to ascend the stairs. "No." He stopped. "Bring two."

He filled a glass to the brim when the decanters arrived, and took a large gulp of brandy, which burned its way down his throat and into his stomach. And then he stared down into the liquid for a long while. His worst enemy. He had proved it before. It had helped him kill Dick. It had made a terrifying hell out of the months that had followed. He had used it since then only in public, as part of the image he had chosen to give the world of a man who really did not give a damn.

Was he to use it again now in private—his worst enemy in the guise of a friend? Always in the guise of a friend, but in reality nothing but the archenemy. Nothing but the devil himself.

His glass shattered against the washstand a little distance away from him. The two decanters would have followed, but at the last moment he had mercy on the poor maids who would have to clean up the mess. Already it was bad enough.

He got to his feet and wandered through into his bedchamber. So what really had happened? He had been rejected by an unlovely and unattractive bluestocking, and one of not quite impeccable virtue, either. She was no great loss. If he could just force his mind back to three weeks ago, before Vauxhall, he would realize that she was no great loss.

He had never believed in love—at least he had not for many weary years. It was no time now to start believing in it. Not at the age of thirty-six, when no decent woman could be expected to afford him a second glance.

What could he do? He must do something to drag himself out of the gloom that assailed him at frequent intervals, this time caused by a foolish infatuation for a woman.

The Season was at an end, to all intents and purposes. He could go to one of the spas as he often did during the summer. Or to Brighton. He thought with distaste of Brighton. He could go to the Continent, travel about for perhaps a year or so. Or he could go down into Hampshire. His estate there was not really far away, and yet it was almost two years since he had been there last.

Perhaps he would go there. It would be soothing perhaps to be in the country with nothing and no one to remind him of a wasted life.

Yes, he thought with sudden decision, he would go into the country—the very next day.

He rang the bell for his valet.

9

MARY WAS ANGRY. A WEEK HAD PASSED SINCE THE garden party at Lady Eleanor's, and he had kept his promise. Oh, he had kept his promise, all right, but in such a way that she began to despair of ever being free of him. He had done it deliberately. Somewhere he was laughing at her, knowing very well what he had done to her.

She hated him with a passion.

In many ways it had been a gratifying week. She had seen Viscount Goodrich every day or evening— sometimes both—and he had been flattering in his attentions to her. If he had indeed hoped to make her his mistress the week before, he had not pressed the matter since. He had even apologized to her the day after the garden party. He had called on her during the morning.

"You are not well?" he asked her after they had greeted each other. He was looking closely at her.

She had cried for an hour the night before, and lain awake for at least another two. She smiled. "Just a little headache," she said. "Nothing some fresh air will not blow away."

And so he took her for a late-morning walk in the park. And asked her politely about the day before. She told him how she had liked Lady Eleanor and how the lady had said she would try to attend Mary's literary evening the following week.

That was when he apologized. He covered the hand that was resting on his arm with his own and looked down at her. "Forgive me for my manner and words two evenings ago," he said. "I was behaving in a possessive manner that I have no right to—yet. And I am afraid the suggestion I made was very improper. Please believe that it arose purely from my deep concern for your safety and peace of mind."

"You are forgiven," she said, smiling at him. "And I was indeed upset that evening. But no longer. I will be seeing no more of Lord Edmond Waite." Strangely the words were like a heavy weight on her shoulders.

He squeezed her hand. "I am glad to hear it, ma'am," he said. "Such a man can only mean you harm. I am convinced that there is not a decent bone in his body."

She did not immediately reply. *I will stay away from you. I will keep my promise to you because I love you.* She did not want to remember those words. After she had cried bitterly over them for a whole hour, she had no longer believed them. She agreed with Lord Goodrich. *And be happy, Mary. That is all I want for you.* No, the man was a fiend. The very devil. How could she be happy?

"I believe you are right," she said.

They went walking and driving together over the coming days, and visited the Tower and Westminster Abbey, where they spent a happy hour reading the tombstones and epitaphs in Poets' Corner. They attended the theater and the opera and a concert in the home of the Earl of Raymore.

He talked to her of his home in Lincolnshire and of his two sons, who were away at school and of whose existence she had not known before. He was very close to declaring himself, she was sure. And she would accept, she had decided. She liked him. Life with him offered stability and security and the chance for a permanent contentment.

She wished that he would kiss her, but he never kissed more than her hand. She wanted him to kiss her. She had some ghosts to banish, and she needed him to banish them. But apart from that one suggestion during her literary evening, his behavior toward her was perfectly correct.

It was a happy week. She was deep into what appeared to be a serious courtship, and her friends approved. Both Penelope and Hannah were relieved at the abrupt ending of her association with Lord Edmond, and delighted with the development of her attachment to the viscount.

She was happy. Lord Goodrich could offer her all the companionship she had known with Marcus—though there had been a very special affection between her and Marcus that had not yet developed with the viscount. But it would develop in time. And Lord Goodrich could offer more. He could offer her the permanency and respectability of marriage, with none of the uncertainties and dangers that had marked her marriage with Lawrence.

She was happy. And yet anger grew in her as the week progressed. Lord Edmond Waite—she had grown to hate the very sound of his name—had proved even less honorable and less of a gentleman than in her worst fears. For if he had continued to pursue her, she could have been righteously angry with him. She could have fought him. And if he had broken off his connection with her as he had promised, she could have been exuberant with the relief of being rid of him. But he had managed to do both and neither.

He had made very sure during that drive home that she had felt again all the unwilling attraction for him that she had denied since Vauxhall. He had played on that attraction until she would gladly have lain with him right there in his aunt's carriage if he had chosen to take her. Or she would have gone with him again to that most vulgar love nest. She did not know quite how he had aroused such feelings of surrender, but he had. And she could not even openly blame him for them. He had used no apparent coercion. Indeed, he had given her a way out and then scrupulously allowed her to take it.

So that she would look back in longing? So that she would continue to ache for him long after he had gone? So that she would forever regret that night, which they might have spent together?

To her horror, she had been quite like a puppet on a string. She had done all of those things. All week, while her mind—her real self—was happy with Lord Goodrich and looked forward to a more permanent relationship with him, her body longed for Lord Edmond.

She had cried and cried for him after he had left her that one evening. For one mad hour she had convinced herself that he really did love her. Worse, she had been convinced that she loved him, too.

The fiend! He had planned it all. And now he very carefully kept himself out of her sight. She looked for him—unwillingly—wherever she went, but never once set eyes on him. He was doing it deliberately. He knew that if she only saw him again, she would see him for what he was and be free of him.

She began to fear that she would never be free of him.

MARY HAD SENT an invitation to Lady Eleanor to attend her next—and last—literary evening. The Season was over and London was emptying fast of people of *ton*. Many people were removing to one of the spas or to the seaside or to their country estates. Lady Eleanor sent an acceptance and the added assurance that she was vastly looking forward to the evening.

Perhaps her nephew would accompany her, Mary thought, and hoped not and tried not to expect such a thing. He would not come, surely, after keeping his promise for almost a whole week. Unless he wanted to see what effect the week of his absence had had on her, of course.

Lady Eleanor came alone. She sat and listened to one of the two poets who had accepted Mary's invitation, and joined in the lengthy and vigorous discussion that followed. And then she sought out Mary.

"A splendid evening, my dear Lady Mornington," she said. "It is a while since I enjoyed myself so much. What a pity that Edmond is not here."

"I have not seen him for almost a week," Mary said.

"He went into the country the day after my garden party," Lady Eleanor said. "Did you not know? I would normally have been glad, since he does not spend a great deal of time on his estate and needs to be there more often. But I must confess I was sad to find that my guess must have been wrong. I thought that the two of you had a *tendre* for each other, my dear."

"Oh," Mary said, flushing. "No."

"It is a great pity," Lady Eleanor said. "You are just exactly the woman for him, my dear, if you will excuse me for saying so. You are someone who might have brought him back to himself."

Mary looked at her warily.

"And the sort of atmosphere that is here tonight might have brought him back, too," Lady Eleanor said. "If he is to be brought back at all. It has been a long time. Most people, I would imagine, think that he is unreclaimable. What do you think, Lady Mornington?"

"Ma'am?" Mary frowned.

"I was under the impression that you were quite

closely acquainted with him," Lady Eleanor said. "Perhaps I was mistaken? Perhaps you know very little of him? I do beg your pardon, but I assumed, you see, that you probably would not have been with him at all if you had not known him well. He does have a deservedly shocking reputation, I am afraid."

"My acquaintance with Lord Edmond is slight, ma'am," Mary said.

"Ah," Lady Eleanor said. "I shall say no more, then." But she sighed and continued anyway. "As a young man, Edmond would have been very much at home here, Lady Mornington. He would quite possibly have been one of your poets, though doubtless his poems would have been written in Latin or Greek and almost no one would have understood them."

Mary stared at her.

"He was too bookish," Lady Eleanor said. "His head was never out of a book. My brother and sister-in-law were worried about him. He would never be able to live in the real world, they used to say. His only ambition was to study for the church, and he was doing so, even though he had not been destined for the church. That was to be his elder brother's position in life—my brother always believed that Richard's sweetness and gentleness would make him an ideal clergyman, though I had my doubts. But it was the life Edmond chose for himself." She chuckled. "He would not have made a good clergyman, either, though. He knew nothing of life. Poor Edmond. He was always my favorite, Lady Mornington, though Richard was almost everyone else's."

Mary listened in disbelief. Was the Edmond Lady Eleanor was talking about the same Lord Edmond she knew? He could not be. There must be some mistake. But how could there be? Lady Eleanor was his aunt.

"At the time, I used to wish that he were a little more worldly," Lady Eleanor said. "And yet now I look back and long to see that quiet, serious, studious boy again. If only the accident had not happened. Do you know about the accident, Lady Mornington, or is everything I am saying mystifying you?"

"The death of his brother?" Mary asked.

"Ah, you do know," Lady Eleanor said. "But I must be boring you, dear, if you have no more than a passing acquaintance with my nephew. And I am keeping you from your guests."

But Mary set a hand on her arm as she turned away. "Please," she said, "you called it an accident. Are you merely being diplomatic? Or is that how you would really describe it?"

Lady Eleanor looked at her for a moment and clucked her tongue. "I suppose Edmond has been telling you the usual story," she said, "and the one that seemed to take root here in town. About his killing Richard and all that nonsense? He is quite as bad as my brother and my eldest nephew. The truth is, Lady Mornington, that Richard was not the best of riders, but rode anyway and took a foolish and unnecessary risk and died as a result. It was everyone's fault and no one's. It was an accident. But it changed Edmond's life—totally and unbelievably. And I suppose I am unrealistic to hope that he will ever come back to himself again."

"But . . ." Mary said. She was interrupted by the viscount, who came up behind her and took her by the elbow. He was smiling.

"Ma'am?" he said to Lady Eleanor. "I hope you are enjoying the evening. You have outdone yourself this time, Lady Mornington. Everyone seems eager to be a part of both groups at once."

Mary smiled at him.

"Goodrich?" Lady Eleanor said. "I always discover good things when it is almost too late. But no matter. I shall be a frequenter of your salon next year, Lady Mornington, my dear."

"Supper must be ready," Mary said. "I should go and see."

"Allow me," the viscount said, squeezing her elbow before striding from the room.

"So that is the connection," Lady Eleanor said, smiling at Mary. "And a very eligible one, too, my dear. I wish now that I had not thought of you in association with Edmond. I find myself disappointed that it is not so. But no more of that. You are staying in town for the summer?"

"I have no plans to remove anywhere else," Mary said.

"Then I shall see you again," Lady Eleanor said. "I shall send you an invitation. Perhaps I will include Goodrich in it. That would not be out of line?"

Mary blushed. "I think not," she said.

Lady Eleanor nodded and turned toward the group whose conversation she had not yet sampled.

It was later that evening that Viscount Goodrich kissed Mary for the first time and asked her to marry him. He stayed until everyone else had left, even Penelope, who looked from Mary to the viscount in some amusement, shrugged her shoulders, and bade them a good night.

They were in the hallway. Mary turned to look at him inquiringly. He was not, surely, about to renew his offer of the week before. He took her by the elbow, guided her back into the salon, out of the sight of her servants, and closed the door behind them.

"Lady Mornington," he said, possessing himself of one of her hands, "you cannot, I think, be insensible of my feelings toward you."

She looked up at him and said nothing.

"I hold you in the highest regard," he said. "In the deepest affection, I might make so bold as to add."

"Thank you," she said, curling her fingers about his. "Thank you, my lord."

"And if you are in any doubt about my intentions toward you," he said, "let me clarify them without further delay. They are the most honorable. I wish you to be my wife, ma'am."

She stared at him. He was going to be her husband. She was to grow as familiar with him—with his appearance, his speech, his habits—as she was with herself. She was to live with him in the daily intimacy she had known with Lawrence. Her mind felt satisfaction, even elation. It would be a good match. It was what she had wanted for several years. It was what she had never been able to have with Marcus.

"Will you?" He had her hand in both of his. "Will you do me the honor, Lady Mornington?"

He was too bookish . . . He wanted only to study for the church . . . He knew nothing of life. Poor Edmond . . . that quiet, serious, studious boy. The words, in Lady Eleanor's voice, had been revolving in Mary's head since before supper. She had not been able to rid herself of them. She could have wished Lord Goodrich's timing had been a little better.

"I . . . I don't know," she said.

But she did know. She did. She wanted to marry him. She wanted to be married. She wanted to be a mother if she could.

"Ah." He squeezed her hand. "I have spoken too precipitately. You need more time."

"Yes." She smiled at him in relief. She needed time to rid her head of the strange and bizarre images of Lord Edmond Waite that his aunt had put there. "A little more time, if you will, my lord."

"I can wait," he said, "as long as you can assure me

that there is hope, Lady Mornington. May I have the privilege of calling you by your given name?"

"Yes," she said, and when she swayed slightly toward him, she realized that she had done so almost deliberately. She wanted the images gone from her head. She wanted to be convinced that Lord Edmond meant nothing to her. "Do call me Mary."

"Mary," he said. And he released her hand, set his hands on her shoulders, lowered his head, and kissed her.

It was not close enough. He made no move either to open his mouth or to draw her closer. It was not close enough. She wanted to feel him against her, holding her close. She wanted to feel his mouth over hers. She wanted desperately to feel the same sensations she had felt the week before. She needed to be convinced that it was a man she needed physically. Not just one particular man. She wanted to be able to choose her man with her mind and know that the physical was very much less important because it was the same with every man.

A foolish wish. It was not the same with every man. Lord Goodrich's embrace was . . . pleasant.

"I had better take my leave," he said, lifting his head away from hers and looking at her with smoldering eyes. "Or I will not be able to leave at all, Mary."

She looked at him in blank surprise. Was he speaking the truth? Had he found their embrace arousing? She had not—not to even the smallest degree. She had not thought she was meant to.

"Mary?" He was looking at her intently. "Do you want me to leave?"

"Yes, please, my lord," she said.

"Simon," he said.

"Simon."

He dipped his head and kissed her again briefly.

"Good night, then, Mary," he said. "You will come walking in St. James's Park tomorrow afternoon?"

"I shall look forward to it," she said.

"And I, too."

She walked out into the hall with him and saw him on his way. And she wondered as she climbed the stairs to her room why she was not now officially betrothed to him. No, she did not wonder. She knew the reason. How had Lady Eleanor phrased it? He had changed totally and . . . How? Unbelievably. He had been quiet and bookish, too unworldly for his own good. He had wanted to be a clergyman. He had been studying to become one. Lord Edmond Waite? It was impossible, surely. Oh, surely it was impossible!

He had written Latin and Greek poetry. Lord Edmond Waite!

He had gone into the country. That was why she had not set eyes on him since the day of the garden party.

He was the reason why she was not now officially betrothed to Viscount Goodrich—Simon. She could not shake him from her mind. And now it was far worse than it had been all week. Now she had begun to see that perhaps, once upon a time, there had been a totally different Edmond, that perhaps the Lord Edmond she knew had been shaped by guilt and rejection and grief and other factors that she knew nothing of.

But she wanted to see none of those things. She wanted to marry Lord Goodrich. She wanted to be quiet and contented with him. She wanted to have a family with him before she was too old. She did not want to be thinking of Lord Edmond Waite at all.

But try as she would to direct her thoughts toward the future that had been definitely offered to her that evening, she could think only of Lord Edmond as she tossed and turned on her bed. And she could dream only of him after she had fallen asleep—strange, frightening dreams. In one of them he was on horseback and laughing at her as she soared over the high gate that he had just cleared. Except that she was not on horseback, and she was falling slowly, and he was running—on foot, not on horseback—slowly, much too slowly, to try to break her fall. She woke up before she touched the ground—or his outstretched arms.

TWO WEEKS WENT by, weeks during which the heat of the summer became more oppressive in the city. And yet they were not unhappy ones for Mary. Her friends Hannah and Penelope both left, one for the North, the other for Brighton. But the viscount remained and continued his almost daily attentions. He did not renew his marriage proposal during that time, but both of them behaved as if they had an understanding.

True to her word, Lady Eleanor sent an invitation to dinner for both Mary and Lord Goodrich, and they discovered that there was only one other guest, an elderly baronet of Lady Eleanor's acquaintance, who had been invited to make up the numbers, she explained, without seeming to offend her friend.

It was a pleasant evening, followed by a pleasant drive home. And if Mary's treacherous mind kept making comparisons, then she ruthlessly suppressed them. She was becoming accustomed to the unwelcome images and memories and was learning not to fight them too ruthlessly, but to patiently and determinedly replace them with others.

She was succeeding, she believed, until one morning when she was going through her mail—much diminished now that the Season and its flood of invitations was at an end. She looked more closely at a letter with unfamiliar handwriting, only to discover that it came from Hampshire, where he had his estate. She slit the seal with impatient and shaking hands and spread the letter on the breakfast table before her. Her eyes went first to the signature, large and bold at the bottom of the page—"Edmond."

Mary drew in a deep breath and closed her eyes. It was not a long letter, she had noticed. She opened her eyes again.

"My dear Mary," she read, and paused before reading on. "Contrary to what you may suppose, I did not arrange it. I knew nothing of it until my own invitation arrived this morning. I am inclined to accept because she is my aunt and has always been kind to me. And she will have only one sixtieth birthday, I suppose, unless she refuses to grow any older. However, if you have already accepted your invitation or want to do so and do not wish to see my face again, I will make some plausible excuse. All my tenants and servants can come down with smallpox or some such calamity. May I beg the favor of an immediate reply? Your obedient servant, Edmond."

Some mysterious invitation from his aunt to a sixtieth-birthday dinner? Mary frowned and thumbed through the rest of the pile of mail, and there it was. She opened the letter with the already familiar handwriting and read the note.

But it was not an invitation merely to dinner or an evening party. It was an invitation to spend a week at Rundle Park, Lady Eleanor's country home in Kent, in celebration of her sixtieth birthday. A few other family members and friends were to be there, too, Lady Eleanor explained. She very much hoped that Lady Mornington could be among their number. She had sent an invitation to the Viscount Goodrich, too, she added.

Mary folded the invitation and tapped it against her palm as she stared off into space.

It would be courting disaster to meet him again when she did not have to do so. She could easily find an excuse to refuse the invitation. She would not even have to resort to dooming all her servants to an attack of smallpox. She smiled unwillingly at the thought. She would be meeting him, if she agreed to do so, in the close confines of a country party. It was a quite undesirable situation.

But if she saw him again, if she spent a whole week in company with him, then she would surely be able to lay a few ghosts finally to rest. She would be able to see quite unmistakably that whatever he might have been as a very young man, before the death of his brother, now he was a man to be neither liked nor respected.

Nor loved.

She would think about it. She would discuss the invitation with Simon when he came later in the morning to take her shopping and to the library.

But she knew already what her answer would be. What it must be.

And she must write to him before the day was out. She must not keep him waiting for his answer.

It seemed so long. She closed her eyes. It seemed so long since she had seen him last.

10

$\mathcal{H}$E DID NOT PARTICULARLY WANT TO BE DOING THIS, Lord Edmond Waite thought as he descended from his carriage and hugged his aunt. He was always pleased to see her, of course, and normally he would have been quite happy to give a week of his time to celebrating a birthday with her, especially as there was to be other company. He had spent several summers at Rundle Park as a boy, when his uncle was still alive, and had pleasant memories of it.

But it had been hard to leave Willow Court just when he was settling there and finding that living in the country in his own home, surrounded by his own land, and served by his own servants, had a certain charm after all. And a certain soothing influence on a turbulent heart.

Yet now he had to face her again after making such a prize idiot of himself the evening of the garden party. She had not taken his hint that perhaps she should refuse her own invitation, since, as Lady Eleanor's nephew, he felt pretty much obliged to accept his. She had written back to say that she had no objection to meeting him at Rundle Park if he had none.

If he had none! Did she not have the sense—or the sensitivity—to realize that he would really rather face the devil than her?

And Goodrich had been invited, too. His mistress and bastard brood were going to have to live without him for a whole week, Lord Edmond thought nastily. Was Mary betrothed to him yet? If she was not, doubtless she soon would be. Perhaps this week in the country would provide a suitable environment for the announcement. Perish the thought!

"Edmond!" his aunt said, hugging him and kissing him on the cheek. "Can I believe the evidence of my own eyes? You are a day early, when you are almost always late."

"Just say the word," he said, grinning, "and I shall take myself off and put up at the village inn until tomorrow, Aunt. Are there any new barmaids there?"

She clucked her tongue. "You will stay here where I can keep an eye on you," she said. "Do come inside, dear. It is an unexpected pleasure to have you all to myself for a whole day before anyone else can be expected to arrive. Perhaps I can talk some sense into you."

"That sounds ominous," he said, setting an arm about her waist and walking up the horseshoe steps with her to the double front doors. "And what the devil did you mean by sending me a partial guest list with my invitation?"

"Watch your language, dear," she said. "I thought you might be pleased to know that I was inviting Lady Mornington, too."

"And Goodrich as well," he said. "I fell all over myself with eagerness to accept your invitation when I knew that he had been invited, too, Aunt. Has he accepted?"

"Both of them have," she said. "I believe they are quite an item. It will be a good match for her."

"She will have the devil of a lot of his attention," Lord Edmond said. "What with the two legitimate sons and his mistress and five bastards. Did you know about them?"

"I always think it unkind to use such a word to describe children born out of wedlock," she said. "They cannot help their birth, after all. Apparently he provides well for them and has a secure future planned for each of them."

"You do know," Lord Edmond said. "Then what the devil are you about, saying that he will be a splendid match for Mary? Any woman deserves better."

"Goodness me," she said. "Your language does leave something to be desired. It is possible that she knows about that other family. Some women do not mind, you know. It enables them to have all the comforts of marriage without any of the, ah, excesses."

Lord Edmond snorted. "Mary would mind," he said. "Believe me, she would mind."

Lady Eleanor looked interested. "Well, then, dear," she said, "perhaps you think you would be a better match."

"Me?" He laughed. "Poor Mary. It would be rather the choice between the devil and the deep blue sea, would it not? At least Goodrich has respectability. He is very discreet about his other life, and that makes it quite acceptable, of course."

"Pour yourself a drink, dear," Lady Eleanor said. She had led him into a downstairs salon. "Who is the devil and who the sea, I wonder."

"No, thank you," Lord Edmond said. "I would prefer tea, Aunt. If you are having some, that is."

She raised her eyebrows but said nothing. She crossed to the bell rope and pulled it. "I thought you had something of a *tendre* for her," she said. "Now I am sure of it."

"For Lady Mornington?" he said scornfully. "A *tendre*, Aunt? What put such a ridiculous notion into your head?"

"A certain way you had of looking at her when you were in Richmond," she said. "And a certain hostility toward a gentleman who we both agree is quite respectable and quite an eligible suitor for her."

"Nonsense," he said. "Anyone with any decency would feel distaste at the idea of a poor woman contemplating marriage with a man while knowing nothing of the very domestic and long-standing arrangement he has with a woman of another class."

She smiled. "I have not heard any speeches of moral outrage from you in many years, Edmond," she said. "Welcome home, dear."

He frowned but said nothing as the door opened at that moment to admit the butler and a maid with the tea and cakes.

"And talking of home," she said when they were alone again, "tell me what you have been doing at Willow Court in the past few weeks. Getting to know your property, I hope, and astounding your bailiff with your interest. And do sit down, dear. You look rather like a cross bear standing there."

Lord Edmond sat.

SHE WOULD REALLY rather not be doing this, Mary thought as the carriage completed its long drive through the park leading to Rundle and turned in the direction of the horseshoe steps. Normally she would have been delighted at the prospect of a week in the country during the heat of August, especially as her hostess was to be someone she liked.

But she would have to meet him again just at a time when she was beginning to persuade herself that she was putting him from her memory. And just at a time when she believed Simon was preparing to renew his offer for her and she was preparing to accept.

She was going to accept. Definitely. She had decided that.

"Here we are at last," Lord Goodrich said from beside her. She had agreed to travel with him, since the journey from London to Rundle Park could be made in a single day. "You will be glad to refresh yourself and have some tea, I am sure, Mary."

"Yes." She looked fearfully from the window, but the double doors at the top of the steps were only just opening. No one had yet emerged. "It has been a tiring day."

The viscount was already handing her down onto the cobbles when Lady Eleanor came from the house and down the steps, followed by Sir Harold Wright, the same gentleman who had been at Richmond when they had dined there. There was no one else, Mary saw in some relief, except servants.

"How wonderful!" Lady Eleanor smiled at Lord Goodrich and hugged Mary. "Now everyone is here and yet it is still not quite teatime. All my guests can become acquainted before the afternoon is out."

Mary shook hands with Sir Harold, who was asking the viscount politely about the journey.

"Do come inside, dear," Lady Eleanor said, taking Mary's arm. "I shall take you to your room myself, and you may take some time to freshen up. It always feels good to change one's gown and wash one's face after a journey, does it not? And on such a hot day, too. Is the weather not glorious? I just hope it holds for the week so that everyone can find plenty of entertainment outdoors. Ah, good. I see that your luggage and your maid have arrived. And Lord Goodrich's valet, is it?"

Mary smiled and looked about her in interest at the neatly tiled hall of the manor. She had always wished that she had a home in the country. But Lawrence, though he had left her comfortably well-off, had not been a wealthy man.

"You are not quite the last guests to arrive," Lady Eleanor said. "But the others are not to arrive for a few days yet and are to be kept a secret." She smiled mysteriously. "Being sixty years old, Lady Mornington—I am going to call you Mary if you do not mind—makes one bold. One realizes that there is not limitless time left and that certain things that need doing and perhaps have needed doing for years must be done now if they are to be done at all. Along here, dear. I have given you a room facing across the park to the front. I have always preferred this view to that of the hills and trees at the back, though many people prefer the wilder aspect there. Here we are."

"How lovely," Mary said, looking about her at the Chinese wallpaper and screens of her room and at the floral curtains and bed hangings.

"I knew you would like it," Lady Eleanor said. "I shall leave you, dear, and send my housekeeper in half an hour to direct you to the drawing room for tea."

"Thank you." Mary smiled at her hostess and wandered to the window after she had been left alone. The driveway ran very straight behind formal gardens, flanked on either side by rolling lawns and stands of trees. It was all very green. Very beautiful. She would have a country home, she thought suddenly, if she married Simon. *When* she married Simon.

Some of the guests were to arrive a few days later, Lady Eleanor had said. Perhaps he was one of them. Perhaps she would not have to face him that day. Perhaps there would be a few days first in which to relax.

There was hope in the thought. And also, inexplicably, a twinge of disappointment. She wanted the meeting over with. If it had to happen, then it might as well be now.

Her maid arrived at that moment with a manservant

carrying her trunk, and Mary turned her mind to getting ready for tea.

THEY HAD ARRIVED. Together. He had watched them from an upstairs window, alighting from their carriage and greeting his aunt and Sir Harold. They were quite an item, his aunt had said. Well.

Lord Edmond ensconced himself in the corner of the drawing room farthest from the door and exchanged reminiscences with Peter and Andrew Shelbourne, nephews of his uncle, no blood relations of his at all. He had met them often at Rundle Park when they were all boys. Peter's wife, Doris, sat silently at her husband's side. She disapproved of him, Lord Edmond thought, and did what he often did under such circumstances—he fixed her with a steady look until she lowered her eyes. Now she would be a little afraid of him, too. It was so easy to intimidate women.

There were twenty-one guests in all, including Sir Harold Wright, his aunt's faithful friend since long before his uncle's death. Rumor had had it once upon a time that they were lovers, but if it were true, they were very discreet about their affair and had made no move to marry after his uncle's death. Perhaps they were just friends, Lord Edmond thought. Perhaps it was just that gossip could not accept anything so dull and unscandalous as a platonic relationship. Anyway, it was none of his business.

It was a larger gathering than he had expected, but he welcomed the numbers. It would be easier to keep his distance from her. And apart from her presence, it was an unthreatening gathering. He had always been a little afraid at his aunt's parties that he would unexpectedly run into some other member of his family. But she had always been tactful. She had never tried to entertain his father or his eldest brother and him at the same time. He was the only guest at the party from her own family.

But then, she had always declared quite openly, even when he had been a puny and bookish and quite uninteresting boy, that he was her favorite. Bless her heart.

And then, just when he was chuckling over some long-forgotten memory with Peter and Andrew and was feeling quite off his guard, she came into the room. He knew it even though he was not looking directly at the door at the time. And sure enough, when he did look, there she was. Their eyes locked almost immediately. She had come into the room alone—without her watchdog.

He favored her with his expressionless stare, since he could not at the moment quell from his mind the memory of the abject misery with which he had taken his leave of her the last time he had seen her. She lifted her chin and then inclined her head. She did not smile.

Well, he thought, turning away to resume his conversation with his childhood friends, that was that, then. He had seen her again and he was still feeling relatively sane. The room had not crashed about his head. Many of those present—Doris Shelbourne, for example—would undoubtedly derive huge amusement from the knowledge that he had been waiting in fear and trembling for the arrival of one small, not particularly beautiful lady. Well, it was over.

He thought of an escapade that had got him and Peter into some trouble many years ago—one that the poker-faced Doris would not find quite proper—and began to tell it. To hell with the woman, he thought. If she expected vulgarity from him, then he was more than willing to oblige her.

Goodrich had entered the room and was standing beside Mary, their shoulders almost touching. He was smiling at her possessively. He looked almost as if he might set an arm about her shoulders at any moment. If he tried it, Lord Edmond thought, he would have to go about for the rest of his life minus one arm. And catching the drift of his thoughts, he redoubled his efforts to make the telling of his story quite as outrageous as he could. Peter and Andrew were already chuckling. Doris had not cracked a smile.

Devil take it, Lord Edmond thought as that arm came briefly about Mary's waist to turn her to greet a couple who were approaching them. Hell and damnation! Was he to be subjected to this for a week? He muttered something to his companions and strolled across the room.

"Ah, Mary," he said in his haughtiest manner, quite rudely ignoring the viscount and the couple with whom they were speaking, and not at all caring about the impression he was making. "So you have come to rusticate, have you?"

"I would hardly call spending a week in the country at a party with more than twenty other guests rusticating, my lord," she said, turning toward him so that his rudeness to the other three would not seem quite so obvious.

"Would you not?" he said. "What would you call it, then? A great yawn? It keeps you from your books and your poets and your politicians. It must seem like a massive waste of time."

"Heavens!" she said. "What a strange impression you must have of me. Life has more to offer than just books and intellectual conversation, my lord. And more than idle amusement, too. Life has an infinite variety of experiences to offer, and I like to sample all of them."

"All?" He widened his eyes and looked down deliberately at her mouth.

"Very well, then," she said, flushing. "Many. Words should be chosen with care, as you have just implied."

"I wish you had meant the *all*," he said, his eyes caressing her.

"You are trying to put me to the blush, my lord," she said calmly.

"And succeeding," he said. "Did you cry, Mary?"

"Cry?" She looked at him inquiringly.

He smiled at her arctically. "My only regret," he said, "was that I could not follow you invisibly into the house. But I will wager that you cried. Women cannot resist a broken heart, I have found, especially when they think themselves the breaker."

"You did not mean a word of what you said, then?" she asked.

He raised his eyebrows. "Did you think I did?" he asked. "Poor Mary. If I was to endure the mortification of a rejection, I felt justified in meting out a little punishment in return. I succeeded, did I?"

"You flatter yourself," she said. "It has been obvious to me from the beginning of our acquaintance that you are quite incapable of experiencing any of the finer feelings, not to mention love. Your charade would not have convinced an imbecile."

"Mary of the acid setdowns," he said, his head to one side. Her fine gray eyes lent her whole face beauty when they were flashing with indignation, he thought. "You really must give me lessons one of these days."

"You forget," she said, "that we are to have no future dealings at all, that you have a promise to keep. I believe this gathering is large enough that we can keep from having to exchange any future words, my lord."

"At which point I am to crawl abjectly back into my corner, I suppose," he said. "Mary, Mary, when will you learn that a libertine and a rogue is without honor? I needed to be in the country for a few weeks. Tedious business to attend to and all that. I have scarcely stopped yawning since I left town. Did you really think that I was keeping my promise to you?"

"Yes, I did," she said. "It was one small thing—one very small thing—for which to respect you."

He shook his head. "And with that short speech you expect to blackmail me?" he asked. "I don't want your respect, Mary, remember? I don't care a damn for your respect." He lowered his voice. "I want your body. And the campaign is about to resume, my dear. Remember that I have the added incentive of knowing that you also wanted mine on the return from Richmond. Very badly, as I recall."

"It seems, then," she said, "that I am a better actor than you, my lord. I convinced you?"

He grinned suddenly. "That was unworthy of you, Mary," he said. "It was not even a good try. You have merely made yourself look remarkably foolish."

She blushed and had no answer, he was interested to note.

"Why the letter?" she asked. "Why the warning, if you were planning to be so unscrupulous?"

"Ah," he said. "I know something of human nature, Mary. I thought the letter would pique your curiosity. I thought you would not be able to resist casting your eyes on a man sick with love for you. And behold you here. And behold me, your lovesick swain."

"You are despicable," she said. "If you will excuse me, my lord, there are other people I should be talking to."

As if on cue, the Viscount Goodrich, having managed to finish his conversation with the other couple, drew Mary's arm protectively through his and nodded stiffly to Lord Edmond.

"Waite," he said.

"You had better hang on to her," Lord Edmond said conversationally. "I had plans for ravishing her in the middle of my aunt's drawing room, Goodrich."

"Such sentiments, flippant as they are, are not for a

lady's ears," the viscount said. "And I can imagine what your plans are, Waite. Forget them. Mary has me to protect her, and I will do so, though I would much regret any public unpleasantness during the festivities for your aunt's birthday."

"But you would not regret private unpleasantness?" Lord Edmond pursed his lips and considered for a moment. "Neither would I. It can be arranged anytime you so choose, Goodrich."

"Please." Mary's voice was quiet, but Lord Edmond knew, though she showed no outward sign, that she was furious. "Enough of this. There will be no wrangling over me and no fighting. Are you two schoolboys to be coming to fisticuffs over nothing at all? And am I a youthful beauty to be fought over? Lord Edmond, you are doing this deliberately, and it will not succeed. Simon, escort me across to the tea tray, if you please."

Lord Edmond watched them go. Her back was very straight. Her hips swayed pleasingly, though without any conscious provocativeness, beneath the loose folds of her muslin dress.

He wondered what on earth had possessed him. Some demon quite beyond his control. He had not planned any of the things he had said to her. And everything had been a pack of lies.

Good Lord, he thought, the wise thing for him to do was to pack his bags and return to Willow Court as fast as horse could gallop. Otherwise there was no knowing to what dishonorable depths he would fall with regard to Mary or what asinine sort of duel he would end up fighting with Goodrich. He might even find himself telling Mary about the plump mistress and the brood of bastards, and despising himself for the rest of his life.

"Ah, Edmond," his aunt said, linking an arm through his. "I did not wish to interrupt you while you were renewing your acquaintance with Mary, but now that you are alone again, you really must meet the Reverend Samuel Ormsby and his wife—she was Phillip's cousin, you may remember. Samuel believes you and he were at Oxford together for a while."

"Oh, Lord," he said.

"Precisely, dear," she said. "I am surprised that he has recognized you."

Instead of rushing from the room to pack his bags, Lord Edmond allowed himself to be led toward the gentleman in the clerical garb, who was beginning to look somewhat familiar.

Oh, Lord. It was like something out of another lifetime. Out of another era. Another universe.

"THE AIR FEELS good," Mary said, closing her eyes and breathing it in with the scent of flowers. "There is the suggestion of evening coolness already."

She was strolling in the formal gardens with Lord Goodrich, tea being over and most of the guests having dispersed to their rooms.

"I knew he was Lady Eleanor's nephew," he said. "I suppose it should have struck me as a possibility that he would be a guest here, too. But I would have expected her to show better taste than to invite him with decent people. I would not have brought you here if I had known, Mary, I do assure you. I am sorry."

"But you did not bring me here," she pointed out. "We each accepted our separate invitations. I think perhaps it would be better, Simon, if you did not show such open antagonism to him. It goads him on into being more outrageous than he would otherwise be, I believe."

"I will be antagonistic to anyone who treats you with anything less than the proper respect," he said.

She smiled at him.

"No," he said, "the best way we can handle this,

Mary, is to become betrothed without further ado. He will not argue with a fiance's rights, believe me."

"It is a rather strange reason to become betrothed," she said.

He stopped walking and took both her hands in his. "Have I given the wrong impression?" he said. "You know otherwise, Mary. You know that I have chosen you as the woman I want beside me as my wife for the rest of my days. And I believe you are ready to accept my suit now, are you not? I have felt it in the past few weeks. Why not make it official now, when there is a good reason?"

"But it is Lady Eleanor's birthday celebration," she said. "We must not try to take some of the attention from her, Simon."

He squeezed her hands. "Somewhere in those words I found reassurance," he said. "Do I take it that you were not saying no but only that the timing is poor?"

She thought. "Yes," she said, "I think that is what I was saying."

"You will marry me, then?" he asked.

"Yes," she said. "I think so."

"Think?" he said.

She drew a deep breath. "I believe I must have been unmarried for too long," she said. "The thought of taking such a step, of voluntarily giving up my freedom again, frankly terrifies me, Simon."

"Then we will not rush into marriage," he said. "I shall give you time to accustom yourself to the idea. Agreed?"

"Agreed," she said after a small hesitation. "But, Simon, I don't believe we should say anything this week."

"Only if Waite proves troublesome," he said. "If he does, Mary, you must allow me to tell him in no uncertain terms that you are affianced to me and that any insults to you, however slight, will be answerable to me. Agreed?"

"Agreed," she said again after another hesitation. "But I think it would be better to ignore him, Simon. He thrives on the sort of attention you give him."

He squeezed her hands once more. "Leave such matters to me," he said. "Relax and enjoy the party."

"Yes." She smiled at him.

"We are betrothed, then," he said, looking at her in some satisfaction. "I am happy about it, Mary."

"And I," she said.

He bent his head and kissed her chastely on the lips.

11

MARY FELT HAPPY FOR THE REST OF THE DAY AND for most of the following morning. Everything she had hoped would be accomplished during the week at Rundle Park seemed to have been accomplished during the first day.

She was to be married. She was to be the Viscountess Goodrich, and her main home was to be a country estate. There she would live out a life of security and contentment with a man she liked and respected. She was only thirty years old. There would be children—two perhaps, even three. She would like to have a son, though of course Simon already had his heir. And a daughter, too. She would like at least one of each.

She was glad that he had asked again and that she had had the courage to say yes. And she was a little sorry during the evening that she had asked for their betrothal to be kept a secret during the week. She wanted to tell everyone. She was fairly bursting with excitement.

And that other had been accomplished, too. She had seen Lord Edmond Waite again and the spell was broken. All the unwilling feelings of attraction and regret had fled, and as she had hoped, she could see him again for what he was. He was an unprincipled scoundrel.

She was so glad she had come and had not refused her invitation, knowing that he would be there, too. It was true that he had declared himself to be in pursuit of her again, but she did not care about that. Once he knew that she was betrothed to Simon, he would have no choice but to leave her alone. Besides, she would put up with the nuisance of his attentions now that her greatest dread had been put to rest—that she was falling in love with him.

He made no effort to seek her company during the evening, being seated at quite the opposite end of the table from her at dinner and contenting himself with a few amused glances across the drawing room at her afterward as she and a few other ladies played the pianoforte and sang. He directed his attentions to Stephanie Wiggins, the shy young daughter of one of Lady Eleanor's friends. He did so, Mary suspected, only because the girl's mother was looking on with almost open alarm.

And the following morning, when Sir Harold led several of the guests on a ride to a distant hill, from which there was a pleasing prospect of the surrounding countryside, Lord Edmond expressed a preference for billiards. Mary rode at the viscount's side with a feeling of enormous relief. Those words at tea the previous afternoon must have been spoken merely to tease her. It seemed that he was going to be civil after all.

It was a beautiful day, as nearly every day for the past three weeks had been. They would have to pay for such a glorious summer, Doris Shelbourne said gloomily. Doubtless they would have an early winter. Mary smiled to herself. She had learned during the brief years of her marriage that the moment of happiness had to be seized. Certainly troubles were ahead—they always were, just as more happiness was ahead. But why cloud the joy of the happy times with a fear of the unhappy?

"I cannot imagine a lovelier day or more pleasant surroundings," she said, turning her head to smile at the viscount.

"You have been nowhere else but England except for Spain," he said. "There are lovelier climes and far more spectacular surroundings, Mary."

"But I don't think any could bring me greater happiness than England," she said.

"That is a typically insular attitude," he said, smiling at her. "I shall persuade you to change it. I plan to take you to every corner of Europe on our wedding journey. I shall keep you away from these shores for a whole year at least, Mary. Perhaps two or even three. Paris, Vienna, Rome, Venice—you shall see them all, and more."

"Mm," she said with a sigh. "How wonderful it will be. I will have to pinch myself to believe that it is all real."

"Oh, it is real," he said. "I promise you."

"But you did exaggerate." She laughed. "A whole year, Simon? You could not enjoy being away from home so long, surely. And away from your sons?"

"They are at school," he said. "And they have relatives with whom to spend the holidays. They are beyond the age of having to be coddled. I never did encourage them to be dependent on me."

She pulled a face. "But you must be a little dependent on them," she said. "Your own sons, Simon. You do not have to feel obliged to take me on an elaborate wedding trip, you know. Just to be with you and at your home will be happiness enough."

He smiled at her. "Ah, but I intend to make your happiness the main goal of my life," he said. "We will travel, Mary, and when we return, we will always be where it is most fashionable to be. There will always be something to amuse you."

"I am thirty years old, Simon," she said. "Did you know that? I am sure you must have. I make no effort to try to hide my age." She flushed. "I cannot delay too long if I am to give you a family."

"I have a family," he said. "You do not have to worry about that tedious duty, Mary. I have no intention of burdening you with children."

"Burdening?" she said. "Oh, no, Simon. It would be no burden. It would be a joy."

They did not argue the matter. They were riding in company with other people, and soon it became necessary to converse with others. Besides, it was very early in their betrothal. Such matters could be discussed with more seriousness later. There would be time enough to convince him that domestic joy for her meant a country home and a husband and family of her own.

Nevertheless, a little of the joy had gone out of the morning. What if their goals for happiness should really prove to be incompatible? But she pushed the thought from her mind.

HIS AUNT WAS trying to throw them together. She was matchmaking. He had suspected it right from the day of the garden party, when she had unexpectedly invited them to stay to dinner. She liked Mary and for some strange reason had conceived the notion that she would make him a good wife.

He had suspected even more strongly when he had received his invitation to this week at Rundle Park and his aunt had mentioned specifically that she had also invited Mary and Goodrich. He had been even more sure of it after he had arrived and talked with her.

If she was hoping to match the two of them, of course, there were those who would have thought it strange that she would also invite Goodrich, since in her own words he and Mary had become an item. But that was just the way his aunt worked. She confronted problems head-on. By inviting the three of them into the country, she hoped that he would oust Goodrich from Mary's affections and that she would see that he was the better man.

Ha! The better man.

What his aunt had done was force him into becoming a blackguard. Or into remaining a blackguard. He did not have much honor or reputation left to lose, if any.

He tried. After that disaster of an opening tea, he did try to keep his distance from her. He even looked over the slim pickings of unattached females at his aunt's party and tried determinedly to show a gentlemanly interest in Miss Wiggins, though the girl was almost young enough to be his daughter and seemed never to have heard the word "conversation." And he denied himself the pleasure of a morning ride merely because Mary was to be one of the party.

But in the afternoon he could no longer avoid being in company with her. His aunt had filled up two carriages with guests interested in the ancient Norman church and churchyard in the village. She had craftily offered Goodrich the seat next to her before the man realized that only those who could fit into the two carriages were to go. Mary was not among them.

For those guests who remained, Lady Eleanor suggested a walk across the pasture and through the trees past several follies to the lake. She was sly, Lord Edmond thought. Not by the merest hint had she suggested that both he and Mary join the walkers. Certainly there was no evidence that she had even dreamed that they walk together. But she had set the scene nicely, he had to admit that. He caught Goodrich's eye as the viscount escorted his aunt out to the waiting carriages, and inclined his head. He noted with the greatest satisfaction the tightening of Goodrich's jaw.

And the rest was inevitable. He was one of the first of the walkers to arrive downstairs, and Mary was the first unattached lady to put in an appearance. Perhaps he might have hung back and waited to offer his arm to Miss Wiggins or to the widowed Lady Cathcart, who had been married to his uncle's cousin. But Mary made the mistake of catching his eye and raising her chin stubbornly. His very self-respect set him to sauntering across the hall to her side.

"Mary?" he said. "You are walking and have reserved no one's arm on which to lean? Allow me to offer mine." Which he proceeded to do with a courtly bow.

"Thank you," she said, her voice chilly. "But I am not sure I will need anyone's arm."

He raised one eyebrow and looked at her.

"Very well," she said, one foot beating a light tattoo on the tiles. "Thank you, my lord."

Everyone else came downstairs in a large and noisy body.

"Doris and I will lead the way," Peter Shelbourne said. "This was the route of many a childhood romp. Remember, Andrew? Edmond? I could do it with my eyes closed."

"A rather pointless though impressive offer," Lord Edmond said. "Go ahead, then, Peter. Lady Mornington and I will bring up the rear so that we can rescue any stragglers who happen to get lost."

"Nicely done," Mary said as they descended the horseshoe steps at the back of the group. "I suppose you intend to lag so far behind that you will have me all to yourself."

"It is a fine idea," he said, "though it had not occurred to me until you mentioned it."

"And I suppose you arranged it that Simon go on the drive," she said, "so that I would be unprotected."

"Far from it," he said. "My knees are still knocking from a certain nocturnal visit I was paid last night."

She looked at him in inquiry.

"It seems I am to keep my eyes and my hands and

every other part of my body off you," he said, "since you are now someone else's possession."

Her jaw tightened. He wondered at whom her anger was directed.

"I gather that my jaw and my nose and several other parts of my anatomy are at risk if I choose to be defiant," he said. "I believe that even a bullet through the heart or brain would not be considered excessive punishment."

"Well," she said, "at least now you know."

"I do indeed," he said. "Mary, are you really going to marry him?"

"I am," she said. "I have been a widow long enough. I want the security and contentment of marriage."

"Ah," he said. "And I thought that it was a new lover you were in search of. No wonder you rejected my suit, Mary. I should have offered you marriage."

"How ridiculous!" She looked at him scornfully. "As if I would have married you. And as if you would have offered marriage. You would be quite incapable of the type of commitment that marriage calls for. Fidelity, for example."

"Do you think so?" he said. "Though perhaps you are right. I had not the smallest intention of being faithful to Dorothea had I married her. And she was too civilized to have expected it. She would have preferred me to reserve all amorous activities apart from the begetting of an heir for a mistress, I suspect. On the other hand, I did intend to be faithful to Lady Wren. She was the most exquisite creature I have ever seen. Yourself included."

"Thank you," she said. "I have never had any illusions about my own beauty."

"I could have been faithful to you, though," he said, his eyes roaming her face. "I don't believe I would have ever wished to stray from you, Mary."

"Nonsense!" she said. "We have nothing whatsoever in common."

"Oh, yes," he said. "There was something."

She looked about her. "Why are we walking around the formal gardens instead of through them like everyone else?" she asked.

"A question unworthy of you, Mary," he said, though he had not noticed until that moment that they were not following the others, "when the answer is so obvious. So that we may fall farther behind, of course."

"If you think to seduce me," she said, tight-lipped, "you have a fight on your hands, my lord."

"A tempting thought," he said. "But let us be civil. Talk to me, Mary. Tell me how you like this house and what you have seen of the park."

She relaxed somewhat as they rounded the end of the formal gardens and proceeded after the others in the direction of the stile leading to the path across the pasture.

"Oh, I like it very well," she said. "I cannot imagine why anyone with a country home can bear to leave it in order to live in town."

"The pursuit of pleasure," he said, "and company. The escape from self. One does not have to come face-to-face with oneself so often amid the clamor of town entertainments."

"Is that why you live almost all the time in town?" she asked.

"As usual, Mary," he said, "you know unerringly how to wound. You think I find facing myself unpleasant?"

"Do you?" she asked.

He lifted her hand away from his arm so that he could climb over the stile and turn to help her over. He could not resist lifting her down and lowering her close to his own body. She flushed, but she smoothed out her dress calmly enough and took his offered arm again.

"Why should I?" he asked. "I have almost everything

a man could ask for in life. I have wealth and property and position. I have had a great deal of pleasure in my life."

"And peace of mind?" she said. "And self-respect? And a place to call home, and loving people to fill it?"

"Ah, you would be enough for that, Mary," he said.

"No." She looked up at him and shook her head. "Absolutely not. For whenever I am with you, my lord, I am doing what you always object to. I am wounding you, if it is possible for you still to feel wounded. I am your conscience. You are a fool if you think you could ever be happy with me."

He sighed. "My small attempt to keep the conversation light and general has failed, has it not?" he said. "We are back to the wrangling. Tell me, why exactly are you marrying Goodrich? Is it just that you think you are of an age when you ought? Is it just for security and contentment? They are very dull words. Is there no love, no fire, no magic?"

"My reasons are my own concern," she said, her voice frosty.

"By which words I understand that there are none of those elements in your relationship," he said. "You are not the sort of woman who can live permanently without any of the three, Mary."

"Oh," she said crossly, "how can you pretend to know anything about me? You know nothing beyond the fact that I am terrified of thunderstorms and behave very irrationally when one is happening."

"I know you, Mary," he said. "I know you very well, I believe."

She clucked her tongue. "Everyone else is across the pasture and in the woods already," she said. "I think it ungentlemanly of you to keep me so far behind, my lord."

"You will insist," he said, "on telling me I am no gentleman on the one hand and expecting me to behave like one on the other. Is he going to take you to live in the country? You will like that, at least."

"He wants to take me traveling," she said. "He wants us to spend a year and perhaps longer traveling about Europe after our wedding. He wants to make my happiness the focus of his life, he says."

"Then you should be ecstatic," he said. "Why are you not?"

She was looking ahead to the ancient trees that made up the woods surrounding the lake. "I want a home," she said. "I did nothing but travel during my first marriage. We never had a home at all except for a tent and sometimes some rooms for a billet. And though I have my home in London now, it can sometimes be lonely."

"So the traveling holds no lure for you," he said. "If your happiness is indeed his main concern, Mary, then all you will have to do is tell him so."

"But he seems so set on it," she said. "And so set on making pleasure the object of our life together. I want a family, but he says he will not burden me with children."

"He is set on bringing himself pleasure," he said quietly, "and on not burdening himself, Mary."

Her eyes flew to his suddenly and she flushed rosily. "Oh," she said, "how did you do it? How? What on earth could have possessed me to confide such things to you? To you of all people?"

"Sometimes a sympathetic ear can loose even the most tightly knotted tongue," he said.

"Sympathetic!" She looked at him in distaste. "What use will you make of these confessions, I wonder. You will tell everyone, I suppose. You will make me the laughingstock. And you will anger Simon."

He swung her around to face him and grasped her by both arms. "When have I ever made public anything I know about you?" he asked. "At least absolve me of that, Mary. And is it so shameful anyway to admit that you want a home and family with the man you are planning to marry?"

She laughed bitterly. "At least," she said, "you can be thankful that I did not somehow maneuver you into offering for me. Can you imagine a worse hell than living with a woman with such lowly ambitions?"

"I have a country home I might have offered you," he said. "If it is solitude and domesticity you crave, Mary, you would like it. I have neglected it for years. It needs redecorating and refurnishing from stem to stern. I have just been there for a few weeks. It needs a woman's touch. But it is cozy. Not as large as Rundle Park or Goodrich's estate, I will wager. It was the smallest of my father's properties—a suitable one to which to banish me. I might have offered it to you."

"So that you might neglect me, too?" she said. "What nonsense you speak. Sometimes I think you almost believe your own words. Do you know yourself so little?"

He released one of her arms to set the backs of his fingers lightly against one of her cheeks. "And you might have had my seed," he said, "as you did that one night. I might have been able to offer you babies, Mary."

She opened her mouth to speak, but the muscles of her face worked somewhat out of her control for a moment.

"Only you could possibly say such a very improper thing to a lady who is not even your betrothed," she said.

"We might have changed that, too," he said. "If only I had met you fifteen, sixteen years ago. You were a child then, were you not? And I, too, Mary. I was the veriest child until my twenty-first birthday, and a man the next day. What a coming of age it was. The weight of ages."

"You merely reaped the consequences of drunkenness," she said.

"Yes." He dropped his hand from her cheek. "So I did. You are in the right of it there." He turned to walk on, his hands at his sides.

She hurried to catch up to him. "Why did you not stop," she asked, "after the accident? Did it not teach you a lesson?"

He wanted to stride away from her suddenly. He wanted to be alone. But he could neither stride nor leave her. They were among the trees and had to wind their way carefully to the site of Apollo's temple with the circular seat within and the view down to the lake.

"If you had killed your brother, Mary," he said, "would you slap yourself on the hand and promise that you would never be bad again? Would you promise to be a good little girl for the rest of your life? With your brother dead at the age of twenty-three? No life left at all? No second chances? And for you one mistake and a lifetime of hell to face before death brought the real thing for the rest of eternity."

"One mistake," she said. "Was it the only time you drank? Or was it the only time that you brought nasty consequences?"

He felt inexplicably like crying. His nose and his throat and his chest ached with the need. He clasped his hands tightly at his back.

"It was the only time," he said. "The first. You would not believe what I was like, Mary. An innocent. A prude. A bookworm. A moralizer. I lived with my head in the clouds. And so they set themselves to get me foxed for my birthday. Not Dick, but the others—Wallace, my father, my friends. They succeeded beyond their wildest dreams. I was still foxed the morning after, when I lifted him up from the ground with his broken neck and stroked his hair and told him all would be well and scolded him for doing anything as foolhardy as to attempt that gate."

She had stopped walking. She was looking at him, her eyes wide.

"You look as though you had seen a ghost," he said. "Do you want to take my arm again?"

"Oh," she said. "I did not know. Though I might have begun to guess. Is it true, then? *Were* you different before the accident? You were at university? You were going to be a clergyman?"

He laughed. "The joke of the century, is it not?" he said.

He watched her swallow. "And you have never been able to forgive yourself?" she asked.

"For murder?" He shrugged. "It was all a long time ago, Mary, and I am what I am. Perhaps it is as well that you despise me so. If you liked me just a little, you would be trying to reform me. Women are famous for that, are they not? I am thirty-six years old. Beyond reform."

"It was not murder," she said. "There were others equally to blame, including your brother himself. Your aunt was right when she explained a few things to me—it was just a terrible accident."

His smile was twisted. "Pat me on the head, Mary," he said, "and I will feel all better. Where the devil is everyone else?"

They had reached the temple, only to find it deserted, though there was the sound of distant voices.

"Ahead of us," she said. "You deliberately planned it so that we would lag behind."

"Did I?" he said. "Was I planning to steal a kiss from you?"

"Probably," she said.

He indicated the stone seat inside the folly and sat down on it himself. "I have probably incurred the undying wrath of your betrothed already anyway," he said. "I suppose I might as well try to deserve it to the full. If you would care to move a little closer, Mary, I will attempt that kiss."

"I was right, was I not?" she said. "You do hate yourself."

"Devil take it," he said, reaching out and taking her hand in a firm clasp. "Do we have to have this conversation? What does it matter if I am not overfond of myself? At least I thereby make the opinion of the world unanimous."

She took him completely by surprise suddenly by sliding along the seat until she was close beside him. She had not pulled her hand from his. "I am sorry about Dick," she said, "and sorry about the hell you have carried within you ever since. I truly am sorry about the nasty and unfeeling things I have said concerning that incident. But hell need not be eternal unless one chooses to make it so. Did your brother love you?"

"Dick?" he said. "He was deservedly everyone's favorite. There was not a mean bone in his body. Why do you think he came galloping after me? No one else did. They all watched me on my way with laughter. Dick came to save me, the fool."

"He came to save you," she said. "Would he have condemned you to fifteen years of hell and perhaps a whole eternity?"

He got abruptly to his feet. "Enough, Mary," he said. "Who mentioned hell anyway? Me? I tend to overdramatize sometimes. Had you not noticed that about me? There are many men who would give a right arm for a share in my particular type of hell, you know." He reached out a hand to draw her to her feet.

"Yes," she said. "The more fool they."

"Does he kiss you?" he asked. "Do you respond to him as you have always responded to me?"

She shook her head. "Don't," she said. "Please don't."

"Don't what?" he asked. "Ask those questions? Or kiss you?"

"Both," she said.

But she did not fight him as he drew her against him. Her breasts pressed against his coat, and her hands, lightly clenched into fists, rested against his shoulders. She lifted her face to his and closed her eyes.

He kissed first her eyes, feathering his mouth across them before lowering it to brush her lips lightly. He deepened the kiss, savoring the softness and warmth of her, parting his lips only slightly.

And he hated himself anew and ached with his love for her.

She opened her eyes and looked up into his. It was a look of naked vulnerability. She was his in that moment, he knew. And the temptation was almost overwhelming.

"So, Mary," he said, "what is the answer to my question? Does he kiss you? Does he arouse passion in you? Does he bed you?"

"Don't," she said. "Don't look at me like that."

He did not know how he was looking at her. Only that he was steeling himself against temptation.

"Don't sneer," she said. "Sometimes I think I glimpse someone—someone I might like, someone wonderful— behind your eyes. But I am mistaken. There is no one, is there? Perhaps there was, once upon a time. But no longer. I wish there was not this."

"This?" he said.

"This attraction," she said. "This longing for you to kiss me properly, not with the restraint you just showed." She pushed herself away from him suddenly and straightened the ribbons on her bonnet. "Where are the others? Shall we follow them?"

"A good idea," he said. "More invitations like that, Mary, and you might well find yourself being tumbled on the hard ground and complaining bitterly to me afterward about my lack of restraint. If you want me, you have but to say the word and we can make the proper arrangements. But I like my mistresses in civilized surroundings."

"In scarlet rooms," she said. Her voice was scornful. "And mistress, did you say? Not wife any longer?"

"Why marry you," he said, "when you seem so very available without benefit of clergy?"

She drew away from him and began to walk along the path toward the next folly, a tower which had been built ruined. Miss Wiggins was standing fearfully at the top, on the very safe ruined parapets, clinging to the arm of Andrew Shelbourne, and everyone else was either looking up at them or gazing out across the lake, which was close by.

"I have quite lost touch with you over the years," the Reverend Samuel Ormsby said to Lord Edmond. "Ever since you were sent down from Oxford most unjustly."

"It was hardly unjust," Lord Edmond said. "I did call such a hallowed personage as a don an ass, you may recall."

"At a time when everyone knew you were beside yourself with grief over the passing of your brother and the grave illness of your mother," the Reverend Ormsby said. "Several of us signed a petition on your behalf, you know. But it seemed to do no good. What have you been doing with yourself since?"

"Perhaps you should tell me about yourself first," Lord Edmond said.

Mary, he noticed when he turned to look at her, had joined a few of the other guests. Yet others were going in search of the grand pavilion, which was hidden away among the trees farther along the shore of the lake.

12

Lady Eleanor gave a few interested guests, mostly ladies, a guided tour of the greenhouses the following morning. Not that there was a great deal of attraction in the greenhouses, she explained to them, when it was summer and the gardens were bright with flowers. The winter was the time to wander in the warmed buildings and enjoy the summer beauties of nature while all was winter bareness outside.

Mary hung back as everyone else strolled from the last of the greenhouses on the way to the rose arbor.

"Ma'am?" she said as their hostess made to follow them. "May I have a word with you?"

Lady Eleanor smiled at her and closed the door. "What is it, Mary, my dear?" she asked.

Mary fingered the velvety leaf of a geranium plant. "I need to know . . ." she said. "That is, there are certain gaps in my knowledge. It is really none of my business, of course, but . . . I need to know," she ended lamely.

"Of course you do, dear," Lady Eleanor said, and she took Mary's arm and began to stroll with her back along the length of the greenhouse. "Sometimes we cannot order our lives as we would wish, can we? We should be able to secure our own happiness with logical planning, but life does not always work that way. You have planned well, and look to be succeeding admirably—on one level. On another you wonder why it is you cannot force yourself to feel happy. Of course you need to ask more questions."

"You know?" Mary said.

"It was very obvious to me the first time I saw you together," she said. "An exceedingly odd couple, I overheard someone say, and I would wager that she was not the only one to say it that afternoon. But not as odd as it would seem, dear, to one who has known and loved Edmond all his life."

"I do not wish to have any interest in him at all," Mary said. "I have fought against his persistence and against my own feelings."

"It would be strange if you had not," Lady Eleanor said. "Edmond is probably the most disreputable member of the *ton* now gracing its ranks. He is fortunate that he is still being received at all. Only his title and his fortune have saved him from complete ostracism, I believe. No lady in her right mind would willingly fall in love with him."

"I did not say I have fallen in love with him," Mary said hastily. "Only that I—"

Lady Eleanor patted her hand. "If only you knew for how many years I have waited for him to meet you, Mary," she said, "or someone like you. I had almost given up hope. Dorothea, of course, was all wrong for him. And Lady Wren, too, though I heard about his attachment to her and was pleased at first. She is a beautiful lady and must have had a dull marriage to her elderly first husband, though I never heard a whisper of scandal surrounding her name. But she was in love with her Mr. Russell, and Edmond could not see it."

"Please," Mary said, "I did not mean to give the impression that I am going to—"

"Of course not," Lady Eleanor said, and turned at one end of the greenhouse so that they could walk back along its length again. "What exactly did you need to know?"

"Yesterday," Mary said, "he told me much the same story about his brother's accident that you had told. Except that he added that his father and his eldest brother had deliberately set out to get him drunk. It must have been easy. He had never drunk before, he said."

"Very likely," Lady Eleanor said. "I would not doubt the truth of that."

"They laughed when he insisted on going riding the next morning," Mary said. "They thought it all a great joke, even though he was still drunk."

"Unfortunately," Lady Eleanor said, "we often laugh at those who are inebriated, my dear. There appears to be something funny about people behaving differently from their normal selves. Seeing Edmond foxed must have seemed hilarious. He was always so very serious, so very much in control of himself."

"But if that is all true," Mary said, "they were more to blame for what happened than he was."

"I have always thought so," Lady Eleanor said, "though I was not there at the time to know exactly what happened. They were not a vicious family, Mary, none of them. And they were a very close and loving family, though I used to think that perhaps Edmond suffered from Richard's great popularity. They were alike—both quiet and home-loving. They both adored their mother and looked up to Wallace and my brother as types of heroes. Edmond was by far the more intelligent of the two, but Richard had the gift of sweetness, which Edmond never had. I think perhaps Edmond was a little jealous of Richard."

"And therefore his guilt would have been stronger," Mary said. "He would have felt as if unconsciously he had wanted his brother dead."

"Oh, dear," Lady Eleanor said. "Yes, I suppose that is

altogether possible. Edmond always looked inward far too much for his own good. He always had too tender a conscience."

"He was banished, he said." Mary frowned. "He was cast out from the family. And yet it was not his fault, or at least it was no more his fault than anyone else's. How could they have treated him so cruelly?"

"Tragic accidents need scapegoats," Lady Eleanor said. "At first, of course, it must have seemed that Edmond was entirely to blame. He was the one who had been drunk and reckless. He was the one who had not listened to Richard's pleadings. Of course they turned on him. It was cruel, naturally, and unjust and despicable. But people are never quite rational at such times. And they did not heap more blame on him than he heaped on himself."

"Did they not realize?" Mary swallowed, surprised to find that her voice was not quite steady. "Did they not realize that they were destroying him? Have they never realized that they lost both brothers on that terrible day?"

"Oh, if you are talking in the present tense," Lady Eleanor said, "then I think the answer must be at least partly yes. At the time, they were too consumed by their grief for Richard and by their concern at the complete collapse and rapid decline of my sister-in-law. And Edmond's running away and his expulsion from Oxford and his failure to put in an appearance at either funeral did not help his cause. Those absences angered even me at the time. It is hard to understand and make allowances for human nature when one's own emotions are raw."

"But now?" Mary said. "They will have nothing to do with him?"

"Overtures were made years ago, I believe," Lady Eleanor said. "But we are talking about human nature here, Mary. I did not read any of the letters that passed, but I know my brother and I know Edmond quite well. My guess is that there was too much pride on both sides, and too much willingness to assume guilt on the one side and not enough on the other. And then, as invariably happens with family quarrels, too much time had passed."

"They have never met one another since?" Mary asked.

"Both sides are at great pains not to do so," Lady Eleanor said. "London is understood to be Edmond's domain, the north of England my brother's and Wallace's. Whenever I issue invitations, I have to be careful to issue them separately. For years my brother would always ask if I had invited Edmond, too, and Edmond always asked if I had invited his father or Wallace. Fortunately they gave up asking some time ago, confident in the belief that I would never distress them by bringing them together unexpectedly."

"There must be so much need of healing," Mary said. "On both sides. Perhaps too much need. Perhaps it is too late."

Lady Eleanor opened the door of the greenhouse and motioned for Mary to precede her out onto the dark lawn. "It is a pity to miss the fresh air," she said. "We do not know when we are to lose this glorious weather, do we?"

"It is surely the best summer I can remember," Mary said.

"I have been saved from lying this time," Lady Eleanor said.

Mary looked her inquiry.

"Had either side asked this time if the other was to be here for my birthday," Lady Eleanor said, "I would have been forced to lie, Mary. I am sixty years old, or will be in just a few days' time. My brother is four years my senior. We are getting old. We cannot delay much longer."

Mary's eyes widened. "He is coming here?" she asked. "Lord Edmond's father?"

"And Wallace and his family," Lady Eleanor said. "They should arrive sometime tomorrow. Perhaps I am doing entirely the wrong thing, Mary, especially with other guests at the house. Sparks may fly at the very least. But it is time, I believe. Much past the time, in fact."

Mary said nothing.

"Now, tell me I am right," Lady Eleanor said. "Please tell me I am right, my dear. I respect your opinion."

"Yes." Mary drew a deep breath. "You are right, ma'am. Whatever the outcome, you are right. I do not know the Duke of Brookfield or his eldest son—I am afraid I do not know his title."

"Welwyn," Lady Eleanor said. "The Earl of, my dear."

"I do not know them," Mary said. "But as far as Lord Edmond is concerned, I do not believe more harm can be done. On the other hand, good may come of it."

Lady Eleanor squeezed her arm. "How wonderful you are, my dear," she said. "I waited with bated breath for your verdict. I was very much afraid I had done the wrong thing. And it is still possible, of course. Perhaps they will not even alight from their carriages tomorrow if they discover that Edmond is here. And perhaps he will leap onto the back of the nearest horse and gallop for London when he sets eyes on them. Who knows? One can only try."

"Yes," Mary said. She hesitated. "Was your invitation to me all part of your master plan?"

Lady Eleanor laughed a little ruefully. "It is a gamble, I must admit," she said. "I merely wanted you to see your two men together for a whole week, Mary. I wanted to set your reason at war with your heart. And I have succeeded, have I not? But again, I do not know if I have done the right thing. What if your heart wins and you end up living unhappily ever after? It is entirely possible. I am not altogether sure that Edmond is capable of having a loving relationship with anyone."

Mary turned her head and smiled at her hostess. "I will not have you feel guilty," she said. "I must tell you that since my arrival here I have accepted Lord Goodrich's offer of marriage. It is what will be best for me, I am sure. And Lord Edmond has never offered me more than *carte blanche,* you know. Does that shock you? I would not accept either that or a marriage offer from him. I could not possibly be happy with him—or he with me, either. But at least I do not despise him as I used to do, and I am glad of that. You are partly responsible, ma'am, and I am grateful to you. And for this lovely week in the country. Sometimes I pine for the countryside."

"You are very gracious, my dear," Lady Eleanor said. "Very. *Carte blanche,* indeed. Does the man have no sense left whatsoever? Does he think to satisfy those needs with you and waste everything else you have to offer him? Men! Sometimes I could shake the lot of them."

Mary smiled.

HE WAS NOT enjoying himself. And that was an understatement of the first order. He wished himself back at Willow Court, if the truth were known. He had never had much use for his country estate, finding life there far too dull for his tastes, but he had found a measure of peace there during the past few weeks, and he longed to be back. Alone. Away from people. Away from her.

For all his worst suspicions had been confirmed during the past couple of days. He was not only in love with her. He loved her. And that changed everything—everything by which he had lived for fifteen years. All his adult life.

Ever since he had rammed the barrel of a dueling pistol into his mouth late on the date of his mother's funeral and had sweated and shaken and finally thrust the weapon from him and cried and cried until there were no tears left and no feeling, either—ever since then he had decided that love, family, commitment to other people could bring nothing but pain and disaster. And so he had lived for himself, for pleasure. Pleasure had become the yardstick by which he measured all the successes of his life. If he wanted something, he reached for it. And if it brought him enjoyment, then he clung to it until the pleasure had cloyed.

Perhaps the nearest he had come to being selfless in all the years since had been his comforting of Mary at Vauxhall. Even when he had mounted her there, he had done so not from any selfish desire for personal gratification but from the desperate need to shelter her from her fear. He had drawn her as close as one human being can draw another.

He cursed the chance that had brought him that invitation to Vauxhall and the whim that had made him accept. For it had changed his life as surely, if not as dramatically, as Dick's death had done. And he did not want his life changed yet again. He had grown comfortable with it. Almost happy with it.

He loved her. And so he could no longer even try to take advantage of her. He could easily do so. She had actually told him that she was attracted to him, and her body had told him as much every time he had touched her. Her eyes told him the same story every time he met them, even though she masked their expression with coldness or disdain or hostility.

He could have her if he wanted her. It would take very

little effort on his part. And he did not think he was being merely conceited to think so. He could have her.

Devil take it, he could have her.

And yet she did not want him. Every part of her except the basely physical recoiled from him. And justly so. She should not want him or like him. Or love him. And if she did, or thought she did, he would have to disabuse her. For he could not take her in any way at all. He loved her, and he was the last man on earth he would wish on her.

And yet there were four days of the country party left, and he felt obliged to stay at Rundle Park despite the longing to get away. Four days in which Mary would see him and perhaps continue to be troubled by her unwilling attraction to him. And four days during which he must fight the temptation to dally with her or to try to ingratiate himself with her.

And yet, he thought, riding out alone during the morning while several of the ladies, Mary included, were touring the greenhouses, perhaps his very best course was to pursue the first of those temptations. Perhaps he should dally with her, as he had done to a certain extent the afternoon before. Perhaps he should make himself quite as obnoxious as he possibly could. It should not be at all difficult. He was an expert at being obnoxious.

He had told her too much the day before. He had felt her sympathies begin to sway his way. It was strange, perhaps, when he had never felt the compulsion to tell anyone else about that worst of all days in his life. He had never felt the need to justify himself or to try to give anyone a glimpse into his personal hell. Only Mary. But of course he loved Mary, and against all the odds and all the urgings of his better nature—if there were such a thing left—he wanted her to love him.

But he did not want her sympathy or her affection. It

would be too unbearable to know that her feelings had softened toward him at all. It would be better by far if she continued to despise and even hate him as she had always done. And there was only one way to ensure that that happened.

Lord Edmond laughed rather bitterly to himself. He would probably end up fighting a duel with Goodrich before the four days were at an end.

But it would be worth it. Once he had made her hate him in true earnest, then she would be safe from him. And he from her.

He smiled to himself and spurred his horse into a gallop across a fallow field, heedless of the possibility of rabbit holes or other irregularities in the ground. If there were a high gate to be jumped, he thought with grim humor, he would jump it without a second thought, since there was no one coming along behind him to imitate his foolhardiness and break his neck.

And this time he was not even foxed!

"WE ARE GOING to get storms out of this weather before it changes, you mark my words," Doris Shelbourne assured the people within earshot of her later that evening. "And then summer will be over. We will have an early autumn. We cannot expect to enjoy weather like this and not suffer for it."

"Storms," Mrs. Leila Orsmby said, looking up at her husband, who was standing beside her chair. "I do hope not. The children are terrified of them."

"Children usually are," Viscount Goodrich said, one hand on Mary's shoulder as he stood behind her chair. "The best medicine is to ignore both the storm and their wailing. They quickly learn that there is nothing to fear."

"That is easily said," Leila said, "but it is more difficult to do. When children are crying and they are one's own children, one feels constrained to comfort them."

"Then one is merely making a rod for one's own back, if you will forgive my criticism, ma'am," Lord Goodrich said. "Children must be taught fortitude."

"I am not sure that fortitude can be taught in that way," Mary said quietly. "The fear of storms is a dreadful thing and one must remember that there is something very real to the fear."

"Nonsense!" Lord Goodrich said. "Pardon me, Mary, but I must disagree most strongly. A little healthy thunder and lightning never did anyone any harm."

"It killed four soldiers in the tent next to my husband's and mine in Spain," she said. "Since then, I have not taken storms so lightly."

"In fact she is driven into a blind terror by them."

Mary looked up at Lord Edmond, who was lounging against the wall in Lady Eleanor's drawing room, his arms crossed over his chest. He was half smiling down at her in a manner that suggested that they shared some very personal secret. It did not soothe her indignation to remember that they did indeed. But only the day before he had declared quite seriously that she must absolve him of ever having shared any personal knowledge of her with anyone else.

"I have seen it happen," he said.

Mrs. Bigsby-Gore was playing determinedly on the pianoforte for several dancing couples, Lady Eleanor having been persuaded by the young people to have the carpet rolled up so that they might have an evening of informal dancing.

"Yes," Mary said, lifting her chin. "I am afraid of storms. I can sympathize with your children, Mrs. Ormsby."

"Mary." Lord Goodrich squeezed her shoulder. His tone was teasing. "You should be ashamed of yourself.

You cannot spend the rest of your life quivering at the approach of a storm just because you once had the misfortune to be close to men foolhardy enough to get themselves killed by one. What were you and they doing in tents during a thunderstorm anyway?"

"Trying to keep dry," she said more tartly than she had intended. "We were bivouacking, Simon. Camping. We were part of an army on the march."

"And the army could do no better for you?" he said. "That is quite shameful. Surely there must have been buildings available. Your husband was, after all, an officer. You ought not to have been subjected to the unpleasantness of being so close to those deaths."

"I do agree that the four poor devils who did not survive the storm should have had the good taste to die elsewhere," Lord Edmond said. His voice, Mary noticed, was heavy with boredom. "As for Mary's fears, Goodrich, you should perhaps thank providence for them. She likes to be held tightly. Ah, very tightly."

Mary's eyes blazed at him briefly. How could he! But she was aware of Leila Ormsby's and Doris Shelbourne's discomfort at the suggestiveness of his last words.

"I know it is a foolish fear," she said. "I do my best to conquer it and almost succeed if I am safely inside a large building. But, anyway." She smiled brightly at Doris. "I hope your prediction does not come true after all, Mrs. Shelbourne. I hope that one morning—a long time in the future—we will awaken to good English drizzle and find that our glorious summer has disappeared quietly in the night."

Fortunately, Sir Harold Wright arrived at that moment to ask her to dance and she got gratefully to her feet.

She glanced at Lord Edmond several times while she danced. He continued to stand against the wall, watching her, that half smile on his lips. She did not like it. It looked malicious. And he had proved himself to be malicious. What possible reason could he have had for saying what he had about her behavior during storms? The comfort he had given her at Vauxhall was almost the only kindly memory she had of him. And now he had tarnished that.

She felt very cross with herself. She realized suddenly that ever since the day before, and especially since her talk with Lady Eleanor that morning, she had been looking for redeeming points in him. She had been looking for something to like, something to excuse the way she felt about him physically. Despite everything, she had been trying to change her opinion of him.

It was foolish in the extreme, she realized. Perhaps he had been very different once upon a time—undoubtedly he had. And perhaps the fault for what had happened to his life was not entirely his own. Perhaps he was to be pitied. But those facts did not excuse him for present obnoxious behavior. They did not make him more likable or more worthy of respect.

For the past day she had allowed feelings to obscure judgment. But she had not liked his contribution to the conversation on storms. She had not liked it at all. And she would not forget again, she decided.

She was standing with the viscount and the Reverend and Mrs. Ormsby later in the evening when Lord Edmond touched her shoulder.

"Waltz, Mary?" he said. "Mrs. Bigsby-Gore is playing one, I hear. And you dance it awfully well, I remember. Though the last time we danced it, I believe we did not spend the whole time, er, dancing. However, there is, alas, no balcony outside the drawing room here, and no large concealing potted plants on the nonexistent balcony." He smiled.

The viscount drew breath to make a reply. He was

going to make a scene, Mary thought, in front of the reverend and his wife.

"Thank you," she said quickly. "It would be pleasant to dance, my lord."

She hoped that her smile was as arctic as it felt.

13

I T WAS NOT BY ANY STRETCH OF THE IMAGINATION A ball. There was merely a lady seated at the pianoforte, her playing making up in enthusiasm what it lacked in finesse. And merely a few couples dancing about the cleared floor of the drawing room, while others stood or sat about watching or conversing. It was certainly too confined an atmosphere for a quarrel.

Mary schooled her features to bland amiability. "You have just surpassed even yourself in vulgarity," she said.

"Have I, by Jove?" he said. "Thank you for saying so, Mary."

Still that half smile, she noticed. She would have liked—oh, yes, she really would—to slap it from his face. "What do you mean," she said, "by suggesting that you have held me tight during a thunderstorm and dallied with me behind a potted plant?"

"Suggested?" His eyelids drooped over his eyes and he looked down to her lips. "Suggested, Mary? If I remember correctly—and I am quite, quite sure I do—I held you very tightly indeed during a certain storm. I do not believe I could have been closer to you if I had tried. The female body is capable of only a certain degree of penetration, you know."

Her eyes widened as she willed herself not to flush. "You are disgusting," she said. "Perhaps you would like to return to the group and repeat those words there. You missed a grand opportunity to sink a few degrees lower in public esteem. Better still, perhaps you would like to stop the music and make a public announcement. It is too delightful a detail to share with only a select group."

"Smile, Mary." His voice drawled annoyingly. She hated men who drawled. There was such affectation involved. "Unless you want the world to witness your indignation, that is."

She smiled. "If I were just alone with you for a single minute," she said, "I would have your ears ringing before I was done with you. Be thankful, my lord, that we are not alone."

"Thankful?" he said. "I could dream of no greater bliss. But it would have to be for longer than a minute, Mary. Considerably longer. Even on a certain tabletop, I believe it took me longer than a minute. Smile!"

Mary smiled. "I choose to end this conversation," she said. "We will dance in silence, if you please."

"You may credit me with some sense of propriety," he said. "You may safely trust me not to make public the fact that we have enjoyed the ultimate intimacy together. No, no, close your mouth. You have just expressed your desire to dance in silence. You need not say 'Enjoyed!' with all the venom and hauteur that you planned. You did enjoy it, Mary, much as you may wish now that you had not. There is no point in denying it. I was there, if you will remember."

She clamped her teeth together and smiled.

" 'As if I could possibly forget,' " he said. "You see? I am even supplying your side of the conversation. Mary, what sort of an ass would ask you what you were doing in a tent in Spain in the middle of a thunderstorm when he knew you were with Wellington's army? I almost asked him myself, but I remembered your objection to my use of that particular word in your salon."

"You will leave the name of my fiancé out of this conversation—no, out of this monologue, if you please," she said.

" 'Ass' is more suitable than his name anyway," he said. "Is he good, Mary? Rich he certainly is, if rumor is correct on the matter. Have you slept with him? I believe I have asked you that question more than once, but you have never answered it. Have you?"

She gave him a glance of cold contempt before looking away to smile vaguely at the room at large.

"Do you sleep with him here?" he asked. "If not, perhaps you would care to leave the door of your bedchamber unlocked, Mary. Is it ever locked, by the way? What I mean is that I could come to you at night and you could explore the full extent of this attraction you claim to feel toward me."

She drew in her breath slowly.

"Was that an indication of assent?" he asked. "Tonight, Mary? We could do together all those things we did in a certain scarlet room. And there are far more things I want to do to you and with you, and far more things that I want you to do to me."

"I am betrothed." They were the only words she was capable of at that particular moment.

"That will not worry me," he said. "I will not think about it while we are about our business. I am not quite the three-in-a-bed type, but I believe I can learn to share you, provided I have you alone in bed when it is my turn."

"Does this particular tune go on and on forever?" she said. "Will it never end?"

"Oh, it will," he said. "Patience, Mary. The night will come. And I will come with it. All you need is a little patience."

She looked fully at him and forgot the need to smile. "I have been a fool," she said. "An utter fool. For the

past day I have been trying to convince myself that if
you were human once upon a time you must still be so
deep down. But you are not. You spoke yesterday to
arouse my pity, did you not? So that I would climb into
your bed to comfort you."

"I have never wanted your pity, Mary," he said. "Anything and everything but that."

"I despise you now more than ever," she said. "We are
all ultimately responsible for our own words and ac-
tions, my lord. Perhaps circumstances cause major
changes and stresses in our lives, and perhaps we can be
excused for crumbling beneath the weight of those
circumstances—for a certain time. But the real test of
the strength of our characters lies in our ability to go
forward with our lives unbroken, to rise above circum-
stance. I lost a dear husband in all the useless cruelty of
war. I found his body myself. He was naked on the bat-
tlefield after the local peasantry had completed their
stripping and plundering of the dead and wounded. My
husband, who had died for their freedom. You are not
the only one to have suffered."

For a moment he gazed into her eyes, his face drained
of all color and expression. But only for a moment. He
sneered.

"I suppose your point is that you have greater strength
of character than I," he said. "Well, I will not argue the
point, Mary. You are undoubtedly right. But I will wager
that I have had greater pleasure from life than you."

"Pleasure!" she said. "That is all that matters to you.
Pleasure! Not pride or honor or joy or happiness. Just
pleasure."

"You see?" he said, drawing her to a halt with a firm
hand at her waist. "While your mind was otherwise occupied, the music came to an end after all. Time does
pass, you see. Tonight, Mary?"

"I will not lock my door," she said, looking steadily

into his eyes. "I will not cower behind locked doors. But if you set so much as a finger on the knob outside my door, my lord, I shall scream so loudly that even the most distant groom will come running. And if you believe that I am afraid of the scandal that would be caused, then try me."

He smiled and raised her hand to his lips. "Fascinating," he said. "Has she told you any of these stories of Spain, Goodrich? Thank you for the dance, Mary."

"Simon." She smiled up at him as he came up beside her and set an arm protectively about her waist.

"All the rest of the dances this evening are mine, Waite," the viscount said. "I believe my meaning is clear?"

"I always hate that question," Lord Edmond said. "It is quite impossible to say no, and yet one feels remarkably foolish saying yes. One always wishes one could think of some witty reply. Ah, I do believe my aunt is calling me. If you will excuse me, Mary? Goodrich?"

And he sauntered away to quite the opposite corner of the room from where Lady Eleanor was deep in conversation with Sir Harold and Lady Cathcart.

"I warned him," the viscount said. "I went out of my way to do so quite privately and civilly so that there need be no public unpleasantness. But such a man is quite impervious to the decencies, it seems. He did not repeat any of his vulgarities while you danced with him, Mary?"

"No," she said. "He was quite civil, Simon."

But in truth she seethed and she mourned. Seethed at his outrageous behavior that evening, far outstripping anything else she had suffered from him since their acquaintance began. And mourned for a love that had been born and struggled for existence, only to die just when it had seemed that perhaps it would survive and grow after all. And she castigated herself for even allowing that love conception and birth when it was a hopeless and an undesirable thing. For once something had been born and died, it had existed. It had been a part of one's life and must be forever a part of one's memory and therefore a part of one's very being.

She had loved him for a day. For a day she had let down her guard and loved him.

And dreamed. She had allowed herself to dream. Foolish, foolish woman.

Deny it as she would, she had allowed both to happen. For a day. For a permanent part of her life.

HE HAD PROBABLY given her a sleepless night, he thought as she came rather late into the breakfast room the following morning. Her face looked pale and a little drawn. She had probably lain awake waiting for the sound of his hand on the doorknob. And of course, being Mary, she would have scorned to lock the door merely so that she could sleep without fear.

If only she knew how long he had lain awake fighting the temptation. Part of him had wanted to go and had rationalized his wish. If he went and she screamed as she had promised to do, then there would be a dreadful scene and he would be forced to leave. He would have his excuse to return to Willow Court, to be done with her once and for all.

And if he went and she did not scream—and he did not think she would—then they could renew their argument. He could find more and more outrageous words to disgust her. He could try to seduce her. Perhaps he would even succeed. He believed he had enough power over her physically that she would succumb to his caresses if he set about the seduction with enough determination. Either way, her hatred of him would be intensified once it was over and she had returned to her senses. His goal would be accomplished.

If he went and she did not scream, then he would have one more chance to talk with her privately, one more chance to touch her, perhaps to kiss her. Perhaps to make love to her.

Perhaps to impregnate her.

The thought had put an abrupt end to his dreaming. He had remembered that she wanted children, that she felt herself almost too old to begin a family, that Goodrich was unwilling to saddle himself with yet another family—seven children, it seemed, were quite enough for him. And strangely, Lord Edmond had thought, he himself had wanted children, too, while she had talked to him—children by her body, children to make her happy, and himself, too. He had never thought of children except in terms of an heir. He had never wanted children.

He had stayed away from her and resigned himself to a sleepless night and imagined her sleepless, too. He watched her now the following morning pick up a plate and fill it from the dishes on the sideboard. Though "fill" was not quite an accurate word. The plate was almost as empty when she sat down—as far from him as she could find an empty chair—as it had been when she picked it up.

"Another sunny day," Andrew Shelbourne said. "Is this England? Can it be England?"

"It can be and is," Lady Eleanor said firmly. "I put in a special order for another week of fine weather during my prayers last Sunday. So everyone can relax and enjoy it. Such prayers are always answered, are they not, Samuel, my dear?"

The Reverend Ormsby grinned. "I cannot answer for God," he said, "but for myself, I would consider it quite uncivil to ignore such a prayer."

"It seems that God is a civil gentleman," Andrew said.

"Even so," Doris said after the general laughter had died away, "I am not sure that we should be venturing as far as Canterbury today. Fourteen miles." She frowned. "It would be a treacherous journey in a storm, and a storm is going to be the inevitable outcome of this long spell of heat, mark my word."

"Doris is going to be thoroughly disappointed if she proves to be wrong," her husband said with a twinkle in his eye.

"And my children will be worse than disappointed if she is right," Leila Ormsby said with a sigh. "Especially if I am from home. Should we perhaps stay, Samuel?"

The Reverend Ormsby laughed. "We might be at home forever, Leila," he said. "They will have their nurse in the unlikely event that the weather does break in the course of the day, and a whole army of other servants in the house."

"And me, too, dear," Lady Eleanor said. "I will be unable to come to Canterbury, I am afraid, though I love it above all places on this earth."

There was a chorus of protesting voices about the table.

"I am expecting some callers," she said, "on this very day. Annoying, is it not? I invited them, and I cannot put them off without seeming quite rag-mannered."

"What a shame," Mrs. Wiggins said politely. "Perhaps we should postpone our drive until tomorrow."

"By no means," Lady Eleanor said. "You are all to go and enjoy yourselves. I live close enough, after all, that I can go to Canterbury any day of the year."

The trip had been suggested during the course of the evening before, and the idea had been received with enthusiasm by all the guests, who were about equally divided between those who were eager to shop and those who wished to view the cathedral.

Lord Edmond was tempted not to go at all. He would

stay and keep his aunt company and make himself agreeable to her callers, he thought. But he changed his mind again. Perhaps Mary was not yet convinced. Perhaps somehow she had persuaded herself that his behavior the evening before had not been so bad after all. Perhaps his failure to make any attempt to enter her room during the night had redeemed him somewhat in her eyes. He would take this one more day to convince her. And then he would leave her alone. He would stay as far away from her as it was possible to when they were both guests at the same country home.

"What?" he said to a question Mr. Bigsby-Gore had just asked him. "Oh, yes, assuredly I am going. I would not miss such a pleasure trip for the world."

THERE WERE TWO days still to go to Lady Eleanor's birthday and the grand celebration she had organized for the occasion. And then one more day after that before the party was at an end. It was not long. But it was far too long. Mary would not be able to endure that long. She would have to leave, return to London.

She sat in one of the carriages on the return from Canterbury late in the afternoon and let the conversation of the other three ladies flow about her without participating in it to any great degree. She felt weary, sick, and quite unable to face another three days at Rundle Park.

She could not do it. She had been foolish enough to love him for one day, and now the persistence and vulgarity of his attentions were no longer merely offensive. They were nauseating. Literally nauseating. She wanted to retch and retch and then cry herself dry and empty. She wanted to sleep and to forget. She wanted to get away. She had to get away. Away from Rundle Park and away from him. And, yes, away from Simon, too. She was not sure of anything at all any longer. She needed to be alone. She needed to think. She needed to lick her wounds.

It had been a horrid day. Somehow there had been a minor misunderstanding between herself and Simon, with the result that when they had arrived in Canterbury and she had been handed from the carriage—the ladies had traveled in carriages, while the gentleman had ridden—he had already committed himself to escort a group of shoppers, whereas she had attached herself to a party set to view the cathedral.

It had not seemed a serious matter. After all, even when they were married, they would not expect to be inseparable. And if he preferred to shop while she preferred to feast her eyes on history, then it was perfectly desirable that they go their separate ways for an hour or two. It had not seemed serious, because Lord Edmond, unmannerly brute that he was, had attached himself to neither group, but had stridden off alone as soon as his horse had been stabled.

But he had reappeared at the cathedral, as she might have expected he would. And he had attached himself to her left side until the gentleman with whom she had been walking moved off from her right to hear some comment that Stephen Wiggins was making.

"You like these old, cold, moldering edifices, Mary?" Lord Edmond had asked.

But she would no longer believe either his ignorance or his lack of taste. "And so do you, obviously," she had said, "or you would not have come here quite alone, with no coercion at all."

"Ah," he had said, "but I came here to be with you, Mary, having guessed that you would choose this rather than the shopping trip. Had I made my intention clear, Goodrich would have been here, hanging on your arm like a leech."

"What a very unpleasant simile," she had said.

"Like a watchdog, then," he had said with a shrug. "Isn't Chaucer or someone buried there?"

"No," she had said. "He is buried in Westminster Abbey, as I am sure you are very well aware. You are thinking of the *Canterbury Tales*."

"Ah," he had said. "Memories of school days and forbidden readings of 'The Miller's Tale.' A fine story. Have you read it?"

"You are becoming very predictable," she had said. "If I had had to guess one story from the *Tales* that you would choose as your favorite for my benefit, it would have been that. What else?"

"And no blushes?" he had said. "A shame."

Their conversation had ended at that point as the whole group came together to stroll about and see all that was to be seen.

It had not been bad—only the sort of encounter she was learning to expect. What had been bad—and especially bad when she considered that they had been inside a church—was the way he had grasped her arm as everyone went outside, and twisted her around so that her back was against a heavy stone pillar and she was suddenly quite out of sight of anyone who was not making a deliberate search. She had been taken so much by surprise that she had made no resistance at all to the press of his body to her own and to his practiced kiss, which immediately opened her mouth so that his tongue could thrust inside.

Looking back on the embrace as she rode home in the carriage, now totally oblivious of the conversation of the other ladies, she could find no way to describe it except with the word "carnal." It had been horrible. None of his other embraces had been like it. There had been no tenderness, no gentleness, no teasing or persuasion or . . . or anything except the most nauseating lust. His hands had grasped her breasts, hurting them. His groin had ground itself against her, parting her legs and setting her off balance.

His eyes had been glittering when he had lifted his head to look down at her. "You see now why I wanted to separate you from the leech?" he had said. "You see, Mary? I want you. And you want me. Admit it."

She had done the only thing she had been capable of doing. She had imposed relaxation on her body, though the lower half of his own was still pressed against her, and she had stared back at him, her face expressionless.

The half smile had been back on his face, the expression that helped her to hate him. "You are a coward, Mary," he had said. "We could have so much pleasure together that we would have to invent a new word for it. But you are afraid to admit to anything as unladylike as sexual desire. 'Attraction' was the word you used. It is a weak euphemism for what you really feel, my love."

"I have nothing whatsoever left to say to you, my lord," she had said, her voice flat. "Not reproach or pleading or denial. Nothing. You will do what you must to pursue your own pleasure, but you will find no more pleasure from me. There will be no further response to whatever approach you care to take with me. You might as well pursue a fish. Now, shall we go? Or would you like to press more kisses on me while you have me imprisoned here? If so, proceed. I have nothing to say."

"Mary." His voice had been amused, but he had pushed himself away from her. "I could arouse response in the snap of my fingers if I so chose. But the time and place are not quite right, are they? Later, my love. Later."

"If you say so," she had said.

He had bowed before her just as if he had been treating her the whole time in the most courtly of manners. "Shall we rejoin the others?" he had asked. "Take my arm?"

"If you wish." She had turned toward the doors. "And if you insist." She had taken his arm.

She closed her eyes in the carriage. It had been a dreadful day. Dreadful. And she could take no more. She had had enough. If she had to face one more of those scenes, she would surely crack.

She was going to have to leave. Rude as it would appear, and much as she hated to throw any sort of blight on Lady Eleanor's birthday celebrations, she was going to have to go away.

14

$\mathcal{H}$E WAS FEELING RATHER SICK. PHYSICALLY NAUSE-ated with self-disgust. It was rather a new feeling. He supposed that Mary had been right when she said that he hated himself. When he thought about it, he had to admit that she had a point, though he had never consciously hated himself through the years—not since the rawness of pain and guilt over Dick's death and his mother's had receded, anyway. Rather, he had turned the feeling outward and looked on the world and all that made it meaningful to many people with contempt. His most habitual expression, he guessed, though he rarely looked at himself in a mirror, was a sneer.

So this disgust with himself was a new thing. He would not use even the most degraded whore with the coarse vulgarity he had accorded Mary in Canterbury Cathedral—in a church, of all places. But the setting was perhaps a fitting one for him. The final degradation. The final thumb at the nose to the world and to God and what they had done to his life—to what *he* had done to his life. There was no point in starting to blame God. He had never done that. At least he had never become a whiner.

He was riding beside Andrew Shelbourne as they turned onto the driveway to Rundle Park, Peter and Bigsby-Gore close behind them. Two of the carriages were ahead, one of them containing Mary. He had not participated a great deal in the conversation on the way home.

He was going to have to leave. He did not want to do so. He loved his aunt and he owed her a deep debt of gratitude. He was not quite sure how he would have fared if all ties to his family had been broken when he was so young. But there were two days to go to her birthday. He could not hold out that long. Two days was an eternity. And he did not know how he was to face Mary again.

He eased his horse to the back of the group as they approached the house. The ladies would need to be helped from the carriages. Only Goodrich and Wright were up ahead. Perhaps he would not help at all, he thought. Perhaps he would disappear in the crowd and withdraw to the stable block. After all, most of the ladies did not expect perfectly courtly behavior from him anyway.

But before he could suit action to intention, his aunt appeared at the top of the horeshoe steps, and with her another lady and two gentlemen—doubtless the callers for whom she had had to stay at home. Lord Edmond glanced at them with little curiosity. He did not know the lady. She was perhaps his own age, perhaps a little older. She was elegantly, if quietly, dressed. His eyes moved on to the elder of the two men, the tall white-haired one—and then jerked quickly to the younger man, whose hair was only beginning to gray at the temples.

And then he was off his horse and thrusting the reins into the hands of he knew not whom and striding he knew not where. He was looking for someone—he did not know whom. Desperately looking. Looking in a panic. And then he saw her and he was beside her and his hand clamped onto her wrist.

"Come with me," he said, and he jerked her into motion so that she almost fell.

"Take your hand off me," she said coldly.

"By God, Waite, you will answer to me for this," Lord Goodrich said, his voice low and furious. "Take your hand off Mary this instant or this whole gathering will witness the breaking of your jaw."

Lord Edmond did not even hear either of them.

"Come," he said. "Come."

Mary looked up at the top of the steps and back to Lord Edmond. "It is all right, Simon," she said. "I will go with him."

"Mary!" the viscount protested.

"It is all right," she said.

But Lord Edmond did not hear the exchange. His eyes were on the corner of the house at the end of the terrace. He knew only that he had to reach the corner and round it. His hand was like a vise on Mary's wrist, but he did not know it. She had to take little running steps to keep up with him.

She should dig in her heels and stop. She should demand release. She should rant and rave at him, scream if necessary. She had had enough of him. More than enough—a raging excess. She should claw and kick at him.

But she did none of those things. She had looked up and seen the two unfamiliar gentlemen with Lady Eleanor and she had understood. And she had looked into Lord Edmond's face and seen the whiteness of it and the wildness of his eyes. And she did none of those things. She half ran beside him around the corner of the house and down the side, past the rose arbor, and diagonally across the back lawn toward the closest of the trees.

At first there was pain in her wrist and then numbness, and then pins and needles in her hand. But he did not release her or relax his hold on her. And she said nothing. She hurried along at his side.

They were among the trees at last, and he swung them around behind the huge trunk of an ancient oak, set his back against it, and pulled her hard against him. One arm came about her waist like an iron band. The other hand tore at the ribbons of her bonnet, tossed it carelessly aside, and cupped the back of her head. Her face was against his cravat, pressed there so that there was no possibility even of turning her head to one side in order to breathe more easily.

"Don't fight me," he said, though she had done no fighting at all. "Don't fight me."

She closed her eyes and relaxed against him. He was leaning backward slightly against the tree. Her weight was all thrown forward against him. She breathed in the warmth and the scent of him, and she listened to the wild thumping of his heart.

She did not know how long they stood there thus. Perhaps it was five minutes, perhaps ten. It felt much longer even than that. But in all the time, his hold on her did not relax at all, though his heart gradually quieted.

She did not care how long it was. Although her mind was quite calm and quite rational, she knew only that she was where she had to be, where she was needed— and where she wanted to be. She knew without panic or horror—they would come at some future time and in some future place, but not now—that she loved him. That despite everything, she had to be with him—for now, at least.

His hand behind her head relaxed finally and joined the other at her waist, and she raised her head and looked up at him. His own was thrown back against the tree trunk, his eyes closed. His face was as white as it had been when he first grasped her wrist.

And then pale blue eyes were looking down into hers,

dazed, not quite seeing her until they gradually focused and he lowered his head to kiss her.

It lasted for several minutes. But it was not at all a kiss of passion. It was one of infinite tenderness and need—the need for human closeness and touch. And she gave back gentleness and tenderness and love, holding her mouth soft and responsive and slightly open for him. She set both arms up about his neck and held him warmly.

"Do you know what this is all about?" He lifted his head away from hers eventually and set it back against the tree again, staring off somewhere over her head as she lowered her arms to rest her hands on his shoulders.

"Yes," she said.

"Ah." His voice was expressionless. "Then it was no accident. It was planned. And you knew about it, Mary, and did not warn me? But why should you? You must have been privately gloating."

"No," she said.

"No?" He ran the fingers of one hand absently through her hair. "And what am I to do now? Run off, dragging you with me? Abduction to add to my other crimes? Would you kick and scream the whole way, Mary? Why have you not been kicking and screaming now?"

"It is time to go back," she said.

He laughed, but there was no humor in the sound. "There is a whole wealth of meaning in those words, is there not?" he said. "You do not mean just to the house, do you, Mary?"

"No," she said.

"Time to go back," he said. "We can never go back, Mary. Only forward. There is no point in going back. The past can never be changed. My brother was not Lazarus, nor I Jesus."

"Sometimes we have to go back," she said. "Sometimes we have lost the way and need to go back."

His eyes looked down into hers again. "Is that what

happened to me, my wise, philosophizing, sermonizing Mary?" he asked. "Have I lost the way?"

"Yes," she said.

"Fifteen long years ago," he said. "Too long ago. All the highways and byways will be overgrown with weeds so high they will have become forests."

"Edmond." She touched his jaw lightly with the backs of her fingers. "You must go back. There is nothing ahead if you do not."

"Edmond," he said. "You say it prettily, Mary. Have I made you blush? Had you not realized that you were using my name for the first time? And is my case so desperate? You make me sound like a lost soul."

"You are a lost soul," she said.

He smiled at her slowly and lazily. "It cannot be done, you know," he said. "I cannot be made over into the sort of man who might be worthy of you."

"I am not thinking of me," she said. "You need to become a man worthy of your own respect. Don't smile at me like that."

He continued to smile. "How do you come to be here with me?" he asked. "Did I bring you?"

"I have the bruise on my wrist to prove it," she said.

He took her hand in his and ran his fingers over the still-reddened wrist before raising his eyes to hers. "I have done nothing but bruise you in the past two days," he said. "I should take myself off, Mary, away from them and out of your life. It is what I intended to do on my return from Canterbury."

"No," she said. "You must go back. You must."

"Tell me," he said. "Were they as surprised as I? Did they know that I was here?"

"No," she said.

"So my aunt is playing devil's advocate," he said. "Well, there is no reason why we cannot all be civil to one another, I suppose. It was all a very long time ago."

"Yes," she said. "You must go back."

"But only if you will come with me," he said. "My feet will not know how to set themselves one before the other across that lawn if you are not there to hold my hand, Mary. You must come with me. Will you?"

"Yes," she said.

"Holding my hand?" He chuckled. "The leech's face will turn purple at the sight, I would not wonder."

"Don't," she said. "He is my betrothed."

He sobered instantly. "Yes, he is," he said. "But no more worthy of you than I, Mary. At least my crimes are all open ones. Promise me that you will look more closely into his background and history before you marry him."

"Let's go back," she said, trying at last to pull herself upright and away from his body.

But he caught at her waist and held her to him. "Promise me," he said.

"If there is something about him that I need to know," she said, "then perhaps you should tell me. But not mere spite, please."

"Promise me," he said.

"Very well, then," she said. "I promise. Let's go back."

He released his hold on her and she moved away from him, brushing the creases from her dress and bending to pick up her bonnet. He was still leaning against the tree as she tied the ribbons beneath her chin. His smile was somewhat twisted.

"Do you have any inkling of how hard this is for me, Mary?" he asked. "I feel paralyzed in every limb. I don't believe it can be done."

She held out her hands to him and he looked at them, surprised, and set his own in them.

"Yes, it can be," she said, "because there is nothing else to be done." She tightened the pressure of her hands in his.

"Well." He squeezed her hands before releasing them and finally straightening up away from the tree. "Perhaps you are right. And perhaps at some future time, when I have your back to a bed and I am between you and the nearest door, I shall say the same words and you will admit the truth of them as meekly as I have just done."

"I would not count on it," she said.

"Let us go and face this unfaceable situation, then," he said. But when she would have taken his arm, he took her hand in his, laced his fingers with hers, and tightened his hold. "After which I may well throttle my aunt."

They stepped out from the cover of the trees and began the walk back across the lawn to the house.

THE DRAWING-ROOM DOORS were open and a buzz of sound issued from inside. The guests were partaking of refreshments, though it was far too late for tea, yet too early for dinner.

Lord Edmond Waite fixed a footman standing outside the doors with a steely eye. "Her ladyship is inside?" he asked.

"Yes, m'lord." The servant bowed.

"Then ask her to step outside, if you please." His fingers were still laced with Mary's.

Lady Eleanor appeared no more than a minute later. "Edmond, Mary," she said brightly. "Where on earth did you disappear to after such a long journey?"

"They are inside there?" Lord Edmond asked curtly, nodding in the direction of the drawing room.

The brightness disappeared from Lady Eleanor's face. "No," she said. "They are upstairs. It was as much as I could do to prevent them from calling out their carriage and loading up their unpacked trunks again." She smiled fleetingly.

"And you have Mary to thank that I am not twenty miles off by now," he said. There was no softening in his expression. "Why did you do it, Aunt?"

She looked helplessly at Mary and then back at her nephew. "Because I will be sixty years old," she said, "in two days' time. Because I have one brother and two nephews. Does that make sense to you, Edmond? Probably not."

He looked stonily at her. "Well," he said, "there is no avoiding the matter now, is there? Let us have it over with, then. Will they see me?"

"They are in my sitting room," Lady Eleanor said without really answering the question. "Will you come up now, then, Edmond?"

"Now or never," he said. "This is not easy, you know, Aunt. Did you expect it to be?"

"Nor for me, dear," she said. "And no, I did not expect it to be easy for anyone. Even for myself. I did not know—I *do* not know—if I am perhaps bringing even worse disaster on anyone. But there is no worse, is there?" She looked at Mary, smiled at her briefly, and turned to lead the way up the stairs.

Mary stood where she was and tried to free her hand, but Lord Edmond's tightened about it.

"Mary comes, too," he said firmly. "I will not do this without her."

Lady Eleanor looked back, her expression interested. "Very well, dear," she said. "If Mary wishes it."

"She has talked me into it," he said, his voice grim. "She had better wish it."

"Such a gentlemanly way to ask, dear," Lady Eleanor said, clucking her tongue, but Mary had moved up beside Lord Edmond again, drawn by the pressure of his hand, and was accompanying him up the stairs.

"I will come," she said quietly.

His aunt preceded them along the upper hallway to her suite of rooms. Lord Edmond did not look at Mary. Indeed, he was almost unaware of her presence at that moment. But he did know that if she once released her hand from his, he would lose all courage. His aunt opened the door into her sitting room and stepped inside. He drew Mary to his side and entered with her.

It was rather like a carefully arranged tableau, he thought irrelevantly. His father stood with his back to the room, looking out of a window, down onto the formal gardens. His brother stood behind and to one side of an easy chair, his hand on the shoulder of the lady who must be his wife. No one was moving or smiling or talking.

"Well," Lady Eleanor said brightly. "Here is Edmond returned at last, Martin."

His father turned to look at him. He was so very much the same, even after fifteen years, except that his hair, which had been partly dark, partly silver then, was now completely white. People had always said that Edmond looked like his father—tall, inclined to thinness, the face long and austere, the nose prominent, the lips thin. His father looked the picture of elderly respectability.

Edmond had a sudden image of his father standing straight and immobile beside the bed on which Dick had been laid out the morning after his death. His father's face had been stern, more like a mask than a face. He had looked across to the doorway where his youngest son had appeared.

"Get out!" he had hissed so low that the words had seemed to reach Edmond by a medium other than sound. "Murderer! Get out of my son's room."

The last time he had seen his father. The last words he had heard him utter.

"Sir?" he said now, and he was aware with one part of

his mind of Mary flinching beside him. He eased the pressure of his fingers against hers. He inclined his head into what was not quite a bow.

"Edmond?" His father's mouth scarcely moved. There seemed to be as little sound as on that morning in Dick's bedchamber.

"And Wallace is here, too," Lady Eleanor said heartily. "And Anne. You will not have met your sister-in-law, Edmond."

They had married almost thirteen years before. Although they had had a big wedding, he had not been invited, of course.

"He called me murderer." Edmond had staggered to his eldest brother's room and thrown the door open without knocking. "He called me murderer, Wally."

"And what would you call yourself?" Wallace had been standing at the window, his hands braced on the sill, his shoulders shaking with the sobs that had racked him.

Edmond had stood there for a few moments, cold and aghast. And then he had left. His mother had been too sick to see him. Or so her maid had told him. But he had heard his mother's voice tell the maid not to admit him. She never wanted to set eyes on him again.

So he had left, taking nothing with him but his horse and his purse and the clothes he had stood in.

"Wallace?" he said now. "Ma'am?"

"Edmond?" his brother said.

There was something farcical about the conversation, that part of his mind that had learned to look on the world with scorn and amusement told him. But he felt no amusement.

"Edmond?" his sister-in-law said, getting to her feet and coming across the room toward him. She was a little overweight, he noticed, elegantly dressed, rather plain. She held out a hand to him. Her chin was up and she looked very directly into his eyes. "I am delighted to make your acquaintance at last."

And finally he had to relinquish Mary's hand in order to take his sister-in-law's.

"And I yours," he said. "Anne."

Anne smiled and looked a little uncertainly at Mary. Lord Edmond set an arm about her waist and drew her closer to his side. "May I present Mary, Lady Morningston?" he said. "My friend." He looked at his father belligerently. "And that is not a euphemism for any other kind of relationship."

His father's elegant eyebrows rose. "I would not dream of suggesting otherwise, Edmond," he said. "How do you do, Lady Mornington?"

Mary curtsied. "I am well, thank you, Your Grace," she said.

"My father, Mary," Lord Edmond said. "The Duke of Brookfield. And my brother, Wallace, Earl of Welwyn. And my sister-in-law, Anne."

"Well," Lady Eleanor said when the civilities had been exchanged, "now that the first awkwardness is past, shall we all sit down while I order up refreshments? I am sure my guests downstairs can entertain themselves for an hour or so."

And incredibly, Lord Edmond thought, they did sit down. And they conversed on a variety of safe general topics. A little stiltedly, it was true, but nevertheless they talked—all of them. Perhaps the ladies were most to be thanked. Anne talked about her three children, two sons and a daughter, and Mary talked about Canterbury Cathedral, and his aunt talked about mutual acquaintances and the weather. He asked his father about his health and Wallace about their journey. And they asked him about Willow Court.

It seemed unreal. How could they be sitting there, the three of them, conversing together politely about nothing of any importance when they had parted fifteen years before with a bitterness that had completely broken close family ties? And yet that was exactly what they were doing.

Was that that, then? he thought when his aunt rose to announce that it was time to retire to their rooms to change for dinner. Had Dick's death and his mother's and the fifteen years since been of so little significance that the past half-hour had erased all the unpleasantness, all the suffering, all the guilt? Was there nothing of any more importance to be said and settled? There was a feeling of anticlimax to succeed the utter panic that had seized him on his return from Canterbury, when he had looked to the top of the steps and seen them standing there with his aunt.

And then, too, there was another strange feeling of emptiness, of something not quite completed, when Anne left the room with Mary and both disappeared in the direction of their bedchambers. He stood looking after them for a moment before hurrying off to his own room to avoid having to walk there with his father and brother, who were coming out of the room after him.

Nothing was finished at all. Nothing was settled. He and his father and brother were polite strangers. And Mary? What had been happening with Mary in the past couple of hours? He had worked hard in two days to give her enough of a disgust of him that she would quell any attraction that she felt toward him. And yet as soon as he had seen that danger to all the protective armor he had built up around himself in fifteen years, that threat, he had forgotten everything except his selfish and overpowering need of her.

Even his love for her could not redeem him, then. Selfishness, it seemed, was ingrained in him, and he had just put her in a difficult situation indeed. "My friend," he had told his father, setting an arm about her waist.

And he did not believe that he had the heart to spend another evening and another day tomorrow making her hate him all over again.

He just did not have the heart. He was too selfish. His love for her obviously was not a great enough force.

15

SO WHERE WAS SHE NOW? MARY WONDERED. HER hatred for Lord Edmond had wavered, as had her resolve to leave Rundle Park without further delay. Far worse, she was somehow deeply involved with him now, aware not only of the fact that she loved him but also of the fact that he needed her.

She could not forget the way in which he had dragged her off with him, not even aware of what he was doing, and of how he had held her as if she had been the only firm and solid thing left in his world. And of how he had kissed her, not with the coarse suggestiveness of his embrace in Canterbury Cathedral, but with warm need. And of how he had clung to her hand for a long, long time, even taking her in to the momentous first meeting with his father and brother. And of how he had introduced her as his friend.

His friend! Surely she was anything and everything but that. And yet somehow, in the course of just a few hours, they had become friends. Mary frowned at the thought. Was it possible? Was there any way in which she and Lord Edmond Waite could be friends? And yet they were.

And now Simon was angry with her—and justifiably so, she had to admit. She was his betrothed. They were in the drawing room, with several of the other guests, awaiting the call to dinner.

"I was shamed, Mary," he said, "left standing there like that while you rushed off for a walk with Waite. How must it have looked to everyone else?"

"No one knows we are betrothed," she reminded him.

"But everyone must realize that we have an understanding," he said. "It is in the poorest taste to give another man your private time. And what on earth could you have been doing to have been gone so long?"

"I told you," she said. "He was shocked to see his family after such a long period of separation. He needed to recover himself before meeting them. And then he wished to present me to them."

"Why?" He frowned. "They are staying, are they not? We will all be presented to His Grace and the earl and countess in time. Why did you need a special introduction? Is there something you are not telling me, Mary?"

She felt annoyed until she remembered again that he had a right to ask such questions.

"I am sorry, Simon," she said. "I suppose that in some way Lord Edmond thinks of me as a friend."

"A friend?" he said, his brows drawing together. "A friend, Mary? He has strange notions of friendship. I don't like it. I want you to stay away from him, do you hear me? And I want no more of this calling me off when I am dealing with him, just because you fear there will be a scene. Sooner or later there is going to have to be a scene, or the people here will believe that I do not know how to protect my own."

"Simon," she said, setting a hand on his arm, but Doris Shelbourne and Mr. Bigsby-Gore approached them at that moment.

"A wonderful day," Mr. Bigsby-Gore said. "A most impressive cathedral, would you not agree, Lady Mornington? I had not seen it before, strange as it may seem."

Mary took gratefully to the new topic of conversation.

A few minutes later Lady Eleanor entered the room on the arm of her brother, the Earl and Countess of Welwyn behind them. There was a buzz of renewed animation as the other guests were presented to the new arrivals.

"Lord Edmond resembles his father," Doris said quietly to Mary. "Is it true that they have not met since Lord Edmond killed his brother? The meeting today must be very awkward for His Grace. Have they met yet, do you think?"

"I would have to say that it is very decent of His Grace to be willing to stay at the same house as Lord Edmond," the viscount said, "considering the life of dissipation he has led since the killing."

"Perhaps we should not judge without knowing the whole of the inside story," Mary said, and won for herself a cold stare from her betrothed.

Lady Welwyn smiled when she saw Mary, and slipped her hand from her husband's arm. "Lady Mornington," she said, "how pleasant to see a familiar face, though I met you only an hour or so ago. I am afraid that we have kept so much to the north of England since my marriage that I know almost no one from the south. This is something of an ordeal."

Mary smiled. "But I am so glad that you have come," she said.

"For Edmond's sake?" Anne said. "It is high time that old matter was cleared up, as I am sure you would agree. Are you the Lady Mornington who is famous for her literary salons in London?"

"Am I famous?" Mary said. "But, yes, my habit of inviting literary or political figures to my weekly entertainments has attracted many regular visitors."

"My friend Lydia Grainger has spoken of you," Anne

said. "How fortunate you are to live in town. Sometimes I pine for it, though I must not complain. The country is wonderful for the children, and we have many close friendships with our neighbors. And Wallace takes me to Harrogate for several weeks almost every year."

Mary warmed to Lord Edmond's sister-in-law.

Lord Edmond was late for dinner. He came wandering into the dining room when everyone was already seated and the footmen were bringing on the first course.

"So sorry, Aunt," he said, waving a careless, lace-bedecked hand in the direction of Lady Eleanor. "My valet could not seem to get my hair to look quite disheveled enough. It was looking too unfashionably tidy."

His words won a titter from Stephanie and some laughter from the gentlemen. The duke's lips thinned, Mary noticed, glancing hastily in his direction, and the earl frowned and looked down at his plate. She could have shaken Lord Edmond. If he wished to make a good impression on his father and brother, could he not at least have been on time for the first meal he was to share with them? And did he have to make such a foolishly foppish excuse for being late?

But of course, she thought, forcing herself to relax and turning to make conversation with the gentleman on her left, it had all been quite deliberate on his part. Just as so much of his behavior was deliberately designed to give people an unfavorable impression of him.

He was, she realized fully at last, a man who wore a mask. And she realized, too, perhaps, why she loved him against all reason. She had seen behind the mask.

She looked curiously at him as he took the empty chair between Mrs. Wiggins and Mrs. Ormsby. He looked along the table at her as he did so and winked.

He winked! *Heavens,* Mary thought, *whatever next?* But a quickly darted look across the table assured her that the viscount was deep in conversation with Lady Cathcart and had not noticed.

LORD EDMOND WAS out early the following morning, riding alone as was his custom. He would have been on his way home now, he thought with some regret, if it had not been for the totally unexpected arrival of his father the afternoon before. And yet, he had to admit, perhaps it was for the best, after all. He had always had the feeling that he could not expect to go through the rest of his life without meeting his family again. Now the dread meeting was over, and really, apart from the inevitable embarrassment, it had not been so very bad.

They had met and been polite to one another. They had spent an evening, first in the same dining room, and then in the same drawing room, and been polite to one another. There was one day to his aunt's birthday, two to the end of this country visit. If they were all careful—and polite—those days could be lived through without any major confrontation, and forever after they would not all live in dread of being brought face-to-face with one another.

And as for Mary—well, there were two days during which he could avoid her as much as possible and be polite to her when he could not avoid her company. It could not be that difficult a time to get through if he set his mind to it.

As luck would have it, there were two ladies walking in the formal gardens as he made his way back from the stables, and one of them was his sister-in-law. He somehow never expected to encounter ladies until close to noon at the earliest. She saw him, raised a hand in greeting, said something to Lady Cathcart, and made her way toward him. Well, at least, he thought, neither Wallace nor his father was in sight. And he had liked Anne the day before.

"Good morning," she said, smiling at him. "Have you been riding? I wish I had known. I would have come with you. Or do you prefer to ride alone?"

"I would have been happy to have your company," he said politely. "Do you always rise early?"

"Oh, always," she said, laughing. "I'm a creature of the country, not the city, Edmond. I am so glad your aunt arranged this little surprise. I have wanted to meet you since long before my wedding."

"The black sheep?" he said. "The skeleton in the closet? The prodigal who did not come home?"

"The missing part of Wallace's family," she said. "The member rarely spoken of but always missed." She laughed. "I have always said that Nigel is like his grandfather, and everyone has always been quick to agree. But he is far more like his uncle. So like that I cannot help but laugh when I look at you."

"Nigel?" he said.

She clucked her tongue. "The estrangement has been almost total, has it not?" she said. "And quite foolish. Nigel is our older son. He is eleven years old. And then there are Ninian, nine, and Laura, six. They are here with us. You must meet them. You are their only uncle on their father's side."

Lord Edmond looked somewhat uncomfortable. "I did know that Wallace had children," he said. "I am afraid I have never had a great deal to do with children."

"It is not obligatory in order to get along well with them," she said with a laugh. "We all were children ourselves, after all."

"Not I," he said.

"You always had your head in a book, did you not?" she said, looking closely at him. "I have learned some things about you over the years, you see, from chance remarks that have been made. You did not play a great deal."

"I have made up for it since," he said. "I have done nothing but play since I reached my majority."

"Oh, yes," she said. "You do not need to look at me with that deliberately cynical look, Edmond. The fame of your reputation has reached us in the north of England, believe me. Each detail is like a knife wound to Wallace and your father."

He shrugged. "Each one convincing them that I am incorrigible?" he said. "Well, I am, Anne. You are not about to try to find redeeming features in me, are you? Females have a tiresome tendency to do that."

"Oh, dear," she said, "one would hate to aspire to the mediocrity of being a typical female. What I meant was that each detail of your . . . your wildness, I suppose I must call it, reminds them of their own guilt, though they would not admit to that even if the Inquisition were let loose on them, of course. I hope the three of you do not mean to be polite to one another for two days. That would be a dreadful anticlimax."

"It is just what I have been hoping for," he said. "Would you prefer that I was rude to them, Anne? I can be dreadfully uncivil when I want to be. And dreadfully annoying, too. I have cultivated the art with great care."

"Like insisting on having disheveled hair before appearing at dinner," she said.

"Oh, that was real enough," he said. "You do not know how lowering it would be for a London gentleman to appear unfashionable, Anne."

She laughed. "Your aunt has said that this is to be a free day," she said. "Everyone may arrange his own entertainment. Wallace and I are to take the children for a picnic with your father. Will you come with Mary?"

"With Mary?" he said.

"I like her," she said. "Do you notice how we are on a first-name basis already? And if she is your friend, Edmond, I cannot think you quite beyond hope. She is a very sensible and interesting lady. So it will be a waste of your time trying to shock me or make me frown on you. I shall merely laugh. Will you come?"

"I think you have the wrong connection," he said. "It is Mary and Goodrich, Anne."

"The viscount?" she asked, turning her head to look at him. "Oh, no. That would be a disappointment. Are you sure?"

"I had personal and private notice from his own lips," he said, "that they are betrothed. You had better not try to matchmake, Anne. He might challenge you to a duel."

"How alarming!" she said. "Would the choice of weapons be mine? I should choose knitting needles. I shall have to invite them both to the picnic, then, and another lady. Whom shall I ask?"

"No one," he said. "I shall stay at the house and challenge someone to a game of billiards."

"Coward," she said. "You must come, if only to meet your niece and nephews. And why did you bring Mary to meet us yesterday if she is only a friend and betrothed to someone else? You looked to be squeezing her hand hard enough to hurt, Edmond."

He narrowed his eyes and looked down at her. "You see altogether too much," he said. "I was terrified, I would have you know. Shaking in my boots. Knees knocking. Teeth clacking. If I had not been clinging to Mary's hand, I would probably have disgraced myself and tripped over a rose in the carpet or something equally foolish."

Her smile softened on him. "They were terrified, too," she said. "Wallace's hand was like a vise on my shoulder, so that for a moment I wondered if Mary or I would be the first to scream with pain. And your father had been pacing the room enough to wear a hole in the carpet for you to trip over. You must come this afternoon, Edmond. The time has come, you know. It can no longer be avoided."

He looked at her broodingly. "You talk just like Mary," he said. "If it were not for her, I would probably still be running straight due west. And now you are trying to make me jump right into the hornet's nest, just when I have been hoping to tiptoe about it for the next two days."

She smiled. "You will come, then," she said. It was not a question. "And we might as well go today. If Mrs. Shelbourne is to be believed, this glorious weather is bound to break with earth-shattering storms any minute now."

"She has been telling us so *ad nauseam* ever since we came here," he said. "I don't know why the woman cannot simply enjoy the sunshine."

"For some people, happiness consists in waiting for some disaster to overtake them or the world," Anne said. "It takes all types to make life interesting, Edmond. Would you really rather I did not invite Mary?"

He gave her a sidelong look and did not answer. He should answer, he knew. But he did not.

"Ah," she said. "I heard you loudly and clearly. I am to please myself, and then any blame for what happens must fall on my shoulders. Well, they are broad ones. I am not as slender, alas, as I was when I married. I can hardly believe that I have met you at last, Edmond, and am strolling with you here just as if you were any ordinary human being and not the monstrous skeleton in the family closet that you mentioned earlier. Good old Aunt Eleanor."

"Old fiend Aunt Eleanor, I would be inclined to say," he said. "But I am pleased to have met you, Anne. Wally made a good marriage, I can see. But then, he was always the most sensible of the three of us."

"I must go to my children," she said as their strolling brought them to the foot of the horseshoe steps. "I shall look forward to this afternoon, Edmond."

"Likewise," he said, releasing her arm and making her a bow.

But he felt rather like a condemned man who has just learned that his execution is to take place that very day. A whole afternoon with no one else for company except his family—a father and brother from whom he had been estranged for fifteen years, two nephews and a niece whom he had never met, and a sister-in-law whom he liked but who seemed determined to force a confrontation. And perhaps Mary and Goodrich, though their company would be no consolation to him at all.

Perhaps he should, after all, have left for Willow Court that morning, he thought.

MARY WAS FEELING a little guilty, though it really was not her fault that she was spending the afternoon as the sole outside member of a family picnic while Simon was driving off with several of the other guests to explore a ruined abbey six miles away. Well, almost not her fault anyway.

The countess had found her writing letters in the morning room and had invited her to join the picnic.

"I intend to invite Lord Goodrich, too," she had said. "I understand that he is your fiancé?"

"Oh," Mary had said, "it is not official yet. Nothing at all is settled." She had felt a little guilty over the last sentence, since it was not strictly true. She had said it only because for some reason she did not want Anne to know the full truth.

The countess had looked strangely pleased. "Ah, I have heard wrongly, then," she had said. "But I shall invite him anyway. Will you come?"

"I would love to," Mary had said. But she had guessed that Lord Edmond would also be a member of the group, and she knew that perhaps she should have made some excuse.

Just before luncheon she had met the viscount and asked him if he had had his invitation to the picnic.

"After I had already agreed to join the party to the abbey," he had said. "I was relieved, of course, to have an excuse not to accept. It would be a pleasure to become more closely acquainted with His Grace, but since Waite is to be of the party, I am thankful that we are not."

"But I am going," she had said. "I accepted Anne's invitation, since she was going to ask you, too."

"She did, but too late." He had frowned. "But I have said you will be coming to the abbey, Mary."

"I am sorry," she had said. "But I cannot go back on my word now, Simon."

A brief argument had ensued, which had left him angry that she would go on a picnic that included Lord Edmond without his escort, and which had left her indignant that he was trying to order her life before they were even married. Both had kept to their original plans.

And yet she felt guilty. She understood that Anne had not issued the invitation to Simon until the abbey party had been all arranged. Had Anne held back deliberately, hoping to separate them? Because she, Mary, had denied that there was a betrothal, perhaps? Mary sensed that Anne liked her and was prepared to like her brother-in-law, too. However it was, she was part of the picnic group and Simon was on his way to the abbey.

The picnic was to be at the lake, and they were retracing the route by which a larger group had come there a few days before. His Grace was going with the carriage and the food by an easier and more direct route. But this time it was the earl who helped Mary over the stile. Lord Edmond and Anne were up ahead with the children. Lord Edmond was in close conversation with the older boy, Nigel.

"You have known my brother long, Lady Mornington?" the earl asked politely.

"Not very," she said. "We were members of the same party to Vauxhall one evening just this summer. Then Lord Edmond attended one of my literary evenings and took me a couple of weeks later to meet your aunt, who was eager to make my acquaintance and has since also come to my salon. Hence my invitation here."

"Edmond attended one of your literary evenings?" he said in some surprise. "Is that not out of character for him?"

"Mr. Beasley was expounding on some of his radical social theories," she said. "Lord Edmond was the only guest present willing to argue against him. Everyone else was awed by his fame, I believe. It was a lively evening." She did not know quite why she spoke of that evening as if Lord Edmond's behavior had been exemplary.

"He is so very different," the earl said. "I scarcely recognized him, Lady Mornington. Oh, the physical differences are not so great, except that he has aged as one would expect a man to do in fifteen years. But in every other way. I expected it, of course. We have heard enough about him. But I suppose I still expected the old Edmond when I met him again."

"What was he like?" Mary could not resist asking the question of yet another person who had known him.

"Quiet. Serious." The earl thought for a moment. "He loved the world of books. He used to write poetry.

He lived more in his imagination than in reality, I believe. And yet I am not sure that is quite true, either. He always had a strong sense of justice and fairness, but a grasp of the realities of life. He used to feel that the wealthy and privileged had a great responsibility to the poor and downtrodden."

"He was at university," she said.

"Yes." There were another few moments of silence as he thought back. "He never seemed to know how to have fun. Poor Edmond. We used to worry about him. We used to plan ways to force him to enjoy himself." He laughed without amusement. "We need not have worried if we had been able to look into the future, need we?"

"Did you plan his twenty-first birthday party?" she asked.

He looked uneasy. "We all did," he said. "It seemed fitting that he enter full adulthood in a more manly way than with his nose buried in a book. Unfortunately, Lady Mornington, he was unable to hold his liquor. But enough of that. Your late husband fought in the Peninsular Wars? Did you follow him there?"

They talked about Spain and Waterloo and Wellington and the peace for the rest of the walk to the lake.

But the Earl of Welwyn, Mary decided after their brief conversation about Lord Edmond, probably felt as guilty about the death of his younger brother as Lord Edmond himself did. If only they could talk to each other freely, offer healing to each other. And they were so close—together again for the first time since the day after the disaster. And yet not close at all.

But it was none of her business, she told herself as they reached the lake, glancing at the duke, who was seated already beside the water and was smiling at the children and beckoning them, ignoring his youngest son, or perhaps not knowing how to include him in his welcome without great awkwardness.

Her heart ached suddenly for Edmond. And she realized that even in her mind she had thought of him by his given name without his title to prefix it.

16

*H*E FELT DEUCED UNCOMFORTABLE, IF THE TRUTH were known. And if he had imagined that the worst of the embarrassment was over after that first meeting, then he was discovering that he had imagined wrongly. He found himself directing all his conversation toward Anne and his niece and nephews—especially toward Nigel, the elder, who had inexplicably chosen to discuss Latin poetry with him during the walk to the lake. It was a novelty, he was finding, to be an uncle. But he could think of nothing that would not sound trite to say to his father and his brother. And he dared not talk to Mary. He certainly did not want to be alone with her.

"I believe that after that lengthy walk we should eat before exploring the shores of the lake," Anne announced when they had joined the duke on the grassy bank.

"Hoorah!" cried Ninian, who was rather inclined to share his mother's tendency to be overweight, Lord Edmond noticed, looking critically at the boy.

And so blankets were spread on the grass and the baskets carried from the carriage by the footman who had accompanied it from the house. And the children waited impatiently for Anne to hand around the food.

Lord Edmond could have sat beside his father, who had Laura seated on one side and him and empty blanket on the other. He sat down instead close to Mary, not looking at her, addressing some remark to Anne.

They sat thus through most of tea, seated close to each other, turned slightly away from each other, conversing with other people. It was the most uncomfortable meal he had ever taken, Lord Edmond thought. The food tasted rather like straw. Though perhaps that was unfair to his aunt's cook. The truth was that he did not taste the food at all. He would not have been able to say afterward what he had eaten.

And then, halfway through the meal, he set his hand down on the blanket to brace himself, to find that Mary's hand was there, too, their little fingers almost brushing. He should move his hand, he knew. He expected her to move hers. And yet neither moved until a couple of minutes later their little fingers rested quite unmistakably against each other.

Lord Edmond had to concentrate his attention on his wine when the thought struck him that the light brushing of two fingers could be as erotic as the most intimate of sexual contacts. He would not answer to what might have happened if there had not been three other adults and three children present.

"May I go and play, Mama?" Ninian asked impatiently when the adults seemed to be lingering over their meal.

"As long as you promise to stay away from the water's edge," Anne said. "Let Nigel and Laura go with you. I do not trust you otherwise not to get at least your shoes and stockings wet."

"I want Grandpapa to come with us," Laura said.

"Grandpapa is still eating," the earl said.

"I am merely enjoying more of Cook's good food than is good for me," the duke said, getting slowly to his feet. "Where do you want to go, little poppet?"

Lord Edmond had a feeling that his father was relieved at the excuse to get away from the uncomfortable atmosphere on the blankets.

When after several more minutes and another glass of wine Anne suggested a walk to the pavilion, Lord Edmond got to his feet quickly and stretched out a hand to help Mary up. But he did not quite look at her. He was hoping that the walking arrangements could be as they had been earlier. He did not want to walk with Mary. He turned to Anne.

"Have you seen the pavilion?" she was asking Mary. "It is supposed to be almost as large and splendid as the house. In which direction is it, Wallace?"

"Around there," the earl said, pointing off to the denser trees and the bend in the lake. "But you exaggerate somewhat, Anne. I daresay it is not one tenth the size of the house."

"Large enough for the birthday tea and celebrations anyway," Anne said with a laugh. "Come along, Mary. We will explore."

And Lord Edmond found that the situation was much worse than the one he had feared. He was to walk with neither Mary nor Anne, but with his brother. And already the ladies were striding off along the bank of the lake, in the opposite direction from that taken by his father and the children. He clasped his hands behind his back and pursed his lips.

"Trust Aunt Eleanor not to do anything as uncomplicated as organize a dinner and dance at the house," his brother said.

"Her love of the unexpected has always been one of her greatest charms," Lord Edmond said. "Do you remember the time when she had a group of traveling players performing at the house, and had them stay for several days afterward, mingling with the other guests just as if it were proper for them to do so? Mama almost had a fit of the vapors when she knew we had been subjected to that. I think she thought that perhaps your virtue had been assailed by some of the actresses. Dick and I were too young and too uninterested in such matters to worry about."

The earl made no comment.

"Of course," Lord Edmond added, hearing his words almost as if they issued from his mouth independently of his brain or his will, "as it turned out, I am the one she should have worried about. Actresses are far more interesting offstage than on, in my experience."

He had the dubious satisfaction of seeing his brother's lips thin. "Hardly a matter for general conversation," he said.

"General?" Lord Edmond looked at his brother in surprise. "But I am talking to you, Wally. You used to like to regale us with tales of your exploits at Oxford and all the delights that were in store for us there. Not the intellectual ones, of course."

His brother flushed. "For God's sake, Edmond," he said. "We were puppies then. We are middle-aged men now. Some of us have taken on responsibilities and have answered the demands of respectability."

Lord Edmond winced. "Middle-aged," he said. "Is that what we are, Wally? And no longer capable of enjoying ourselves? Is that what one gives up with youth?"

"Obviously you have not," the earl said, his voice low and furious. "Your excesses seem to grow with your years, Edmond. I just hope that you do not try to corrupt my children."

Lord Edmond's nostrils flared. His voice was icy when he spoke. "Actually," he said, "on the walk here I was enlightening Nigel on the sensual pleasures that Eton will have to offer him—with not a woman in sight, of course. I shall try to have the same conversation with Ninian on the return walk. As for Laura, I must take her aside within the next day or two and give her some early

instructions on how to entice her man away from cour-
tesans. Girls can never learn too early, can they?"

His words were interrupted when his brother's hand
grabbed him by the cravat and swung him around to
face him.

"It was not enough, was it," he said through his teeth,
"for you to kill poor Dick and Mama? But you must
destroy Papa, too, with your wildness and your debaucheries. And now you must attempt to sully my family with the products of your vile mind. Leave here,
Edmond. Do something decent in your rotten life and
leave today."

Lord Edmond made no move to release himself. He
spoke quietly. "Sometimes, Wally," he said, "when people expect certain behavior of someone, he will oblige
them. If you expect the worst of me, then devil take it,
the worst you will get. What did you expect, you and
Papa—and Mama, too, though she never said it in
words—when you called me a murderer? What did you
expect when you drove me away? That I would finish
my studies, become a clergyman, and spend the rest of
my days doing pious penance? Is that what you expected?"

"That is what anyone with a sensitive conscience
would have done," the earl said.

Lord Edmond laughed and brushed his brother's hand
away. The ladies had already disappeared among the
trees, he saw. "Then perhaps I do not have a sensitive
conscience," he said. "Do you?"

"I beg your pardon?" The earl's voice was haughty.

"How did you absolve your conscience for getting me
foxed for the first time in my life and laughing at the
spectacle I made of myself?" Lord Edmond asked.
"How did you forgive yourself for allowing me to take
that ride, and even thinking it a huge joke, and for not
stopping Dick from coming after me?"

The earl was nodding his head. "Oh, yes, I see how it is," he said. "I might have expected it. It is often the case, I believe, that a guilty man will try to shift the blame onto someone else's shoulders."

"No," Lord Edmond said. "I was as guilty as sin. I killed them just as surely as if I had taken a gun and shot them. But I was not quite alone in my guilt, Wally. And I certainly do not need you to point out to me how rotten my life has been. I know it better than anyone—I have lived it. But I do not like to mire innocents in my hell, for all that. Your children are safe from me. You may rest easy."

The earl seemed uncertain of what to do with his anger. He clasped his hands behind him and swayed on his feet. "We did not drive you away, Edmond," he said, his voice uneasy. "You went. We searched for you and you were gone. And we wrote to tell you of Mama's passing. You might have come for the funeral."

"When the letter told me that the shock of Dick's pointless death as a result of my drunkenness had driven her to a premature end?" Lord Edmond said. "It was scarcely an invitation home, Wally."

"Neither was it a command to stay away and break Papa's heart with a rapid decline into dissipation," the earl said. "You might have come home, Edmond. You might have made your peace with us. You might have found us ready to forgive."

Lord Edmond's laugh was more sneer than laughter. "Perhaps I was not ready to forgive you," he said.

"Good God, Edmond!" The earl's voice was exasperated. "How were we to know that you would be so little able to hold your liquor? You were twenty-one years old. A man, or so we thought. It seems we were wrong. You proved quite unable to control either your liquor or your life."

Lord Edmond laughed again. "I was a boy," he said.

"A little bookworm of an innocent and naive boy. It is not easy for a boy to adjust his life to the sudden fact that he is a murderer and has lost his family. I needed you—you and Mama and Papa. I needed you to tell me that all would be well, even though it could not possibly be true with Dick gone. I needed you to tell me that you loved me, even though my part in his death would have made it a strain to do so. I needed you to tell me that we were still a family and that nothing could ever change that, even though Dick was gone. I needed to cry. I did so finally alone on the day of Mama's funeral. And if there is a worse misery than crying alone, Wally, I wish you would tell me what it is so that I can direct all my energies to avoiding it for the rest of my life."

"If you had just written and told us that," the earl said, white-faced. "If you had just come, Edmond. Do you believe that we would really have turned you off? Things would have been strained for a long time, but we had always been a family. We would have come through it together. Instead we were left to believe that you did not care at all. First of all getting yourself expelled from Oxford and then all that followed it. And finally humiliating Lady Dorothea and running after a woman who did not even want you, by all accounts. What were we to think, Edmond? The evidence was all against you."

Lord Edmond smiled. "I suppose I have always made the mistake of believing that other people have imaginations as acute as mine," he said. "We had better walk on, Wally. The ladies will be thinking we have both fallen in the lake."

"Anne set this up," the earl said. "I know her quite well enough to be certain of that, Edmond. And you may be sure that before you leave here there will be a similar confrontation arranged with Papa. Anne does not realize that after fifteen years the rift is beyond healing."

"Women," Lord Edmond said, "are incurable romantics. They believe that if only two people can be made to talk, all their problems will be solved. Mary is the same."

"What in the name of all that is wonderful is she doing in your life?" the earl asked. "She is an intelligent and a decent lady, Edmond."

"Thank you," his brother said dryly. "And I will not wait for you to add hastily that you did not mean the words exactly as they sounded, because you did. She is too good for me, you think? Far too good? On that we are agreed. The lady will not be long in my life. I meant it when I said that I do not like to corrupt innocence. And if you think the renunciation will be easy, let me add this. I love her. Do you understand me? I do not mean that I lust after her, want to bed her. I mean that I love her."

He instantly regretted the anger that had made him speak the words aloud. His love for Mary was to have been a private matter, locked deep within the most secret recesses of his heart.

His brother sighed. "I thought you were gone completely, Edmond," he said. "Apart from your looks, which tell me unmistakably that you are my baby brother fifteen years after I saw you last, I have found nothing to recognize in you. Almost as if someone else were in possession of your body. But there spoke Edmond for the first time. Ever the idealist, ever the romantic."

"Romantic?" Lord Edmond frowned in puzzlement.

"Loving," his brother said, "and renouncing that love from the noblest of motives. You did it with Sukey Thompson once upon a time. Do you remember?"

"Sukey?" For the first time Lord Edmond's laugh had

a tinge of amusement in it. "With the blond ringlets and the big blue eyes and the pout?"

"You were deeply, painfully in love with her," the earl said. "You were seventeen, if I remember correctly, and she was nineteen. You renounced your love for her because you had nothing to offer her of greater value than the life of a country parson, and even that quite far in the future. You were heartbroken for days, perhaps even weeks. You wrote reams of poems."

Lord Edmond snorted. "And she did not know I existed," he said. "Did she not have a *tendre* for you, Wally? Do you know, I had not thought of that girl for years and years."

Both brothers laughed. Then they looked at each other rather self-consciously.

"Perhaps it was partly my fault," the earl said quickly. "Do you think I have not always been plagued by the thought? Only the way you turned out reassured me, Edmond. You must have been heading for bad ways, I have always thought, and we had just not seen it. But perhaps part of the guilt was mine. No." He passed a hand over his eyes. "There is no perhaps about it, is there? I wanted to see you foxed—grave, serious Edmond making an idiot of himself. It was great fun. Perhaps it was all my fault."

"I did not have to drink," Lord Edmond said. "Neither you nor Papa nor anyone else at that infernal party ever held me down and poured liquor down my throat. I drank because I wanted everyone to see that I was now a man. I wanted to be like you—grown-up and self-assured and popular with the ladies. You were always my hero—everything I could not seem to be. All I could do was hide behind my books and pretend that life perfectly suited me that way."

"Oh, God!" The earl closed his eyes and passed a hand over them again.

"I am afraid I was not nearly a man," Lord Edmond said. "I was still a child despite my twenty-one years. A child who played with fire and got burned."

"Edmond," his brother said wearily, "how is it possible to go back? It has been so long and the damage has been so great. And not only to you. We all lost a family on that dreadful day. You more than Papa and I, it is true. But we all lost. At least that is what Anne has been telling me for years. But how can we go back?"

"I think we just have," Lord Edmond said. "Perhaps you will never know, Wally, what it means to hear you admit that you were a part of the whole guilt surrounding Dick's death. What it means to hear you say that I was not the only loser. It makes me feel that I have been missed, that perhaps I was of some importance in your lives."

"Of some . . . ?" The earl looked at his brother with mingled incredulity and exasperation. "What the devil are you talking about?"

Lord Edmond shrugged. "You were as I have described you," he said. "Dick was more like me, but gentle and sweet—everyone's favorite. And then there was me, with nothing but my proficiency in Latin to commend me."

The earl stared at him. "Did you not know how much we were all in awe of your learning?" he said. "How Mama and Papa almost burst with pride every time they could boast of you to someone new? We all basked in the glory of your accomplishments."

Lord Edmond laughed rather shakily. "Well," he said. "Well."

"I think we had better go and find the ladies," his brother said, "before we do something that would embarrass us both, like falling into each other's arms or something."

"Quite right," Lord Edmond said. "And I have to go through something like this with Papa, too, you say?"

"I will wager that Anne will arrange it somehow," the earl said.

Lord Edmond grimaced and looked down at the hand his brother stretched out to him.

"Shall we at least shake hands?" the earl asked. "Will you at least do that, Edmond, to show that you forgive me for my cowardice through the years? I have let you bear it all alone."

Lord Edmond stared at the hand for a long moment before placing his own in it. And then, after all, they were in each other's arms, slapping each other's backs, wordlessly choking back the tears that would have made their humiliation complete.

"Nigel is keen on the classics," the earl said, frowning as they drew apart and each tried to pretend that nothing out of the ordinary had happened. "I have always boasted to him about how his uncle was such a Latin scholar. He has not begun to pester you about it yet, has he?"

Lord Edmond laughed. "All the way here," he said. "Though I would not describe his behavior as pestering. Actually I have been tickled pink to think that anyone would consult me as a Latin expert. My intimates in town would roar with laughter and not stop for a week. I would never live it down."

"Edmond—" his brother began.

"I am not going back," Lord Edmond said quickly. "Not for a long time, anyway. I am going home after this party, Wally. I was there for a few weeks before coming, and rather fancied myself as the country squire. I am thinking of taking to striding about my property with a stout staff in my hand, a foul-smelling pipe in my mouth, and a faithful shaggy hound at my heels."

His brother chuckled.

"Besides," Lord Edmond said, "Mary lives in town."

"IT IS TRULY magnificent," Anne said, "and a total folly to have it built out here in the middle of nowhere, glorious and wondrous as that nowhere is. We are agreed, Mary?"

"Oh, yes," Mary said. "And a wonderful if improbable setting for a birthday party."

"And having said as much to each other in a dozen different ways during the past fifteen minutes or so," Anne said with a smile, "shall we confess to what is really on both our minds?"

"Are they not coming here?" Mary asked. "Have they turned back?"

"Either way," Anne said, "I can only read hope into their absence. If they had continued embarrassed and tongue-tied in each other's company, they would have hurried along on our heels, would they not, for fear of being left alone together?"

"You think they have talked?" Mary asked. "And come to some sort of an understanding?"

"Or bloodied each other's noses," Anne said with a laugh that sounded a little nervous. "I have wished for this for so long, Mary, that I hardly dare hope. Wallace has never been quite happy. Always, even at our most joyous moments—our wedding, the birth of the children, their christenings, a few other occasions—always I have been aware of something. And I have known him long enough to be quite aware by now of what that something is. It is guilt and grief. Grief fades when a person is dead, Mary. You would know that as a widow. But it does not go away when the person grieved for is still alive."

"I have not known Lord Edmond long," Mary said,

"and cannot pretend to know him or understand him well. But I am sure that it is guilt and this family rift that have . . . oh, that have kept him from being the person he might have been."

"You love him, do you not?" Anne asked quickly.

Mary stared at her. "I am betrothed to—" she said.

Anne waved a dismissive hand. "Oh, yes," she said. "But you are not serious about that, Mary. You will not make the mistake of marrying him, I think. And I must confess to some guilt of my own. I maneuvered this situation—him going to the abbey and you coming here. Am I not dreadful? You love him, do you not?"

"Lord Edmond?" Mary said. She hesitated. "I have grown fond of him."

Anne chuckled and then sobered. "Oh, here they come," she said. "We must pretend to be admiring this pillar, Mary. Corinthian, is it? I have never been able to remember what name goes with which kind of pillar."

"It is Corinthian," Mary said.

They both glanced with disguised curiosity at the two men when they came up, but absurdly they all admired and conversed about first the column and then the whole of the domed round pavilion in which Lady Eleanor's birthday party was to take place the next day.

Five minutes or more passed before Lord Edmond grabbed Mary by the wrist, rather as he had done the afternoon before on their return from Canterbury, and drew her outside to look down on the lake.

"Well, Mary," he said, "you insisted that I go back. I went back yesterday and I have been back today."

"And?" she said.

"And I believe I have a brother," he said, gripping her wrist so tightly that she began to lose the feeling in her hand.

She drew in a deep breath but said nothing.

"And a damned managing sister-in-law," he said. "It

seems that nothing on this earth can stop her from setting up a similar ordeal with my father."

She looked at him and smiled.

"And what the devil do you mean by that damned smirk?" he asked her.

"It is a smile," she said. "And your language belongs in the gutter, my lord."

"Which is where I live and picked it up," he said. "And we are back to 'my lord' again today, are we?"

"Yes, my lord," she said.

"Ah." He looked out at the lake and said nothing for a while. "It is as well. If you called me by my given name again, I would as like be trying to steal kisses or more from you again, Mary. And it would not do with the good, rich man waiting to lead you to the altar, would it?"

"No," she said.

His grasp shifted to her hand suddenly and he raised it to his lips before releasing it entirely. "Thank you, Mary," he said. "Thank you for making me go back."

17

$\mathcal{I}$F IT WERE POSSIBLE, THE DAY OF LADY ELEANOR'S birthday party was sunnier, more cloudless, and warmer than any other day of the glorious summer so far. Everything was perfect, everyone agreed, for the day of celebration. All morning, servants made their way to and from the pavilion, doing last-minute-cleaning and taking the food and the punch. An orchestra, a surprise addition to the party, arrived from Canterbury and made their way to the lake after taking refreshments at the house.

It was bound to storm before the day was out, Doris Shelbourne declared. She could just feel it in the air. But everyone either ignored her or politely agreed that it was a distinct possibility, but perhaps some other day.

Many of the guests walked to the pavilion during the afternoon. Others rode there in carriages. A few select neighbors had been invited. It was difficult to put a name to the entertainment, Lady Cathcart complained to Mary as they strolled across the pasture. It was not strictly a tea, since they were expecting to stay at the pavilion until dusk or perhaps even later. It was certainly not a dinner, since no hot meal was to be served. Though of course a veritable feast had been taken from the house, so they would not starve by any means. Had Lady Mornington observed the extent of it?

Lady Mornington had.

It was too formal for a picnic, Lady Cathcart declared. Yet it was not a ball, was it? There would not be enough guests. Besides, they were wearing day clothes, not nighttime finery. But there was the orchestra. Merely to entertain them as they ate and conversed? Or was there to be dancing? Had Lady Mornington heard?

Lady Mornington had not.

"It is all very provoking," Lady Cathcart said. "One likes to be able to give a name to the type of entertainment one is attending, does one not, Lady Mornington?"

"Whatever it is," Mary said with a smile, "we are all certain to enjoy it. Just the weather and the surroundings are sufficient to lift the spirits. Add the pavilion and the orchestra, the food and the company, and I believe Lady Eleanor has excelled herself."

"Do you believe so?" Lady Cathcart asked doubtfully.

Mary smiled. But in fact she was not convinced. It was true that all those ingredients for a happy day were there, and true, too, that if anyone did not enjoy himself, then the fault must be entirely his. But she was not expecting to enjoy what remained of the afternoon or the evening.

She had been overhasty earlier in the week. Her desire to be married again, to enjoy all the security that marriage could bring, had clouded her judgment. Affection had been the single most prominent factor in her first marriage. She had not given enough attention to it in her plans for the second. Worst of all, perhaps, she had accepted Simon's offer as much to escape from feelings she wished to deny as to embrace a life she did want.

It was true that no public announcement of her betrothal had been made, but her private word had been given. And she was sorry for it. Oh, it was as good a match as she could hope to make, and it had everything to offer her that she had ever dreamed of—security, a home in the country, a husband who appeared to care for her. Everything except children, perhaps. She had not broached the subject with Simon again, but she feared that perhaps they could never be in agreement on that point. For him two sons seemed to be family enough.

That important difference notwithstanding, she would be mad, she thought, to end the betrothal. The only possible reason she could have for doing so was that she loved another man. Though when she verbalized the fact in her mind, she had to admit that it was a very major reason indeed for ending an engagement.

And so end it she must. And she feared that it would have to be done on the day of the birthday party. With her decision firmly made, she did not believe she could dissemble for a whole day. Besides, it did not seem fair to do so. Simon had a right to know of her change of heart.

The opportunity did not come until well into the evening. From the start the party was a great success. There was music to listen to and food to eat and punch to drink and conversation to be enjoyed. Later, there was dancing. There was the bank of the lake to be strolled along. The guests mingled freely so that there was little chance of any private *tête-à-tête*.

Mary stayed away from Lord Edmond, a task not difficult to accomplish, since he seemed equally intent on avoiding her. She also stayed away from the viscount as much as she was able, and acknowledged to herself that she was being cowardly, deliberately avoiding the moment that she knew must be faced.

But he finally sought her out and suggested that they join the Ormsbys, Stephanie Wiggins, and a gentleman from the neighborhood in a stroll up through the woods. It seemed that the moment could be avoided no longer,

Mary thought, smiling at him and taking his arm. Though there was perhaps safety in numbers.

They walked up past the follies to the edge of the trees and the beginnings of the pasture.

"Oh, dear," Leila Ormsby said, pointing to the west. "That is why the heat is still so oppressive though it is evening already. Look!"

She did not need to point. They could hardly avoid seeing the heavy dark clouds banked in the western sky.

"Rain will be welcome," the Reverend Ormsby said. "Though it would have been better timed had it waited until tomorrow. Perhaps the clouds will pass us by after all."

"Those are rain clouds if I ever saw any," Mr. Webber said, shading his eyes.

"At least Doris's predictions of a storm are unlikely to prove right," the Reverend Ormsby said. "There is not a breath of wind."

"That is the very fact that makes me expect one," his wife said. "Do you think we should hurry back to the house, Samuel, to be with the children?"

He laughed. "And miss the rest of the party?" he said. "There are so many servants at the house, my love, that our presence would be supremely redundant. I suggest we get back to the pavilion in case the rain does come over."

"I would look a perfect fright if I got wet," Stephanie said, pulling on Mr. Webber's arm and turning back to the woods.

The Ormsbys followed them, but Mary and Lord Goodrich by common but unspoken consent strolled out into the pasture.

"I have had so little time alone with you in the past few days," he said. "Country parties are not the best occasions to enjoy a new betrothal, especially a partly secret one."

"No," she said. "Simon—"

"I am selfish, Mary," he said. "I want you to myself. Waite has seen more of you than I. You are sure he did not harass you yesterday? I was more than annoyed at the unhappy chance that sent us in different directions."

"It was a pleasant family picnic," she said. "Lord Edmond spent much of the time with his brother. It seems that they are reconciled, and I can feel nothing but happiness about that."

"I suppose so," he said. "Certainly they went off riding together this morning. I cannot help feeling, though, that Waite is making a dupe of Welwyn."

It was so easy when something unpleasant was to be said, Mary was finding, to grasp at any conversational straw, to put off the evil moment.

"Simon—" she said.

He covered her hand on his arm with his. "You are not really enjoying that party, are you, Mary?" he asked. "I expected something altogether more glittering and formal. I thought we would go to the house and spend some time alone together."

They were halfway across the pasture, she noticed. She also noticed at the same moment a distant flash of lightning from among the heavy clouds. The old terror clamored for attention. Her breath quickened.

"It is going to storm," she said. "Did you see that?"

"All the better," he said, smiling down at her. "The others will stay at the pavilion until it is well past. We will have the house to ourselves, apart from the servants."

There was a low rumble of thunder, so distant that it was felt more than heard.

"Perhaps we should go back to be with the others," she said.

There was a suggestion of coolness against their faces.

The trees off to their right, at the edge of the pasture, were beginning to rustle in the breeze.

"Nonsense!" He chuckled. "Are you really afraid of storms, Mary? I will protect you, you know. It would be my pleasure."

Vivid images of Vauxhall flashed into Mary's mind with the next fork of distant lightning. "Simon," she said, "let's go back." She held on to rationality. She tried not to want to reach the safety of Edmond.

"Look," he said, laughing, "we are at the stile already. Come, Mary. We will be at the house before the clouds move over or the storm really begins. By that time I will have you warm and safe in my arms." He vaulted over the stile, disdaining to use the stepping stones, and he held out a hand to help her up.

"Simon." She stayed on her side of the fence and gripped the sides of her dress. "I have been trying to say something all the way across the pasture. I cannot seem to force the words out."

He looked at her closely and dropped his hand.

"I am afraid I have to go back on my promise," she said. "I cannot marry you. I cannot feel comfortable with the idea, and it would not be fair to marry you just for the security I crave."

He stood staring at her for a few moments and then extended his hand again. "Come over the stile," he said, as she set her hand obediently in his. "It is absurd to talk in this manner." He lifted her down when she had swung her skirt carefully over the top bar. "Is it persuasion you want, Mary?" He drew her to him and kissed her.

"No," she said, turning her head away. "I am sorry, Simon. I know I am treating you shabbily, but there is no decent way to break a betrothal. I am sorry."

"It is Waite, is it not?" His voice was tight with anger. "You prefer to sink to the gutter than to marry me, Mary?"

"Please," she said, "let us not get unpleasant."

"I was willing to take you despite a sullied reputation," he said. "And I am to be rejected in favor of London's most notorious libertine? And you expect me to smile and wish you well, Mary?"

She had stiffened. "A sullied reputation?" she said.

"Everyone knew you were Clifton's whore," he said. "I was prepared to overlook that fact."

"Perhaps you should not have done so," she said quietly. "You cannot expect honorable behavior of a whore, can you?"

"Obviously not," he said.

He looked up at the sky, drawing Mary's eyes up, too. The clouds had moved fast, and the breeze was now steady on them and increasing into a wind. Lightning flashed even as they watched.

"There is no time to go back," she said regretfully. "We will have to make a run for the house."

"Yes," he said grimly, and they hurried side by side, not touching, in the direction of the house.

They reached it in time, though it would not be long before the rain came down and the storm moved overhead, Mary guessed. She turned to her companion when they were inside the hall.

"I am afraid we should have turned back to the pavilion earlier, Simon," she said. "Now you are stuck in the house alone with me and the servants and a broken engagement. I have managed things badly. I am so sorry."

"For my part," he said, "I have no intention of wasting the evening, Mary. I am returning to the pavilion."

"But you will be soaked." Her eyes widened.

"Perhaps." He shrugged. "I believe there is still a little time before the rain begins in earnest. But better a soaking than remain here to an evening of boredom."

She drew a deep breath. "So I am to be left all alone," she said.

"As you said, there are plenty of servants." His expression and voice were cold, and despite her fear of the storm, Mary was suddenly glad that she had had the courage to speak up. Life with this man would not have been easy, she saw. He did not like to have his will thwarted.

"Yes," she said, "and so there are."

But there were none in the hall, which seemed large and dark and frightening after the doors had closed behind the viscount and she was left alone. Most of them would be either at the pavilion or belowstairs enjoying some free time, with family and guests away.

Mary hurried up to her bedchamber and closed the door firmly behind her. She could always summon her maid, she told herself. She need not be entirely alone. But she was determined at least to try to remain alone. She was in a large, securely built mansion. She was quite safe. And it was time she conquered her fear.

She stood rigidly in the middle of the room, hands clasped firmly to her bosom, as lightning flashed outside the window. She counted slowly, waiting for the rumble of thunder that would follow.

IT CAME ABOUT much as he had expected it would. He would have been surprised if the day had passed without its happening. He danced with Anne and at the end of the set she smiled at him and linked her arm through his.

"What a warm evening," she said. "Let us walk down by the lake, Edmond, shall we?"

He put up no resistance, even though he knew what was about to happen, just as if it were a play for which he had written the script. His father was sitting close to the door, talking with Sir Harold.

Lord Edmond smiled and gave her his arm. "That would be pleasant," he said.

He watched with mingled amusement and despair as she pretended to notice her father-in-law for the first time as they were about to pass him.

"Father," she said, delight in her voice, "how fortunate that you happen to be right here. I need a gentleman for my other arm. Do come for a stroll by the lake."

His father looked as delighted by the prospect as he himself felt, Lord Edmond thought. But Anne, he was beginning to realize, must have been a manipulator all her life. A benevolent one, perhaps, but a manipulator nevertheless. Like puppets on a string, the two of them were soon wandering down to the lakeshore with Anne between them.

And of course—oh, of course—after a mere five minutes, despite the fact that it was such an oppressively warm evening, Anne shivered and felt the absence of her shawl and excused herself to go and fetch it. Both Edmond and his father knew that she would not return.

"I do believe she is right," the duke said, squinting off to the west. "There is a cool breeze and those are rain clouds moving in. I hope this does not mean we are to be stranded here for the night. Eleanor would be delighted beyond words."

And indeed all the signs were there, Lord Edmond had to admit when he looked, and thought about the heavy atmosphere of the evening and the freshening breeze. It was not just rain. There was a storm brewing. And despite his embarrassment at being left alone with his father, his thoughts leapt to Mary. There was a storm coming. She would be terrified. She had gone off walking with Goodrich and a few other couples. He hoped Goodrich would have more sense than he himself had had at Vauxhall and would bring her back to the pavilion before the storm started. He would not like to think of her having to take shelter—especially with Goodrich, of all people—in one of the small follies.

"A storm," he said. "Doris is to be proved right, it seems. She will let us all know of it, too, for the rest of tonight, and probably all day tomorrow."

"Edmond," his father said quietly, "I never stopped loving you, you know."

Lord Edmond's body went rigid. He continued to stare off to the west.

"But I have been quite unable to bring myself to talk to you in the past two days," the duke said. "I know myself terribly at fault. I have known it all these years, but not seeing you has made it easier to suppress the guilt. I cannot recall what I said to you to make you run off. It must have been something dreadful."

"You called me a murderer," Lord Edmond said quietly.

"Ah." There was a short silence. "Yes, I knew that. I just hoped it was not true. I lashed out at you from my pain and guilt. And then, when you left and everything else started to happen, I convinced myself that you must truly have been guilty. At least I convinced a part of myself."

"It is old history," Lord Edmond said. "It is best forgotten."

"No." His father sounded sad. "I have ruined your life, my boy. I have known it all these years, although perversely I have only railed against you and half believed my own condemnations. Too much time has passed. Too much wrong has been done. How can I ever ask forgiveness for the enormous wrongs I have done you? I am sorry, my boy. I will have to go away from here tomorrow and leave you to what I can only hope will be a happier future."

Lord Edmond turned to look at him. "Tell me what

you said at the beginning of this conversation," he said. "Say it again."

"That I have never stopped loving you?" The duke looked into his son's eyes. "You want my love, Edmond? After all I have done to you?"

"I want it." Lord Edmond's eyes were intense.

"I love you," his father said. "You are my son. Can you ever forgive me?"

Lord Edmond swore. He stared at his father for a few moments, hesitated, and then drew him into a hug even more bruisingly hard than that he had exchanged with his brother the day before. For perhaps a minute both were oblivious of the people who strolled about them, and of Anne, who appeared briefly in the doorway of the pavilion and then disappeared again.

"You must come home," the duke said at last. "You must come back home, my boy. You have been too long away."

Lord Edmond smiled. "I am going home, Papa," he said. "To Willow Court. I am in the process of learning what it means to be a landowner. But yes, I will come to stay with you and with Wally and Anne and my nephews and niece. Perhaps for Christmas." He laughed. "Or perhaps you can all come to me. Is this really happening?"

The duke looked up at the sky. "It is indeed, my boy," he said. "And the storm is about to happen, too. Those clouds are moving faster than I expected. Did you hear that thunder?"

They walked back to the pavilion, looking at each other in some wonder when they stepped inside to the brighter candlelight, and smiling rather self-consciously.

"I knew when Anne got you and Wallace together yesterday," the duke said with a chuckle, "that my turn would come today. I have a gem of a daughter-in-law, Edmond. Perhaps I will have another eventually?"

"Perhaps," Lord Edmond said evasively.

But they were separated at that moment when Lady Cathcart called to His Grace to make up a hand of cards while the younger people danced.

"It looks as if we might have a long night of it," Lady Eleanor said to Lord Edmond. Predictably she looked thoroughly pleased by the possibility. "Doris is already circulating with the proud tidings that she has been right all along. Will the storm be bad, do you suppose?"

Lord Edmond looked about the room after she had wafted off to talk with someone else. The Ormsbys were dancing. They had gone walking with Mary and Goodrich. Stephanie had been one of the group, too, if he was not mistaken. She was sitting with her mama at the other side of the room. There was no sign of Mary or Goodrich. And he could hear rain against the long windows.

Damn Goodrich! He hoped at least that they were inside a folly and not sheltering beneath a tree. Surely they could not be that foolish.

And then he breathed a great sigh of relief. He caught sight of the viscount close to the doors, brushing raindrops from the sleeves of his coat. They had returned just in time, too. The rain outside was becoming a deluge, so that many of the guests stopped what they were doing in order to look toward the windows. There was a buzz of excitement at a flash of lightning.

Lord Edmond wondered if Mary would be frightened in the midst of a crowd. He looked for her. But she was nowhere in sight. He looked more carefully.

He strolled toward the viscount, who was laughing at something Mrs. Bigsby-Gore was saying. "Where is Mary?" he asked, interrupting their conversation without preamble.

"Lady Mornington?" The viscount looked at him haughtily. "Somewhere in the house, I would imagine."

"The house?" Lord Edmond frowned. "The house as opposed to the pavilion? What is she doing there?"

"How would I know?" the viscount said. "I am here, as you see. And I imagine that Lady Mornington's movements are none of your business anyway, Waite. Ma'am, will you dance?" He turned back to Mrs. Bigsby-Gore.

But Lord Edmond clamped a hand onto his arm. "Is she alone there?" he asked. "Did you leave her alone to return here?"

Lord Goodrich looked pointedly at the hand on his arm. "The house is full of servants," he said.

"She is terrified of storms," Lord Edmond said, his eyes narrowing. "With very good reason. You knew that."

"Childish nonsense!" the viscount said. "If you would be so kind as to remove your hand from my arm, Waite, I can lead the lady into the dance."

"You left her," Lord Edmond said, his voice tight with fury, "knowing that." He lifted his hand away from Lord Goodrich's sleeve as if it had burned him. "Your own betrothed."

"Lady Mornington is nothing to me," the viscount said, and he turned away as thunder rumbled in the not-so-far distance.

Lord Edmond strode across the room, but a hand on his sleeve stayed him as he was about to open the door.

"Edmond?" his aunt said, laughing. "You cannot go out there, dear. I fear we are stuck here for many hours to come. Is it not dreadful?" She smiled cheerfully.

"I have to go back to the house," he said. "Mary is there alone."

"At the house?" She frowned. "But Lord Goodrich is here."

"The bastard left her there alone, knowing her terror of storms," he said.

"Oh!" She looked shocked, though not, apparently, at

his choice of words. She lifted her hand from his arm. "Go, then, Edmond. Go quickly, dear. And don't try to come back."

He was gone without another word, shutting the door firmly behind him. Lady Eleanor enjoyed a private smile at the closed door before turning back to her guests.

18

SHE LICKED DRY LIPS WITH A DRY TONGUE AS SHE paced. She glanced several times at the bell rope, one tug on which would bring her maid in just a few minutes. But she did not pull it. It was merely a matter of waiting out the storm, she told herself. Storms did not last forever, and usually they were directly overhead for no longer than a few minutes. And storms did not strike large stone mansions or harm the people safely lodged inside them.

She tried to remember how she had used to feel about storms as a child. But she could remember only Lawrence's voice muttering more to himself than to her in their tent in Spain that someone was surely going to get it. And the terrified screaming of horses. And then . . . the rest of it.

She rubbed her hands against the sides of her dress. Moist palms. And a dry mouth. Lightning flashed and she counted only to eight before the thunder followed. She looked at the bell rope again.

And then she swung around toward the door, relief flooding her. Her maid had come without being summoned. Somehow she must have heard that her mistress was at home. The door opened after a quick tapping.

"Oh," she said, and the relief was still there—and something else, too. "You look like a drowned rat." She laughed, the sound nervous and almost hysterical to her own ears.

"Hm," he said. "You are supposed to gasp out something like 'My hero!' and rush into my arms."

"Am I?" she said, and bit her lip and smiled at him a little uncertainly. "What are you doing here?"

"Dripping onto your carpet," he said, looking down.

She swallowed. "Did you come because of me?" she asked.

"I seemed to recall that you are susceptible to seduction during thunderstorms," he said. "Of course, I came because of you, Mary."

"Don't," she said. "Don't use that voice. It is the one that comes with your mask."

"Mask?" He raised his eyebrows.

"Oh, Edmond," she said, "do go and change. You will catch your death."

But a particularly loud clap of thunder had her scurrying a few steps toward him before stopping. She licked her lips again.

He dragged off his coat, grimacing as he did so from the wetness of it. He pulled free his neckcloth and began to unbutton his shirt.

"By the time I go to my room and change and comb my hair in a fashion that suits it when wet, and don a few jewels to impress you," he said, pulling his shirt free of his pantaloons and drawing it off over his head, "the storm will be over and I will have lost my chance with you, Mary. Besides, by that time you will probably be a blithering idiot." He grinned at her. "It is going to be overhead soon. I think my arms had better be dry and available for you when that happens. Your teeth are beginning to chatter."

She clamped them firmly together, swallowed as he pulled off his Hessians and moved his hands to the buttons of his pantaloons, and turned jerkily away.

"I shall fetch you some towels from the dressing room," she said. But another flash rooted her to the spot.

"No need," he said. "A blanket from the bed should do. I will be able to cover myself quite decently, I do assure you. If you do not want to watch the next installment, Mary, you had better turn away again for a moment."

She did, and crossed the few feet to the bed to pull free one blanket. He took it from her hand before she turned back to him, and had wrapped himself in it by the time she did.

"Come a little nearer," he said as the storm grew closer and louder and more intense. "But I have had second thoughts about these dry arms holding you, Mary. All this stripping off to the skin and talking of seductions has made me dangerous. Not to mention certain delicious memories of the last storm. Just stand close and we will talk our way through the height of the storm."

She moved closer and curled her hands into fists at her sides.

"Don't you think I should have a laurel wreath for my hair, and perhaps rope sandals for my feet?" he said. "Is that what the ancient Romans wore on their feet? I think this blanket looks distinctly like a toga, don't you, Mary? How did they fasten the things about them? Do you know? They surely did not stride about the streets of Rome clutching them as I am forced to do. How would they shake hands with anyone? Did the Romans shake hands? And what if a particularly nasty gust of wind came along? It could all be a trifle embarrassing, don't you think? You are not being fair, you know, Mary. I have asked enough questions to form the basis for a fifteen-minute discussion, and you have answered none of them. Help me out. It is your turn."

"You were a classics scholar," she said. "You must know all the answers."

"I merely follow the methods of Socrates," he said. "He never told his pupils anything. He merely asked endless questions. Yes, it is close, is it not?" he said as she cringed. "Must I hold you? Don't trust me, Mary. I don't trust myself."

His pale blue eyes gazed intently back into hers when she raised them to him. She was almost past reason.

"I have been trying so hard," she said. "I know it is something I must conquer."

But the lightning and thunder happened simultaneously even as she finished speaking, and she found herself being drawn against warm and naked safety. Strong arms came about her, enclosing her in the blanket. She buried her face against warm chest hair and rested her hands against it, too.

"It is all right, Mary," he was murmuring, his cheek against the top of her head. "I have you safe, love. Nothing is going to hurt you."

He rocked her in his arms during the five minutes or so that the storm was overhead. She listened to the rain lashing the windows and to the strong steady beat of his heart. And the terror was suddenly all gone. She could almost enjoy the fury of the elements while she relaxed in her warm and living cocoon.

She drew back her head and looked up at him.

"No," he said. "A big mistake, Mary." And he set one hand behind her head and drew it none too gently against his chest again. "Don't look at me. If you don't look at me, I can pretend you are a frightened maid or my niece or my sister-in-law or some elderly dowager. If you don't look at me, I have a chance."

"Edmond," she said.

"Christ!" he said. "And that was no blasphemy, Mary.

That was a fervent prayer. What has happened to 'my lord'? Call me 'my lord.'"

Through the thin muslin of her dress she could feel the stirrings of his arousal. And she could feel a tightening in her own breasts. Edmond! She kept very still.

"Whose idea was this blanket, anyway?" he said. "What I should have done, Mary—but hindsight is always pointless—was take you along to my room and stand you with your back to me while I changed into dry clothes . . . into decent armor. You know enough about human anatomy to know very well what is going on here, I suppose? No, don't answer that. You might try to be tactful and say no, you had not noticed, and that would be a dreadful blow to my masculine pride. Why am I the only one babbling?"

"Edmond?" She raised her head again and looked up into his eyes.

He sighed. "You will have no respect for my title, then?" he said. "Listen, Mary, if you do not want what is about to happen to happen, you had better drag up some courage from somewhere and remove yourself from this blanket. And I mean now, or preferably five minutes ago. The storm is moving off, I do believe. Devil take it, woman, I am only human. Too damned human, I'm afraid."

"So am I," she said. "Too damned human."

"Such language," he said, and his head moved down to hers and his eyes closed and he spoke against her lips. "God, Mary, I have not wanted this to happen. Not any longer. I have been trying to do something decent at last. But it seems one cannot change oneself after all when one has lived a selfish and self-indulgent life for years."

"Then let it be said that I have seduced you," she said, her arms going up about his neck. "You are merely my victim."

He groaned. "There is only one thing more exciting

than your naked body against mine, Mary," he said. "I have just discovered it. It is your clothed body against my nakedness. I don't have a chance, woman. I swear I don't."

"I know," she said, and she angled her head and opened her mouth wider, inviting him to deepen the kiss.

He accepted the invitation without hesitation, widening his mouth over hers, teasing his tongue over her lips, up behind them so that she shivered with a sharp ache, and into her mouth, sliding over surfaces, circling her tongue, and finally beginning a firm rhythm of thrust and withdrawal in promise of things to come.

"I have always loved long hair on women," he said against her throat, pushing the fingers of one hand into her hair. "Hair to wrap about the breasts and waist. But your short curls drive me wild, Mary. Don't ever grow them out."

His hands roamed over her, finding the hardened nipples of her breasts, fitting themselves to her small waist, spreading over her hips. And her own hands followed suit. She felt the muscles of his shoulders, the rippling muscles of his back, the narrow waist and hips, the firm, hard buttocks.

"I suppose," he said, "I had better make the ultimate admission of defeat and undress you and lay you on that bed, had I not?"

"Yes," she said.

"You are no help at all, Mary," he said, feathering kisses over her face.

"No."

"So be it, then," he said, and he slipped his hands beneath her dress and shift at the shoulders and slowly drew them down over her arms until, loosened about the waist, they fell away to the floor.

"Ah," he said, drawing her against him again, speaking against her mouth. "Maybe I had better take that back about clothed bodies after all, Mary." The blanket was also in a heap at their feet.

She drew breath slowly. She was far more aware of what was happening than she had been on the Vauxhall night. She could feel him with every part of her body. He was all hard muscle and warm flesh and hair. He was magnificent. And she loved him. She rested her hands on his shoulders.

"Edmond," she said against his mouth.

"You have me persuaded," he said. "You do not need to say more. Onto the bed, love."

She wondered as he turned back the bedcovers and she lay obediently on the bed if she realized what he was calling her. She reveled in the endearment. Even if it were only the occasion that was provoking it, it was enough. The occasion was enough.

"Mary." He came immediately on top of her, his hands moving down her sides, his mouth finding hers. "I don't want to wait any longer. Do you? Say no."

"No," she said.

"Good girl," he said. "I like obedient women. Have I told you how much I like you?"

Like! She smiled ruefully against his mouth. But her body was on fire for him, and her love needed to be fed by him in this physical way—just one more time. One more time would be enough.

"This much," he said, parting her legs with his knees, pushing them wide. "This much." He positioned himself at the entrance to her so that she could hear her own heart beating. "This much, Mary." He came into her, stopping only when he was deeply embedded in her. "I like you this much. Do you like me? Just a little? Tell me you like me just a little. You would not allow this otherwise, would you?"

Light blue eyes looked down into hers in the candlelight. There was a hint of anxiety behind the passion in them.

"I like you." She smiled at him. "This much." She lifted her legs from the bed and twined them about his. "And this much." She pressed her hips into the mattress, tilting herself to him so that he was deeper in her. "And this much." She tightened inner muscles, drawing him deeper still.

"God in his sweet heaven, woman," he said, burying his face in her curls. "Are you trying to prove that I can still perform like a gauche schoolboy? Let me take a few minutes over this, will you?"

She relaxed beneath him, letting his body play with the hum of desire in her own, letting him focus it and build it until she could control her reactions no longer, but tightened her arms about him and twisted her hips, drawing him deep to give her the release she craved.

"Edmond," she pleaded.

"Yes, love," he said, finding her mouth with his again. "Oh, yes. Oh, yes."

And they found it together, that center of the universe, which only lovers experience in the moment of fulfillment. Her body shook beneath his as his relaxed weight bore her down into the mattress.

"There," he said five minutes later as he moved to her side, drew a sheet up over them, and settled her head on his arm. "So much for reformations of character, Mary. They just do not happen. I am sorry. The temptation was too great."

"Yes, it was," she said.

"I did try," he said. "If only the rain had not made my clothes so infernally wet. I think I might have had a will of iron if I had not had to remove all my clothes."

She chuckled.

"It's not funny, Mary," he said. "Once this storm is over . . . In fact, I think it is already over—have you heard any thunder lately? Anyway, once this night is over, you will realize, as you did last time, just what horrors your terror drove you into. And as usual, I was here to oblige with the grand seduction scene. During the next thunderstorm you had better make sure that you are on a different continent, an ocean between us."

"Edmond." She turned onto her side and touched his cheek lightly with the fingers of one hand. "Don't feel bad. It was not seduction."

"I was not exactly invited into your bedchamber, was I?" he said. "Do you want me to challenge Goodrich? Do say yes. I would like nothing better than the opportunity to draw his cork."

"I broke off our engagement," she said. "I am afraid I have behaved very badly to him. He had every reason to be annoyed with me."

"There is still such a thing as gallantry," he said. "Did you really, though, Mary? It is some relief, anyway, to know that I have not just been bedding someone else's fiancée."

"Have you spoken with your father?" she asked.

He grimaced. "And we cried and slobbered all over each other," he said. "It was in the best spirit of sentimental melodrama, Mary."

"And all is well?" she asked.

"He asked me to forgive him," he said. "*Me* forgive *him*. Can you imagine?"

"I am so glad," she said. "I am so happy for you."

"Are you?" he said.

She nodded and smiled at him.

"Why are your eyelids drooping and your words slurring?" he asked her. "I was not that good, was I? Tell me I was that good."

She closed her eyes. "You were that good," she said. "Now you must return the compliment and tell me that you are sleepy, too, and that I was that good."

"I am talking in my sleep," he said. "And you were . . . oh, some superlative."

She continued to smile. She loved him. And he liked her. She wondered what he would say if she told him her feelings. She wondered if it would make any difference to anything. But it was surely wiser to keep her mouth shut. She had always considered that they were as far apart as the two poles, in everything except physical attraction. Surely not enough had changed to make any sort of relationship between them a possibility. He was right. It was the storm that made everything seem possible. It must be the storm.

And a good loving.

She fell asleep before she could decide whether or not to say the words aloud.

HE DID NOT sleep. He lay staring up at the moving patterns of the shadows cast by the candles and listening to the rain easing outside and the distant rumbles of thunder. He lay awake memorizing the feel of her and the smell of her.

And regretting fifteen wasted years, years given up to every imaginable excess of debauchery, years in which he had lost reputation and even honor. He had nothing whatsoever to offer a decent woman, nothing to offer the woman he loved. All he could do, all he could look forward to, was making amends in the future, perhaps making something out of his remaining years. Perhaps eventually, although he was already thirty-six years old, there could be marriage and children. Perhaps eventually he would deserve them.

But not with Mary. Too late for Mary. And so the possibilities brought no comfort.

She stirred finally and opened her eyes. She smiled at him.

"You are awake," she said.

"Mary," he said, and he kissed her mouth, tasting her, memorizing the taste, "this is good-bye. You know that, don't you? After tomorrow you will no longer be plagued by me. And it is a promise I will keep this time."

The smile held on her face. Her eyes looked back into his.

"Tell me something," he said. It was something he would rather not think of, but reality was reality. "Is there any chance I might have got you with child?"

She flushed, though she did not look away from him. She appeared to be thinking. "Yes," she said.

He swore.

"Such language," Mary said.

"Listen, Mary," he said. "If it is so, then you must write to me. Promise? I will come to you in London and marry you. I'm sorry about it. I know it would be a dreadful fate for you, but the alternative would unfortunately be worse. Promise that you will write? I would find out anyway."

"I would write," she said after a lengthy pause.

"The rain is stopping," he said. "Even so, it is bound to be hours before the others will attempt to drive home. The thought is tempting."

"Yes," she said.

The look in her eyes and the warm languor of her body told him that she was still amorous after the storm, as she had been in his scarlet room after Vauxhall. The temptation was almost overwhelming. One more time. She was willing. Just one more time.

He kissed her.

One more time. One more chance to plant his seed in her at a time when she was likely to conceive.

He drew his head away, eased his arm from beneath her head without looking into her eyes, and sat rather hastily on the side of the bed.

"Lord," he said. "Wet clothes or the Roman toga. Which is it to be? If I stagger out of here tripping over the hem of the toga, the servants are bound to be lined up outside your door all prepared to enjoy the show."

He walked naked across the room, aware of her eyes on his back, and looked with some distaste at the heap of his clothing, still quite unmistakably wet. His pantaloons were a little apart from the rest. They were damp. Damp and chilly. He drew them on and pulled a face.

"Just what I need to cool my ardor," he said. "The storm has passed. I don't believe it will return. You will be all right, Mary?" He looked back to see that she was sitting on the edge of the bed, wearing a blue silk dressing gown. Her face was flushed and her dark curls adorably rumpled.

"I will be all right," she said.

"Good night, then." He opened the door resolutely after scooping up his wet clothes, stepped through it, and closed it behind him without allowing himself the luxury of a glance back.

SHE HAD STOOD at the window for a long time gazing out into the darkness. Even the final distant flashes of lightning with no sound of thunder had passed. The rain had completely stopped. Soon perhaps the carriages would return, unless the rain had been heavy enough and had lasted long enough to make the roadway slippery with mud.

He had wanted her as his mistress. His bedfellow. His plaything. But he had changed since that time. He had just lived through a turbulent emotional time and it seemed that the rift with his family was healed, and with it all the bitterness and guilt that had blighted his adult life. He was different and seemed to want to make the changes permanent. He no longer wanted her as his mistress. His reluctance to make love to her earlier had been proof of that. She feared that perhaps she really had seduced him.

However it was, there was nothing to suggest that perhaps he would want her as his wife. He liked her, he had said even when he was making love to her. Liked, not loved. Clearly he found her attractive. But attraction was not love. He would marry her if she was with child, he had told her. But that did not mean that he would marry her willingly, that he wished to do so.

Better to leave things as they were, she thought. Better that than to embarrass him by hinting that she loved him, that perhaps, after all, she wanted a future with him. But not a future as a mistress. As a wife. Perhaps he would feel honor-bound to offer for her if she hinted at any such thing.

But what if his reluctance, his admission only of liking, his good-bye, were all motivated by his belief that she wanted none of him? What if at last he was doing something noble in his life?

What if they lived apart for the rest of their lives because of a misunderstanding? Because neither had the courage to speak the heart's truth? The thought was unbearable.

And so she must risk the hint, she decided, and stood at the window and went through all the arguments yet again—for surely the dozenth time.

But her decision was the same again at the end of it all, and she could not bear to wait until the morning, when she knew she might see everything differently, when the harsh voice of reason might silence her. If her love was to stand a chance—and if she was to risk rebuff and humiliation—then it must be done now.

She turned resolutely from the window and moved toward the door. But she had taken no more than three steps before a swift tap on the door heralded its opening and he stepped inside as he had done earlier. But this time he was wearing a brocaded dressing gown, its blue color several shades darker than her own.

He closed the door behind his back.

"I am a very poor risk, you know, Mary," he said. "Unreliable. Totally undependable. No one would be willing to wager on me. If there were a bet on me in one of the betting books at the clubs, there would not be a single taker for me. Only hordes against. The chances that I will ever make anything meaningful out of my life are slim, to state the case optimistically. You would have to agree with me, wouldn't you?"

She swallowed and said nothing.

"Anyone would be a fool to trust me and take me on," he said.

"Edmond," she said, "I was on my way to your room. Why have you come back here? What are you trying to say?"

"I am going home, Mary," he said. "Home to Willow Court. To stay. I know almost nothing about it except what I learned in the few weeks before I came here. I know nothing about crops and tenants and drainage and rents and all that. But I intend to learn. I am going to become that very dull English type—a country gentleman. So boring that within a year everyone will snore at the mere mention of my name."

He flashed her a grin and she tried to smile back.

"The house is unbelievably shabby," he said, "and the garden, too. I don't have any ideas about houses and gardens. All I know is that they look shabby and unlived-in and uncozy. They need a woman's touch."

Mary licked her lips.

"And the house needs children," he said. "Noisy, laughing, mischievous children with muddy feet and jam-smeared mouths."

"Edmond," she said, "I love you."

But he rushed on with what he had come to say. "I cannot offer any evidence that my determination to change will really bring about change," he said. "Perhaps I will fail miserably, Mary. Perhaps it is all so much dreaming. I would not envy any woman who was decent and kind enough to give me a chance. She would be likely to end up hurt and disillusioned. I think that must be right, don't you? Any woman would be a fool."

"Edmond," she said, "I love you."

"But it is up to you," he said, rushing on. "I am going home, Mary, and I want you to come with me. You would have your home in the country and your children, if I am capable of begetting them. And a husband who would try to love you always as he does today and would try to give you a good life. Will you come? I am sure you would be well advised to say no." He paused and looked at her fixedly. "*What* did you say?"

"I love you," she said.

"It's the thunderstorm," he said. "It does make you a little . . . strange, Mary, you must admit."

"Then you will have to take a risk, too," she said. "Will I mean it tomorrow and next week and next year and twenty, thirty, forty years from now? The whole future is a risk. That is the excitement and wonder of life. When do you want me to come?"

There was incomprehension in his eyes. "You are saying yes?" he asked. "After everything I have done to you? After all the aversion you felt for me in London?"

"I was afraid," she said. "I was afraid that I would love where there could be only lust in return, and even that for only a short time. Edmond, I want that home in the country more than I can say. And those children. Plural? Oh, I hope so. And I want all of it with you. Not with anyone else. Only with you."

He laughed. "And I pictured myself hurrying out of this room two minutes after entering it," he said, "with

a flea in my ear and a slap on the cheek and perhaps a slipper at my rear end. But I had to come, Mary. I could not risk losing you only because I was afraid to ask for you. You will marry me?"

"Yes." She came across the room to him and set her hands on his shoulders. "When, Edmond? Please soon. Oh, please soon."

"One month from now," he said. "At the very worst, our first child must be no less than an eight-month baby. We can say he was born early and hope he does not weigh twelve pounds. Was tonight really a bad time for you, Mary—or a good time?"

"I think the worst—or the best," she said.

"Was it, by Jove?" he said. "Is it?"

"Yes." She slid her hands beneath the silk collar of his dressing gown and reached up to kiss him beneath one ear. "That means it will also be the best on our wedding night, Edmond. But speaking for myself, I have no objection to an eight-month baby. None at all."

"You aren't trying to seduce me again, by any chance, are you?" he asked her, setting his hands at her waist and arching her body in against his. "You have a shocking tendency to do that, you know, Mary."

"Edmond." She wrapped her arms tightly about his neck and raised her face to his. "You said you always want to love me as you love me today. Tell me how much you love me."

"I'll write a poem about it tomorrow, if you wish, love," he said. "In Latin. For tonight would you not rather that I showed you?"

She thought for a moment and then smiled. "Yes," she said. "Love me, Edmond, and make me an eight-month baby."

"God in his heaven, woman," he said. "Is that an invitation or is it an invitation?"

"It is an invitation," she said against his mouth. "Love me."

"With all my heart," he said. "And that other, too, Mary."

He kissed her and steered her backward to the bed. And he proceeded with slow thoroughness to do both simultaneously.

*Get ready to fall in love
with a brand-new series from Mary Balogh. . . .*

WELCOME TO THE SURVIVORS' CLUB.

*The members are six gentlemen and one lady,
all of whom carry wounds
from the Napoleonic Wars—some visible
and some not. These tight-knit friends have helped
one another survive through thick and thin.
Now, they all need the perfect companions
to teach them how to love again.
Learn how it all begins in:*

The Proposal

Featuring the beloved Lady Gwendoline Muir from
One Night for Love and *A Summer to Remember*.
Available from Delacorte in hardcover.

Turn the page for a sneak peek inside.

1

G WENDOLINE GRAYSON, LADY MUIR, HUNCHED her shoulders and drew her cloak more snugly about her. It was a brisk, blustery March day, made chillier by the fact that she was standing down at the fishing harbor below the village where she was staying. It was low tide, and a number of fishing boats lay half keeled over on the wet sand, waiting for the water to return and float them upright again.

She should go back to the house. She had been out for longer than an hour, and part of her longed for the warmth of a fire and the comfort of a steaming cup of tea. Unfortunately, though, Vera Parkinson's home was not hers, only the house where she was staying for a month. And she and Vera had just quarreled—or at least, Vera had quarreled with *her* and upset her. She was not ready to go back yet. She would rather endure the elements.

She could not walk to her left. A jutting headland barred her way. To the right, though, a pebbled beach beneath high cliffs stretched into the distance. It would be several hours yet before the tide came up high enough to cover it.

Gwen usually avoided walking down by the water, even though she lived close to the sea herself at the dower house of Newbury Abbey in Dorsetshire. She found beaches too vast, cliffs too threatening, the sea too elemental. She preferred a smaller, more ordered world, over which she could exert some semblance of control— a carefully cultivated flower garden, for example.

But today she needed to be away from Vera for a while longer, and from the village and country lanes where she might run into Vera's neighbors and feel obliged to engage in cheerful conversation. She needed to be alone, and the pebbled beach was deserted for as far into the distance as she could see before it curved inland. She stepped down onto it.

She realized after a very short distance, however, why no one else was walking here. For though most of the pebbles were ancient and had been worn smooth and rounded by thousands of tides, a significant number of them were of more recent date, and they were larger, rougher, more jagged. Walking across them was not easy and would not have been even if she had had two sound legs. As it was, her right leg had never healed properly from a break eight years ago, when she had been thrown from her horse. She walked with a habitual limp even on level ground.

She did not turn back, though. She trudged stubbornly onward, careful where she set her feet. She was not in any great hurry to get anywhere, after all.

This had really been the most horrid day of a horrid fortnight. She had come for a month-long visit, entirely from impulse, when Vera had written to inform her of the sad passing a couple of months earlier of her husband, who had been ailing for several years. Vera had added the complaint that no one in either Mr. Parkinson's family or her own was paying any attention whatsoever to her suffering despite the fact that she was almost prostrate with grief and exhaustion after nursing him for so long. She was missing him dreadfully. Would Gwen care to come?

They had been friends of a sort for a brief few months during the whirlwind of their come-out Season in London, and had exchanged infrequent letters after Vera's marriage to Mr. Parkinson, a younger brother of Sir Roger Parkinson, and Gwen's to Viscount Muir. Vera had written a long letter of sympathy after Vernon's death, and had invited Gwen to come and stay with her and Mr. Parkinson for as long as she wished since Vera was neglected by almost everyone, including Mr. Parkinson himself, and would welcome her company. Gwen had declined the invitation then, but she had responded to Vera's plea on this occasion despite a few misgivings. She knew what grief and exhaustion and loneliness after the death of a spouse felt like.

It was a decision she had regretted almost from the first day. Vera, as her letters had suggested, was a moaner and a whiner, and while Gwen tried to make allowances for the fact that she had tended a sick husband for a few years and had just lost him, she soon came to the conclusion that the years since their come-out had soured Vera and made her permanently disagreeable. Most of her neighbors avoided her whenever possible. Her only friends were a group of ladies who much resembled her in character. Sitting and listening to their conversation felt very like being sucked into a black hole and deprived of enough air to breathe, Gwen had been finding. They knew how to see only what was wrong in their lives and in the world and never what was right.

And that was precisely what *she* was doing now when thinking of them, Gwen realized with a mental shake of the head. Negativity could be frighteningly contagious.

Even before this morning she had been wishing that she had not committed herself to such a long visit. Two weeks would have been quite sufficient—she would actually be going home by now. But she had agreed to a month, and a month it would have to be. This morning, however, her stoicism had been put to the test.

She had received a letter from her mother, who lived at the dower house with her, and in it her mother had recounted a few amusing anecdotes involving Sylvie and Leo, Neville and Lily's elder children—Neville, Earl of Kilbourne, was Gwen's brother, and lived at Newbury Abbey itself. Gwen read that part of the letter aloud to Vera at the breakfast table in the hope of coaxing a smile or a chuckle from her. Instead, she had found herself at the receiving end of a petulant tirade, the basic thrust of which was that it was very easy for Gwen to laugh at and make light of her suffering when Gwen's husband had died years ago and left her very comfortably well off, and when she had had a brother and mother both willing and eager to receive her back into the family fold, and when her sensibilities did not run very deep anyway. It was easy to be callous and cruel when she had married for money and status instead of love. Everyone had *known* that truth about her during the spring of their come-out, just as everyone had known that Vera had married beneath her because she and Mr. Parkinson had loved each other to distraction and nothing else had mattered.

Gwen had stared mutely back at her friend when she finally fell silent apart from some wrenching sobs into her handkerchief. She dared not open her mouth. She might have given the tirade right back and thereby have reduced herself to the level of Vera's own spitefulness. She would not be drawn into an unseemly scrap. But she almost vibrated with anger. And she was deeply hurt.

"I am going out for a walk, Vera," she had said at last, getting to her feet and pushing back her chair with the backs of her knees. "When I return, you may inform me whether you wish me to remain here for another two weeks, as planned, or whether you would prefer that I return to Newbury without further delay."

She would have to go by post or the public stagecoach. It would take the best part of a week for Neville's carriage to come for her if she wrote to inform him that she needed it earlier than planned.

Vera had wept harder and begged her not to be cruel, but Gwen had come out anyway.

She would be perfectly happy, she thought now, if she *never* returned to Vera's house. What a dreadful mistake it had been to come, and for a whole month, on the strength of a very brief and long-ago acquaintance.

Eventually she rounded the headland she had seen from the harbor and discovered that the beach, wider here, stretched onward, seemingly to infinity, and that in the near distance the stones gave way to sand, which would be far easier to walk along. However, she must not go *too* far. Although the tide was still out, she could see that it was definitely on the way in, and in some very flat places it could rush in far faster than one anticipated. She had lived close to the sea long enough to know that. Besides, she could not stay away from Vera's forever, though she wished she could. She must return soon.

Close by there was a gap in the cliffs, and it looked possible to get up onto the headland high above, if one was willing to climb a steep slope of pebbles and then a slightly more gradual slope of scrubby grass. If she could just get up there, she would be able to walk back to the village along the top instead of having to pick her way back across these very tricky stones.

Her weak leg was aching a bit, she realized. She had been foolish to come so far.

She stood still for a moment and looked out to the still-distant line of the incoming tide. And she was hit suddenly and quite unexpectedly, not by a wave of water, but by a tidal wave of loneliness, one that washed over her and deprived her of both breath and the will to resist.

Loneliness?

She never thought of herself as lonely. She had lived through a tumultuous marriage but, once the rawness of her grief over Vernon's death had receded, she had settled to a life of peace and contentment with her family. She had never felt any urge to remarry, though she was not a cynic about marriage. Her brother was happily married. So was Lauren, her cousin by marriage who felt really more like a sister, since they had grown up together at Newbury Abbey. Gwen, however, was perfectly contented to remain a widow and to define herself as a daughter, a sister, a sister-in-law, a cousin, an aunt. She had numerous other relatives, too, and friends. She was comfortable at the dower house, which was just a short walk from the abbey, where she was always welcome. She paid frequent visits to Lauren and Kit in Hampshire, and occasional ones to other relatives. She usually spent a month or two of the spring in London to enjoy part of the Season.

She had always considered that she lived a blessed life.

So where had this sudden loneliness come from? And such a tidal wave of it that her knees felt weak and it seemed as though she had been robbed of breath. Why could she feel the rawness of tears in her throat?

Loneliness?

She was not lonely, only depressed at being stuck here with Vera. And hurt at what Vera had said about her and her lack of sensibilities. She was feeling sorry for herself, that was all. She *never* felt sorry for herself. Well, almost never. And when she did, then she quickly did something about it. Life was too short to be moped away. There was always much over which to rejoice.

But *loneliness*. How long had it been lying in wait for

her, just waiting to pounce? Was her life really as empty as it seemed at this moment of almost frightening insight? As empty as this vast, bleak beach?

Ah, she *hated* beaches.

Gwen gave her head another mental shake and looked, first back the way she had come, and then up the beach to the steep path between the cliffs. Which should she take? She hesitated for a few moments and then decided upon the climb. It did not look quite steep enough to be dangerous, and once up it, she would surely be able to find an easy route back to the village.

The stones on the slope were no easier underfoot than those on the beach had been; in fact, they were more treacherous, for they shifted and slid beneath her feet as she climbed higher. By the time she was halfway up, she wished she had stayed on the beach, but it would be as difficult now to go back down as it was to continue upward. And she could see the grassy part of the slope not too far distant. She climbed doggedly onward.

And then disaster struck.

Her right foot pressed downward upon a sturdy looking stone, but it was loosely packed against those below it and her foot slid sharply downward until she landed rather painfully on her knee, while her hands spread to steady herself against the slope. For the fraction of a moment she felt only relief that she had saved herself from tumbling to the beach below. And then she felt the sharp, stabbing pain in her ankle.

Gingerly she raised herself to her left foot and tried to set the right foot down beside it. But she was engulfed in pain as soon as she tried to put some weight upon it—and even when she did not, for that matter. She exhaled a loud "Ohh!" of distress and turned carefully about so that she could sit on the stones, facing downward toward the beach. The slope looked far steeper from up here. Oh, she had been very foolish to try the climb.

She raised her knees, planted her left foot as firmly as she could, and grasped her right ankle in both hands. She tried rotating the foot slowly, her forehead coming to rest on her raised knee as she did so. It was a momentary sprain, she told herself, and would be fine in a moment. There was no need to panic.

But even without setting the foot down again, she knew she was deceiving herself. It was a bad sprain. Perhaps worse. She could not possibly walk.

And so panic came despite her effort to remain calm. However was she going to get back to the village? And no one knew where she was. The beach below her and the headland above were both deserted.

She drew a few steadying breaths. There was no point whatsoever in going to pieces. She would manage. Of course she would. She had no choice, did she?

It was at that moment that a voice spoke—a male voice from close by. It was not even raised.

"In my considered opinion," the voice said, "that ankle is either badly sprained or actually broken. Either way, it would be very unwise to try putting any weight on it."

Gwen's head jerked up, and she looked about to locate the source of the voice. To her right, a man rose into sight partway up the steep cliff face beside the slope. He climbed down onto the pebbles and strode across them toward her as if there were no danger whatsoever of slipping.

He was a great giant of a man with broad shoulders and chest and powerful thighs. His five-caped greatcoat gave the impression of even greater bulk. He looked quite menacingly large, in fact. He wore no hat. His brown hair was cropped close to his head. His features were strong and harsh, his eyes dark and fierce, his mouth a straight, severe line, his jaw hard set. And his expression did nothing to soften his looks. He was frowning—or scowling, perhaps.

His gloveless hands were huge.

Terror engulfed Gwen and made her almost forget her pain for a moment.

He must be the Duke of Stanbrook. She must have strayed onto his land, even though Vera had warned her to give both him and his estate a wide berth. According to Vera, he was a cruel monster, who had pushed his wife to her death over a high cliff on his estate a number of years ago and then claimed that she had jumped. What kind of woman would *jump* to her death in such a horrifying way, Vera had asked rhetorically. Especially when she was a *duchess* and had everything in the world she could possibly need.

The kind of woman, Gwen had thought at the time, though she had not said so aloud, *who had just lost her only child to a bullet in Portugal,* for that was precisely what had happened a short while before the duchess's demise. But Vera, along with the neighborhood ladies with whom she consorted, chose to believe the more titillating murder theory despite the fact that none of them, when pressed, could offer up any evidence whatsoever to corroborate it.

But though Gwen had been skeptical about the story when she heard it, she was not so sure now. He *looked* like a man who could be both ruthless and cruel. Even murderous.

And she had trespassed on his land. His very *deserted* land.

She was also helpless to run away.

*And don't miss the next touching story of love,
friendship, and healing in Mary Balogh's new
Survivors' Club series*

The Arrangement

Available in paperback from Dell Books in fall 2013

Turn the page for a delightful sneak peek.

$\mathcal{W}$HEN IT BECAME CLEAR TO VINCENT HUNT, VIS-count Darleigh, that if he stayed at home for the remainder of the spring he would without any doubt at all be betrothed, even married, before summer had properly settled in, he fled. He ran away from home, which was a ridiculous, somewhat lowering way of putting it when he owned the house and was almost twenty-four years old. But the simple fact was that he bolted.

He took with him his valet, Martin Fisk; his traveling carriage and horses; and enough clothes and other necessary belongings to last him a month or two—or six. He really did not know how long he would stay away. He took his violin, too, after a moment's hesitation. His friends liked to tease him about it and affect horror every time he tucked it beneath his chin, but he thought he played it tolerably well. More important, he liked playing it. It soothed his soul, though he never confided *that* thought to his friends. Flavian would no doubt make a comment along the lines of its scratching the boot soles of everyone else who happened to be within earshot.

The main trouble with home was that he was afflicted with too many female relatives and not enough male ones—and *no* assertive males. His grandmother and his mother lived with him, and his three sisters, though married with homes and families of their own, came to stay all too frequently, and often for lengthy spells. Hardly a month went by without at least one of them being in residence for a few days or a week or more. His brothers-in-law, when they came with their wives—which was not every time—tactfully held themselves aloof from Vincent's affairs and allowed their women-folk to rule his life, even though it was worthy of note that none of them allowed their wives to rule *theirs*.

It all would have been understandable, even under ordinary circumstances, Vincent supposed grudgingly. He was, after all, everyone's only grandson or only son or only brother—and *younger* brother at that—and as such was fair game to be protected and cosseted and worried over and planned for. He had inherited his title and fortune just four years ago, at the age of nineteen, from an uncle who had been robust and only forty-six years old when he died and who had had a son as sturdy and fit as he. They had both died violently. Life was a fragile business and so was the inheritance, Vincent's female relatives were fond of observing. It behooved him, therefore, to fill his nursery with an heir and a number of spares as soon as was humanly possible. It was irrelevant that he was still very young and would not even have begun to think of matrimony yet, left to himself. His family knew all they cared to know about living in genteel poverty.

His were not ordinary circumstances, however, and as a result, his relatives clucked about him like a flock of mother hens all intent upon nurturing the same frail chick while somehow avoiding smothering it. His mother had moved to Middlebury Park in Gloucester-shire even before he did. She had got it ready for him. His maternal grandmother had let the lease expire on her house in Bath and joined his mother there. And after he moved in, three years ago, his sisters began to find Middlebury the most fascinating place on earth to be.

And Vincent need not worry about their husbands feeling neglected, they had collectively assured him. Their husbands *understood*. The word was always spoken with something like hushed reverence.

In fact, most of what they all said to him was spoken in much the same manner, as though he were some sort of precious but mentally deficient child.

This year they had begun to talk pointedly about marriage. *His* marriage, that was. Even apart from the succession issue, marriage would bring him comfort and companionship, they had decided, and all kinds of other assorted benefits. Marriage would enable them to relax and worry less about him. It would enable his grandmother to return to Bath, which she was missing. And it would not be at all difficult to find a lady willing and even eager to marry him. He must not imagine it would be. He was titled and wealthy, after all. And he had youth and looks and charm. There were hordes of ladies out there who would *understand* and actually be quite happy to marry him. They would quickly learn to love him for himself. At least, *one* would, the one he would choose. And they, his female relatives, would help him make that choice, of course. That went without saying, though they said it anyway.

The campaign had started over Easter, when the whole family was at Middlebury, his sisters' husbands and their children included. Vincent himself had just returned from Penderris Hall in Cornwall, country seat of the Duke of Stanbrook, where he spent a few weeks of each year with his fellow members of the self-styled Survivors' Club, a group of survivors of the Napoleonic Wars, and he had been feeling a little bereft, as he always did for a while after parting from those dearest friends in the world. He had let the women talk without paying a great deal of attention or even thinking of perhaps putting his foot down.

It had proved to be a mistake.

Only a month after Easter his sisters and brothers-in-law and nieces and nephews had returned en masse, to be followed a day or so later by houseguests. It was still early spring and an odd time of year for a house party, when the social Season in London would be just getting into full swing. But this was not really a party, Vincent had soon discovered, for the only guests who were not also family were Mr. Geoffrey Dean, son of Grandmama's dearest friend in Bath, his wife, and their three daughters. Their two sons were away at school. Two of the daughters were still in the schoolroom—their governess had been brought with them. But the eldest, Miss Philippa Dean, was almost nineteen and had made her curtsy to the queen just a couple of weeks before and secured partners for every set at her come-out ball. She had made a very satisfactory debut indeed into polite society.

But, Mrs. Dean was hasty to add while describing her daughter's triumph over tea soon after their arrival at Middlebury Park, how could they possibly have resisted the prospect of spending a quiet couple of weeks in the country with old friends?

Old friends?

The situation had soon become painfully clear to Vincent, though no one bothered to explain. Miss Philippa Dean was on the marriage mart to the highest bidder. She had younger sisters growing up behind her and two brothers at school who might conceivably wish to continue their studies at university. It seemed unlikely that the Deans were vastly wealthy. They had come, then, on the clear understanding that there was a husband to be had for the girl at Middlebury and that she would return to London with all the distinction of being betrothed within a month of her come-out. It would be a singular triumph, especially as she would be securing a husband who was both wealthy and titled.

And who also happened to be blind.

Miss Dean was exquisitely lovely, his mother reported, with blond hair and green eyes and a trim figure. Not that her looks mattered to him. She sounded like a sweet and amiable girl.

She also sounded quite sensible when in conversation with everyone except Vincent himself. She often *was* in conversation with him during the following few days, however. Every other female in the house, with the possible exception of Vincent's three young nieces, did everything in her power to throw the two of them together and to leave them together. Even a blind man could see that.

She conversed with him upon trivialities in a gentle, somewhat breathless voice, as though she were in a sickroom and the patient hung precariously between death and life. Whenever Vincent tried to steer the conversation to some meaningful topic in order to discover something of her interests and opinions and the quality of her mind, she invariably agreed wholeheartedly with everything he said, even to the point of absurdity.

"I am firmly of the opinion," he said to her one afternoon when they were sitting together in the formal parterre gardens before the house despite a rather strong breeze, "that the scientific world has been in a wicked conspiracy against the masses for the past number of centuries, Miss Dean, in order to convince us that the earth is round. It is, of course, quite undeniably flat. Even a fool could see that. If one were to walk to the edge of it, one would fall off and never be heard of again. What is *your* opinion?"

It was unkind. It was a bit mean.

She was silent for several moments, while he willed

her to contradict him. Or laugh at him. Or call him an idiot. Her voice was gentler than ever when she spoke.

"I am quite sure you have the right of it, my lord," she said.

He almost said "Balderdash!" but did not. He would not add cruelty to unkindness. He merely smiled and felt ashamed of himself and talked about the blustery wind.

And then he felt the fingers of one of her hands on his sleeve, and he could smell her light floral perfume more clearly, an indication that she had leaned closer, and she spoke again—in a sweet, hurried, breathless voice.

"I did not at all mind coming here, you know, Lord Darleigh," she said, "even though I have been looking forward forever to my first Season in London and do not remember ever being happier than I was on the night of my come-out ball. But I know enough about life to understand that I was taken there not *just* for enjoyment. Mama and Papa have explained what a wonderful opportunity this invitation is for me, as well as for my sisters and brothers. I did not mind coming, truly. Indeed, I came willingly. I *understand,* you see, and I *will not mind* one little bit."

Her fingers squeezed his arm before letting it go.

"You will think I am forward," she added, "though I am not usually so outspoken. I just thought you needed to know that I do not mind. For perhaps you fear I do."

It was one of the most excruciatingly embarrassing moments of Vincent's life, as well as being almost insufferably infuriating. Not that she infuriated him, poor girl. But her parents did, and his mother and grandmother and sisters did. It was quite obvious to him that Miss Dean had been brought here not just as an eligible young lady whom he might get to know with the possibility on both their parts of deepening their acquaintance in the future if they liked each other. No, she had been brought here fully expecting that he would make her an offer before she left. Pressure would have been brought to bear by her parents, but she was a dutiful daughter, it seemed, and accepted her responsibility as the eldest. She would marry him even though he was blind.

She very obviously *did* mind.

He was angry with his mother and sisters for assuming that mental deficiency was one effect of blindness. He had known they wished him to marry soon. He had known that they would proceed to matchmake for him. What he had *not* known was that they would choose his bride without a word to him and then practically force him into accepting their choice—and in his own home, moreover.

His house, in fact, was not his own home—that realization came like an epiphany. It never had been. Whose fault that was must be examined at some future date. It was tempting to blame his relatives, but . . . Well, he would have to think the whole matter over.

He had a niggling suspicion, though, that if he was not master here, the fault lay with him.

But for now he was in an impossible situation. He felt no spark of attraction toward Miss Dean, even though he believed he would very probably like her under different circumstances. It was clear she felt nothing for him but the obligation to marry him. He could not, though, allow both of them to be coerced into doing what neither of them wanted to do.

As soon as they had returned indoors—Miss Dean took his offered arm and then proceeded to steer him along with gentle but firm intent even though he had his cane with him and knew the way perfectly well without any assistance at all—Vincent went to his private sitting room—the only place in the house where he could be assured of being alone and of being himself—and summoned Martin Fisk.

"We are going," he said abruptly when his valet arrived.

"Are we, sir?" Martin asked cheerfully. "And what clothes will you be needing for the occasion?"

"I will need everything that will fit into the trunk I always take to Penderris," Vincent said. "You will doubtless decide for yourself what *you* need."

A low grunt was followed by silence.

"I am feeling especially stupid today," Martin said. "You had better explain."

"We are going," Vincent said. "Leaving. Putting as much distance between us and Middlebury as we possibly can in order to evade pursuit. Slinking off. Running away. Taking the coward's way out."

"The lady does not suit, does she?" Martin asked.

Ha! Even Martin knew why the girl had been brought here.

"Not as a wife," Vincent told him. "Not as *my* wife, anyway. Good Lord, Martin, I do not even *want* to marry. Not yet. And if and when I *do* want it, I shall choose the lady myself. Very carefully. And I shall make sure that if she says yes, it is not simply because she *understands* and *will not mind*."

"Hmm," Martin said. "That is what this one said, is it?"

"With the softest, gentlest sweetness," Vincent said. "She *is* sweet and gentle, actually. She is prepared to make a martyr of herself for the sake of her family."

"And we are running away *where*?" Martin asked.

"Anywhere on earth but here," Vincent said. "Can we leave tonight? Without anyone's knowing?"

"I grew up at a smithy," Martin reminded him. "I think I could manage to attach the horses to the carriage without getting the lines hopelessly tangled up. But presumably I won't have to risk it. I suppose you will want Handry to drive us? I'll have a word with him. He knows how to keep his lips sealed. Two o'clock in the morning, shall we say? I'll come and carry your trunk out and then come back to dress you. We should be well on our way by three."

"Perfect," Vincent said.